BAD AXE COUNTY

BAD AXE COUNTY

A NOVEL

John Galligan

ATRIA BOOKS

NEW YORK   LONDON   TORONTO   SYDNEY   NEW DELHI

ATRIA
BOOKS

An Imprint of Simon & Schuster, Inc.
1230 Avenue of the Americas
New York, NY 10020

First Atria Books hardcover edition July 2019

ATRIA B O O K S and colophon are trademarks of Simon & Schuster, Inc.

For information about special discounts for bulk purchases, please contact Simon & Schuster Special Sales at 1-866-506-1949 or business@simonandschuster.com.

The Simon & Schuster Speakers Bureau can bring authors to your live event. For more information or to book an event, contact the Simon & Schuster Speakers Bureau at 1-866-248-3049 or visit our website at www.simonspeakers.com.

Interior design by Kyoko Watanabe

Manufactured in the United States of America

1 3 5 7 9 10 8 6 4 2

Library of Congress Cataloging-in-Publication Data has been applied for.

ISBN 978-1-9821-1070-3
ISBN 978-1-9821-1072-7 (ebook)

BAD AXE COUNTY

PROLOGUE

Whistling Straits Golf Course, The American Club, Kohler, WI

Afternoon, July 9, 2004

The clammy hand of state representative Cyrus Johnsrud (R-Portage) has released her elbow and is drifting down her spine, stopping to savor each vertebra through the fabric of her gown. The representative is about to grope her royal behind, for sure, when the queen spots her chaperone anxiously scanning the crowd—searching for Her Highness, who else?

When she wears heels, Heidi White, nearly eighteen, becomes a young woman of average height, but in addition to her gown and sash, she wears the tiara of the Wisconsin Dairy Queen. This should make her easy to find. But her chaperone, Mrs. Wisnewski, is trollishly short and also too vain to wear her eyeglasses at swanky affairs. So the Dairy Queen hangs in there, clarifies a faraway pocket of Wisconsin geography for the representative, the distinctive place where she is from.

"No, I'm from Crawford County. Bad Axe County is one county to the north. They kill us in baseball, but we beat the hide off them in rodeo. We're the Vanguards and the Bobcats, they're the Blackhawks and the Rattlers."

"Excellent," he says. "You betcha."

"We're both the coulees, though. We're a different world from you guys."

"Oh, you betcha."

"We never had the glacier, so we're like a million years old." A camera flashes in her face. She doesn't flinch anymore. "We actually have bobcats and rattlesnakes. We have more caves than the Ozarks. Blackhawk ran away there to hide from the army."

These points of pride are lost on the representative from the rolling cornfields and pastures of the central state. His fingers have fathomed her tailbone. She can feel him delicately sorting out her layers—gown, slip, nylons, panties—mentally getting her undressed.

"Well, the folks in the coulees must be real proud of you, young lady. You just gave a heckuva speech up there."

She has given it dozens of times. It is not a speech, really. She won the Crawford County and state dairy crowns nine months ago with a real speech about her family's heartwarming struggle to survive as small milk producers in the rugged southwest corner of the state. But since she became queen, her role has been to deliver a promotional message, scripted for her by the Wisconsin Milk Marketing Board. She begins by reporting new scientific findings that chocolate milk is good for recharging the body after intense athletic workouts. She next announces upcoming opportunities such as the Grilled Cheese Academy—people think she's joking, but she isn't—and the Master Cheesemaker certification program, as well as entry deadlines for various Dairy Youth Fund scholarships, "of which I myself have been a recipient." She goes on to note consumer cheese trends, identifying "eight ways Americans will eat cheese in 2004." Following that—and she does this all in seven minutes—she invites one and all to look for her on the floor after the program, where she will be handing out samples of seasonal cheese flavors as well as information on cheese-and-beverage pairings and easy-cheesy recipes. As a closing act, pure vaudeville, her own touch but approved by the marketing board, she starts to count as fast as she can, with no given reason—letting the suspense build—then gives up and shouts: "Thirty-five billion! That's how many dollars are generated by the Wisconsin dairy economy!"

Then she goes, "Phew!" and grins—she is a naturally beautiful girl, wholesome and healthy—and chugs a glass of chocolate milk to cheers from audience. She has three more months of Dairy Queen duties to go.

She is doing her floor show now, big smile, two hands beneath a platter of cheeses, cameras flashing away. State rep Johnsrud has progressed, plying her underlayers with a sensitive horizontal stroke. Mrs. Wisnewski has plunged off in the wrong direction, toward the golf clubhouse—probably because the chaperone has forbidden her Dairy Queen to enter what is clearly adult male territory. Heidi White is a good girl, but she is also headstrong, curious about boys versus men, and bored with the demands of a cheese queen. Meanwhile, Johnsrud is asking her why—pretending that she fascinates him—why did she compete for the throne?

"I admire my parents, my grandparents, I admire all farmers, all the incredibly hard work it takes to run a farm and treat animals well and make a good product and feed people and take care of the land and make the world a better place, and I want to do my part . . ."

He chuckles gently. She knows her answer sounds pat. Everybody knows girls just want to defeat rival girls, wear pretty dresses, and get attention from men. Coming from a backward corner of the state, she must seem too naïve to cover her tracks. Good time to strike, Johnsrud ascertains. She reads all this without alarm. People are basically good. No worries.

"You are just blowing me away with how wonderful you are. Smart and beautiful, and, gosh, what energy."

His hand finally connects with her rear end: a faintly brushing touch, a probe for permission, deniable if she takes offense. The state rep could bounce a quarter off what he's about to grab. In addition to farmwork, Heidi White competes in roping and barrel racing and plays high school softball. The 2004 Wisconsin Dairy Queen looks good in her gown, for sure, but it's another thing entirely to see her in faded jeans and a snug tee, a John Deere cap with her red-blond ponytail out, wearing her shit-kicker boots—in her real element.

"You really melt a guy's cheese," he confides into her ear. "Ya know?"

The farm girl from remote Crawford County keeps two hands on the silver platter, bearing up ten pounds of Colbys, Swisses, Cheddars, Havartis, and one firm chèvre.

"Tell you what. That speech you gave, you said your dream after high school is you want to be a public servant, get into law enforcement, live out there in the boonies, run a little farm on the side, make some babies, milk some cows, but, heck, how about instead you come look me up at the state capitol? I got a job for you in my office. How about you really use your talent?" He brushes her butt again. "That sound good? You come to Madison, be my girl Friday?"

The grope is about to occur. But so what? She has perfect balance. On her mind is a late supper of her mom's pork chops and potato salad, after which she will bottle-feed a motherless calf and curry her horse, and after that there is supposed to be a kegger tonight—a half barrel off the tailgate of some boy's pickup, a bonfire, fireworks, good kids having good times on a bend of the Kickapoo River. All things considered, the 2004 Wisconsin Dairy Queen will probably just step free of the grope and shrug the whole thing off, keep smiling as she takes her cheese platter and goes elsewhere—

But then this happens instead.

Mrs. Wisnewski is completely frantic as she elbows herself between important men in suits. She has even put her eyeglasses on. They magnify the black mascara streaking down her wrinkled face. She is crying about something. Unbelievable. Mrs. Wisnewski is crying.

"Uh-oh, spilled milk."

State rep Johnsrud tries to joke. He uses the opportunity to loop an arm around the queen's waist, handle her at the hip as if he needs to squire her clear of the charging crazy lady. Instead Mrs. Wisnewski stiff-arms him into a waiter bearing flutes of Door County cherry lambic. She forcefully tows the Dairy Queen—cameras flashing, cheese ungluing from the platter, slinging out—through an exit door onto a patio. Across the crisp green golf course, Lake Michigan lies still and silver beneath an early-evening sky.

"Oh . . . oh, dear Lord . . ." gasps Mrs. Wisnewski.

"What?"

"Oh, Heidi . . . your mom and dad . . ."

"What about them?"

She will always remember how slowly she caught on. She was thinking that her parents had decided to give up struggling and sell Cress

Springs Farm to Royce Underkoffler, the bankruptcy specialist preying on farmers across the coulees. So Mom and Dad finally did it, she is thinking. OK. Well. So now they move to Florida. They stop breaking their backs every day while sinking deeper into debt. Her dad gets his anxiety under control. Her mom quits clerking the night shift at the Kwik Trip. The land by itself is worth a small fortune, so her parents stop fighting with each other, head down south, and take it easy. She is thinking, yeah, it was dumb of her to try to save it all, to romanticize the past with the Dairy Queen gig, which has become tedious and lame, on top of being a shill for Big Ag. But her queenship won't last forever. Like her parents, she will move on . . .

"Sit down," Mrs. Wisnewski commands her.

"Why?"

"Heidi White, I'm telling you to sit down." The chaperone takes a clawlike grip on her forearm. She lunges toward a wire bench, choking out her words. "Sit down, young lady."

"What happened?"

"They were shot."

"What?"

"They were shot at the farm."

"My mom and dad?"

"After you left this morning . . . first your dad shot your . . ."

Mrs. Wisnewski gasps, can't finish.

"I . . . he . . . what? He shot who?"

"Your . . . oh, my dear girl . . . your mom . . . and then he shot himself . . ."

Her abilities to think and speak and hear—these dissolve. She stares at a golf course against a vast silver lake without any idea what either thing is. Little Mrs. Wisnewski, crouched on the paving stones in her black formal dress, becomes a gargoyle clawing at her hands. State rep Johnsrud looms in, expressing concern. Mrs. Wisnewski leaps and snarls as if to bite his face. The Dairy Queen whispers, "No."

This word becomes the entire shape of her response. No becomes her universe. No! The tiara—like a talon on her head—she tears it off with a shriek—No!—in a terrible handful of strawberry blond. No! No!

Mrs. Wisnewski has to stop her from running into the resort's driveway, where huge buses loom with their crushing weight. Then somehow she is inside the car, contained by a seat belt, a fiery sunset ahead, landscape streaming in dusk light. This is not real, no. This cannot be real.

"You're lying," she blurts. "Somebody's lying. Dad would never do that."

"The deputy told me—"

"Dad was stressed, but he would never . . . Just last Sunday morning someone stole a trailer full of hay from our neighbors . . . Mom and Dad must have caught somebody stealing. It's a lie."

"I don't think anyone is lying," says Mrs. Wisnewski from behind the steering wheel, her face stained, her voice stiff. "Nothing was stolen, the deputy told me. They don't think anyone else was involved. These things just happen. Somehow we have to accept them to survive."

Her whole world is no. No, no . . . never, never. A thousand kinds of no and never, across two hundred miles of landscape to a rugged place that now frightens and bewilders her.

She will go to war with no and never and "nothing was stolen." She will fight to accept and survive. But former Dairy Queen Heidi White will need twelve hard years, many of them black-souled and lost, before she can call her beloved coulees home again.

NIGHTFALL

Jerry Myad @thebestdefense
@BadAxeCountySheriff lets hope she gets hit by a
milk truck #dairyqueen

Angus Beavers saw that Sheriff Gibbs had died two months earlier when an old issue of the *Bad Axe County Broadcaster* caught up with him at the team's spring training facility in Jacksonville, a long way from Lost Hollow Road.

April was a hot stench already in Florida. Waiting his turn on chemical-green outfield grass, this rough kid from the Wisconsin coulees dreamed of skunk cabbage unfurling in the seeps, trillium blooming on the bluff sides. As he tracked fungoes in the sodden sky, he yearned to see eagles soaring in spring air at the ridgetops. As he whiffed on curve-balls, he remembered chopping good dry oak. Four years gone from the Bad Axe, he was sick for the sensations of the place he came from. He wanted to start over. But until the news about Gibbs arrived, he had never seen a way back.

Coach Hernandez had slapped his chest with the newspaper.

"Hey, Meat. Great piece in there about a truck that hits a cow, the cow goes airborne—somehow this all occurs at a gas station—and then—"

But Angus had felt a charge from the headline: BAD AXE MOURNS LONGTIME SHERIFF RAYMOND GIBBS.

———

"About time you went to hell," he told Gibbs later inside his small, nearly empty Jacksonville apartment. He clenched a fist. So who would be the new sheriff?

He took a shower, microwaved a frozen cheeseburger, and got an ice pack from the freezer. He lay down on his narrow bed with his sore back arched over the ice.

. . . after thirty-one years of doing the county's most dangerous job, Sheriff Gibbs died of natural causes while relaxing with friends aboard the River Princess . . .

Bullcrap. What Gibbs did was cruise around the Bad Axe in a spanking new Dodge Charger, hobnobbing with his cronies. The *River Princess* was a casino boat that operated on neutral water in the Mississippi River, where no state laws applied—as in booze, gambling, and lady friends for hire.

. . . according to Bob Check, chairperson of the Police and Fire Commission, the Bad Axe County Board of Supervisors will appoint an interim sheriff to preside until a special election in July . . .

Angus let the paper fall. Best don't ever come home, his dad had told him. Best just live the dream. But with Gibbs now dead . . .

———

An hour later, around midnight Wisconsin time, Angus Beavers called home. His heart thumped. His hot face gleamed. No one answered.

He called again at three a.m. His little sister, Brandy, answered, sounding drunk.

"Mmm . . . what? Who is this?"

"Where were you? It's Angus, and it's the middle of the night."

He waited. Beyond his window an old lady started freaking out in Spanish.

"Angus? Are you shitting me? When was the last time you called?"

It was Christmas, from winter ball in Mexico. He had bought a phone card and called from a *mercado*. No one had answered. The house on Lost Hollow Road had no machine. He hadn't been sure what to say anyway. He felt out of place and alone, in a life he never wanted.

"That doesn't answer where you were, all hours," he told his sister.

"Are you shitting me?"

Shirtless in boxers, Angus slumped in a sweat on the edge of the bed. His ice pack had wet a photo of the dead sheriff saluting veterans where the story continued on page three: BAD AXE MOURNS GIBBS.

"Who'd they make the new sheriff?"

"Huh?"

"Gibbs kicked it. The paper said there was going to be an interim sheriff. Who is it?"

"Some lady."

"Not Boog Lund?" Surprised, Angus stood. Boog Lund was Gibbs's chief deputy. "You're sure, some lady?"

"Yeah. See, Horst Zimmer hacked up this couple down at Bishops Coulee." His sister yawned like it happened every day. "Then he set a fire. This lady deputy found the bodies. Then she figured out that Zimmer did it. She busted him trying to sell their Xbox off his tailgate for twenty bucks to get some tweek. So suddenly she was a big deal and they made her the temporary sheriff." Brandy yawned again. "But not for long."

Angus peeled the two-month-old newspaper off himself and looked at it briefly. The crime Brandy was talking about hadn't happened yet. But a thing like that was not too much of a surprise, if you knew how it was with drugs in the coulees. The surprise to Angus was a lady sheriff— but not for long. He began to pace.

"Let me talk to Dad."

"Dad's too sick to get out of bed."

Hungover, Angus imagined. "What's wrong with him?"

"Cancer."

"What? Where?"

His little sister lit a cigarette, blew smoke across the mouthpiece of their black rotary phone. "Where do you think?"

"What?"

"Everywhere," Brandy said.

Angus didn't know what to feel. Their dad would have bigger and better cancer than the next guy. That old lady screeched Spanish. The foul air stung his eyes. And the sirens, always. He shut the window.

"Since when?"

"He was in the hospital at Christmas."

"Who's taking care of him?"

"I am."

"Who's taking care of you?"

"I am."

He had to catch his breath. He had to shut his eyes, jump the sadness for now and figure this out. Gibbs was dead. There was a new lady sheriff. His dad was too sick to stop him. Maybe there was a way.

"Can you do something for me?" he asked his sister finally. "You know that chest freezer that used to be outside my bedroom wall? Dad put it on the forklift and moved it to the Quonset shed."

"What about it?"

"Can you look inside for me?"

"Why?"

"Or just check and see if it's still working?"

She must have put down the phone by the TV. Angus listened to Aspinwall Ford offer "dynamite deals on closeout-model work trucks." Then came that old Clausen Meats rant—*"Nobody packs more meat!"*—that he had heard all his life.

"It's still working."

"Is there still all that frozen fish inside?"

"I couldn't tell you."

"Why not?"

"I couldn't open it."

"Why couldn't you open it?"

"Why do you think, Angus? The big-ass lock and chain that Dad put on it."

So maybe he was right. All this time, he had never believed his dad would burn the body.

———

He left Jacksonville in the morning. He flew through Charlotte. By midafternoon he was in Chicago, unable to rent a car because his Wisconsin driver's license had expired when he turned eighteen two years ago. He put himself on a bus from O'Hare bound for Madison, packed between college students going back to school after spring break. In Madison, the taxi driver's mouth fell open. "A trip out there is gonna run you three or four hundred dollars, bro. You sure?"

"Let's go."

Halfway to the Bad Axe, late afternoon, Angus directed the driver off U.S. 14 onto a county highway that ran northwest through Crawford County toward the Mississippi River. He watched the landscape wrinkle into the steep bluffs and narrow hollows of his home. Past his window flowed the tiny hard-luck farms, the cinder-block taverns at the junctions, the dusty milk trucks on evening rounds, the Amish buggies clip-clopping on the shoulder, the gas stations pushing cheese curds and lottery tickets. By the time they crossed into Bad Axe County, a storm was on the way. The half-wild coulee cows told him so by their instinct to lie down.

"So what brings you home?"

Angus heard this question as the cab slowed through gusting winds for entry into the town of Farmstead, the Bad Axe County seat.

"Get my life back," he told the driver.

He had to think what he meant.

The life he wanted—it hadn't ever really begun.

"Mommy?"

Here were today's numbers. If you counted back, she was thinking, present to past, today's numbers were 11, 17, 20, 22, 53, and 4,290. You could also count them in the other direction, past to present. Or you could scramble them, which was more how she felt.

"Mommy . . . you're not paying attention."

"I'm sorry, sweetie. What?"

"I said, what is a queen?"

"You know what a queen is."

"I know, but what does it *mean*?"

Her five-year-old, Ophelia, was asking. Whenever she could, Opie hung around to watch her mother get dressed. The process involved a lot for a little girl to take in. First, off came the ancient Seneca High Indians sweatpants and the faded Crawford County 4-H Horse Club sweatshirt. This revealed straps, scars, freckles, stretches—the truth about a thirty-ish mother of three. She met her daughter's eyes in the mirror.

"A queen is married to a king, for one thing."

"I know that. But who is she?"

"It really depends on if she's the one who is actually descended from the royal line—" Too complicated. "She is the wife of the king, and they are the bosses of the country."

"Oh."

Today, for the storm that was coming, she pulled on the silk long johns that Harley gave her for Christmas, which went on tight and wouldn't bunch beneath the uniform. For private pretty, she put on pink socks, a birthday gift from her three-year-old twin boys. Next she put on brand-new boots, black tactical Reeboks, right out of the box. One hour ago, and twenty-two days since she had responded to the crime at Bishops Coulee, she had finally lit fire to the boots that had become blood stained inside that poor young couple's house. Out the window over Opie's head she could see smoke still rising from the barrel. She was trying.

"Is a queen powerful?"

"She can be. She probably tells the king to jump, and the king asks her how high. You know how it works in this house, with me and Daddy."

"Ha," said Opie. She was protective of her daddy. "Ha, ha, very funny."

Next came the Kevlar vest, which squared her off in the front and made her look like a LEGO figure to the twins. But Opie was old enough to know what the vest meant. She was quiet until all the Velcro was snugged into place.

"Is a queen pretty?"

"You'd better tell the queen she's pretty, or she'll have your head chopped off."

"Ha, ha."

Now the long-sleeved uniform shirt, in hideous tan, with all its pockets and epaulets and patches and pins. She buttoned it up all the way. She liked a black bow tie.

"But America's Dairyland is not a real country, right?"

Crap. How did she not see this coming?

"No. America's Dairyland is an idea people use to sell cheese. And cheese is not a country either. Not even Swiss cheese. Hon, what is it? Is someone teasing you at school?"

"No. Not teasing."

"No? OK, good."

"But is she bad?"

"Is who bad, sweetie?"

"The Dairy Queen?"

She looked at her daughter. Her little chin trembled.

"No, of course the Dairy Queen isn't bad."

"Then why do they say 'the f-word Dairy Queen'?"

"Who said that?"

"Mr. Kussmaul."

Ah, the school bus driver, a Gibbs man. She leaned into the bureau mirror—good skin, a sprinkle of freckles, intense green eyes—her face still a strong part of the Mighty Heidi package. She tucked her red-blond braids under the beige cow pie of a hat. She strapped on her duty belt and organized it: cuffs, Taser, OC spray, radio base, flashlight, baton, omni-tool, pistol. Finally, and today was day seventeen already, she pinned the gold badge over her shirt pocket: *Heidi Kick, Interim Sheriff, Bad Axe County.*

"Mr. Kussmaul is just sad that Sheriff Gibbs died. He's only had fifty-three days to get over it. And he's never had a woman sheriff before. He'd feel better if your mommy stayed home and made easy-cheesy recipes."

"You shouldn't f-word the sheriff."

"Right on, girl. Off with your head if you f-word Sheriff Dairy Queen."

"Ha, ha. Very funny. But why are you getting dressed?"

"I have to work."

"Did another really bad thing happen?"

"No, sweetie. It's just because the weatherman says a storm is coming."

"Can I do the geese with you?"

"Not today. I need to be alone with them."

"I know what that means." Her daughter frowned. "It means some-body is teasing *you.*"

"Just a little," she admitted. "But Denise is teaching me how to be ready."

She touched Ophelia's silky head, kissed her on the ear, and together they left the privacy of the bedroom into the world of twin little brothers.

"Dylan, Taylor, Mommy's leaving."

She gathered three hot little bodies into a group hug.

"Bye, darlings. I love you. Be good for your daddy. I'll see you in the morning."

She was a day counter. For the first 6,407 days of her life, she hadn't been, but then her life changed—life itself became visible to her—and since then she had counted, at least certain kinds of days.

Today, as she had just told Opie, was fifty-three days since Ray Gibbs had died unexpectedly, and more evidence of Gibbs's sloppiness and corruption had trickled in on almost every one of those fifty-three days, much of it also implicating his chief deputy, and now hers, Elvin "Boog" Lund.

Today also made twenty days since she had cuffed Horst Zimmer for the bloody double murder at Bishops Coulee, and therefore twenty days that she had been privately fixated on the emptiness of Zimmer's motivation: theft of an obsolete Xbox, a toaster oven, and a chainsaw. If she hadn't caught Zimmer trying to sell his paltry loot off his tailgate in the parking lot of a tavern, her report might have reached a familiar and haunting conclusion, one she had been forced to accept 4,290 days ago: *Nothing was stolen . . .*

One more count: today marked the eleventh day since she had come to understand how unprofessionally she felt about it all. Instead of arresting a killer and becoming the interim sheriff, she secretly wished—and for eleven days she had vividly fantasized—that she had blown out Zimmer's zombie brains.

———

But meanwhile there was the *other* today. Meanwhile there was the job to do, protect and serve, and therefore there was the matter of thinking clearly and reacting calmly. This meant she had to prepare for how men in the Bad Axe seemed to feel about her as the first female sheriff in Wisconsin. Teasing hardly described it.

F-word Dairy Queen.

Look out, geese.

She scooped a beer pitcher full of cracked corn from the sack by the washing machine and headed past the burn barrel out to the pen. Aside from landing a great job back home in the coulees, the rest of her dream was to farm again, to milk cows, birth calves, cut hay. But she and Harley had three kids and two jobs, and her husband was a town kid and a baseball jock, not a farmer. That's why after they had secured a lease on the old Pederson farm, they had agreed, in the same way that young couples try a puppy before a child, on a flock of sixteen geese.

As she swung open the pen door the creatures rushed her with one collective squawk, snowy white feathers ruffling, bright orange beaks and feet flashing in the scrum. She held the corn behind her back. Since she had become a target in the Bad Axe, she and the geese had worked out a routine.

"Attention, please."

Sixteen pairs of black beady eyes looked up, less shoving and nipping, orderly for geese.

"OK . . . let's see . . . so why is going to Subway for a sandwich like seeing a prostitute?"

She rattled the pitcher of corn. They were all ears.

"You pay a stranger to do your wife's job."

This raised a mostly dissatisfied goosey murmur. Queen Gertrude nipped Cordelia. Squash Blossom tried to flap an end run behind the sheriff to the corn. She raised the pitcher higher. "Not good enough? Remember you're just practice cows, so don't get cocky. Do any of you smart-asses know why you should never lie to a woman who has both PMS and GPS?"

They waited for it.

"Because that woman is a bitch . . . and she will find you."

There was a bit more raucous honking, for sure. But that certain synergy had yet to occur. She got the jokes from Denise Halverson, her night-shift dispatcher, and she tried to remember a better one. Denise was a genius. She always predicted the next encounter with the male mind, and with a joke she inoculated accordingly.

Above the pen, the sky churned. Lightning rippled beyond the hog-back ridge that nestled the farm. She counted nine seconds before thunder grumbled over the hollow. So, OK, then. The vaccine she required had to be raunchy, sexist—*and about the weather*. She had one. She faced the geese and lowered her voice. "Darlin' . . ."

She imagined taking a shot of Rumple Minze to facilitate a hiccup and a slur.

"I'm no weatherman . . . but darlin' . . ."

She released a drunken eyeball to glide across the waiting birds.

"But . . . *hic!* . . . you can expect about six inches tonight."

It was probably the eyeball and the hiccups, but the geese went nuts for this one, squawking and honking and nipping at her. As she threw the corn, she realized the awful joke had worked. Her brain felt cleansed and cooled, ready to reimmerse in the male world of the Bad Axe County Sheriff's Department.

Now go, she told herself, wondering where her husband was. *Hold that and go.*

———

"I'm rolling," she told Harley when she found him waiting in the Peder-sons' defunct milking parlor, which they used as a garage. "Sorry. I don't have time to talk."

He looked handsome in a pool of antique-yellow barn light. That didn't stop her from feeling bothered that he held an aluminum base-ball bat he had taken from his pickup, which was parked alongside her Charger and loaded with bat bags and milk crates full of baseballs. It was a blurry number of days since anything had been easy between them.

"I saw you burned your boots," he began.

"Sure did."

"I'm glad. Because I've been thinking . . ."

He ran his fingers along the barrel of the bat, touching smears made by groundouts, pop-ups, squibs, every kind of mishit.

"I know what you think."

"You do?"

"I know what you want."

He smiled at her. "Aside from dry ground, and at least one guy who can throw strikes, what is it that I want?"

"You want me to tell the county board I can't do this. You want me to say that Boog Lund waited his turn, he was Gibbs's chief deputy, he's got thirty years of experience, he deserves it. I've had enough, I want out, and I won't run in the election. In Harley-speak," she said, and this annoyed her lately, "if I can't hit the ball square, don't swing. And after Bishops Coulee, you think I can't even *see* the ball."

Here it came.

"Hon, it's good you finally burned your boots. But as for hitting square, you're the sheriff of Bad Axe County, which is more than enough to worry about, but then I hear that you were down in Crawford County last week, and I hear that you were—"

"Do you hear *that*?" she interrupted, pointing toward distant thunder. "That is snow, sleet, and freezing rain, headed our way. I've got three deputies, my whole crew, and no overtime budget. Do you really need to psychoanalyze me right now?"

She rounded the bed of his pickup. As she pulled her door open, her radio squawked. She reached in, hit TALK. "Go ahead."

Her day-shift dispatcher, Deputy Rinehart Rog, said: "Sheriff, Red Wing has freezing rain. Weather Service has issued flash-flood warnings. If it's snow and ice, we're going to see lines down and power out. Looks like it'll be on top of us in about half an hour. Your crew meeting starts in nineteen minutes."

"Thanks, Rhino."

As she turned back to her husband, she felt a telltale tightening in her chest.

"I'm fine."

"I'm not psychoanalyzing. I just get worried when someone tells me that you were down in Crawford County demanding to see the case file on your parents—"

"I was requesting. I've been meaning to do it for a long time. There is no reason that file should be sealed. I'm fine."

"But, Heidi, then I heard you were making the rounds of those sleazy taverns down around Soldiers Grove, asking about one of your dad's farmhands from twelve years ago, some dirtball with a rap sheet, sure, but no record up here in the Bad Axe."

Her mind walled up. She began to back the cruiser out, using the last crack in the rising window to say, "Good-bye. I love you. I'm fine."

———

But it was day eleven for the truth that her loving husband was just now sensing. As she processed the depravity of the Bishops Coulee crime, her past life and her present life had become scrambled. She was seeing zombie killers everywhere.

She could feel it happening now as she reached the outskirts of Farmstead and waited for traffic to pass through the highway intersection. Speeding toward the intersection through the storm-jaded twilight was a busted-up dark blue panel van, doing about sixty against the limit of forty-five.

She leaned forward and squinted to focus. Piece-of-shit vehicle with dealer plates, zombie strike one. Doesn't even notice her and slow down, zombie strike two. Behind the cracked windshield, his tattooed neck and shaved head, his jabbing finger and angry ranting mouth, his victim on the passenger seat just a big-eyed girl, zombie strikes three, four, and five. Then he blew through the town's one and only traffic light, solid red.

Six strikes and you're dead. She closed her eyes. She mashed the gas and yanked the Charger onto the highway, chased him down and ripped him from his van, knelt on his neck and put her service pistol to his skull—*you sick-brain bastard, so many of you out there hurting people and killing people, one of you took two of mine*—and pulled the trigger.

It would have felt so good.

She turned the other way and headed for her meeting.

"Hey . . . I think I've been here before."

The girl in the passenger seat, Pepper Greengrass, blurts these words in surprise as the van blows through the red light. Dale Hill, the driver, an ex-con supporting his gambling habit by working Pepper and two other underage girls out of a motel in a resort town two hours to the east, snarls back, "Tell me why I care."

"I think my big brother played baseball here."

The Wisconsin Dells, where they just came from, is surrounded by the level sands of central Wisconsin. Over the rugged terrain of the Bad Axe, Dale Hill's driving style has nearly killed them several times, though Pepper Greengrass, only sixteen, has hardly noticed.

"Yeah. I'm pretty sure I've been here. For one of Bennie's baseball games."

"I said tell me why I care."

She puts her knee-high black boots up on his dashboard.

"Bennie played shortstop for the Wisconsin Dells Scenics. I was eleven years old."

"Boots," Dale Hill orders. "The fuck off."

Pepper lowers her boots and watches a sign go by: FARMSTEAD, WISCONSIN / POP. 2,364 / HOME OF THE BLACKHAWKS. She watches another sign: BAD AXE COUNTY LIBRARY over a free–Wi-Fi icon and an arrow pointing down a side street.

She remembers something about rattlesnakes, though, not Blackhawks. So maybe this isn't the place. She watches the town go by: three taverns, a yarn shop, a diner, a Kwik Trip gas station where a Greyhound tilts at the curb, spewing exhaust into a sky bunched and ready to storm. Then, through empty storefronts, she gets a glimpse of a scoreboard and stadium lights.

"Look! There's the baseball diamond!"

She gets Dale's trademark snort of compressed dog breath.

"See it? That's the field, down in there, with bluffs around it."

"What I'm looking for is the place where I sign your ass up. The Ease Inn."

"You're not going to believe this. That game, my brother Bennie hit six home runs."

"You're right, I don't believe it."

"You think I'm lying?"

"With the odds against that? Yeah. I think you're full of shit."

Dale Hill is easily annoyed. She has known him less than a week, but already Pepper Greengrass has the hang of it.

"You wanna bet me?"

"I'm not going to bet you."

"Why not? You quit betting? You're in recovery?"

"Nobody ever hit six homers in one game, never in the history of baseball. The odds of that are like twenty million to one. It's bullshit."

"Then why don't you bet me?"

"Why don't you shut your stupid blowhole and help me find this place. It's called the Ease Inn."

"Well, OK, I'm glad you quit," Pepper says. "Gambling isn't good for you. I read that in my psych class. They say it increases irritation behavior."

She unzips and peels off her boots, puts her long brown naked legs up on his dash.

He grits his teeth. "Off. Put that shit away unless you're making money off it. Anyway, you can't afford to bet. You're already in the hole."

This is true. Almost seven days in, Pepper still owes Dale for everything, from room and board at the Pine Cone Motel to what she wears: the pink lip gloss, the leopard-print top, the tall black boots and the short black skirt, the red Shopko panties underneath. But the only way she can't afford to bet is if she loses. And she can't lose, because it really happened, here.

"Come on. Twenty bucks. Give me my phone back. I'll Google it."

Dale leans to squint through his windshield. A frigid mist has spattered it.

"You've got the odds in your favor," she says, "so why not double or nothing? I'm wrong, I owe you forty more. Just put it on my tab."

"I'm not betting you."

"You're chicken. Gimme my phone back."

"I'm not giving your phone back. Won't be any reception in a shithole like this anyway."

Pepper Greengrass hooks her thumbs beneath her tiny bra cups and makes chicken noises at the man she contacted via a number she found on the internet, a site called Backpage.com, then met for an "interview" behind the liquor shelf at the exit 37 truck stop outside the Dells.

He crushes his brakes, backs up, rolls down his window to look at a Kwik Trip gas station, where a dirty red-and-white taxi cab sits at the pump. He hollers at the heavy-shouldered guy in a red ball cap who emerges bearing foam boats of heat-lamp food. The guy freezes. Then he points in the direction they just came from. Pepper watches him stuff the ball cap down into the Kwik Trip garbage. He pulls his sweatshirt hood over his head.

Dale floors the van through a U-turn. Pepper glimpses that stadium again—yup, that's it. She puts her legs up on the dash. "Off!" He flails a fist, but she leans away. Sleet strikes the window at her shoulder. There is that sign again: BAD AXE COUNTY LIBRARY.

"So what, no reception," Pepper says. "I know a place where we can get Wi-Fi."

"I said I'm not betting you."

"Triple or nothing," she taunts him, squeezed against her door.

Interim sheriff Heidi Kick had debriefed her day-shift deputies and sent them home. Storm or no storm, "No more overtime" was her mandate from the Bad Axe County board of supervisors as they tried to sort out the suspicious spending patterns of Ray Gibbs. Overtime abuse was an easy issue to correct. As for Gibbs's Public Outreach budget, the board's directive was "Not one penny more until we figure out what's been going on."

After a face splash of cold water in the bathroom, a preemptive wise-crack from Denise, a glance at the kids' pictures on her phone, and the clean squeak of her new boots on the tile floor, she was ready to assign her night crew, made up of patrol deputies Rob Schwem and Kevin Eleffson and her Gibbs-tainted chief deputy, Boog Lund.

"So here we go, guys. This storm is going to hit us with folks coming home from the regional wrestling meet in Richland Center, with all those Amish buggies leaving the Yoder auction. Tonight is also euchre and darts league. Lots of action on the roads."

She paused so Schwem and Eleffson could collect their game faces. She had no illusions. Boog Lund outweighed her by thirty years and two hundred pounds and was the only declared candidate for the permanent sheriff's position. As such, they considered Lund their real boss. She forged on.

"We'll get up to seven inches, according to the National Weather Service, and we could end up with flooding as early as midnight if it's mostly rain. If we get down to thirty degrees and it snows, or if it's a little warmer and it's ice, we could have power outages, so be ready for welfare checks. Anything frozen is going to melt fast, so either way we have flash floods to think about, at least through tomorrow night."

Chief Deputy Lund grumbled something, left his chair, and headed for the Mr. Coffee at the back of the room.

"Now, you guys remember last April when the relay got iced over and the radios didn't work. And as we all know, cell coverage is spotty in the hollows. Obviously we're going to have to work extra hard on communication."

Deputy Schwem put his hand up.

"Go ahead."

"Is it OK to say this?" Meaning he would say it anyway. "You sound just like my wife."

"I'm sorry?"

"She always wants me to work harder on communication." Eleffson rewarded him with a snicker, and Schwem beamed proudly. "Just kidding. You forgot to mention the Lutheran potluck in Coon Valley."

"Thank you."

Eleffson whispered, "You give the little lady up to seven inches, Schwem, she'll understand you better." The sheriff grimaced inwardly. She and the geese had nailed it. To cover himself, Eleffson's long arm went up. "Rolf Dunkel's funeral was today. Open bar at the VFW after the burial. Dunkel's gonna have a lot of friends now that he's dead."

"Wonderful."

"Plus this weekend is Cabin Fever Days at the Ease Inn. So tonight is Cabin Fever Days' Eve. Tap beers for a dollar."

The sheriff chewed her cheek. Open bar, dollar taps, a major storm at freezing point.

"All important to know. Thanks." She mapped the county in her head. Farmstead was neatly on the main ridge down the center of it, a little north of dead middle. To the west was the roughest terrain, the deep coulees cutting to the Mississippi—Snake Hollow, Dog Hollow, Lost Hollow—and the rowdy river towns like Blackhawk Locks and Bishops Coulee. She would send her wiseguys that way. "So we're going to take zones. Deputy Schwem, northwest. Deputy Eleffson, southwest. I've got the girls' volleyball karaoke fund-raiser at the Ease Inn, so I'm going to take northeast, closest to home." She meant *home* as in the Public Safety Building, but her family's rented farm was in the northeast quadrant too. "I'll remind them at the Ease Inn not to serve minors or intoxicated individuals. Chief Deputy Lund, you do the same at the VFW and then take the southeast quadrant, please."

Southeast was Zion, Blue Mills, Mastodon, and other tiny, quiet villages in the usually more law-abiding region of Bad Axe County that touched the level center of the state. The assignment was a courtesy to Lund. He finally joined the meeting, lumbering away from the pot at the back of the room, managing three, not four, foam cups of bad coffee. He smiled as he passed her, retracting his lower lip to show ground-down gray incisors, a look she knew well, having grown up around aging male livestock with treacherous intent. Her dad's last stud bull, Samson, came to mind.

She asked Lund, "Did you have something to add?"

He emitted his *who me?* chuckle. "Golly. I wish I did." He played this to the eager grins of Schwem and Eleffson. "But somehow, even though we've got us a Dairy Queen running the show, we're still out of creamer."

He cut too closely through her personal space, his massive body forcing her to step back. She waited with her tongue bit while he distributed cups to the other two. It gave her time to count: after Gibbs's death, Boog Lund had been acting sheriff for thirty-six days before the county board removed his title and made her interim. As he turned to retake his chair, she snatched the cup he had poured for himself.

"Thank you, Deputy."

Up close he smelled like hashed browns and Brylcreem. Heat prickled under her shirt as she looked him in the eye.

"From now on, I'm gonna take mine black."

She turned to the window to hide the rush of blood to her face and was surprised by snow slanting through the lights over the parking lot. She watched it a moment, sipping the terrible coffee. Her deputies hadn't caused her sudden spike of discomfort. No, it was the unexpected recollection of Samson the big black bull, isolated and angry and increasingly feeble when his breeding days were done. But it wasn't the connection to Lund that she was thinking of anymore. A nagging memory from her Dairy Queen days was of Samson staggering along a fence through a snowstorm with a bloody gash between his eyes and one horn shattered.

Looking into both new and remembered snow, she now recalled a face. Who was that twitchy, sniffly guy with the pale eyes and the crooked smirk, the one her dad had fired for smashing poor Samson in the head with a shovel? He had claimed self-defense. He made threats as he was thrown off Cress Springs Farm. There was a zombie with a motive. She would put him on her list. But what was the name that went with the face?

Shit. She had dribbled coffee down her shirt. She heard chuckles.

Boog Lund said to the others, "Hey, whatever puts hair on your chest."

Dale Hill hits the brakes and wrenches the van into the Ease Inn. This is a truck stop, a mini-mart, a tavern, and a motel, like the place in the Dells where Pepper Greengrass met Dale six days ago, except even under its harsh plaza lights, this place has a run-down, soggy look to it, a yellow-brown color scheme gone dumpy, a lariat-and-horns Western theme that fails to match the muddy field and the grain depot that Dale's beams highlight in the background.

He pulls through the pump area into the tavern lot, stops the van with a jerk that tosses his pack of Basic Lights to the floor. She retrieves them, replaces them on the console, squares them with her fingers lingering. Dale gives her a look of hard suspicion. Thunder rumbles over. Wet snow splatters the windshield. Pepper says, "What? You told me not to. I'm a good girl."

He pulls his keys. He slams his door. He ducks around the van's front end into a plastering gust. Pepper cracks her door and calls after him, "Come on! Bennie Greengrass! Six home runs, twenty bucks, triple or nothing!"

While Dale is gone she thinks back to the game. It was a night game, under the lights. There was a water tower above the third-base side that must have said FARMSTEAD. She had climbed to the tip-top of natural stone bleachers that were carved up a bluff, under pine trees. Bats chased insects through the lights. The crowd was rowdy. Bennie gave her money and she had feasted on popcorn, a hot dog, and a blue-raspberry snow cone. She had possessed a stolen cigarette and lighter in her sock. She was going to be twelve in two days—three twelves, she remembers—so that made it August 12, 2012. When she smoked that cigarette, people stared. There had been a fight after the game. She and Bennie had celebrated his ridiculous six home runs by barhopping all the way home, taking a nap at a rest stop, eating burgers for breakfast at Culvers in the Dells, that whole night a wonderful blur and the last time she remembers her brother alive.

She retrieves Dale Hill's pack of Basic Lights from the console. She sticks one between her glossed lips, lights it with a Bic mini from the bottom of her tiny red purse. The van gets cold fast. She smokes and rubs her bare thighs. She thinks about Montana, real lariat-and-horns country, where her sister Marie is. She considers how Big Sky Country might be different. Probably no signs that say WE HAVE CHEESE CURDS and UFF-DA! and TURKEY PERMITS HERE. She wonders where that Greyhound bus is going, pausing with a hiss at the highway intersection before wallowing into the push of the storm.

On the phone the night before Pepper ran away, her sister had finally let it drop where she and Kevin and the kids had disappeared to last year: Hungry Horse, Montana. Right away Pepper had found it on a Google map, out there 1,379.3 miles to the west. Kevin was driving a tour bus in Glacier National Park and Marie was waiting tables at a casino on the Flathead reservation. Marie had never said, *Come on out.* Pepper had listened for it, but she had never heard any kind of solid invitation. Still, she reminds herself now, a one-way Amtrak ticket from the Dells to Whitefish, near Hungry Horse, is only $165 plus tax. Once she pays back what she owes Dale, she can make $165 in a snap.

He does not ease out of the Ease Inn. He charges back against what is now sideways snow, his blazer flapping to show how he keeps his phone in a holster on his belt like a big boy. Pepper hasn't seen her phone since he took it away five minutes after she met him. He slams back in, empties his fist of a drink coaster and a teeny paper umbrella.

"Gate fee," he fumes. "Can you believe that? For a party in a barn?"

"How much?"

He glares back at the tavern. One irritation behavior of Dale's, noted by Pepper, is berating service people—waiters and cashiers and bartenders—and demanding their names.

"Your online post didn't say shit about a gate fee, *Ladonna*."

"Maybe you could win it back off me."

"The bitch tells me, 'Unless you're going to the party to dance, everybody pays.' *La-fucking-donna*. I go, 'I'm going in there to dance? I *own* the dancer. I'm management.'"

"How much?"

"Is that my cigarette? Little thief."

Pepper releases the cigarette from her lips and holds it out, half smoked. Dale throws it out his window. "You're gonna be real sorry," he warns, "next time you steal from me."

You can't hurt me, Pepper tells him silently.

"How much is the gate fee?"

"A hundred bucks cash just to get in, for a spectator, like I wanna watch your skinny ass up there with a bunch of Holsteems."

"You wanna say Holsteins."

"What?"

"Holstein is the kind of the cow you mean."

"You wanna get hurt right now?"

"Come on. Bet me. Bennie Greengrass. August 12, 2012. Six home runs. Twenty gets you sixty."

"How you gonna prove it?"

"I saw a sign for a library. They'll have Wi-Fi. Give my phone back and let's go Google it."

Pepper watches his eyes. She hadn't known Dale Hill past those first five minutes before she knew this: a deep fear of missing easy money drives everything about him. Her stepdad, Felton Henry, a long-haul trucker who gambles all over the country, is just this way.

"You don't have twenty," he accuses her.

She uncrumples two tens from her purse. Dale swells up. He snatches her hand, but the wrong one. She holds the money over by her door. He squeezes hard, folding her bones.

"The hell you get that?"

"You can't hurt me. I stole it from my mom."

"Every cent you make is mine."

"I stole this before I accepted you as my personal savior. But OK, how about quintuple or nothing? You win, you put that whole gate fee on my tab."

He throws her hand back. "Never, ever touch my cigarettes." He glowers through his windshield into the storm's enclosing swirl. "So where's this fucking library?"

Pepper celebrates with a grin into the snow. "So does that mean we're on?"

7

Angus Beavers directed the cab driver along a stealth route to the baseball field that players called The Hole. From the Kwik Trip, this meant heading out of town on the highway about a half mile, then turning west on Viking Road into an onslaught of wind and sleety snow. Where Viking crossed Third Avenue, he told the driver to turn left. Another left turn put the cab in a dark alley behind a pair of defunct grain elevators. From there they snuck behind the library and trespassed through the parking lot of Bad Axe Manor. The driver crept the cab along with his phone in his hand.

"According to this, The Hole is not a place—and now I lost the signal."

"Just keep going through this parking lot—"

"It says *No Thru Traffic.*"

"It says *Manor* too." It was a government home. Angus pointed from the backseat. "Around the building where those big trees are. You'll see the outfield fence. That's The Hole."

The driver hunched closer to his windshield. The cab's headlights struck the outfield fence, then filtered through snow into the stadium sunk inside a bowl of limestone, its bleachers chiseled into soft blond rock collecting whiteness. "Just follow the fence around—"

"Drive on the grass?"

"Follow the fence around. That's the clubhouse over there."

"OK. I see it. A clubhouse? And the high school plays here?"

"No. The high school has its own field. This is semipro. Stop here."

Though the clubhouse was always locked, to Angus's knowledge it had never been secure. The Rattlers were the adult summer league team, but Angus had made the roster when he was sixteen, after his season as a high school junior, when he had hit .397 with twelve home runs and run the forty-yard dash in 4.5 seconds. A Minnesota Twins scout had recommended more playing time against better competition, but while Angus could have started at almost any position and batted at the top of the order, he had hardly seen the field. The Rattlers were men like Harley Kick, ten years older, at least. Angus mostly sat on the bench, glad to be there, watching and learning the game, waiting his turn, listening to the older players. This is how he had heard about the technique that Scotty Clausen, Wade Gibbs, and some of the others had used to jimmy open the flimsy clubhouse door. Those guys took girls inside the clubhouse at night, so they claimed, and banged them ceremonially on the wobbly benches or the cold floor or among the boxes of old uniforms in storage. This was how Angus learned about the Cave Girls. He felt ashamed now to recall how eagerly he had listened.

"Turn your lights off," he told the cab driver. "Can I borrow your pen? I'll be back."

He became cold in a familiar way before he cleared the fence. A spring storm in the Bad Axe: four o'clock you stood in shirtsleeves under a fly ball in the outfield, five o'clock you were soaked to the bone with your truck slid into the ditch. He shouldered the loose steel door. With the pen he tripped the plunger on the lock. The door swung open.

The smells stood him still for a moment. Baseball was baseball— leather, tar, sweat, soil, and grass—but at this moment, finally back home, the familiar aromas stirred him as if they were brand-new. As the lightbulb warmed he saw there had been a remodel of the clubhouse, now padded chairs instead of wobbly wooden benches, now lockers with players' names on them, a refrigerator, the rattlesnake logo freshly painted on the wall. This excited him too. Before, all he had ever wanted was to play for the home team. It was different now. What he had dreamed of lately was a home team that he could want to play for.

But he had to hustle. If he got caught here, they would know why he was back.

8

Deputy Rinehart Rog maundered down from the dispatch room, pausing for a bisonlike slurp from the bubbler outside the sheriff's office. He filled her doorway, his great black beard dripping onto the shelf of a gut too large to fit behind the wheel of a cruiser anymore.

"I just took a call from the library," Rhino began. "Harold Snustead wants to close early, make it home before the storm gets too bad. But Walt Beavers won't get off the internet."

"Thanks. Denise should be here soon. Then you can head home."

"He's probably looking at porno."

"I'll pay a visit on my way to the karaoke fund-raiser. Thanks."

"Sounds like Coach Beavers has had a few."

"I'm sure he has."

"Weather Service now says up to ten inches. Power lines are down across the river in Allamakee County."

"Got it."

"Did I tell you Buttercup finally had her baby?"

"Congratulations. Give her hay from me."

"It's a girl calf."

"Lucky you. Girls rock."

"Heidi," he said solemnly.

"Yes, Rhino? What is it?"

"No, I mean me and Irma named her Heidi. In your honor. First lady sheriff in the state."

She felt a dizzying flush of emotion. The people here, their chronic kindness, exactly how her mom and dad had been, their fundamental goodness and warmth. She forced a smile. "I'm not sure interim counts, but thank you. That's sweet."

He still plugged her doorway, eclipsing the corridor's light.

"Was there something else?" she asked.

"Um, yeah. I figured it out."

"You figured what out?"

"Why Denise and you tell those nasty jokes about ladies. Irma helped me. It's like flu shots. Then the real jokes don't make you sick."

"You nailed it."

"Irma said don't ever try any jokes like that myself."

"You nailed that too."

He grinned proudly, saluted her, and disappeared. But one word stayed with her. *Sick.* Downing Boog Lund's cup of bad coffee had felt like power in the moment, but twenty minutes later her mood kept falling, her stomach churned, and her nerves jangled. That creepy zombie farmhand who hit Samson in the face with a shovel—what has his name? But she had to get her mind back in the present. Thinking it might help to call home and tell the kids she loved them and good night, she carried her phone to the window, where she could see her night dispatcher, Denise Halverson, banging the old flatbed truck she called "Old Alimony" into the lot.

As Denise swung the truck around, aiming to park next to the ambulance, a voice behind said, "Sheriff?"

She turned to find town of Dog Hollow supervisor Bob Check, dressed in a stiff new Bad Axe County jacket and ball cap, both black with orange lettering.

"Oh, hello, Bob. You're the EMS captain tonight?"

"Yours truly."

"You guys are going to be busy. I mean, let's hope not, but . . ."

The retired dairy farmer held up a folder with a hand missing its two middle fingers.

"Signatures," he said. "We've got 143. We need 200 to file your nomination papers."

She felt a flood of acid rise from her stomach. "OK, Bob. Good work. I appreciate it."

His smile was dentures in a half grimace, his face so weather-beaten she could barely see his eyes. But their intense blue was on her directly. "Nomination papers are as good as a hole in a bucket, Sheriff, if you're not gonna sign 'em. We've got seven days left."

"I understand. Thank you, Bob. Harley and I are talking about it . . ."

"That knucklehead." He widened her view of his dentures. It was a smile, she reminded herself, and *knucklehead* was a term of endearment. The baseball-crazy Bad Axe–loved Harley Kick. "With a wife like you, he ought not to talk, he ought to listen. We need you, Sheriff. You're a natural."

"Well . . . I'm not sure what I am . . ."

"You're a gal who's got her head screwed on tight."

"I'm glad it looks that way. Thanks. This interim job is a privilege. I just don't know that I'm ready to do it permanently."

"You're exactly what we need"—as he leaned closer and lowered his voice, she smelled hay on his clothes, meat loaf on his breath—"to eliminate a gut worm like Boog Lund."

That startled her. *Gut worm.*

"I'm vermicide?"

As Bob Check guffawed, the wind hitched. Lightning crackled, vivifying acres of snow-crawled sky and colorizing Denise as she speed-waddled in. The sheriff watched her dispatcher handle her snacks, her thermos, her spinal pillow, her paperback novels, her Aaron Rodgers bobblehead. Somewhere, secreted among her daily luggage, was Denise's tin of wintergreen Skoal, illicit in the "tobacco-free zone" she was about to enter.

"Anyway, as you can tell," Bob Check continued, "a bunch of us feel strongly. We want you to run against Lund—and beat the skin off him."

What should she say? "Harley and I are discussing it, Bob. Thank you. Seven days?"

"Right. And we'll have enough signatures by tomorrow. One of us will bring the papers by and hopefully you'll be ready to sign—"

A scorch of lightning stopped him. They both looked out the window as the trailing boom sent hail plunging faster than the snow.

"Opening day of baseball tomorrow," the old farmer remarked. "So a storm like this is a Bad Axe tradition. Problem is, this year the ground is saturated. My crick is over the bank. I've been telling my daughter to get the cattle off that low pasture before they drown. The storm is the easy part. This is all going to melt."

Denise burst through the back door.

"Rider on the storm! Fat bitch, incoming!"

The sheriff attempted a deep breath. Out the other door went Rinehart Rog, hatless and in short sleeves, snow and hail sticking in his beard as he shambled to his truck. She raised a wave, wishing him a safe trip home. She turned and Bob Check was leaving her doorway, reminding her with the folder of signatures before he headed toward the fire-and-rescue end of the building. The sheriff went the other way and caught up with Denise offloading her snacks into the squad room refrigerator.

"Thanks for being early. We're patrolling quadrants tonight."

"Ten-four, my queen." Denise closed the refrigerator. "Are you OK, Heidi?"

"I'm fine."

"You look like you saw a bogeyman. Can I goose ya?"

"Well . . ." She thought about their elderly librarian. "Harold Snustead does like to recommend early-reader books about female heroes, like what I need is a dose of the Amelia Earhart story, which is actually about a woman who disappeared into a black hole." She gathered air to continue. "But Harold means well. So have you got a gentle one?"

Denise stuck a finger her into her cold plump cheek and tilted her head to think.

"Hmm. Something quaint, yet offensive. Sure. Why did God invent high heels?"

"Hell if I know why She would do a brutal thing like that."

Denise giggled. "High heels were created to benefit our work in the kitchen, so that we can reach the dishes on the top shelf—but hang on, I'm getting a 911 call."

Denise barreled down the hallway. The sheriff could hear her big voice responding to the caller. "Oh, dear. That's awful. But he's gone now? You stay safe, little one. I'm sending an ambulance. And Chief Deputy Lund is nearby. He'll be there right away."

Denise barked at Bob Check over interoffice to activate his volunteer EMS crew to the Bad Axe County Library. She reappeared breathless. The sheriff stiffened.

"Heidi, it was that little Grimes girl who kinda lives at the library. Some shithead freak came in there with a girl and he punched Harold Snustead in the face. He's on the floor in a big pool of blood. Lund just left the VFW. I figured I'm gonna send him."

A shithead freak and a girl? That sounded familiar.

"I've got it," she told her dispatcher. "I was headed to the library already."

The blood came from the librarian's nose, which appeared broken, and also from a cut on his scalp, where Harold Snustead had hit his head as he fell. Gabby Grimes, a seventh grader who took sanctuary in county buildings, had apparently seen it all but wasn't quite making sense. A man had punched Harold Snustead in the face. Then he had dragged a long-haired girl out of the library. This is what Sheriff Kick understood so far.

"Catch your breath, Gabby. You're safe. Mr. Snustead is going to be OK."

She hoped he was going to be OK. She had outraced Bob Check's volunteer crew to the library by five minutes and counting. Meanwhile, Bad Axe County's seventy-six-year-old librarian had roused himself to his desk chair, where he sprawled with his head tipped back. His blood grew sticky around the sheriff's boots as she applied pressure with a pinch between his eyes while holding a blood-sopped wad of tissue against his head wound. It appeared from blood tracks that he had been assaulted in the library's common area, near a table that supported an oversize book with a dull-red cover.

"Gabby, what happened over there?"

Wide-eyed, the girl tried to answer. She was a spindly waif in old clothes and broken glasses, a ponytail wrenched across her tiny skull. Deputies answered regular domestic disturbance calls at the Grimes home on Kickapoo Street.

"It was . . . old newspapers. Mr. Snustead . . . he was helping her get information."

"Helping who?"

She shrank a little. She ungripped her damp white hands to show that she didn't know. "This tall girl with long black hair."

"How old, do you think?"

Gabby shrugged. "High school? She wore a really short black skirt, like, a leopard top, and black boots."

"How tall?"

Gabby stood up and showed her. Taller than either of them. "And pretty skinny."

"OK . . . and what did the man look like?"

The librarian gurgled blood, like he wanted to answer. Gabby waited a moment. Seeing Harold Snustead couldn't speak, she said, "Short. Kind of chubby. He was wearing a blazer and jeans. His head . . . was shaved . . . like my dad's."

"Did you see what vehicle they came in?"

Gabby hadn't. The librarian managed to shake his head. He hadn't either. The sheriff made her guess: dark blue van with dealer plates. Shaved head, hollow eyes, ugly, ranting mouth. She shifted in the blood puddle to reach a fresh handful of tissue off the desk.

"Was anyone else in the library, Gabby? Did anyone else see this?"

"Coach Beavers was on the computer. Mr. Snustead said I could stay until he locked up, he could give me a ride, but he wanted Coach Beavers to get going."

The sheriff reflected on Walt Beavers for a moment. He was "Coach Beavers" because he dithered around in the first-base coaching box for the team that Harley had long starred for and now managed, the Bad Axe Rattlers of the Mississippi Valley League. She had asked Harley once, but he couldn't explain how a rummy like Beavers had been entrusted with such a sacred duty. Harley had inherited the situation. *This is the Bad Axe.* That was all he had to say.

The sheriff looked around the library.

"Are you still with us, Mr. Snustead?" He had closed his eyes. He didn't answer. "Gabby, did Coach Beavers see the man punch Mr. Snustead?"

"Yes. But he left right after that, when I was calling 911. He wouldn't go before, but as soon as I said Deputy Lund was coming, he just zipped right out of here."

"Do you have any idea why the man punched Mr. Snustead?"

She watched fear flicker through Gabby Grimes's eyes. The girl's dad made a practice of punching her mom. Her mom never cooperated with the sheriff's department.

"You're safe, sweetheart. It's important that you tell me everything you saw."

"She . . . That girl had a phone, and she was trying to use the Wi-Fi to look up something about a baseball game. A Rattlers game. But Mr. Snustead told her the *Broadcaster* only went online last year, and then he got her this book of old newspapers. That one over there."

"But why would that make the man punch Mr. Snustead?"

"She made him mad. She was teasing him, I guess."

"Teasing Mr. Snustead? No? You mean the girl was teasing the man she came with?"

Saucer-eyed, Gabby nodded. "She won a bet from him, I think. He was mad because Mr. Snustead found her that book with the newspapers, and then he found the article she wanted. It had her brother in it. That was what the bet was about. I guess she was happy because she won money, so she kissed Mr. Snustead."

Hold on. What? Beneath the gob of tissue, his bloody skull tipping up and down, the elderly librarian had tuned in enough to tell her, "Yes, she kissed me."

"Why did she kiss you?"

His mouth opened. That was all he could do.

"Gabby?"

"She said, 'Thank you for helping, you're so cute,' and she kissed him. Then the guy just, like, *wham*, he pounded Mr. Snustead right in the face. Then he grabbed her phone and yanked her out of here, and I called 911."

"That was good, Gabby. You did the right thing. So when did Coach Beavers leave?"

"The lady on the phone told me Deputy Lund was coming. As soon as I said that, he went over really fast and closed the book of newspapers on the article they were looking at. Then he took off."

"Do you know why he closed the book?"

"I don't know, I mean, the Rattlers lost? He heard them talking about it? And he didn't like it? He's a coach, right?"

Finally in came the EMTs, stomping wet boots, the creases in their jackets spilling snow. Bob Check's crew consisted of Kent Tainter and Lana Kussmaul. As those two connected their eyes to the sheriff, she absorbed the moment—that double take by Boog Lund supporters—*Oh, yeah, you, but not for long.*

"Hurry home, Gabby. Here's my card with my cell phone number on it. You can always call if you think of something else. If I need to, I'll come by and talk to you later."

Gabby Grimes collected her things and pushed out the doors. Kickapoo Street was only eight blocks away.

The ambulance crew was waiting.

"Welcome to the party, folks," she began. "As far as I know, Mr. Snustead was struck once with a fist in the face, then fell and hit his head on the corner of that table over there. It seems like he's stable." She looked at the librarian. The EMTs hadn't touched him yet. Bob Check was masking and gloving. His crew just stood there. "Or not. It looks like he just passed out."

"Uff-da," said Lana Kussmaul. "Too much *Goodnight Moon.*"

"Has anybody called the sheriff?" asked Kent Tainter. Lana Kussmaul hooted. Tainter cuffed the sheriff on her stiffened shoulder. "We're just kidding!"

"You two get your heinies in gear." A scowling Bob Check waded in to assume the sheriff's pressure positions against Harold Snustead's injuries. "Any idea who hit him?"

She repeated what Gabby had said. Two strangers, a bet about a baseball game, then the loser, the man, had roundhoused their elderly librarian, who had helped the winner, the girl, by looking up the game in a book of old newspapers. They could have been almost anyone, she reasoned out loud. Storm permitting, she would be tracking down Coach Beavers to find out what he saw. Coach Beavers—now she was thinking to herself—who had rushed to shut the book of bound newspapers. What was he worried about when he fled the scene?

She looked across the library at the big red volume closed on the table, Harold Snustead's blood spattered around it.

———

After the EMTs had stretchered Harold Snustead away, she went to the table in the center of the library. The book was a cheaply bound tome, thick and wide, nearly three feet tall, made from all the issues of the weekly *Bad Axe Broadcaster* in the year 2012.

A spatter of blood arced across the table and stopped exactly where the opened book would have been. She reopened the volume, its front cover fitting perfectly into the clean spot on the table. So where was the blood? She began to flip randomly forward and back within the year 2012, looking for spatters on open pages. But she was dealing with what had to be five hundred pages of newsprint. She was due at the karaoke fund-raiser twenty minutes ago. She scribbled a note and left it on Harold Snustead's desk: *Taking 2012 Broadcasters. Will return.*

With the heavy book held awkwardly under one arm, she once more headed for the doors. She had put one foot down into two inches of snow before she stopped again. Shouldn't she at least know what dirty old Coach Beavers was doing on the internet?

10

Looking past all the big-league-style upgrades inside the Rattlers' clubhouse—the Gatorade cooler, the plush red towels, the five-pound tub of Dubble Bubble, the washer and dryer—Angus Beavers turned his attention to the tubs at the back of the equipment room, packed with air-sealed bags of old jerseys.

If the Rattlers were the official Bad Axe religion, like people said they were, then their uniform shirts were sacred objects. After Aspinwall Ford sprang for new unies every season, the old road jerseys were auctioned off for fund-raising. Some nutty woman once paid five hundred bucks for number 7, Harley Kick. Meanwhile, the old home jerseys were preserved. Angus found the tub from 2012. He peeled back the lid. Inside, each jersey was sealed in its own plastic bag by the same machine that Clausen Meats used to package beef jerky. His was on top: *Beavers 23*. It would be too small for him now. He had hardly broken a sweat with it on.

He sorted out the jerseys that he wanted: Wade Gibbs, nephew of Sheriff Ray Gibbs, number 10; Scotty Clausen, son of the Rattlers' manager back then, Pinky Clausen, number 4; Sherman Ossie, whose family owned Ossie Implement, number 32; Curtis Strunk, his dad a Rattlers Hall of Famer, number 2. Angus closed the tub and turned out the light.

———

The cab driver, his face blue from the glow of his phone, had news for Angus.

"This is Rattlesnake Bowl, also known as Clausen Meats Field."

"Some people call it that."

"That was the Aspinwall Ford clubhouse, remodeled and rededicated last fall."

Angus tucked the jerseys into his bag. "That means Suck's still playing center field."

"Sorry, what?"

"Suck Aspinwall. He sucks, everybody can see it, but he still played instead of me, even when I had pro scouts look at me in high school. Shit like that drove my dad and uncle Walt—"

He stopped. That was not his story. He had been OK with waiting his turn. But the sight of him sitting on the bench behind players like Suck Aspinwall, who came from wealth and status in the community, had driven his dad and uncle Walt out of their beer-pickled minds. Their Beavers pride was a big part of how he lost the life he wanted.

"I don't get it," said the cab driver.

"Aspinwall Ford."

"I still don't get it."

"This is the Bad Axe. This is coulees. Where did you grow up?"

"Somewhere else," the driver said.

"That's why you don't get it."

———

Angus had one more errand. He directed the driver out on U.S. 14 north beyond town, then left on County Highway ZZ, then north on Toole Coulee Road. He confirmed that Clausen Meats was still there, just as he remembered it: the low brick building, the retail store in the front, the processing room and meat locker in the back, the fleet of reefer trucks, the roadside sign—a ham, struck with a cleaver—glowing through the slash of sleety snow.

Back on the highway, Angus told the driver to pull over at the junction with Lost Hollow Road. The junction still lacked a sign because nobody except the Beaverses lived on the road. That suited Angus right now, counting bills into the driver's hand.

"With an extra two hundred, in case you need to pull off somewhere and spend the night."

"That's really cool of you."

"And another hundred to forget what just happened."

"Got it, bro."

"Drive careful."

He watched the taxi's red and white dissolve in the stormy distance. He slung his bag over his shoulder, winced it around to where his back could stand it, and from there the pitted gravel road went down, curved, went down again, curved again, and suddenly there was a hush. The coulee walls had cut the wind. Immense soft snowflakes swirled down upon him as Angus Beavers descended into silver darkness, silent but for creaking trees and crunching footfall and the whisper in his mind.

11

Around her left wrist Pepper Greengrass wears a thick rubber band, red or blue, the kind that comes around asparagus or broccoli stems at the Piggly Wiggly grocery store in the Dells where her mom works. Pepper's habit is to snap the rubber band, feel the sharp sting, and listen to a voice say, *That doesn't even hurt.*

After the scene at the library, after Dale Hill tows her out and hurls her into his van, Pepper begins to snap the rubber band against the sensitive tissue on her inner wrist.

That doesn't even hurt.

Dale drives in a silent conniption fit until his rage gets the best of him. Then he jerks the van to the side of a deserted road outside Farmstead. Pepper has been watching wet snow plaster the ribs of Holsteins standing in a field. Dale's arm lashes out. He snatches Pepper under the jaw.

"Give it back."

The crush of his grip makes her talk funny. "Gib wha ba?"

He sweats. He lost easy money. He punched a sweet old man. His fingers touch her teeth through her cheek. "It's mine unless it's paid for."

"Whaz yers?"

His grip narrows until he has her by the bottom lip. He twists the lip like he wants to rip it from her face. Pepper gasps and draws her knees up, stations her tall boots like a shield over her crotch and belly and boobs. With her head twisted, this is when she sees the backseat of the van and is startled. Her backpack is there. But she didn't bring it.

Dale's face looms two inches from hers. She tastes his fingers, Basic Lights.

"I'm not playing. I own that shit. Put it back."

"K, k, sorry, leggo."

He releases her lip. She scrapes the kiss, the one she gave the cute old librarian, back across Dale's stubbled jaw. That restores his property, and now he stomps on his gas pedal. The van snakes back onto the road. "You got help," he informs her when he is speeding again. "So that cancels the bet."

He slams on into the storm, following his own mutter-back of the directions he received from *fucking Ladonna* at the tavern. The road descends. Pepper snaps her rubber band, snaps it, snaps it—*doesn't hurt*—watching through a screen of sleet as leafless woods pass on one side and dripping rock walls pass on the other. The road plunges, twists, plunges again, hairpins back the other way. Finally it hits bottom with a jarring passage across an iron bridge over the sluggish spread of the creek. It is dark down here. Dale jabs his headlights through another quarter mile before they shine on a broken sign that points them onward and says MISSISSIPPI.

"What the fuck just happened?"

"River," Pepper tells him. She snaps extra hard. "Why is my backpack in the van?"

"None of your goddamn business. This is supposed to be Wisconsin. What the fucking hell just happened?"

She shivers. She can see the river. Dale doesn't know what it is. He revs the van's engine at the shattered sign. Pepper hears her sister's hesitation on the phone. *You're asking could you come visit in Montana? . . . I guess . . . maybe . . . I mean, does Mom say it's OK?* She snaps the rubber band as hard as it will snap. "As in Mississippi River," she informs Dale.

"How the fuck?" is his reply.

"You went too far west. That's Iowa on the other side."

"The fuck do you know?"

"My ancestors crossed the Mississippi every summer to hunt buffalo on the plains."

"Fuck your ancestors."

"You missed your chance," Pepper tells him. "But you're welcome to visit the casino."

He jerks the van through a five- or six-point turn, manly in intent but not in execution. As his headlights dial back the other way they filter through the storm and strike a wall of yellow-brown rock, layered, clumped with moss and pocked with cliff swallow nests, too tall to see the top of. She is shivering now, can't stop.

"If it's not my business why you brought my backpack, then whose business is it?"

"It's none of your goddamn business whose goddamn business the fuck it is."

———

One ridge and two valleys later, through what now are snowflakes so big that they drop straight down like gob-spit off a bridge, Dale spots the sign for the road that he has been calling a cocksucker for as long as Pepper can seem to remember. He hits his brakes too hard. The van slides, does a 360, and shanks into the ditch.

For a while Pepper watches the spectacle of a grown man shrieking like a hysterical old witch while he spins his tires and the van sinks deeper. Then she says, "I know how to drive, so let me. Because you're gonna have to push."

He slams his door. Pepper slides over. She feels the creepy heat of him in the seat and the damp grime of his hands on the wheel. She turns the tires toward the road, runs the window down to listen for him. Those heavy snowflakes splatter in, making her colder. She presses the brake, puts the gear into low. "Are you stupid?" Dale screeches. By this he means *go*, so she gives a bit of gas, just enough to keep the weight of the van on the tires. She eases it up to the road—and suddenly she has maybe five seconds.

At two seconds, she looks into the mirror to see Dale slogging out of the ditch. At three seconds, she understands she has a chance. She has her backpack, all of her stuff, even though she didn't bring it, and the van is hers if she takes it now, and maybe she can make it all the way to Hungry Horse. At four seconds, Pepper's hands have left the gears and steering wheel—she is snapping her rubber band: *it doesn't hurt*—while in her mind's eye she is arriving in Hungry Horse, seeing Marie's face, trying to read if her sister is truly, honestly, happy to see her . . .

Then it is too late.

Walt Beavers had bolted without logging out, and his history on the library computer was more eclectic and ambitious than she might have expected.

He had begun by shopping for insulated boots. After that, he had priced a crossbow. Then he had compared joint-lubrication formulas. After that, he had looked at water volumes at Lock & Dam No. 9 on the Mississippi, probably a place where he liked to fish. After that, like he was sneaking up on it, Coach Beavers had finally opened a porn site. There he had taken just a couple of nips of "Big Boob Teenies" before sending the browser to a website called Backpage.com. And that was a different place entirely.

The sheriff used her cell phone to call Denise. Instead of hello, Denise answered, "Harold Snustead is going to need surgery."

"I'm not surprised."

"So is the cocksplat who punched him, if he ever crosses the path of Denise 'Thunder Thighs' Halverson."

"I hear you." She was thinking zombie more than cocksplat, but it steadied her to hear Denise's sass. "I'm hoping somehow Walt Beavers can lead the way."

"I'm staying in touch with the hospital. I'll let you know."

"Good. Here's why I called you: a website called Backpage.com."

"Are you asking me what it is?"

"I can see what it is."

"And?"

"There's just this weird feeling I have about Walt Beavers on a sex-for-sale website at the same time as what seems like a pimp and prostitute show up in town. I'm on the library computer, about to go in, following the sticky trail of Coach Beavers. I need a vaccination."

"God help you. OK. What's the difference between a hooker and a whore?"

"Tell me."

Denise gave her punch line a manly oomph. "Frankly, in my experience, there is no difference."

"Hmm."

"Too abstract?"

"Yeah. Also, my research indicates they're called escorts."

"How about a limerick?" asked Denise.

"Have you got one?"

"You think? 'There once was a whore from Peru, / Who filled her vagina with glue. / She said with a grin, / "If they pay to get in, / They can pay to get out again too.'"

"Oh my God, Denise, you are a genius." A decent breath filled her lungs. Her brain felt cleaner. "Keep me posted on Harold."

Coach Beavers had clicked efficiently through Backpage.com from "Social" to "Parties" to "Wisconsin"—and, yes, it was a live link, something a sheriff should know about—to "Bad Axe County," where the most recent listing was a haiku-length notice that said *4/8, dancers, gate fee, Ease Inn for Singapore Sling.*

Based on the computer's history log, Coach Beavers had been looking at boots again when the black-haired girl had worried him by reading from the *Bad Axe Broadcaster* about a baseball game in 2012. Sheriff Kick memorized the Backpage.com listing: *4/8, dancers, gate fee, Ease Inn for Singapore Sling.*

She headed out into the storm with the big red book half wrapped inside her jacket. It probably didn't matter what a Singapore Sling was. Something fruity. A code phrase. As she steered behind slapping wipers toward the south end of town, heading for the Ease Inn, she put the pieces together. The *4/8* was April 8, today. In the context of

Backpage.com, *dancers* probably meant strippers. A *gate fee* suggested a private event. So, a private party, tonight, with strippers? This man who punched their librarian—was he bringing a stripper? More than a stripper? For Walt Beavers and his ilk to enjoy? She rapped her knuckles on the cover of the red book as it rode on her passenger seat. Was there something in those pages that Coach Beavers didn't want her to see?

The roads were bad and getting worse. She whooped her siren and flashed her lights at a grimy red tractor-trailer coming too fast into town. She turned into the lot of the Ease Inn, rolled past the pumps and past the front window of the tavern. The place was busy—dollar taps, she remembered—and she could hear the karaoke leaking out of the banquet room in the back, under way without her. Someone was mangling the Otis Redding great about sitting on a dock by a bay.

No, she would not go in and ask for a Singapore Sling. She would get the drink if she asked for one, not access to a party with strippers. She could see through the window that the bartender was Ladonna Weeks, an especially toxic ex-flame of Harley's. No, she would not go inside at all. On top of swapping paint in a collision with Ladonna, she might get spotted by someone from the fund-raiser.

She needed a different strategy. Easing past the motel doorways, she noted a few vehicles positioned deliberately beyond the lot lights, where long-haul drivers parked their rigs overnight. She rolled past a blue-and-corrosion Chevy sedan. It looked empty. But inside the next vehicle, a red club-cab pickup, a head ducked down.

She parked and went to the driver's window, motioned that she wanted it down.

"Wow. Brand-new truck. You're gonna wreck this one from the inside out?"

She was asking this of Calvin Fanta as marijuana smoke poured out, almost choking her.

"Come sit in my car," she said.

"Aww . . . Missus Kick . . ."

"Sheriff Kick. Come on."

Fanta, tall and knock-kneed, was one of Harley's high school players, a left-handed junkballer who had graduated last summer, failed to make the Rattlers' rotation, and now was fading into Bad Axe baseball history. As he sat down in her cruiser, she said, "You were getting stoned behind the wheel, Calvin."

"I wasn't gonna drive like that."

"I know. You were going to go inside and drink tap beers for a dollar while the roads got a whole lot more icy. *Then* you were going to drive 'like that.' "

"Aww, come on . . . Missus Kick!"

"Calvin, you're talking to *Sheriff* Kick. And that pretty new truck tells me that maybe you're not just smoking, you're dealing. I search that truck, am I going to find evidence of that?"

"Shit."

He slumped in defeat, his knees banging her onboard computer.

"Let's work together. Here is what I want. Go to the bar and order a Singapore Sling—"

"A what?"

She repeated it, a Singapore Sling, a cocktail.

"Then come back and tell me all about it. Bring me anything and everything Ladonna gives you, except the glass it came in. Remember anything she says to you."

"What? I don't get this."

"You don't need to get it. Here's a twenty. Tip Ladonna one dollar and bring my change back. Then we'll talk about how to handle your possession-with-intent-to-deliver charge. You got it? Singapore Sling. Go."

She turned her dome light on and opened the volume of *Broadcasters* against the wheel. Why had Walt Beavers shut the book? She began to flip back and forth, looking for the pages where Harold Snustead's blood was spattered. Then she found them. The spray of blood continued over the two sports pages of the August 15, 2012, issue, and on those pages were the prep football preview, rodeo results, a badly overexposed photograph of a guy with a good-size sturgeon, and, finally, a brief story about a game between the Bad Axe Rattlers and the Wisconsin Dells Scenics. Given the choices of what Coach Beavers might have been concerned about, Gabby Grimes seemed right to suggest that something about this article was the reason he had closed the book and rushed out of the library.

She squinted at the small print. The game was a Wisconsin Baseball Association first-round playoff matchup, a game the Rattlers were expected to win. But the Scenics, from the Dairyland League, had blitzed the home team, 19–3. That was a shocker. She went back to the top of the article. The game had been on Sunday, August 12. Less than a month before, she had given birth to the twins. That would explain why she didn't remember. She was on maternity leave from the Dane County Sheriff's Department. She and Harley were living in Middleton, a suburb west of Madison, two hours away. Harley was driving out here for Rattlers games, staying overnight with friends.

But a glance through the box score surprised her. Harley had pitched? And given up nineteen runs? Twenty-one hits? Six home runs to one guy? Those were T-ball stats. Her husband must have pitched left-handed. Or with his feet. And *that* was a story she would have remembered. But what was Walt Beavers worried about?

With her phone, she took a picture of the story with its box score. She would ask Harley. When she found Coach Beavers, she would ask him too.

———

In five minutes Calvin Fanta returned, pigeon-toeing through the slush away from the tavern. She moved the volume of *Broadcasters* onto the backseat. Fanta slid in beside her with a sweetly alcoholic exhalation. He handed her two things: a tiny paper umbrella and a coaster.

"How was your Singapore Sling?"

"I hate pineapple."

"And Ladonna gave you these? Was it Ladonna?"

"Yup."

The word *skank* traveled through the sheriff's mind. She pushed it out with a deep breath. She tipped the umbrella under the dome light: a number was written on the underside. It looked like a Bad Axe County fire number, the kind posted to identify a rural property. The coaster was so brand-new that it smelled like ink, with a faint hint of pineapple. It

advertised a place called Come Back Saloon. No such place existed in
the Bad Axe, nor south in Crawford County, as far as she knew. Maybe
Vernon County, north? Why would the Ease Inn give out another
tavern's coasters?

"This is it?" she asked.

"Yup."

"Any conversation?"

"She said, 'Bottom Road.'"

"Anything else?"

"Nope."

"How about my change?"

"Missus . . . I mean, Sheriff Kick . . ."

Calvin Fanta was shaking his head, exhaling ruefully, and rubbing his
palms on his pant legs, like his grip had slipped and he had just grooved
a home run. "I don't know if I shoulda or not, but I figured . . ."

"What is it, Calvin?"

"Well, there actually was a little more conversation. Ladonna said,
'You sure? Once I put that drink on the bar, you pay for it in full, in
cash . . . no refund.'"

"And . . . ?"

"I paid a hundred bucks for that stupid drink."

A hundred-dollar gate fee? Wow. Then she felt surprised that Calvin
had the cash. It probably confirmed that he was dealing. She thought
for a minute.

"That's a lot of money for a drink. How about we call that your fine
for possession?"

"Yeah, sure. That's what I was kind of thinking."

"Now, about the dealing . . ."

At the Ease Inn's side window appeared an unmistakable profile.
Etched by the red neon of a Bud sign, Ladonna's darkly skankish beauty
was still a thing that jerked the eye to it. She must have been suspicious
about Calvin Fanta buying a Singapore Sling. She lingered, seeing Calvin in the sheriff's car, then moved away.

"I'm not dealing, ma'am. That's my dad's new truck."

"You were smoking weed in your dad's new truck?"

"I've got Febreze."

"Well, that fixes it, huh? All right, Calvin. Buckle your seat belt."

Sheriff Kick put her locks down and started her cruiser rolling.

"Wait—what? My dad's truck!"

She dropped him off, stoned, with a Singapore Sling on his breath, at his parents' house. Curtains parted very cautiously, someone watching as he stumbled toward the door. Driving away, she recalled Ladonna's gaze from the tavern window. Ladonna knew that she knew about the party. She would have to find it fast.

———

Five minutes later the sheriff bore the bound volume of *Broadcasters* under her jacket into the Public Safety Building. She left it on her desk. In the restroom, she splashed water on her face, moisturized her lips, did not allow herself to linger on the troubled woman looking back. She hurried down to Dispatch, where Denise's computer screen displayed the property tax roster for Bad Axe County. A sticky note on the back of Denise's hand recorded the property number written on the cocktail umbrella.

"Here it is."

The sheriff squinted. The property was on Bottom Road in Snake Hollow Township, which filled the far southwest corner of the Bad Axe. Denise switched windows to display a PDF plat map of the township that looked hand drafted. She dragged it to her dual monitor. The property in question was on the south flank of Battle Bluff, a local landmark on the Blackhawk Trail. The Bad Axe River ran through the bottomland farm. Enlarged, the handwritten script identified its owner as *E. Faulkner*. Denise said, "Since the title to the property transferred in 2010, those records are online. Someone named Prayleen Brown is the legal owner."

While Sheriff Kick marveled at the name Prayleen—both lovely and absurd—Denise kept tapping her keyboard.

"OK, I know who this is. Prayleen was Emerald Faulkner's daughter. Emerald passed maybe ten years ago. There's a brother in that family, William. Yes, you heard me correctly. High school English class, right? *The Sound and the Fury*? William Faulkner?"

"You're joking."

"Me? Joke?"

"Who in the hell would name their kid William Faulkner?"

"Oh, that's nothing," Denise said. "I have a whole list of doozies like that in my head. Don't get me started. I'll give you one more just for now, and it will blow your freaking mind. Abraham Lincoln. And trust me, Clove and Peetey Lincoln, neighbors of my great-uncle Gunnar, probably never even heard of the other guy. Anyway, our own Abe Lincoln drowned in a bucket when he was three."

She shared this while scrolling to the top of the deed, moving too fast for the sheriff, who looked away, feeling dizzy.

"Prayleen Brown now lives in Topeka, Kansas. And . . ."

Denise switched into Google, typing so emphatically that her Aaron Rodgers bobblehead bobbled. "And William 'Billy' Faulkner, Blackhawk High Class of '85, is now in Chicago. So they're absentee. I bet they rent the land. I have to tell you, this all sounds like a stag party."

"What? Why?"

"People call them stags. It's been a thing in the Bad Axe forever. Secret parties in the hollows. Men only. Except for the entertainment."

"Why hasn't anybody told me?"

Denise answered with a shrug. "I never knew about them until I married Dirk. He always told me he was going to a Ducks Unlimited meeting and came back smelling like chicks instead of ducks."

"Sonofabutt, Denise. I'm from freaking thirty miles away. I never heard of secret stag parties out in the hollows."

"Because you're a good girl."

The sheriff made herself stay quiet. For about six months of her life, after losing her parents, she would have stripped for booze money, easy. Thirty miles away and ten-plus years later seemed to be enough distance, thank God, that most people in the Bad Axe didn't know. Boog Lund could have a field day with her past. Without noticing how it happened, she was drinking coffee from the pot on Denise's hot plate, out of a pink mug that said *I DONUT CARE.* Oh God—had she checked for Skoal spit first? She put the mug down.

"OK, are these like bachelor parties? What goes on?"

"I could never get a straight answer out of Dirk." The way Denise said her ex's name made it sound like a kind of knife. "But drunk men and cheap women, what else? All you can drink. Amateur strip contests. Lap dances. Take it from there, right? Goes all the way back to when Ladonna's grampa Boyd Weeks cooked moonshine and ran a brothel in the thirties. It faded for a while, but when meth hit the coulees, and now there's heroin too, suddenly there was a big new batch of girls willing to party, if you know what I mean. Gibbs was only the latest sheriff who looked the other way. You're surprised?"

"I really shouldn't be. Yet I am. Yet I'm not." Her pulse had sped up. Harold Snustead's assailant was headed for that party, and she might be able to help that girl, maybe more than one girl, if she could get there in time.

She had picked up Denise's mug again. Empty. Her tummy squealed. She retrieved the cocktail umbrella with the property number written on it.

"Wish me luck," she said.

Her move to exit seemed to remind Denise of something. "Oh, Heidi, by the way, while you were at the library, the new Crawford County DA stopped by looking for you."

She paused in the doorway, only semisurprised. "Crawford County?"

"As in, our neighbor to the south, where you grew up?"

"He was looking for me?"

"He was a she," Denise answered. "Kinda young and preppy. She was going home from a meeting in La Crosse, passing through. Something about open records?" Denise frowned now. "There was some kind of conflict with a clerk, it seemed like. She said she wanted to get a little background from you."

The sheriff stalled, feeling suddenly exposed. The problem wasn't open records, it was *closed* records. All those years ago, she had been denied the details of how Sheriff Ken Skog and his medical examiner had arrived at murder-suicide as the cause of her parents' deaths. What was the physical evidence? What suspects had been considered and rejected, and why? Skog had disbelieved her when she said that the murder-suicide weapon, the .38 Cobra he had returned to her after the case was closed, was not her father's gun. Her father's *real* gun, she told Skog, was a family heirloom Colt revolver that shot Whiz-Bang bullets—and that gun was missing, along with a whole box of Whiz-Bangs, *the whole box*, from where he kept it atop a hewed beam in the barn. Skog's explanation was money pressure: the farm was going bankrupt, so her dad sold the valuable old gun and bought a cheap one . . .

"Heidi? Hello?"

But why seal a routine case file? The reason Skog gave—confidential financial information establishing the failure of Cress Springs Farm, in turn establishing her father's motivation—had always smelled like a smoke screen to her. Last week, as her grief and suspicion were reawakened by the Bishops Coulee murders, she had exchanged words with the Crawford County clerk, and in the heat of the moment she had threatened to sue. Anyone wanted background, Crawford County DA or otherwise, that was it.

"She said she'd call you in the next day or two. I said you were kinda busy right now."

"I am."

"I said you had enough to do up here in the Bad Axe."

"I do."

"You don't mean to tell Crawford County what to do."

"I don't."

"And right now you have a party to attend."

"I do."

"Go."

Wish me luck, she nearly asked Denise again. A profound aloneness stopped her. She put on her jacket and headed into the snow toward her Charger.

13

After he is released from the ditch, the next thing Dale Hill does is forget that he found the road before, and he gets lost again looking for it. He drives in stormy circles back to where he went into the ditch. This is once more the fault of *that rip-off bitch Ladonna* at the tavern. He yells at Pepper Greengrass to pay attention, but he doesn't say what to pay attention to. This is men, as Pepper knows them. She tells Dale that he's the one who needs to pay attention. This time he connects a hard fist-strike to her collarbone as she twists away too late.

She snaps and snaps the rubber band against the veins of her wrist. None of this is hurting, not at all. What she can't solve is the presence of her backpack on the backseat.

She did not bring it. Dale did, for a reason he won't tell her. *None of your goddamn business whose goddamn business the fuck it is.* . . . So all this time, the backpack has ridden along behind her like a translation of the day's events, events she thought she understood, into a language that she doesn't know. She snaps the band.

"Why don't you give him a ride?"

They have come up behind that same hooded guy from the Kwik Trip toting a heavy blue bag, in the middle of nowhere, plodding along this tiny potholed road. His breath steams into Dale's headlights as they swing around a curve. He has nowhere to get out of the way. Pepper worries Dale will hit him. She lunges, pounds the horn. He takes one thick hand off the bag strap and raises a go-fuck-yourself bird into the plunging slop. Dale explodes, rushes his window down, and shoves his own middle finger over the van's roof, shrieking that the guy should go fuck himself, himself. Pepper snaps the band.

Finally Dale finds Bottom Road. They cross another iron bridge, then turn down a dark and narrow lane mushy with black mud all churned up in the frozen output of the storm. The lane twists until Dale's headlights flash on a farm gate and a battered pickup parked alongside.

A man in coveralls heaves from the truck and turns out to be almost some kind of giant. The expression *tall enough to hunt geese* travels through Pepper's mind. Someone once said this about her true dad, Bernard Greengrass, carrier of the Plains Sioux genetic code that gave Pepper long legs.

The tall man in coveralls spits brown juice through Dale's headlights, then stoops at his window. With a gnarled and massive hand, he meat-hooks away the coaster Dale got from the tavern—it's a ticket, Pepper sees—then limps across the slushy mud and swings the gate open.

"They're just now telling me," he looms in to notify Dale, "that on account of the storm this party ends at midnight."

"You charge a hundred bucks"—Dale is gearing up to take this guy's name—"you at least oughta give decent goddamn directions."

The big man ignores him. "We don't want folks stuck in here."

"You oughta be ashamed"—Dale stops halfway through the gate—"charging a gate fee for management. A hundred bucks my ass. All I'm doing is bringing a dancer to the show."

"What I'm ashamed of is letting my neck get wet jawing with a horse clod like you."

"Give me your name," Dale demands.

"My name is Ed Burney. But I'm gonna keep it. You're not out this gate by midnight, I'll be seeing you again."

Dale pulls through, still bitching. Around the next curve, the lane is lined with snow-pasted vehicles tilted into the ditch. The lane goes on. Like some weak-ass turkey bitch at a Dells outlet mall, Dale drives all the way in to where the action is—an abandoned farm, broken machinery, boarded windows, a newish metal barn that pulses with energy—and once there, he throws a fit about no parking, then turns around and drives too fast back out to the end of the line. Pepper marvels. Dale and her stepdad, Felton Henry, they share so much.

"Get pretty," Dale commands, snapping on his dome light.

"I was born pretty."

"Don't fuck with me."

Pepper tips the visor mirror down. Cinnamon skin, blue eyes, ass-deep Greengrass black hair. Any beauty issues derive from her half-German mom's cheese wheel of a face, but Pepper knows how to build cheekbones, how to lift out eyes that look slightly poked into her face. She refreshes her lip gloss. She snaps the rubber band. *You can't hurt me.*

"Who needs to fuck with you?" she follows up with Dale. "You're too busy fucking with yourself."

He is drilling a Basic Light into his lungs. As he exhales, he seems to be letting something go, and his calm surprises her.

"Keep it up. See where it gets you."

14

Sheriff Kick's pulse leaped suddenly. A cold sweat broke along her spine. She lifted her right foot, her whole leg trembling.

She had been doing eighty-five on a snow-covered highway, with almost no visibility, ranting at Sheriff Skog for not believing her, then cursing herself for finally giving in, then acting self-destructively, behavior straight from her darkest of nights.

She let the cruiser drift down to thirty.

Now she crawled along, taking deep breaths, squinting through her wipers still at full speed. She was just passing the sign that would have announced her entry into Snake Hollow Township had it not been glommed with sticky snow, when her radio crackled out fragments of Denise that dissolved into static. A moment later her phone stirred in her breast pocket. She camouflaged her inner distress with a dumb bit of banter.

"Did you miss me already?"

"Heidi, the radio relay must be iced over again. I'm glad I caught you before you got down into Snake Hollow. Your cell won't work down there."

"You're not going to tell me I drank your tobacco spit, are you?"

Her dispatcher let pass about three terrifying seconds. "Are you there, Denise?"

"This is a tobacco-free zone, Sheriff. I have no idea what you're talking about. But if I did, the answer would be no, you're good. You just stole the rest of my coffee."

The sheriff pumped her brakes, brought her speed down even

more. She was looking for Weber Ridge, the turn down-hollow toward Faulkner's farm on Bottom Road. "So what's up?"

"You're gonna have to come back. I just took a ten forty-five from Earwig at the home."

The sheriff saw Weber Ridge but didn't take it. She coasted through the junction feeling the slick macadam under the snow beneath her tires. Who was Earwig? What home? In Dane County, where she had memorized the 10 codes, a 10-45 was a stranded boater.

"Sorry. Earl Wiggendorf, night supervisor at Bad Axe Manor, tells me somebody just called in a bomb threat. We have to respond."

"Bullshit."

"A pile of it. But it's a county facility and there's protocol in the county legal code. We have to respond."

"Ladonna Weeks. She saw me with Calvin Fanta after he had his Singapore Sling."

"I wouldn't put it past her. We don't have a number to trace, but Earwig said the caller was a woman. Anyway you'd better turn around."

She had already started, using the narrow shoulder as she tried to picture the layout of Bad Axe Manor. The first hospital in the region was now a sprawl of dilapidated quarried-sandstone structures beyond the right-field fence of the diamond where the Rattlers played. She hit the gas as hard as she dared, heading back toward Farmstead.

"So . . . what's the protocol?"

"I have it right in front of me: 'Bad Axe County Emergency Management Bomb Threat Protocol.' Step one is that I have to notify the emergency management coordinator, who calls the shots, including the deployment of the county sheriff for evacuation and assessment of the threat. So you take orders from the coordinator."

"And that's Marge Joss?"

"It is. And she's a Boog Lund kinda gal. She'd like to deploy you right out of town."

For a harrowing few seconds she considered whether the bomb threat might be the work of one of her deputies. Gibbs had not looked the other way on stag parties all by himself. Denise read her mind. "I know, Heidi. I know. But here's the thing—"

She gasped. She was driving too fast again.

"Heidi?"

"I'm here."

"Here's the thing. We've got a blizzard. Now we've got a bomb threat. We'd like to assume it's bogus, but legally we can't. And consider this: do we *know* the asshole who punched Harold Snustead is at our little party? No, we do not. We're on a major highway. It goes all the way from the Illinois to the Minnesota border. All kinds of people pass through here. Do we know that he's a pimp, and she's underage? We do not."

"Sonofabitch."

"That we do know. But I have an idea."

"I need one."

"All we need is a man, a typical local guy, a decent man, but with some balls, who is *not* at that party right now."

Denise paused as if to listen to herself.

"I know, I speak in opposites, my queen, but if we can just come up with one guy, and give him a camera . . . Buddy Smithback? He doesn't even need to go in. We just need license plates."

"OK. You're right. I'm heading back."

15

To Pepper's eye, the barn that she and Dale go into—if you take away the hundred or so grubby white men—looks like the setup for a Ho-Chunk tribal pancake breakfast, the kind of event with a flea market, a kiddie talent show, handshakes from the tribal vice president, and an information table set up by the American Diabetes Foundation. Pepper's gaze takes in long folding tables and metal folding chairs, bright lighting, concrete floor, plywood stage. A PA system spews garbled music over a voice announcing things she can't understand. She turns a circle. At the far end of the barn, those are ice-fishing tents, the kind she is used to seeing on frozen Lake Wisconsin. So those are for the lap dances, she figures. At the center of the barn, opposite the stage, men gather around half barrels of beer that are iced down inside sawed-off plastic garbage cans. Others crowd a plywood bar stocked with off-brand liquor bottles and red plastic cups. The hundred bucks includes unlimited alcohol, apparently. At the far side of the stage, on more folding chairs, two girls sit huddled over their tits like they're scared of what they've gotten themselves into. This is where Dale drops her off, bossing her over the din, "Stay here," then heading for the liquor bottles.

"Hey, bitches." She opens strong. These girls don't get it. "Whatever. I'm just kidding."

The girl who finally makes a dull reply—"Ha, ha"—is a heavy blonde with a bruised-banana look. Another girl says to Pepper, "You're new, right? Where'd you come from? You're not coulees, right?" She has short thick legs and a bent-looking face under hair that she has dyed cotton-candy pink. This girl volunteers, "She's from Bishops. I'm from Locks."

Pepper says she's from the Dells. The girls from Bishops and Locks find this impressive. The Dells is Wisconsin's most famous place. Water parks, casinos, golf courses, petting zoos, go-cart tracks, half of Chicago on drunken vacation, all kinds of bullshit that these girls are lucky not to have. Pepper keeps looking around. Over by the alcohol, Dale exhorts some idea into the ear of an older man who looks gnomish, even next to Dale's dumpy five seven. This older guy is like a miniman, coiffed with what looks like a toupee, wearing a cheap brown business suit and sensible rubber overshoes.

Never mind. Pepper keeps looking. One of the lap-dance tents shudders. Out escapes a fourth girl, even bonier than Pepper, ginger haired, wobbly fast on tall red heels, bolting back to home base while her client squirts away into the crowd of men. As this girl arrives, Cotton Candy from Locks informs Pepper, "She came over from Iowa. She's got ice if you want some."

Now Dale steers his conversation partner over. Pepper gets a closer look. There is a man you see in casinos, usually small, usually dressed by JCPenney, usually not a gambler, who creeps around in soft shoes with a smile of fascination stuck on his face and the body language of a Peeping Tom. He dreams of sniffing your armpits. Or he wants to sit where you just sat. All while he wears his JCPenney costume and speaks in harmless drivel. This is that man. Dale says to Pepper, "Sweetheart, this fine gentleman wants to buy you a drink."

"But aren't they free?"

The miniman guffaws.

16

Squinting against the snow, Angus Beavers used half-buried fence posts to follow Lost Hollow Road. His mind kept starting over. What if he was wrong? What if she wasn't even there? What if his dad had really burned her?

He set down the Jumbo Shrimp bag. He unzipped it to verify that the stolen jerseys—*Clausen, Gibbs, Ossie, Strunk*—were inside. Yes—he had really done that. Yes—that morning he had been in Florida. For the eternity of a minute he stood with his hot skin melting the sleety flakes, his heart thrumming with adrenaline. He was soaked, freezing, burning up, two hours slogging downhill, nearly home. He took full, gulping breaths, tasting the tangy drift. Rust smelled like blood when it was wet. His dad's scrap yard was just up around the curve.

He shouldered the bag and trudged on. Soon he saw that in his four years away, Beavers Salvage had become a junkyard. It looked like now people drove by and threw trash off tailgates. They used to be afraid to do that. He plodded past busted patio chairs, swollen mattresses, sacks of kitchen garbage that the coons had torn open and scattered. He saw in the luminous storm-dark beyond the littered ditches that Beavers Salvage now spread across his dad's entire ten acres, both sides of the road. He ground his teeth to stop a shiver. Cancer, Brandy had said. Everywhere.

Here was the house. It looked too small to Angus, iced over and slumped inside a reef of junk, its chimney belching smut from the muddy Amish sawmill slag that his dad got from Zooks for free. He climbed the porch and lingered, squeezing his cold-stung hands and gazing out where the yard light cast a pinkish spray of snow over the black maw of the Quonset shed, where Brandy said the freezer was chained and locked.

But something out there looked different. He kept looking. Some basic feature of the scrap yard had changed in a way that made him uncomfortable. His dad had done something big.

He stared until he understood. Since he could remember, runoff from farmland on the ridge had carved a head-deep gully through the scrap yard. The flow down that gully was so cataclysmic after heavy rains that Angus had once tipped a fifty-gallon drum of crankcase sludge into the brown torrent and counted less than ten seconds before the drum was swept like a dry leaf across the flooded road and into the meadow beyond.

That gully was gone. His dad had filled it in. The ground where it had been was a flat downslope. Now Angus knew why he was uncomfortable. His dad had defied gravity and water, and that could not end well. Where did all that water go now? If his dad hadn't figured that out, then this storm right here, when it melted, was going to cut itself a new gully, maybe right under the house.

––––––

He let himself inside. A grown girl he hardly recognized smoked a cigarette in front of an enormous flat-screen TV. Gluey-eyed, Brandy tried to make him out across the dark room, his little sister's face scabby under thick makeup, her body jammed into tight things to make men look, one pale leg hanging over the recliner's arm and showing her panties like she was still ten years old.

"Are you shitting me?" Her voice was sluggish. "What are you doing here?"

"I quit. I'm home. Where's Dad?"

"Are you shitting me?" She staggered up and hugged him hard, butting him in the chest. "What are you doing here?"

He went into their dad's bedroom. People who knew Beavers said that Lyman Beavers gave Angus Beavers his strength and size, his speed and his eyesight, and his dad talked this up as if *he*, not Angus, were the pro-baseball prospect. But when Angus turned the light on he saw a different man, a tiny old invalid curled away in an undershirt and a diaper on the brass-shouldered bed.

For a long time he just stared. He never had the slightest idea how to talk to his dad. Probably no one did. Always a good chance of getting hit, at least before now.

"So then . . . I was looking out at the yard," he began finally. "And I guess I gotta give you big credit. You filled that gully. Big project."

His dad's chance to boast passed in silence.

"Gotta wonder where the water goes, though. We got a spring blizzard now that's gonna melt fast."

Angus turned him over. He was skin and bones. His wet eyes looked afraid.

"You can't outsmart water. I always heard you say that. So I wonder if you forgot—"

"Gaww!" A furious sound burst from the back of his dad's throat, around his dry, immobile tongue. "Gawww!" Like a crow.

"Dad, it's OK, it's me, it's Angus. Are you in pain?"

He switched on the beside lamp. On the dresser he found a bottle and a pill cutter. The label on the bottle said *Oxycodone 80 mg / one tablet every six hours*. The bottle was one-third full of half tablets. The refill was more than two weeks past.

"Are you in pain, Dad? What's going on with your pills?"

Not getting more than another "Gawww!" for an answer, Angus backed out and closed the door. Now he studied the mess, really seeing it for the first time. The house was pretty bad when he lived here, pretty bad ever since his mom passed when he was little, but never like this. The kitchen, living room, and hallway were full of plastic sacks, booze bottles, packaging, shoes and clothes, all things left where they fell. As if triggered by his scrutiny, Brandy got up from the chair. Clumsily, as if her depth perception were off, she prowled the front window that looked onto Lost Hollow Road. The dress she wore grabbed her on the backside. Angus winced at the profile of her spackled face, the red lips, the plum-black fingernails, the green bead stuck through her raw and sniffling nose. He opened the door to his old bedroom. It had become a bin for the Amish slag wood for the stove. Mice scrambled in the pile. Angus was not expected back. He saw that. He closed the door.

"What?" Brandy demanded.

"Who are you waiting on?"

"A friend."

"What friend?"

"Nobody you would know."

"Where are you going?"

"A party."

"A party where?"

"Somewhere."

"When was your friend supposed to be here?"

She turned in sudden fury, flinging her arms and stumbling on thick rubber heels that looked like dirty cheesecake. Mom's shoes, Angus remembered.

"God! I don't know, OK? I'm just supposed to be ready."

"How old is he?"

"Are you shitting me?"

"Are you sharing Dad's pills with this guy?"

She turned to look out the window, showed her heavy ass, her birdy calves.

"Because that stops right now. What's his name?"

She kept looking into what was frozen rain now, stained pink by the yard light, nothing else to see.

"Is Dad's truck running?"

"Do you think I'd be here," his sister fumed, "if Dad's truck was running?"

He checked inside the refrigerator. A jug of orange juice had settled out and gone green across the top. In the door were five eggs and something half eaten inside a crumpled Subway wrapper. In the freezer he found a half gallon of vodka, almost empty, an open bulk package of frost-fuzzed hashed browns, and a dozen or more rock-hard items wrapped in white butcher paper sealed with Clausen Meats stickers. It was pure Bad Axe, Angus thought, the smallness of the place, that his dad would still be a customer.

He dragged his Jumbo Shrimp gear bag like a big wet slug across the kitchen floor. He moved aside the jerseys—*Clausen, Gibbs, Ossie, Strunk*—making sure Brandy didn't see. He lifted out the foam boats of chicken nuggets, mini egg rolls, and spicy fries that he had gathered under the heat lamps at the Kwik Trip. He wasn't hungry but he dipped a nugget in barbecue sauce and crunched it in his mouth, getting Brandy's attention.

"When your friend gets here, I expect to meet him."

"Expect away."

He watched her go hard for the food. Their dad hollered "Gaww!" again. After a minute of chewing noisily she looked up at Angus with sauce on her lips, her eyes exhausted. "I heard you ask him what he did. He's trying to tell you *garbage*."

"Why is he trying to tell me *garbage*?"

"He's proud of it. It's like a waterslide, but underground."

"A waterslide?"

"He buried a big pipe where that gully was. The water off the ridge goes into that big pipe now, and under the scrap yard, all the way under the road and out into the meadow. You should see it. All that water just shoots out. It makes a little lake in the meadow. Then it runs into the creek."

"He dug the road up?"

"He dug the road up. He fixed it back, but the county still fined him. Not that he paid."

Angus watched her attack a chicken wing like a hungry cat. He gave her a napkin.

"Why garbage?"

She looked at him blurrily. "You see all that garbage people throw by the road?"

"I did. People used to be afraid to do that. What about it?"

"When we get a big flood of runoff from the ridge, he takes that garbage up there and drops it into"—she belched unashamed, still his little sister—"drops it into the pipe. He has a hole in it up there by the Quonset."

Angus was only half seeing what she meant.

"A hole in it?"

"A hole in the ground over the pipe, and then a hole *in* the pipe, the top of it. You drop something down there, Angus, it goes for a long dark waterslide under the yard and under the road and ends up in the meadow."

"And he drops garbage in there?"

"Right. When there's enough water flowing in the pipe. It goes underground and shoots out the end of pipe and flows across the meadow and gets in the crick, and the crick takes it back down Bishops Coulee. Get it? Dad sends the garbage back to the assholes who dumped it here."

Angus remembered what their dad had said a thousand times: *This is a scrap yard, not a dump.*

"He's real proud of it," Brandy said. She had tears in her eyes.

———

Angus let her eat. He found a headlamp with semiworking batteries and went outside in one of his dad's jackets that smelled like grime and rust and sweat and old cigars. He wanted to see what Brandy meant. He followed the feel of aggregate beneath the icy snow up toward the top of the scrap yard and found the short patch where the pipe wasn't buried. Down about waist-deep, his dad had peeled open a six-foot steel culvert, like peeling the top off a sardine can. Angus aimed his headlamp. Brown water trickled along the bottom of the pipe. He tossed in a matchbook from his dad's coat pocket and watched it get carried away.

OK. He got it now. Give shit to Lyman Beavers, Lyman Beavers gives it back. Maybe he and his dad were on the same page after all.

———

The old chest freezer was in the Quonset shed, chained and locked, still humming. Angus found bolt cutters, and he found a rusty ax. With the bolt cutters he severed the chain, but the lid was frozen shut. He found a hand torch and traced blue flame inches from the seal. He knocked the lid upward with the butt of the ax, broke the grip of ice. He raised the lid.

Inside was a glacial mass of fish fillets, several hundred pounds, God knows how old. His dad, his uncle Walt, experts, just ask them, know-it-alls on the topic of baseball, of course, but also on fishing, hunting, trapping, on the drunken killing of every live thing they ever touched. They had been so easy to blame.

Angus was just raising the ax to hack at the fish when he heard a horn blow. As he came to the mouth of the Quonset shed, he heard the front door slam. He held on to the ax and came slipping downhill through the scrap in a hurry.

"Hey!"

Brandy cleared the cinder-block steps clutching a little silver purse. She skated on those wedge heels toward a rust-bombed GTO with a homemade plywood spoiler.

"Hey! No, you don't!"

Brandy fell on the ice. The driver blew his horn again, raced his engine. With the ax in his fist Angus came as fast as he could, but from too far. Brandy scrambled in. She had said Angus wouldn't know her friend, but he did know the gaunt figure in the hooded jacket, smirking at him as the car swerved away.

That was ex-Rattler Brock Pabst.

As Angus stalked back to the freezer, he was shaking. He was so blind his first blow was backward, with the fat end of the ax. If Brock Pabst's jersey wasn't one of the Rattler jerseys he had stolen, it was only because Pabst wasn't one of them on that particular night. But there were lots of nights, lots of parties, and that was his sister.

He turned the ax around and swung the sharp end with all the angry strength he had.

17

Pepper Greengrass, many times in her short life, has observed this in men: drop a guy like Dale Hill in alcohol, he swells up like a sea monkey.

His neck thickens.

His man boobs harden into muscles of the mind.

He sucks breath like killer weed, forced to wince from the tremendous impact of himself. When he speaks he looks around like people want to steal his words.

With her second red-cup vodka mixer from the JCPenney miniman, Pepper watches this and overhears Dale say, "I hear you. I do. But I'd like to clear the purse for the dance contest first, you know? Cover the damn gate fee—hundred bucks, can you believe that shit?—and cover my gas to get here."

"OK, yeah, you dang-darn betcha . . ."

In keeping with his brown suit and rubber overshoes, the miniman speaks agreeably in an Old World cadence and accent. Pepper wonders: Swiss? Norwegian? Is he German, like her mom's mom? His *yeah* sounds like *yaw*. His face is pale and plain but fixed in that smile of astonishment. He finds Pepper's eyes and winks. She hears him tell Dale, "OK, yaw, sure thing, every person likes to maximize a situation. However, I would like to move before the storm gets worse."

Dale has an idea. "Look at those sad bitches. My girl is gonna win. How about you pay the purse? Just add it on."

"This is how much, OK?"

"Winning girl gets two hundred."

The noise of the DJ, the men carousing . . . Pepper loses the thread. The drinks are weak, vodka with too much Sunny Delight, but she hasn't eaten all day. She has goofed her way through round one of the "amateur strip contest." This already seems like long ago. She remembers jumping around in her bra and panties, doing some kind of weird impromptu fancy-dance/ballet-type moves while men hooted. She sucks at dancing, but she is the only one here with legs. In the finals she will face the bruised-banana chick with the heavy-duty tits that she has yet to release from her harness of a bra. Probably she will lose to those tits, Pepper predicts. Suddenly a guy is yelling wetly into her ear, "You're a real pretty girl. I like dark. You mixed? You got a little spade in you? You got beaner?"

His grease-black hands hang like hooks at his side. She's got Ho-Chunk, Pepper informs him, snapping the rubber band around her wrist. One-quarter German.

"You got a dick?" His breath wets the side of her face. "That why you're so athletic?"

He swings a hand under her skirt, gropes Pepper's privates for his answer. She snaps the band and keeps her balance. *You can't hurt me.* Marie never said *don't* come. The Amtrak is only $165 plus tax, and Marie did not say *no, don't.*

But Dale has seen the grope. He sea-monkeys over with his foul mouth running and shoves the guy. The guy shoves back. He asks Dale, "You wanna go? You wanna get down?" Dale launches a head-butt, probably something he learned in prison. They go, they get down, whatever, because Pepper clears the hell out, woozing away too drunk now and wondering all over again why her backpack, why all her stuff in the world, has ended up here, in Dale's van.

Some new guy jerks words into her ear. "So, Pocahontas, you like ice fishing? Twenty bucks, you want to see what's biting?"

He is short, smells like manure. Pepper looks across the top of his dirty hat and sees a tiny bird flit through the rafters, trapped inside the barn. Her line of thinking continues: Amtrak is only $165 plus tax to Whitefish, and she will need a cab from there. She would like to bring gifts. She snaps the blue band. "Fifty bucks."

"Going rate is twenty."

"You get what you pay for."

"Sweet piece like you, girl, I'll go thirty."

"Forty."

"Thirty-five."

She heads toward the tents, snapping.

"You don't really bite, do you, Pocahontas?"

"Call me that one more time and you'll see."

———

Sometime later—time drifts—she vomits into the cold slop outside. Back in the barn, she clings to a shadowy space behind the stage and watches the other girls wrestle with the drunken farmers, the road-crew guys, the bikers, and the truck drivers. Her eyes track that little bird—a sparrow, she sees—following its insoluble panic overhead. The outside door opens, again and again. The bird only has to fly through, and away. But it doesn't understand.

"I guess I'm riding back to the Dells with yous guys."

Surprising Pepper with this announcement is Cotton Candy, the girl with the turtle legs and the dyed-pink hair. The girl's lip gloss is smeared. Her spine sags. She offers one of two red cups, more vodka and Sunny Delight. Her eyes plead. Pepper's mouth needs rinsing, so she takes one.

"But he's nice, right?" the girl asks.

"You mean Dale?"

"He said there's a place to stay. He takes care of everything."

"Yeah. Sure."

"And I can make friends."

"There's two other girls, yeah."

"I was at the Dells once. We rode the Ducks."

"Cool."

"My name's Bailey. Dale says we're leaving in five."

"In five?" Pepper thinks this can't be right. "But I'm in the final."

" 'We're leaving in five minutes so get your shit' is what he said. This storm, I guess."

"And he tells you, not me?" Dully angry, Pepper downs the drink.

Now four girls? Packed in that tiny motel room? "Shit. Then I'm gonna use the potty. If you mean by nice, yeah, he'll stop for the bathroom, but only if he's the one who needs to go."

She squishes through ice-cold drizzle to the portable toilet. She pees and comes back in. Shivering, she holds the door. *Come on, out you go.* But the sparrow freaks and flits away in the wrong direction.

Then Pepper cannot find Dale. Cotton Candy is nowhere either. She hurries to the front door. Dale's old blue van is pulling away.

What?

She staggers, flings her hand, catches something slick and cold. She barely stays on her feet as she fights a closing blackness. Her eyes grasp at images, claw for the surface as she goes under: glazed fence posts, boarded-up farmhouse, overarching glitter of tree tops. Then there is engine noise and a horn toot. Headlights ignite a wallowing body—her body—her skirt and legs and boots—but nothing feels like hers.

"OK, hop in, then, yaw?"

Pepper shakes her alien head. *You can't hurt me.*

"Here we go. Hippity-hop."

He steadies her, the miniman in the brown suit and the rubber overshoes, the one who talked to Dale, who gave her drinks.

"Off we go. Fair and square."

She swims her arms, fighting. *You can't hurt me.* He laughs. He opens his passenger door and shoves her and she can't feel the ground. She feels herself lifted like a little girl. She tries to find her rubber band and snap it. On his car seat, the moment before she blacks out, Pepper sees her backpack.

18

Headlights flashed in the sheriff's mirror. Here came the extra school bus Denise had ordered to speed the transfer of Bad Axe Manor residents from Blessed Savior Lutheran, the bomb threat evacuation site, back to their beds at the manor.

But the bus was moving too fast. It was aiming for the breezeway of the main building, slapping its windshield with a single frantic wiper. The sheriff slung herself from her cruiser, waving her arms. She intercepted the bus and pounded on its passenger door. Just as she feared, the wild-haired older woman behind the steering wheel, gumming an unlit cigarette, was Belle Kick, Harley's mom.

"Belle . . . you can't clear the breezeway. The bus is too tall."

"Who's watching the kids?" the woman squawked.

"What do you mean? Harley is."

They stared at each other. Belle pulled this gag every time—*Who's watching the kids?*—and the sheriff was still falling for it.

"The bus is too tall for the breezeway, Belle. We have to unload out here."

With a sigh Harley's mother pulled her emergency brake. She had been driving with a lighter in her fist. "Is my grandson OK?"

"Which? Why?"

"Did Taylor get over his fever?"

"Taylor had a fever? When?"

"Earlier tonight."

"Harley told you that?"

"Who else is he going to tell? Poor guy."

The sky shed fat flakes that fluttered crazily between the sheriff and her husband's mother. Then Belle was out of the driver's seat and coming down the bus steps, sheltering the cigarette and the lighter against her phlegmy bosom. "Let's go, people!" she hollered back in at the elderly and infirm struggling up from their seats. "Chop-chop."

She continued, "I told Harley to give the kid a shot of whiskey and put an ice cube on his neck. He'll be fine."

The sheriff watched her mother-in-law scurry off, looking for shelter to have a smoke. As she helped folks from the bus, she admitted that Ladonna's brutal math had worked perfectly: one call, plus no bomb, equaled three hours later. There was no doubt that she had missed the party. She hoped they at least had a list of license plates.

"There never is a bomb. It's always just some jerk."

The sheriff put her hand up to see through the snow. The observation had come from a pretty young woman who didn't have any legs. She sat heavily in a wheelchair that had side pockets containing a water bottle, a laptop, paperback books, binoculars, and a fly swatter. She had just been lowered from a transport van and didn't seem to notice the snow.

"It's always just some guy who didn't get his homework done. Or somebody who wants to get out of school and party."

"You're right. But we had to check."

"Or keep the cops busy. I mean, why else bother us?"

Now she noticed the snowflakes and put her face up to catch more.

"By the way, Sheriff Kick," she said, smiling shyly, "I've got your back."

"You do?"

"On social media? When people hate on you?" She displayed her smartphone, in a pink case on a lanyard around her neck. "On Twitter, I'm @groundbeef. Get it?"

Beaming expectantly at the sheriff, she waited two seconds. "Ground beef? What do you call a cow with no legs?"

"I don't . . ."

Abruptly the sheriff was breathless, punched by a visceral memory of when her own life had become a carnival of self-loathing. For a full half year, after the wrong gun had been returned—not her father's gun, but no one believed her—she had dreamed of lying down in front of a freight train. Then she had planned it, right down to which train, which spot on the tracks, and which body parts would be severed. Only a worse idea had saved her: use that wrong gun to kill the killer. Steering her mind away from the terrifying memory, she squinted through glassy eyes to read the name tag: Cindy Lemke.

"Well, thank you, Cindy. But . . . I don't think you should call yourself that."

"I think it's funny."

"Well, thank you. I don't even look at the social media stuff. I don't think it's healthy."

"You're right, it's mostly not. That Jerry Myad dude? Did you see where he tweeted that you should be hit in the head with a bat? I'm in his sick face every day."

The sheriff's cell phone vibrated in her pocket. She answered Denise with a lump in her throat. She was suddenly so weary.

"I'm just wrapping this up. Did we get some names?"

"You bet we did," Denise said. "Buddy Smithback just got back from Faulkner's. The party was breaking up already. They were shooing people home, tipped off by Ladonna, of course. But Buddy nailed it."

"I'm ready."

"He photographed every license plate there. I'm using DMV records to construct a roster of names. You're gonna like this, Heidi. All these Ducks Unlimited liars are gonna want to make deals to save their marriages. You're gonna get all the dirt, everything and everybody—"

"Just the dark blue van with dealer plates," the sheriff interrupted as she dropped heavily behind the wheel of the Charger. "He's the one I want right now. Aggravated battery. Possibly pandering and sexual assault of a minor."

"Buddy got a picture of the van just before the guy left. I've got the tag number. Those are actually Illinois dealer plates. So I'm logged in to Illinois DMV, waiting. The website says it's verifying my credentials."

To the sound of Denise tapping her keyboard, the sheriff glanced at the Charger's clock: a few minutes after midnight. She put the car in gear, rolled away into stormy darkness. So where was that girl now? Where were any of those girls?

She had just paused the Charger at the highway, was watching a snowplow splatter past, deciding that she would now pursue Walt Beavers, see what the old porn-hound-in-the-library could tell her about what happened there, when Denise blurted, "Whoa!"

"What?"

"Holy shit. I mean, you know a lot of these guys. And I know *all* of them. This is a regular Who's Who of Bad Axe County. But for your information, no Harley Kick on the list."

As she exhaled a breath she didn't know she was holding—of course Harley wasn't there—the sheriff watched two vehicles approach from the south and pass through her headlights—one red sedan, one black pickup—both drivers properly decelerating for conditions as they entered town. From the north, a semi rumbled down Main Street and accelerated where the street became the highway. But it slowed and turned into the Ease Inn before it reached her.

"No, I say whoa because there's a couple county board members here. Real churchy fellas. Pretasky and Glomstad. Wow. Gosh, boys." Then Denise sighed. "But sorry, Heidi. I'm finally in with Illinois DMV, only to find out those plates were stolen off a vehicle in Wisconsin Dells, probably from some schmuck at the Ho-Chunk Casino."

The sheriff listened as Denise attacked her keyboard. A new set of headlights coming from the south abruptly slowed and wobbled, as if the driver had been startled by something and was now indecisive. Every cop knew the moment. The driver was guilty—almost always it was DUI, very frequently also drug possession—and had just seen her cruiser. Denise was saying, "I just sent Dells PD the picture of the plate and the van, see if they know it."

Now the headlights retreated erratically, the vehicle swerving in reverse. The sheriff leaned forward in her seat, her foot trembling over the accelerator. The vehicle had backed up all the way to Ten Hollows Road, about to turn off the highway. It was still within the range of her headlights. She was about to get a look at it broadside.

"Oh, lovely," Denise went on. "Here's Ricky Schlitz at the party, here's Randy Brundgart, all these guys are Rattlers, big heroes in the community, here's Brandon Delk, here's Kyle Kumpf—"

"Got him!" the sheriff broke in.

"Got who?"

"Dark blue van. He was northbound on the highway. He saw me and ducked off onto Ten Hollows Road. I'm in pursuit."

"Be careful, Heidi. I've got nobody even close to helping you right now. And it's—"

She cut the call. She put her business lights on, surged the cruiser to the Ten Hollows junction, and turned left. Anticipating her, the driver had switched his headlights off, tried to disappear in the night. But Ten Hollows meant ten hollows, and soon enough he was hitting his brakes on the first steep downhill turn, his taillights blooming in the icy mist.

She added siren. He put his headlights back on and sped toward the coulee bottom. She followed only fast enough to keep him in visual contact. As an out-of-towner, her librarian-punching pimp wouldn't know where he was going. There was plenty of nowhere in the coulees. He would make a wrong turn. As she followed, Denise's warning looped through her mind—*no help*—but she didn't want help. Since the Bishops Coulee murders had scrambled her in time, alone was how she wanted to feel, that old dark habit, hidden struggle, her against the world.

But the driver took all the correct turns. It was almost as if he knew that his best chance was to stay with Ten Hollows Road until it climbed back up and crossed County Highway ZZ. From there, going left on ZZ, he could race her back to the highway junction where the Ease Inn was, get himself buried in the tavern's busy parking lot, and claim to have been there all along. It was a reckless, low-percentage ploy that had worked for her a few times in her drunk-driving days. This guy was trying it, just like a native.

Her heart jittered as she coasted the Charger in beneath the Ease Inn's plaza lights, following the van between the pumps. He squirted around the far side of the parking lot, disappearing briefly. When she caught up, he had snugged the van between two pickups. She came to a stop behind him—

Shit. The van was maroon. Not blue.

She shoved the Charger's door open and stepped out. OK, maroon was close to blue. She took two steps before the door burst open on the driver's side. The driver's legs appeared first. She drew her Ruger. "I need to see your hands! Now!" Then his ass came out, his hands still reaching inside. She put two hands to the Ruger and braced herself. Her heart skittered and her eyes stung as they narrowed. She was sure he was reaching for a weapon. Then a beer can fell out, spilling into the slush. The driver lost his grip inside and toppled backward onto his ass.

Shit. He wasn't bald or stocky. He was not a pimp. He knew how to run from her because he was a native, Randy Brundgart. Her gut heaved. With a sweat-slick hand she holstered the Ruger. She swung an unsteady boot at the van's slush-caked rear plates. Shit. Wisconsin. She had come a half second from shooting the Rattlers' first baseman.

"Missus Harley! How's it goin', girl?"

As Brundgart crawled in the slush, more bodies lurched from the van. Soon the entire Rattlers infield greeted her in a slur of voices, Scotty Clausen, Wade Gibbs, Sherman Ossie. "Hey, how's it goin'? What's the problem? We were here the whole time! Damn, you were gonna shoot Randy!"

"He was driving intoxicated." Her voice felt thin and unconvincing. This was not her battle tonight. "He ran from me."

"We were here all night!"

"You were at a stripper party."

"Us?" Now amid the blur of faces and voices she heard the tone shift, heard the snickering. "Who, us? What party? We guys? Harley's buddies? *Us?*"

And more. They surrounded her. "Get away from me," she snarled. She closed them out, slammed her door and sat inside the Charger. This was not her fight tonight.

Again a massive sense of aloneness overwhelmed her. She had not just fanaticized this time. She had practically hallucinated in real time. Not only had she whiffed on the pimp and failed to extract the black-haired girl, but in drawing a gun on the wrong man, nearly shooting him, she had sideswiped her own past. As she sat there trying to slow herself down, her kill-the-killer mistake swept back in a wave. That shitty little Cobra .38 that Crawford County gave back to her was not her dad's antique revolver. She was sure. So where had the Cobra come from? She had gone straight to Cecil Mertz, proprietor of Rolling Ground Shooting Range and a black-market gun dealer. Maybe Mertz had sold the Cobra, and maybe he had seen her dad's heirloom Colt on the market. In other words, maybe Mertz could tell her who had killed her parents. She had been so terribly lost, had been just about to lie down before the midnight ore train out of Duluth, and Mertz, the evil old prick, had toyed with her.

"Sure, darlin', a bone-handled antique Colt .45? And a box of Whiz-Bang .22 shells?"

She could hear his voice oozing contempt like it was yesterday.

"I do believe I was offered those exact same items from one of them drugged-up punks. I gave him cash and that little .38 you got there."

"Who was he? Someone who worked for my dad, right?"

"Well, let me see if I can recall . . ."

Mertz had given her Dalton Rockwell, who the previous fall had hayed at Cress Springs Farm. No more than two hours later, she had found Rockwell exactly where Mertz said he would be, dealing out of a tavern in Lansing, Iowa. She had walked him into snow-swept corn stubble and put that little shit-rocket .38 to the back of his skull. She had felt blissful. Her suffering was over. Done deal . . .

———

She startled when someone rapped on the Charger's window. A pink glove wiped snow away, and a woman's smiling face appeared. She put the window down.

"Sheriff, hi!"

Beside the cruiser, sheltering their faces from the storm, stood the high school girls volleyball coach and her husband. She could not recall their names. They looked plenty tipsy from the fund-raiser that had ended hours ago. The husband moved to block a wet gust, and his wife, Harley's colleague at the high school, said, "We just saw you and I said to Dan we just have to say hello, Dan said maybe she's busy, I said of course she's busy but we just have to stop and tell her what a wonderful job she's doing because it's not easy and we know that, oh gosh, Dan knows that, Dan works for the county too—don't you, Dan?"

Dan tried to say so, but his wife interrupted. "We're sorry you missed the fund-raiser. Just a hoot. A *hoot*! The girls on the team really look up to you and they were so disappointed you couldn't be there. But of course, we all understand, you're so busy doing such a wonderful job. But you're not running in the special election, we heard. We sure hope she changes her mind, don't we, Dan?"

She wasn't sure how long she sat there, not hearing all the good things they said about her, all the reasons she should run against Boog Lund in July. She could just vaguely recall them toddling off into the storm.

Because her execution of Dalton Rockwell had not been a done deal. In that snow-swept Iowa cornfield—she was blind on booze and weed, Rockwell was too—he had thrashed and she had missed him, point-blank, twice, and those were all the shells she had. Rockwell had sworn he was in jail when her mom and dad were killed, and that had turned out to be true. He had been in the Crawford County lockup that entire July, and for guess what. For beating up and robbing Cecil Mertz.

One week later she had checked herself into a rehab clinic in Missouri and begun her long struggle back toward acceptance . . . *nothing was stolen* . . . and survival . . . *life in forward gear* . . . into college, law enforcement, marriage, kids . . . *purpose and love dissolve grief* . . . and finally back to the coulees, under the illusion, obviously, that the past was behind her.

Pulling away from the Ease Inn, she called Denise. "On my way to Walt Beavers's place," she said. "I need his version of what happened at the library. Maybe he can confirm the vehicle, and maybe he'll tell me why he ran away."

"Save it for tomorrow, maybe?"

Denise waited for a reply. The sheriff pushed her Charger up to speed, thinking of the black-haired girl, feeling her. Who knew better than she did that for a lost girl there might be no tomorrow?

"No, I'm fine."

"You sound kinda shaky, my queen. Sleaze abides. Scum never stops scumming. Let's be better safe than sorry."

As the Charger spun along into the blizzard, she couldn't feel if she was moving forward, backward, or both.

"Heidi, did we lose you?"

19

Pepper Greengrass can't see what she is looking at, because everything has gone black. But she wishes someone else could see how this awful little man drives really slow while he's chattering away in his awful little accent. Would someone please look?

Because there is a girl riding into stormy darkness and he is chitchatting about her clothing size. Pepper can't talk except to tell herself that everything smells like the Armor All wipes she uses to clean inside her stepdad's cab and his sleeper, to wipe the sticky trail that Felton Henry leaves on everything, sticky, sticky, Pepper can't pull one thought apart from another. Bad men all talk to her at once.

Don't waste them. Those cost money. And get that backpack out of here.
I didn't bring it. He brought it.
Stop lying.
He brought it from the Dells.
Those are my cigarettes.
No, he took your cigarettes away from me the first time I met him at the truck stop.
Stop lying. You're a woman now. You like it.

Someone, tell Pepper that someone pissed Pepper's skirt but that the miniman stripping her says it's OK because we're at Walmart now. *You like it. Women like it. Thirteen is a woman. Look it up.*

Pepper can only shake and wish for someone to please watch him skate on his rubber overshoes across the parking lot and stuff her wet clothes down the throat of the trash barrel by the doors. Someone, listen to his radio, the teeny-tiny polka. Someone, smell his window glass and the ice slipping down it. Because she can't hear or smell or breathe or blink or snap her rubber band. Through the doorway of his sleeper cab she sees herself under Felton Henry, rolled, pinned, entered.

God made this. It doesn't hurt you. Stop lying.

Someone, tell Pepper to see what he went into Walmart to get. It's a pink woman's training suit, and a blue-checkered apron, and a Realtree camo jacket and matching hat, and a yellow squash and a zucchini, and a jump rope with wooden grips, and a plastic deer with its legs banded to its back, and a roll of wide silver tape, and a bottle of vodka so big it has a handle . . .

His headlights are tubes of sleet-sparkle through darkness. His voice is singsong polka into a phone, into another girl. Can she do it? With his new girl? Now? Tonight? A hundred?

Someone, tell Pepper to answer the phone. *Pepper Pauline Greengrass, answer the phone.* Tell Pepper she feels freezing cold. *Answer the phone. Pay Dale. Save for Amtrak.* But this is not Pepper because Pepper is blacked out this whole time and shivering so hard that her bones might shatter from the explosions, over and over, as each instant blows away the one that came before.

20

Coach Walt Beavers's truck was in his short shank of a driveway. The sheriff fishtailed off the glazed gravel road and parked beside him. The Charger's tail stuck out, but she doubted anyone would come past. The path around Beavers's scabby little Datsun was crimped by neglected thrusts of buckthorn that snatched at her uniform. Beyond, the old man's yard was the typical coulees wasteland of damaged goods and abandoned ideas, failure and loss accented by north-blown snowdrifts. She kept her head down to navigate around the tilted basin of a rusted charcoal grill where Beavers must have once thought to plant flowers. She made it to the door of his decomposing mobile home and knocked.

Waiting, she felt the desolate beauty. In her two years as a Bad Axe County deputy, she had been dispatched to Dog Hollow just once, assigned to investigate smoke rising where it shouldn't rise. Thrashing through a meadow thick with wildflowers taller than her head, she had discovered a meth kitchen in an army tent concealed in a swamp, no one there. Thrashing back, she had startled something large. Stumbling with her weapon drawn onto matted grass where deer had bedded down, she had been slow to understand that she was not about to be ambushed.

She knocked once more on Coach Beavers's door. This time she noticed a single dark key in the knob. The hood of his truck was free of ice. He had come home recently. Beyond his truck, the restless blue flicker against the Charger's windshield meant that her onboard computer searched in vain for a signal.

She turned the knob, pushed inside, and met fetid air, then two long-haired cats that blossomed like pale ghosts and rubbed around her boots.

"Coach?" she called out. "This is Sheriff Kick. I need to talk to you."

This was not like Bishops Coulee. The house was not on fire. There was no blood in the snow. But she kept entering. Call it a welfare check. Call it suspicious circumstances, the key in the door. She shined her flashlight around the squalid living room. The woodstove was open, no fire. But no ransacking, no sign of violence. Maybe he was passed out on his bed.

"Coach Beavers?" She rapped the butt of her flashlight on the stovepipe chimney. "Is everything OK? It's Sheriff Kick."

She found a light switch. His power was out. Her boot rattled something and she jumped back and put her light on a space heater. But no bloody boot prints like she had followed at Bishops Coulee, no gore-smeared walls half consumed by fire. Maybe he was passed out in a house with no heat. Hard-drinking coulee dwellers died like this every winter, Popsicles before they were found.

With the cats around her ankles, the sheriff followed her light beam down the trailer's narrow hallway. Beavers was not in his bed. No one had struggled for their life and been dragged out. She checked the bathroom, occupied by a bad smell only. No one was here. In the hall she lifted his receiver. The ice had downed his phone line too.

Back in the living room, she scanned with her beam for anything significant. She was drawn to a shelf behind the woodstove: a framed newspaper clipping. She came closer. There was a shrine here, a record of loss. Even as a recent transplant to the Bad Axe, she knew that years ago Walt Beavers had chased the walleye bite too close to a rolling dam on the Mississippi and lost his only child, his little girl, in a drowning accident.

So here was a shrine to tiny, goggle-eyed Hannah Beavers, maybe a second grader in the school portrait by Kling Kountry Kamera. Around the portrait, her grieving father had displayed other memorabilia, including a charm ring and what had first caught her attention, a 4-H

Rabbit Club photo clipped from the *Broadcaster*, framed and labeled in pen *3/25/1984*. Combined under a paper clip were other articles that the sheriff presumed mentioned or pictured Hannah Beavers. Maybe he pillaged library archives with a penknife? But this was long ago. The book he shut was 2012. She moved her flashlight beam. Adjacent to the shrine were several Rattlers trophies. Attracted to dates now, she studied them. The Rattlers went back sixty-some years, but this collection of trophies began in 2012. That must have been when then-manager Pinky Clausen made Walt Beavers first-base coach. The twins were born that summer.

She moved her beam back across the shrine to Hannah Beavers. Opposite the Rattlers trophies, Beavers had positioned what looked like a mustard crock. She picked it up. Yes, it was a small ceramic mustard crock with a swing-top stopper. She unclipped the stopper and got a strong whiff of ashes. She shined her light inside: black ashes, chunky, almost char. His daughter's remains?

The sheriff leaned in, blowing dust off what she assumed were more vestiges of Beavers's deceased daughter. Beside the crock was a blue plastic barrette in the shape of a butterfly. Under the barrette was a page torn from a refillable desk calendar, the kind that flipped one day at a time. A birthday, or a death day, she figured. She moved the barrette aside, glanced at the date, then placed the barrette back onto its dust shadow.

Wait. Hannah Beavers had died in the eighties sometime.

She looked again. Her double take was correct. The date on the calendar page was August 12, 2012, the same day as the Rattlers-Dells game at issue in the library, when Beavers had closed the book of *Broadcasters* and run out. She took cell phone pictures of the mustard crock, the barrette, and the calendar page. She opened the crock again. Her mom and dad had been cremated. This did not look like those ashes.

She called out once more to be sure. "Coach?"

Outside, she shined her light onto the floor of his pickup: not there. She heard a moan. She panned her light around the wider bottomland where the rusty double-wide trailer sat at a tilt. She heard the moan again. Touching the weapon at her hip, she made a slow and treacherous tour around the off-balance structure, baby-stepping through an obstacle course of snow-hidden junk, hearing moans all the way around.

She found a place to look between the cinder blocks that raised the trailer on the driveway side. She shined under and saw a grease-gray little head, turned away.

"Coach Beavers, it's Sheriff Kick. What are you doing under there?"

He groaned and rolled over into the flashlight beam. She winced. His head was grossly swollen in several spots, like someone had shoved eggs under his skin. One of his arms flopped toward her at a horrific angle. His lips were ash colored.

"What happened, Coach? Who did this?"

His eyes stared blankly.

21

Angus struck with the ax, struck, struck in fear and rage, scooped shattered chunks of frozen fish from the freezer and hurled them aside on the dirt floor of the Quonset shed, struck again, and again, and—

He reeled back, soaked in livid sweat that chilled him to the bone. The ax fell from his fist. His chest heaved. His back screamed. His hands shook. He staggered amid the mayhem of frozen pike and walleye that lay about the freezer, tails and heads, eyes looking everywhere.

There she was.

He took several gulping breaths and forced himself forward, leaned over. Down the beam of his headlamp, encased in heavy rime, curled and shrunken and discolored, looking like a very old woman . . . there she was.

He made himself continue. His dad had wrapped her in a black garbage sack that shredded as he reached in and peeled it away. There she was, like a very old gray-skinned little woman, yet somehow also still the same exact blond girl that he had found sprawled in his uncle Walt's truck bed that hot August morning . . . staring at him wide-eyed . . . nothing on her but her torn pink panties, her gold necklace, and her two blue hair clips in butterfly shapes.

Only one blue butterfly clung to her frozen hair now. One of her pinkie toes had broken off with the sack as Angus tore it away. A walleye fin was stuck to her neck, behind her ear. Freezer burn had charred the soft parts of her bare thighs. His ax blade had hit her in the shoulder, cut through ice crystals into bone. He staggered away. He went to his knees outside.

When he had finished retching, he went inside the house, emptied out his baseball gear bag, and headed back for the body.

22

"Who did this to you?"

The sheriff had crawled half her body under the trailer. He seemed conscious, but Walt Beavers couldn't answer. It was hard to judge the extent of his injuries. She decided that hypothermia was about to kill him, no matter what else.

She crawled out and went inside. She tore the blankets off his bed in a storm of cat hair and balled them up. She pushed the wad ahead as she squirmed between the cinder blocks and crawled deep beneath the trailer, holding her face just above the rubble of mud-stuck trash. Beavers had kicked booze bottles under here. She batted a pint out of the way. While she was gone he had rolled onto one side, his back to her, and now she saw he wore his Rattlers jacket. The snake stared right at her, the timber rattler coiled around the baseball, beneath *BEAVERS* and the numeral *0*. She covered the shivering man with his blankets.

"Hang in there, Coach. Let's get you warmed up. I'm going to call for help. You're going to be OK. Can you tell me what happened?"

He could not.

"Can you give me a name?"

He could not. She elbowed out, wet and muddy now, teeth chattering. She sat inside the Charger, taking fast and shallow breaths. Her radio had no signal at all. Her cell phone had only a wavering hint of reception.

"Denise, I need an ambulance at Walt Beavers's place. He's badly hurt. Somebody attacked him and he escaped under his trailer. I think Zion VFD can get here quickest."

Denise's response was faint and broken.

"Did you get that? Yes? No?"

She left the Charger in a weird blur of fear and isolation. As she approached the mobile home again, she thought she could hear Coach Beavers saying something—or calling her. She crawled back under his trailer to get closer. He was still and silent beneath the blankets. So it was something else she had heard. She waited. Soon enough she heard a mutter, then a squishing sound. She stopped breathing to listen. There it was again, someone stepping through the icy slush. She twisted and saw a pair of rubber barn boots creep past.

"Who's there?"

Whoever it was, he froze. Then he backed away through the slush.

"This is the sheriff! Stop! Stay right where you are!"

She began to elbow away from Beavers, paddling backward through the trash and muck and booze bottles. As her legs emerged, something glanced across her right boot. She rolled over, pulled back. He had hit her with something. Her ankle stung from the blow.

"Get on the ground!"

The command tore out of her. She was working her body around, planning to come out headfirst with her weapon drawn.

"Get down now!"

"Ha. Dairy Queen?"

The voice, somewhere to her left, was reedy and slurred, intense with derision. "Stupid old stumble-fuck won't tell you nothing now."

"Get down."

"I'll get down with you all right. Come on, let's get down."

As she crawled from beneath the trailer, Ruger first, she saw a descending blur and drew her head back just in time. The chopping blow struck her right upper arm, the weapon thick and hard, bruising her to the bone.

She crawled backward, deeper beneath the trailer, gasping from the pain. She could barely grip the pistol as the rubber boots danced away into the headlights of her cruiser. Where had he come from? Who was he? She had to get a look at him. She inched forward, lowered her head to the mud, and looked up. She saw a scrawny man in filthy jeans and a baggy hooded sweatshirt. The hood was cinched around his face. He snorted, spat from the black hole. Mucus hung on the hood strings. "Baggy old coonfucker don't have shit to say to nobody now." He paced away and muttered to himself. Then, as if he had suddenly remembered what he was doing, he surged back in, spraying icy slop under the trailer. "You wanna get down? Come on, bring it!"

She could see his weapon now: he had struck her with an aluminum baseball bat. He waggled it low, paddling his boots in the slush like a nervous hitter. Her arm felt numb. How did he get here? she wondered. Had he come home with Coach Beavers? And planned to leave in Beavers's truck? Then she arrived? Had he tried to wait her out, then seen a chance to attack when she went under the house?

"Stick that head out here again. Come on, Dairy Queen, you can milk my cock."

He was sky high, she decided, and lethally dangerous. She watched as he released one hand from the bat and honked the grimy crotch of his pants. He took a little hop and a skip and wound up with the bat and bashed out one of the Charger's headlights. Then he did the other. When he danced back, she saw that his rubber boots had a yellow rim stripe and were stuck with dried cow flop. The bat had lost its rubber grip. It had a hole drilled above the knob, a strap looped through the hole. It was a sturgeon wallop now.

"Come on!" She flinched back as he bent to look beneath the trailer. "You wanna get down, let's get down!"

She shined her flashlight in his face. He was nobody she had ever seen before. He was nobody, period. One of the zombies, emerging from the night to take away another life. As he danced back, panting jets of steam from the dark cowl of the sweatshirt, her heart thundered with the urge to shoot him. He jammed the bat barrel into his crotch, made it a phallus. He humped the knob in her direction.

"Come out backward again! Come on! Gimme that royal ass!"

But she couldn't see him from the waist up anymore, couldn't make a lethal shot. She fumbled the Ruger back into its holster. With frazzled imprecision she unsnapped and armed her Taser. She had been good with the weapon at the academy, but practice targets didn't dance around in a meth frenzy. Yet he was gripping high-conducting aluminum, touching the bat to the core of his body. If she could hit him anywhere, put him down, then take her time with the Ruger, it would feel so good . . .

A car horn surprised them both. He paused with the bat jammed into his crotch, looking toward the road. He was motionless for about one second. Now or never. She half squeezed—watched the red laser touch his hip—and then she squeezed all the way.

She watched her shot connect in slow motion. The leading probe traveled about ten feet, and with more luck than she had counted on, it stuck in the bare skin of his right hand. The other probe, delayed an instant, stuck someplace on his left side as he twisted away. With the second contact came a flash and a snap, then a howl of pain like no live-subject demo she had ever witnessed. The bat cartwheeled straight up. He flew backward, disappeared into the black around her flashlight beam. She had him.

But then she didn't. By the time she could scramble upright on the slippery yard and draw the Ruger again, he was on his feet in a burst of superhuman adrenaline, hurling back filthy oaths as he took off in a clumsy sprint behind Beavers's truck, heading for the car idling at the road. It was some kind of low-to-the-ground sport sedan, darkly patched with Bondo and finned in the rear by what seemed to be a spoiler. The passenger door was open, but galloping toward it he screamed at the driver to get out, and the sheriff glimpsed a female, thick and busty, with the sluggish fearful movements of a child as she slipped through headlights around the nose of the car. She just made it into the passenger seat. The car howled away.

She was not imagining this time. She was exploding out of the imaginary into the real. She started the Charger, crushed the gas, and braked to swing the car around. A nearly sightless minute later, plunging into a corner with slapping wipers and no headlights, she saw him doubling back on the ridge above, his crooked high beams dialing through the icy mist. He was aiming down the long descent of County J to the Mississippi, heading out of the coulees to the highway along the river, where there was traffic and he could lose her.

She accelerated into gusts of sleet. As she reached the first switchback of County J's icy decline she was still far behind, but she could see his headlights below through ice-glazed treetops. She was going too fast. She went faster. Two curves down, coming out of it, she saw his taillights. Now she had him. But once more she didn't. She couldn't see the road in front of her, couldn't find the edge of the opposite switchback. Her foot went for the brake. She stopped just short of touching it—then she touched it.

The Charger sailed on ice like a balloon in the wind. Past her window spun the black-on-yellow icon of a truck aimed down the side of a triangle, warning of the steep straight grade that she now slid down backward. She pictured the bottom: one buckshot sign, tight against the Great River Road, commanding STOP; a slippery half second beyond the sign, the Burlington Northern tracks from Duluth to New Orleans; and one more slick half second beyond the tracks, two million gallons of muddy water purling south every second.

She touched her brake again. Faster than a heart skip, the cruiser's rear end launched to the side. With a neck-snapping squeal the guardrail knocked the Charger back into a nose-first slide. Now she could see it all coming. But all for nothing, suddenly. The taillights she was following had vanished. No headlights reflected in the trees. Nothing. He had dodged her somehow. The zombie trick. She was going to die for nothing.

She surrendered the Charger into the final sheer-ice straightaway. There was no way she could stop at the bottom. Whether she braked now or not, she was going to shoot through the stop sign onto the highway—and if she wasn't hit by traffic, she would slide beyond the highway, across the railroad tracks, and into the river.

She put her emergency lights on. She started her siren. Sliding out the narrow bluff cut toward the highway, she released her seat belt, unlocked her doors, reached under the dash for the escape hammer that broke window glass. The distance to the highway closed fast. The Charger was spinning again—but now unexpected light and thunder filled the bluff cut, swelling massively as she slid two hundred yards, one hundred, fifty . . . Then the night was split by the earthshaking horn of a freight train.

The train's power froze her as the cruiser broke from the bluffs. Its huge black body barreled across her windshield view and she knew from her studies in self-destruction that this was the midnight ore train out of Duluth, a hundred boxcars full of iron ore going sixty miles an hour. She closed her eyes and wrapped her arms across her chest. *For nothing.* The siren shrieked. The train horn blared. The car spun.

———

Then it was quiet, except for river water gurgling through the cruiser's front grill.

She felt herself tilted forward, sprawled against her steering wheel. She opened her eyes.

She had slid halfway off the Pool 9 fishing pier. The cruiser bobbed, its nose tipped into the current, its chassis grinding against a girder in the pier frame. She could see in the southern distance a back-hauling freight engine with a half dozen empty boxcars rummaging through a curve along the backwaters of the Bad Axe. She sat shaking for a full minute. That was not the ore train from Duluth. That was a short train. It had missed her.

Walt Beavers. Still under his house. She had forgotten him. Radio. She had just reached for her radio handset when headlights flashed behind. On a manic engine snarl, a pair of crooked high beams surged to fill her mirror. She twisted, saw his cockeyed blazes coming fast. He was ripping down the pier. Then he struck.

23

The massive crunch from behind snapped her head against the headrest, then tossed her into the airbag as the Charger was pounded, nose first, into the Mississippi. The heavy car bobbed vertically for a few seconds while she slashed at the airbag and tore it from her face. She popped the dome lights and they vivified a muddy brown bottom. For a half-conscious moment she stared at sticks and rocks, beer bottles, a crayfish scuttling. Then the car dropped its rear end with a cannonballing crash. The current took over, glide and spin.

Her zombie was reversing away. She could see his headlights speckling the drizzly air and panning the snow-bright bluffs as he raced north along the Great River Road.

The cruiser's tail bobbed up again. Now the car began to sink.

The escape hammer did its job. The glass shattered in, washed over her on a tide of incoming river. She held her breath and squatted on the driver's seat and propelled herself out. She stroked for the surface.

Four pulls and there she was, swept along in the dark, watching the car sink behind her, watching headlights pass in both directions on the highway a few hundred yards distant. She waved, yelled. Then she drifted alone. She had been unsafe, but she did not feel sorry. She had almost died for nothing, but for some reason she was still here.

———

She knew rivers well enough. She reached land about where she had aimed, a place where she could see the silhouettes of ice-glazed trees on the bank, roots and soil, instead of cattails and swamp. Even so, the shore-line was a stinking muddy quagmire. She made torturous progress. Noth-ing worked, not her flashlight, not her radio, not her phone, just her heart and lungs, her churning legs. Through exhaustion and bone-deep cold she fought her way across the downed trees, the icy heaps of rotted flotsam, the sucking pockets of muck. When at last she reached the Burlington Northern tracks, here came the *real* midnight ore train out of Duluth.

This was the train she once had planned for. She had scouted it, timed it, imagined lying down for it, and was severed by it many times over. Now it pounded toward her on a frigid oily gust, the devouring clatter-squeal-roar of a hundred ore cars moving at sixty miles an hour. This time she stood close within its annihilating power. Inside the freight's crushing passage, inside her rejection of the surrender she once had craved, she heard a quiet voice.

I will find you.

The violent pimp, the troubled girl, Coach Beavers's zombie attacker, the killer of her parents, her lost and undone self—yes, events and years had scrambled—but softly and succinctly, like a bullet punch of light through the awful din and darkness in which nothing thrived, she heard the voice again.

I will find you.

When at last the train had passed, she moved on. On frozen feet in squishing boots she staggered south along the Great River Road. The flickering pink neon ahead was the sign for Mudcat's Roadhouse and Marina, a mustachioed catfish standing on its tail and raising a martini. By law the tavern should have closed hours ago, but true to its outlaw status, Mudcat's still served its clientele of bikers, river rats and fisher-man, boyfriends and husbands, still wandering home from the stag party.

"Ahoy!" hollered some black-leathered inebriant from the Mudcat's party porch, raising his plastic beer cup as she stumbled into the light. He kept hollering and she kept coming.

"Ahoy the Dairy Queen!"

DAYBREAK

Jerry Myad @thebestdefense
@BadAxeCountySheriff why dont you drink
bleech and die I will buy the bleech #dairyqueen
#kickherout

24

Angus Beavers fit the girl's wet but still rock-hard little corpse into his gear bag. Curled up, she was about as long as a thirty-four-inch bat. He fit the bag on the floor of the Beavers Salvage truck, passenger side. In the house, his dad moaned against his cold bedroom wall.

"I knew you didn't burn her," Angus said. "I knew them guys couldn't make you do a thing like that."

He kept talking. It was all on him now anyway.

"I'm gonna give her back. Maybe that's why you saved her. I don't know. You save everything. But they're gonna find her in that locker at Clausen's where Scotty keeps all that shit he poaches. They're gonna find her there just like we Beavers found her in Walt's truck. Let them explain how she got into Scotty's meat locker."

His eyes stung. His throat burned from vomit.

"I tried to never blame you and Walt. But you two never had to go to that party. You never had to be there. I'll guess Brandy goes to them parties now. You don't even know that."

He had nothing else to say for a while. He shucked his dad's damp diaper and tabbed a dry one in its place. He fetched the bottle of cut pills from the dresser top and read the prescription again and got a cup of water and gave his dad a dose and a half.

"I never wanted what I got out of it," he said. "I never wanted to leave home."

He stood away in a dim corner of the room and watched the pills work. His dad's body softened. His toes spread. He moaned faintly.

"I could have waited my turn. I didn't want to go to any academy. You know what they do at a baseball academy? Baseball. They don't hunt, they don't fish, they don't drive down gravel roads smelling apple blossoms, they don't go to Mudcat's for fish fry, nothing. Baseball, eat and drink, night and day. And, yeah, I like it OK, maybe I have some talent, but you and Uncle Walt, you're the ones who wanted what I got. I wanted what I had."

He thought a minute. It wasn't quite like that.

"I woulda had what I wanted."

———

He had been willing to wait. That was his story. Even though at sixteen he was the best pure talent ever in the coulees, except maybe Harley Kick when Harley was young, he had been content to ride the Rattlers' bench and wait his turn. That was just how it worked. He was sixteen. He could sit, wait until there was a place for him.

But that was not how his dad and uncle Walt saw the situation. What his dad and uncle Walt saw was that Aspenwall Ford sponsored the scoreboard, so Suck Aspenwall played center field, Angus's natural position. What they saw was that Vossteig Funeral Home paid for the programs, so Vick Vossteig crashed around in right field like a circus bear with his mitt on the wrong paw, yet Angus couldn't replace him. They saw that weak-armed Scotty Clausen, son of Rattler Hall of Famer and then-manager Pinky Clausen, played so-so in left field, played badly at shortstop when Harley Kick pitched, and peaked at .230 with three or four homers in the cleanup spot, the spot where Angus, with his power, should have been in the batting order. What his dad and uncle Walt saw was that the nephew of the sheriff, little duck-assed Wade Gibbs, was third baseman for life. Brick-handed Sherman Ossie, of Ossie Implement, had a lock on second base. And so on, while their boy Angus rode the bench. What they saw was themselves, Beaverses, getting disrespected, getting the coulee-trash treatment, as usual, like they got when they played, and so his dad and uncle Walt went to games and drank beer and bitched and hollered to no result except Angus's shame—and that was the story, right up until a night when there was a bad Rattlers loss, a fight, and a party where a girl got killed. Then the story changed.

———

"Put Angus in the game!"

It was a matchup the Rattlers should have won easily, a state playoff game against a ragged bunch of Ho-Chunk Indians, the Wisconsin Dells Scenics. But for some reason Harley Kick hadn't shown up, and without Harley Kick the wheels had come off in a hurry. By the third inning, the home team was down, 7–0.

"Put Angus in the goddamn game!"

Lyman Beavers, a beer cup slopping in one hand, a half dozen empties under his feet, rattled the backstop and yelled at Coach Clausen, who scowled over the rail of the dugout.

"What are you waiting for, Clausen? You're getting your tail kicked while your best guy is on the bench! You're a chickenshit! Put Angus in the game!"

Meanwhile, Angus's uncle Walt operated ass-to-bleacher down the third-base line, no longer able to stand after loosening up via happy hour at the Ease Inn. "Your kid's a pre-Madonna, Clausen! You couldn't coach Little League! You're afraid to put a Beavers in the game!"

The Rattlers were getting humiliated, at home. The Scenics pitcher was an old guy with a keg belly and stick legs. He threw knuckleballs. Their young shortstop, B. Greengrass, hit three homers in his first three at bats, every time sailing around the bases with a big grin and his long black ponytail flapping—disrespecting the game, according to the Rattlers.

Then it went from bad to worse. By the seventh inning, the score was 19–3. The Scenics were drinking beer in their dugout. Some of the Cave Girls—supposed to be loyal Rattlers fans—were hanging around the dugout corners, having fun, joking with B. Greengrass and a few others. Greengrass had six homers by then. He could really hit. But still it was ridiculous. Everything he touched went over the fence. Then that grin, that ponytail, and after homer number six he put his arms out like an airplane—pure disrespect for the Rattlers and for baseball itself.

"Put Beavers in the game!"

"How long this shit's gotta flow upriver, Coach, before you do something?"

Angus had watched from a corner of the dugout while the whole place got rowdy. Chief Deputy Boog Lund had moved in on Angus's dad, commanded him to shut his beer flap. There was a struggle, curses, threats, an arm bar and handcuffs, cheers from the crowd as Lund dragged Lyman Beavers away. Down the third-base line, Angus's uncle Walt Beavers had begun dancing with a Ho-Chunk woman who was as drunk as he was. Meanwhile, Rattlers players were shouting across the diamond at the Cave Girls, telling them to get the fuck away from the Scenics dugout, and the girls were sassing back, red cheeked with the thrill of it. Then, with two outs in the bottom of the seventh, the game went from bad to worse to ugly: a knuckleball butterflied out of control, hit Scotty Clausen in the neck, and the Rattlers stormed the field.

Angus had watched in puzzlement from the bench. It was just a knuckleball. He had hit himself harder putting a shirt on. But Scotty Clausen and a few others mauled the old-man pitcher, who sat on the mound with his head covered. At the edge of the scrum, B. Greengrass tried to make peace, but Wade Gibbs yanked him back by the ponytail and he spun and dropped Gibbs with one punch. Based on that, Boog Lund bull-charged B. Greengrass, knelt on him, tried to cuff him, but some long-haired little girl about Brandy's age had appeared out of nowhere and launched herself at Lund's head and attached herself there, shrieking and clawing and not letting go until some of the Scenics' women fans took her away. But worse than all of this was watching some of the Rattlers players go after those Bad Axe girls for being friendly with the Scenics, jerking their bare arms, screaming in their faces. Angus saw a girl go down, saw her face bleeding, her shirt torn and her bra showing, saw her crying and limping away.

After the dust had settled, his dad and uncle Walt had dropped Angus and Brandy off at the scrap yard and gone to a party. Angus had dug worms to go fishing in the morning. He had watched TV with Brandy until she fell asleep. He had carried her to bed.

———

From then onward, on a loop in his mind for the next four years, it went exactly like this. At sunrise, he wakes to find Brandy in his bed. Stepping onto the porch with his worms and his fishing rod, he discovers his uncle Walt's pickup drunk-parked halfway onto Lost Hollow Road, a bad place to be with the morning milk truck about to come barreling down the hollow.

He goes back inside, finds Uncle Walt asleep in Brandy's bed. He finds the key in Walt's pocket. He heads out to move the truck.

It is a humid August dawn. Fog hangs across the hollow. His dad's burn pile faintly smolders on its steady diet of trash that lately people have begun to throw onto the property. As Angus comes down the porch steps, two crows lift out of Walt's truck box. They don't go far. They make one tight circle and land on the neck of the yard light. They sit there croaking at him.

Because Angus knows crows, he looks into the truck box, expecting that Walt maybe lopped a decent tail off a road-killed coon, maybe ran over a turtle and meant to eat it later. But there is a girl inside. She is sprawled in a twist, mostly naked, looking up.

He can't have seen that, Angus thinks. He steps back, surveys the scrap yard, his heartbeat suddenly a sour-iron burping motion at the back of his mouth.

He looks again: a girl in only torn pink underpants, blue hair clips, and a necklace, staring up with wide blue unmoving eyes. She seems about his age, about half his size, a small blond high school girl, narrow shoulders, heavy hips, vaguely clotted face, naked breasts like rigid little cones. The necklace is gold. The blue hair clips are shaped like butter-flies. It takes this long before Angus understands that she is dead.

Now he is frantic and sick. He sees her neck is purple, twisted like the neck of a sack. Her knees and elbows ooze bloody scabs, picked open by the crows still croaking above. His vision blurs. His stomach bucks. He runs.

———

His dad and uncle Walt get sober in a hurry. They didn't kill her. Angus never doubts this for a moment. They have no idea how she ended up in Uncle Walt's truck. They remember her from the party, but that's as far as it goes. They remember a girl *like* her at the party, stumbling out of Faulkner's barn with some of the Rattlers—the players drunk and angry—but nothing after that.

Uncle Walt has lost a daughter, Angus's cousin, a girl he never knew, and when Walt catches up with what he's looking at, he begins to weep into a hand clamped across his eyes. Angus watches his dad go shaky and pale, like Angus has never seen him. Then his dad shovels Skoal under his lip, taking pretty much the biggest dip in the history of tobacco. His dad is going to think now. His dad is many things, Angus knows, but another man's fool is not one of them. He will not take credit for a dead girl.

Uncle Walt says finally, "They throwed her on us, Lyman."

"I seen that," his dad snaps. "Don't you think I seen that?"

"Wade Gibbs, Scotty Clausen, them all, that's the drunk stripper girl they took to Faulkner's back barn. Curtis Strunk. Ossie. Them four."

"Don't you think I seen that?"

"God help her poor people."

Uncle Walt is sobbing as he stumbles to the cab of the pickup, stumbles back with his jacket. He covers the girl where he can.

"God help us too, Lyman, we're in trouble now. They throwed her on us and they're gonna say we did it."

"Hell they are."

"They know who's sheriff."

"I know they know who's sheriff." Angus's dad spits down the front of himself. "You think I don't know they know who's sheriff?"

"Wade Gibbs can't do no wrong, big man for an uncle. Scotty Clausen, a big man like Pinky for a dad, he can't do no wrong neither."

Angus's dad spits again. This time the gob gets to the ground and he paces. He goes back and forth past the tailgate of the pickup six or seven times before he looks at Angus and says, "What they don't realize is they ain't the only boys that's got a big man on their side."

This leaves Uncle Walt without words. For a long time there is no more conversation except from the crows croaking to get back on her body. Too dizzy to stand any longer, Angus crumples into the huge open space of a combine tire. He watches buzzards sail against a blue-pink sky, wafts of burn-pile smolder drifting up. The next thing he remembers, his dad is saying, "Knobloch. Clinton Knobloch. Lavern Shirley." His voice rising, ranting. "Doug Ott. Fonda's kid. Them guys seen the same thing we did."

"Lyman, they won't say what they saw."

"They won't have to." His dad snaps at Angus, "Get in the house. Get your sister. Take her fishing. Get. Now."

Stumbling away, Angus believes he hears a siren. For sure he hears his dad say, "Get your balls back in the sack, Walt. Listen up. I'll tell you how this is gonna work."

———

Four years later, Angus now believed that he had imagined the siren. He also now understood how his dad had made it work. He knew why Sheriff Gibbs and his chief deputy, Boog Lund, had arrived quietly at the scrap yard in street clothes and civilian vehicles, with Coach Pinky Clausen pulling up behind.

After that morning, the fix had happened fast. By the next Rattlers game, Uncle Walt was in a brand-new uniform in the first-base coaching box. A week after that, Angus was on his way to the same high school baseball academy in Virginia where Scotty Clausen had gone and gotten kicked out. From the academy, with his talent, it was a done deal to get drafted somewhere: *Angus Beavers, Oakland A's, thirty-second round.*

"But I never wanted it," he told his dad again. "You and Walt did, not me."

He went outside. The storm had mostly stopped. The whole world was locked in ice and felt as if it could shatter. He put air in the tires of the Beavers Salvage truck and jumped the battery. He unzipped his gear bag, assuring himself that the frozen girl was really in there. He turned his sweatshirt inside out, cinched the hood around his head, and aimed the truck for Clausen Meats.

25

For Pepper Greengrass, once she has her vision back, it turns out that she can do this. Just keep hanging it out there, keep it moving. The bright light explodes, explodes, the miniman purring praise and slamming cool white heat against her naked body—not a problem after all—it doesn't hurt a bit.

By break of day, as soft orange light streams through the cracks of the blinds, she is high on something much better than last night. She is comfortable five minutes at a stretch with her bare ass rooting in the air while the miniman pokes her this way and that, like playing pin the tail on the donkey. This is pure pretend: fuck herself with a yellow zucchini, fuck herself with a jump rope handle, put a camo hat on backward and go down on this other big naked bitch in the room. This is just men, as Pepper knows them. Whatever. Whatever she is high on, she likes it.

Just wiggle with her lip bit while this heavy, smelly girl, Tianna, lesbian-humps her on a beach towel. Just glisten with oil and make eyes over the Walmart sunglasses, the whole time feeling like she has to take a major shit. Funny. Goddamn, she is so high.

She is back on track. Hah! Track! She remembers the last time she went on the Amtrak website to check. The price was $165 plus tax for a one-way ticket from Wisconsin Dells to Whitefish, Montana. The ride was twenty-eight hours and seven minutes. So if that's all the time it's going to take, she calculates out loud to Tianna and the miniman, "Then

I can go all the way without eating and save money. Right? Then from Whitefish—right?—they'll have taxis?"

"Would you shut up," Tianna grunts between her legs.

"I could hitchhike. I could steal a horse."

"You're already on a horse," Tianna mutters.

"I mean, she's my big sister. She's gotta be glad to see me, right?"

The camera lowers. The miniman's face is flushed and damp. "Let's try something fun, OK? Sure. You betcha."

"I wouldn't stay with them forever, just until I get a job."

"Tianna, darling, can you reach the toy?"

"There's casinos out there, and there's always jobs when there's casinos. Marie's working in a casino out there." She tips her sunglasses to study the double-headed latex dick, pink and veiny, coming at her in the grip of Tianna's fist.

"In we go, make nice faces, very pretty girls, we're scooting now, coming together like Lady and the Tramp with the noodle, double scoot, very sexy. Tianna, keep your face turned, please. Left side only. Pepper, you're my money girl. Look at the camera. Very fun. OK, there we go, you betcha."

It doesn't feel like her body anyway down there, or anywhere. Good money, right? Sooner or later this puts her on the train. Done deal.

Now Tianna's cell phone rings. She suctions off the double dildo, leaves Pepper hung like a bull with a bubble-gum pink cock, laughing at the sight.

"You *what*?"

Tianna shrieks this into her phone. She pries the camera guy aside, going for her cigarettes.

"Jesus Christ, Brock. You fucking what? Can't you drive yourself? Where's your car?"

She lights a Kool menthol while she listens.

"Someone stole your car? Seriously? I mean, why? And you did *what* to yourself? You were supposed be watching Garthy. OK, yeah, sure, Jesus Christ, you're having a heart attack. I believe you. Sure. *Shit*."

She ends the call with an angry stab at the phone. She glowers at her pile of clothes on the floor. Her tits hang slackly as she coughs out smoke.

"You need to pay me now. I gotta drive all the way to Locks and take that idiot to the ER. It was my night out. He was supposed to be Daddy. He went out and got fucked up."

She jerks her shorts up, crams her tits into a tube top. She demands, "One hundred bucks. Give it."

This is critical, the money. Pepper sits up, crosses her legs, leans back on her hands. Miniman counts off three twenties. Only sixty. Tianna won't touch it.

"You said a hundred."

"Leave early, this is all you get."

Pepper watches Tianna shift into a different part of her brain. "You little cocksucker," she begins. Dug into the bad side of her face, her right cheek, are six deep sores in the shape of the Big Dipper. Her nose is bent toward the one eye stuck slightly in a squint. When she squares her face it's like looking at something from Picasso. "You give me the hundred, like you promised, or I make a phone call and say there's a minor here." She turns that unbalanced face on Pepper. "What are you, girly, like, fifteen?"

Miniman laughs, high and anxious and short. He sets the three twenties on a stool, pads away in his soft white socks, keeping his eye on Tianna, opening a camera bag.

"Nobody believes a meth mommy, OK?"

"Fuck you."

"Take your money now and go."

"Oh, I'll go."

"OK, you betcha. Go."

Pepper's head swivels back and forth. Tianna grabs a camera. He points a square-nosed pistol with two soft little hands. Tianna drops the camera on the floor. She kicks it and something breaks off. Pepper is enjoying this. Miniman grabs his sixty bucks back and swears he's going to pull the trigger if she doesn't leave. Tianna yanks her keys from her pocket. Her cigarette pack comes flying out of her tube top as she slams out the back door. Her car howls past the window.

Now Pepper has half a pack of menthol Kools. After a quiet minute, she lights one. She blows a cloud and a question toward miniman that he doesn't seem to hear. He looks exactly like a troll now, slump shouldered, his glasses skewed, panting, a camera strap twisted around his neck. He lifts the window blind and looks out.

"Bitch."

She asks it again. High as shit. Hardly knows her own voice. Beyond the window all things are pink and orange and sparkly. She can't remember how the world became so pretty.

"I said, What I gotta do to get her hundred too?"

26

It wasn't sleep exactly, more like paralysis. She came out of it with a start: Walt Beavers. Bad Axe County had no hospital, so it took a minute to figure out where she was: Vernon Memorial Hospital, in Viroqua, one county north.

She made her arm work and pressed her call button. Her voice was croaky and faint as she questioned the nurse, who said to her, "Mr. Beavers is in the ICU just down the hall. He got here before you did."

"He's OK?"

"He's in serious condition. He can't talk to you. We're going to watch him for a bit, get him stabilized, then probably transfer him up to La Crosse."

"Can you please open the curtain?"

A soft orange sunrise streamed in. Too much time had passed. The nurse said, "Let's try this again," and approached with a thermometer. A minute later it beeped.

"Good. You're back to normal. Your core temperature was right around ninety-five when you got here, that's mildly hypothermic, and you were exhausted and experiencing some delirium. Mostly you needed to get warmed up and rest."

"My husband?"

"He was here. We assured him you were going to be fine and he went back home an hour ago. Would you like anything to eat or drink?"

"I'm ready to go."

The nurse only smiled at her. A few minutes later, as she sipped warm tea, pink-yellow rays shot upward around the spot where the sun had yet to appear. Next the whole sky took on a fuzzy orange glow that suffused downward into a landscape locked in snow trapped under ice. The beauty gnawed at her memory of the bad night hidden beneath. *I will find you*. She reached for the bedside phone.

"Holy crap, Heidi! You had me worried. Sheesh!"

Denise sounded gassed at the end of her shift. No doubt it had been a long night for everybody. "Oh my God. When they got to you, you were slurring and stumbling around, and Schwem said you couldn't tell anyone what happened."

"I'm fine now. I need a dry uniform, a new cell phone, and a car."

"I've already got the extra uniform from your locker and a new phone, backed up from the cloud, on the way. You will be pleasantly surprised by the deliveryman."

Denise paused then and her voice sounded anxious.

"But, Heidi, really, what happened? I mean, Zion VFD got to Walt Beavers's place and you were nowhere to be found. An hour later you turn up five miles away, crawling around in the parking lot at Mudcat's like a possum who got into the sauce. Right now they're fishing your Charger out of the river. Everybody's talking about it."

It occurred to her, as she watched pale blue seep through orange at the highest point of the sky, that she could explain, or not. Time spent explaining, documenting, accounting for several different kinds of recklessness and bad judgment, time invested in the maze of policy and procedure, covering her ass, was time lost against *I will find you*. It seemed pretty clear to her anyway: she was not permanent sheriff material.

"Like Schwem said, I'm not sure what happened. But I'm sure it will come back to me."

Denise said a lot with her silence.

"Heidi—"

"Denise, I promise. I'll remember eventually. Right now we've got a stag party, a beating, and a girl out there somewhere."

"Well, meanwhile our favorite chief deputy is acting like Christmas came early."

"I'm sure he is. How soon is my stuff going to be here?"

Denise sighed. "The uniform and phone, any minute. But as for a car, I'm sorry, Heidi. Anybody has an accident in a county vehicle—I mean, especially if they can't remember what happened—the county code says desk duty or ride along until an investigation is completed. It's in our insurance policy too. Marge Joss is all over it. What you should do, as soon as the doctor lets you, is go home and rest."

"Sure," she said. "Good idea. Did the Dells PD identify that van for us?"

"Nothing yet. The only other new thing we have is a break-in at Clausen Meats. Some guy in rubber boots and a hoodie put an ax through the front door. Completely routine. No need for you to get involved."

"Sure," she said again. She lifted the sheet to look at herself. They had stripped her naked and put her in a backless lavender gown. Her skin was nubbed with goose bumps and her whole body felt stiff. Her right arm thumped with pain. She sat up and touched her bare feet to the floor. She transferred weight and felt good enough to go. *Some guy in barn boots and a hoodie.*

Denise continued, "But like I said, they're fishing your Charger out of the river as we speak, Chief Deputy Lund presiding. Please think about what happened, Heidi. Otherwise someone else is going to tell the story."

Ten endless minutes later, the delivery Denise had promised finally arrived in the person of Olaf Yttri, her best daytime deputy, bringing her a dry uniform, an operational duty belt, and a new cell phone.

"Sorry, no extra boots in your locker. And I didn't see any, um . . ."

He meant underclothes. "They're in my desk drawer."

"Didn't check there. You gonna be OK, boss?"

"I'm already fine. Thanks."

Deputy Yttri was a bodybuilder, thick and tall, a pure Norwegian blond, his hair cut short and spiked with gel, perfect teeth beneath a perfect little mustache. He was single and a gentleman, and behind his back Denise swooned and called him Olaf the Handsome.

He waited in the hallway until she limped out in the dry uniform, carrying her wet clothes in a hospital sack. Her boots felt soggy and cold. Her nurse, just catching up, was alarmed.

"Sheriff, I'm sorry, you're not ready—"

"I'm fine. Thanks for everything."

She waved Yttri forward. "Clausen Meats," she told him.

Olaf the Handsome exchanged looks with the nurse and then he appraised her almost tenderly, like she was Sleeping Beauty just come awake, making her weirdly aware of being nude beneath the uniform.

"I thought you were cleared to go," he explained. "The thing at Clausen's was just a routine burglary. Nothing was stolen. They just want a report for the insurance claim. No big deal. I can get it later."

Nothing was stolen. She wobbled. He caught her by the elbow. "How about I help you get back in that bed?"

"How about you just take orders?"

She found a smile to soften it. Olaf the Handsome smiled back.

"Whatever you say, boss."

"Thanks for everything," she told the nurse again.

————

Beyond the outside doors, they had to check their steps to avoid a grubby silver Subaru angling erratically out of the ER bay with its passenger door open. Having apparently dropped someone off, the car spurted on a pair of backfires into visitor parking.

Yttri's cruiser was in the other direction. They stopped to watch. A tall and rough-looking young blond woman slammed the driver's door, rounded the Subaru, and kicked the passenger door shut, then stormed back toward the ER entrance. She blew past them, fuming hoarsely into a cell phone.

"Irregular heartbeat? Burns on his nut sack? When he's supposed to be home watching Garthy? And somehow he lost that precious dumbass car of his? You tell me!"

"New plan," the sheriff told Yttri. "There's a girl I need to meet. You find out who she brought here and get Denise to run the plate on that car."

As smoothly and calmly as she could manage to move, she followed the woman back inside the hospital.

27

The blond young woman had disappeared somewhere, but through the half-open door of a triage room, the sheriff glimpsed the passenger she had delivered. Could she be this lucky? She was looking at a wasted young man wearing dirty jeans, a gray hoodie, and rubber barn boots with a yellow stripe around the top. He sprawled in a wheelchair taking questions from the same ER doctor who had treated her last fall for a thumb out of its socket, an Indian woman, polite and reserved, Dr. Patel.

"Nah, I did it to my own damn self. I just need some pain meds and I'm outa here."

A nurse got in front of Sheriff Kick with a questioning look. The sheriff said, "Crime suspect. Likely high on meth."

"OK." The nurse glanced at her clipboard. "We've got Brock Anthony Pabst, twenty-five, no insurance, no permanent address. For occupation I think what he wrote is 'packs meat'? Complains of irregular heartbeat and a burn in his groin."

It could be him. Seeking pain meds, of course. Olaf the Handsome appeared beside her. "Sheriff, a woman named Tianna Ek owns that car. She's twenty-three. Address on the river in Blackhawk Locks." He nodded toward the patient. "Denise had his name already. Hospital intake called it in. They live together. They both have priors. You want to hear?"

"Hang on."

"Where are you burned?" Dr. Patel was asking Brock Pabst in her calm and lilting voice.

"I told you. My freaking nards, lady. It *hurts*, man, I'm telling you. I need meds."

"I'm sorry, I've never heard of nards."

"I'm in pain here. You don't speak English?"

"No better than the queen, I am afraid. What are 'freaking nards'?"

While Brock Pabst squirmed irately under the doctor's placid gaze, the sheriff looked him over more carefully. A beard no better than mildew darkened his face. Where it showed, his skin was gaunt and scabby. Crude tattoos stained his hands and neck. Paranoia bugged his bloodshot eyes. Was this her zombie? The timing was right, the injury was so right it was poetic, and this was the only ER within range . . .

"I just about had my damn ball sack off burned off."

"I see," said Dr. Patel. "So let's have a look."

"Shit. If you don't mind, lady, I'll wait for the doctor."

"I am the doctor, Mr. Pabst. Please draw down your pants and your underpants and let me have a look."

As she noticed the sheriff, Dr. Patel showed the faintest hint of amusement. Pabst muttered, *"Fuck,"* as the doctor closed the door.

"You want to hear the priors now, Sheriff?" asked Yttri.

"OK, hit me."

"His and hers. Ladies first. Tianna Ek, shoplifting, breaking and entering, resisting arrest, and good old child endangerment. And for the gentleman, three DUIs, felony assault, possession of marijuana and methamphetamine with intent to deliver. Also, vehicle theft. Looks like at some point he tried to steal and sell a tractor."

"Lovely. Thank you."

A toilet flush roared from inside the women's lavatory and the door banged open. Tianna Ek was six feet tall, with robust and potentially beautiful genes, but self-abuse had made her egg shaped, stick limbed, and ugly, and she was dressed like a twelve-year-old trying to defy her mother, white tube top and white shorts, both grimy. She snapped obliviously along in her flip-flops, then did a double take. *Now* she saw the cops. She seemed about to run for it. Then some other function of her bad brain kicked in and she headed recklessly toward Sheriff Kick and Yttri, gripping an iPhone and bringing along a gust of menthol cigarettes and intimate body odor.

"Brock's OK, right?"

"You must be Tianna."

"It was *my* night out," she wheezed. "Then he calls and says it's no big deal but he needs me to come home and bring him to the ER. I'm, like, if it's no big deal, why can't you drive yourself? He goes, 'I don't have my car.' I go, What the hell happened to your car? And then I'm like, You burned *what*? How did that happen, if you're supposed be home with Garthy? Asshole won't tell me. He'll probably hog the meds too. But he's OK, Brock's OK, right?"

"How about you find us some coffee?" the sheriff suggested to Yttri.

When her deputy had complied, she looked into the girl's agitated blue eyes. Her face was dramatically made up, almost like a stage actor's. Beneath the foundation and blush, one of her cheeks was deeply pocked. The ruby lipstick wasn't hiding a downwarp in the right corner of her mouth. "Wait!" she blurted. She grabbed the tube top and looked down her cleavage. "Fuck! My smokes!"

"You're Tianna Ek?"

"Uh . . . maybe?"

She bared eroding teeth in an absent smile that was still saying *fuck I lost my smokes*. "I didn't do nothing, I don't even know what happened, so I don't have to say my name, right?"

"You said you were out, Tianna. Anyplace in particular?"

"Here and there."

"Here and There? Is that the name of a tavern I haven't heard of yet?"

"Yeah."

"But then you're still out at six thirty in the morning? In hot pants?"

That pushed Tianna Ek's eject button and she stormed toward the exit. Following, the sheriff decided this was not the same young woman who had delivered the attacker—Brock Pabst, if it was him—to Coach Beavers's place in Dog Hollow. That girl was smaller and younger.

"So where was Brock last night?"

"Home."

"All night? Because it was your night out?"

"Yeah."

"So you live with him? And you two have a child?"

"Yeah."

"How do you know Brock was home all night?"

She sped up. "You can't hassle me."

The sheriff suddenly felt as tired as she was. It had to be whiplash making her spine feel as stiff as a piece of lumber. Her throbbing arm weighed two hundred pounds.

"I'm just asking questions."

"Brock said, 'Take me to the ER.' That's all I did."

The sheriff struggled to keep up. Outside, a maintenance guy threw salt on the pavement. On the highway, a county snowplow barreled along, throwing up a wave of filthy slush. The driver blew his horn two blasts.

"Get away from me."

"You understand that you're talking to the sheriff, don't you?"

"Yeah, right."

Tianna Ek paused alongside her garbage-bagged window. She said, "You mean the so-called sheriff."

"So-called? Is there something else to call me?"

The girl's iPhone chirped. Her thumbs pecked the phone. When she opened the car door something moved on the backseat. A boy toddler sat up beneath the blankets. His mommy shoved the phone into her too-tight shorts. "Twitter?" she answered the sheriff with snotty emphasis. "You really want to know what people call you?" She slammed the door.

The sheriff watched the Subaru putter feebly through the parking lot, then catch a clean burst of gas and squirt onto the highway. Yttri had found her with coffee. She fought a dizzy spell, came back to focus.

"Clausen Meats," she reminded him.

28

No actual Clausens were on-site at Clausen Meats, just the clerk who discovered the break-in, plus a manager who had come in early to deal with it. The sheriff felt relieved. She detested Coach Pinky Clausen, his son, Scotty Clausen, and all things Clausen. She wouldn't even eat Clausen meat. She didn't know them really. Hearing stories from Harley was enough.

The manager, a middle-aged woman named Brenda Nordstrom, led her and Yttri inside the retail area. Instantly they were crowded by shelves of jams and mustards, racks of packaged beef jerky, coolers of cheese and butchered meats. Polka music played. At the rear of the store, behind a glass half wall for everybody's viewing pleasure, three butchers in bloody white jackets hacked and sawed meat. She recognized Ron Yanske, son of a neighbor on Pederson Road. He saluted her with a gore-smeared glove.

"So," began Brenda Nordstrom, "aside from the broken front-door glass, which you saw, this is where the damage is."

She pointed out a few minor divots in the stainless steel around the freezer door, which locked with a keypad.

"And that's it. If you come into the office, we can look at the security footage."

Right away the sheriff saw that the Clausen Meats burglar was not same guy who had hit her with the bat. He was not Brock Pabst, if Pabst was the one. Sure, a hoodie, but this guy was bigger, with none of the meth head in his body language. He rushed in indecisively, more like a sober person committing a crime without a lot of experience. After he put the blunt end of an ax through the front door, he carried a large blue duffel bag to the freezer door. He stood there a few long seconds. Something wasn't right. Then he dropped the bag and hurried out.

"That bag looks heavy," Yttri said.

The sheriff asked Brenda Nordstrom, "Your alarm system was on?"

"No. We always turn it off with a storm coming because thunder and lightning tends to trigger it. I'm guessing that this gentleman knew that. Maybe he's worked for us in the past, or he knows someone who did."

Now on the computer screen the burglar returned with a pry bar that did him no good on the door, which was flush to the wall. Thwarted, he began to panic. With the elbow of his sweatshirt he tried to rub away the pry-bar marks he had left in the steel. "Brand-new freezer," Brenda Nordstrom remarked. "Up until two years ago we had old-school meat lockers that we rented out to anybody. Too much wasted energy. Too much liability, some of the weird stuff people were keeping in here."

Of course he couldn't make the marks go away. He hoisted his bag, staggered as it slung too far around his back, and then hurried off the screen. "Wait for it," said Brenda Nordstrom. Ten seconds later, he came back in a third time, now without the bag. He lurched around the retail space, finally grabbed a handful of beef sticks from a display on the counter, and then he was gone.

"We didn't even notice those were missing until we looked at the recording," said Clausen's manager. "All that work for a half dozen beef sticks. Hard times, I guess. The economy and whatnot. I kind of feel sorry for the guy, leaving with a snack when what he wanted was a side of beef. But we do need to report to our insurance carrier."

The sheriff felt Olaf the Handsome looking at her. She met his fathomless gray eyes, followed them. Through the glass half wall where the butchers worked, meat was everywhere, from sides to cuts. A tub of turkey carcasses sat right under the window. And the door in and out was a two-way swinger with heavy rubber flaps, no lock of any kind.

The sheriff asked, "Is it cold in there?"

"Oh, yes. State code is thirty-six degrees."

She fought through a shiver. "Will they get all that meat processed and packed by the end of the day?"

"Oh, gosh, no. They couldn't. They don't need to. It'll keep."

"So there was meat in there this morning? When this happened?"

The manager realized what she was saying. "Oh. Gosh. Always. So why didn't he take some? Well, that is really strange, then, isn't it?"

———

When they were back on the highway and heading for Farmstead, Olaf the Handsome said to her, "You're right. He wasn't stealing meat. You want me to follow up?"

"I'll let you know."

He looked across at her and smiled. He drove his Tahoe clocked at fifty-five. The highway was clear of snow and ice already, glowingly black. His tires hissed through meltwater. The sun-struck icy landscape made her brain hurt. She felt both hot and cold at the same time, and had to close her eyes.

The text tone on the new phone startled her awake: *Can you come home? The kids and I need to see you.*

29

Angus Beavers shivered in a bright early sun that he wished would stop shining on the rattling, exhaust-spewing Beavers Salvage truck.

It was a sight. It was all colors, a Frankenstein concoction of different body parts with its box made of barn planks bolted to angle irons, its open-air back window rimmed with teeth of broken glass, its coulee-trash cargo rolling and skidding on curves: the bucketless frame of a wheelbarrow, the blade of an Amish plow, the rusty iron gizzard of a thresher—and the inside-out blue gear bag with a girl's thawing body inside.

Hoping to stay mostly out of sight after the disaster at Clausen Meats, Angus had taken the long, long, *long* way home. But on this final stretch, to get around the tower of rock that was Battle Bluff, he had to come down the Great River Road through De Soto and Ferryville and back into Bad Axe County on County B, and take that to Lost Hollow Road.

How did he mess up so badly? Clausen Meats had remodeled, put a new freezer in, stopped renting closet-size meat lockers like the old days. Scotty Clausen didn't keep stuff there anymore. He hadn't known that.

Now he could feel another mistake coming as he piloted the scrap truck between the melting snow-clung bluffs and the long funnels of brown water pouring through the gaps in the rolling dam at Blackhawk Locks. Ahead: a stoppage on the highway, orange cones out, the cherries on a sheriff's cruiser throwing pale sparks in the overwhelming sunlight. There was traffic behind him. Angus had no place to turn around.

The highway had been shrunk to one lane to make room for something that was happening at the Pool 9 fishing pier, where a barge fifty yards offshore supported a crane that was dropping a cable into the current. A smaller shore-side crane had just backed off a flatbed truck. Angus came close enough to see who was directing traffic. He jerked his foot off the gas. It was Chief Deputy Boog Lund. His Tahoe cruiser blocked the southbound lane.

The Beavers Salvage truck decelerated sharply, crap skidding in the box. A heavy horn blew, a semi in his mirror, just about crushing him. At his window, southbound traffic, released by Lund's command, accelerated into the bottleneck. Angus was stuck.

Then Boog Lund saw the truck. Angus looked away. A diver's head broke the surface, his fist in a neoprene glove giving a signal: *We are hooked up.* The smaller crane rooted along the downstream bank, getting into position. This was how they pulled out a vehicle.

"Well, heck-all-golly, Hotshot."

Lund was at his window. Angus couldn't inhale.

"Ain't it baseball season? You're supposed to be where, Florida?"

"My dad's sick."

"Your dad's been sick awhile, Hotshot. You might say all his life."

Lund walked around the truck, looking in the box. Angus ground his teeth, watching in his dirty mirrors. Gibbs's chief crony came back to the window.

"How about I see your driver's license and vehicle registration?"

"I don't—I was just—my dad's sick—"

"You hear OK?"

"I don't have a—I'm not sure the truck's actually . . ."

"Pull over."

Lund lumbered into his stream of southbound traffic and stopped it so Angus could pull through the bottleneck across the highway and into the little gravel turnout beside the truck that brought the crane. He made hand motions: *Stay there*. After he got traffic streaming past himself again, he stood at his car door talking on the radio, looking over at Angus, the Beavers Salvage truck, the gear bag in the box, the whole bad picture.

Angus watched what the barge crane was recovering. Half the car was up, spewing muddy water, before he understood that it was another sheriff's cruiser. In fact it looked like the hopped-up Charger with the bully bar that Gibbs used to drive. Did the new sheriff, the lady, drive that now? Drive it into the river? The towline from the shore crane began to draw the Charger toward the bank.

Lund hung up his radio. He strode over, belly first.

"Don't give me that bullshit about coming home for your dad. Some dumbass with a big blue bag just like yours busted into Clausen Meats. He's on camera. What're you, about six one, two hundred, dark sweatshirt, muddy boots? What's in the bag, dumbass?"

"Gear," stammered Angus. "Luggage. My stuff."

As Lund once more headed around the back of the truck, an oncoming driver hesitated to rubberneck at the scene, leaving a gap that Angus first saw beyond Lund in his rearview mirror. As that gap widened in front of him and became about half enough for the truck, he stomped the gas and barged into the line. With the southbound traffic, he accelerated away.

He never saw how Lund reacted. A few hundred yards downriver, he nipped up Bible Coulee Road, headed toward Lost Hollow, and never looked back.

30

"Mommy! Mommy! Mommy!"

As she appeared in the doorway to the old farm kitchen, the kids left their cereal at the breakfast table and charged her. A spoon clanged to the floor. A chair tipped over. Long-striding Ophelia hip checked Dylan into a pile of muddy boots. In the same fluid motion, the sheriff's daughter stiff-armed the other twin, Taylor, into the side of the washing machine. Both boys were howling protests by the time their daddy appeared with a fistful of yellow daffodils.

"Hey, monsters! Is that what we practiced?"

They settled down as Harley handed her the daffodils.

"I rescued them from under the snow. OK, kids, hit it."

They sang her the "Belly Breathe" song, the one she had taught them, about relaxing under stress, with some new choreography by the twins. Still smiley and teary eyed as they went back to their breakfast, she fit the daffodil stems into a vase and dropped her wet clothes into the laundry sink. She glanced out at Yttri, waiting in his cruiser. Coming up behind her, Harley said quietly, "Hon, can I talk to you?"

Her pulse was up before he closed the bedroom door.

"I'm fine," she said.

"Um," Harley said, and he seemed to count to ten. "You're so fine you put a gun to Randy Brundgart last night."

She stripped off her duty belt, almost too exhausted to bear its weight. She dropped her new dry trousers and stepped out of them. If

Harley was surprised to see her nude underneath, he didn't show it. She felt him looking at the bad bruise above her ankle. Then he watched her shirt come off, exposing the purple-green contusion where the zombie struck her with his sturgeon wallop. The arm moved stiffly as she maneuvered into a bra.

"Look at you. And Randy Brundgart, Heidi. He's about as dangerous as Elmo. What's going on?"

"He was driving drunk. He ran from me."

"But that's not like you, to be all chasey and gun happy. And then later you end up in the river? How did that happen?"

"I'm just getting dry stuff on. I'm not going to talk about it."

"Heidi, last night the kids and I had dinner at Culver's—"

"Aren't you doing that too much?"

"Please don't change the subject. We were eating at Culver's and Don Webb comes up to me and says, 'Hey, what's the deal? I hear your wife's suing Crawford County.' What can I say? Hell if I know, she's just my wife. What *is* the deal?"

"The deal is gossip. I just had a little discussion with the county clerk, that's all. But listen," she said, "when you played for the Rattlers four years ago—"

"I still do. Please don't change the subject."

"No. Listen. In 2012, when we lived in Middleton, right after the twins were born, you were driving out here for games, staying overnight with friends. You guys played the Dells in a regional playoff game. You pitched, you lost, nineteen to three—"

"Hey, hold on." He put his hands up. "First of all, you hate it when I change the subject." He took a breath to slow himself down. "Secondly, the kids and I, we can't lose you, Heidi. Your job is dangerous enough. If you're out there chasing ghosts from the past . . ."

Standing at the dresser, weaving with fatigue, she chose fresh underwear from the dresser. She had to sit to put them on.

"You pitched in that game, and you lost, nineteen to three."

"I hardly gave up nineteen runs in a season, let alone one game. I quit pitching the year my ERA broke 2.5. I don't know why we're talking about a baseball game. Let's talk about why you were at Ralph

Dunleavy's farm the other day, asking about a guy who used to milk for your dad."

"How could you not remember losing nineteen to three?"

"Because that never happened. Can we talk about suing Crawford County?"

"Why, four years later, would somebody be interested in that game?" A detail from the box score came to her. "Some guy named Greengrass hit six home runs off you."

"It didn't happen."

"Six home runs. You could not possibly forget that."

"Exactly."

She shut the bathroom door in his face as he attempted to follow. What the hell was going on? She put on the fan and ran the water. Why would he deny playing in the game? Her guts cramped hard. When she finished on the toilet, she washed her face, applied lotion and lip balm, rebraided her hair and repinned it. Coming out, she said, "I love you."

"I love you too."

"So let's try again. You gave up nineteen runs, six dingers to one guy, and you don't remember?"

"Why does it matter, Heidi, when we almost lost you last night?"

"Last night?" She gritted her teeth as she snapped and buckled and belted. "Last night, two people, a man and an underage girl, came into the library looking for information on that game. The man punched Harold Snustead after Harold found the box score in a book of old newspapers. Nineteen to three, losing pitcher Kick. Walt Beavers was at the library. He literally closed the book on that game. Later someone beat him with a baseball bat and nearly killed him."

Harley hung his head a moment, then he looked at her.

"I wasn't at that game."

"You're in the box score."

"I'm in the box score *because* I wasn't at the game. Pinky Clausen gave me all the shitty stats to punish me for not showing up."

"Why didn't you show up?"

"I promise you it doesn't matter. It was a small mistake I made. And

I have no idea why anyone would care about that game, or beat up Walt Beavers over it."

He held her gaze. She had been on leave, in recovery from giving birth to twins. She had been breast-feeding, leaking everywhere, and fighting postpartum depression. Was her husband telling her not to ask what kind of trouble he could get into, the kind of "small mistake" he could make, when he drove back to the Bad Axe for Rattlers games? When he "stayed with friends" overnight?

"I promise you," he repeated.

Now he was showing her a thumb drive.

"Back on topic. You left this in the desktop."

She put her hand out.

"Heidi, you're investigating a twelve-year-old closed case in another jurisdiction. There is a spreadsheet on this drive, names, dates, criminal histories, guys you think might have killed your parents—am I right? You started this after the Bishops Coulee murders? You can't be doing this, sweetheart, for so many reasons. You could lose your job, you could lose yourself . . ."

She kept her palm open, staring him down.

"You want to promise me? Then let me promise you," she challenged him. "I'm fine."

He put the thumb drive in her hand. They faced each other silently for a long moment until he hugged her stiffly. Then he sighed. "So let me fill you in on what's happening around here. You're supposed to be off today—"

"You have no idea—"

"I know. So I asked my mom, and she—"

"No. We agreed. Your mom does not watch the kids."

"We also agreed you'd take Saturday mornings off, no matter what. Once today's game was canceled, I scheduled practice on the parking lot, freshmen, JV, then varsity. Nine, noon, and three. So I asked Mom—"

"Harley, please."

"She came at four a.m. so I could go see you in the hospital."

The upstairs floor creaked. Next the stairs. Then a coughing fit racked the house.

"Hon, Mom slept over. She's already here."

"Long time no see," Belle Kick greeted her. "Look, kids, it's your mom."

The jab hit her like the cup of coffee that she craved.

"Whoo-ee," Belle followed up. "I woke up, looked out the window, and just about broke my neck looking at the man in uniform out there. He oughta run for sheriff. He's got the filly vote for sure. Did you catch the jerk who did the bomb threat?"

Harley passed through. "Home about five. Thanks, Mom."

The kids followed him out. Meanwhile, Granny Belle had found her purse and was shaking out a cigarette.

"Belle, I really wish you wouldn't."

Harley's mom waited with her wild gray eyebrows arched as if to say, *You wish I wouldn't what?* Then she shrugged, stuck the cigarette behind her ear, and pulled a folded sheet of paper from the purse.

"This was under the flag on your mailbox when I drove in at dark-thirty this morning so Harley could go to the hospital."

The sheriff unfolded a photocopied page from a Blackhawk High School yearbook. She was startled to see, circled in red marker, a headshot of her eighteen-year-old husband-to-be rocking a mustache-and-mullet combo. The caption said *Harley Kick, Lady Killer.*

"He was so handsome, so popular," his mother reflected, touching the photo with a tobacco-stained finger. "Charm the Jesus off a nun, that boy."

The sheriff bit her tongue. What the hell? She twisted to look out the window. Harley's truck was already at the far end of the driveway, crashing through the flooding ditch. Yttri was in his Tahoe talking on the radio. The kids were petting one of the barn cats, the pregnant gray one with white socks.

"Who would drive out here to put this on my mailbox?"

"Oh, some woman," Belle said, "for sure."

"Why?"

Belle's chest rumbled and she coughed. "Kind of like a bomb threat, isn't it? Get you all stirred up over nothing?"

The sheriff stood from the table. Her arm throbbed, her calf had stiffened even more. Leaning over the laundry sink, she searched the pockets of the wet uniform for the Come Back Saloon coaster that Calvin Fanta had bought for a hundred bucks. She set the coaster on the windowsill to dry.

OK. Sure. Go with Ladonna. Double Ladonna. But this is over something, not nothing.

———

"Beautiful spot to raise a family," Yttri said awkwardly when she came out. The kids were throwing wet snowballs at the pasture fence. "You guys nailed it."

She hardly heard him. *So Ladonna figures out I know about the stag party. She calls in a bomb threat to stop me from getting there. Then she trolls me with a picture of my husband, Lady Killer? Why? And why now?*

"Anyway, Sheriff, breaking news."

Yttri sounded solemn. She noticed he wasn't getting into his Tahoe. She stopped at the passenger door. He said, "They got your Charger out of the river."

"That's good."

"But there was a problem."

"Sure. What was the problem?"

"It looks like you hit something."

"I see."

"There's a huge guardrail swipe on one side, and the back end is crunched in. The headlights are smashed out, and your Taser was in there, discharged."

"Really?"

"So . . . yeah. Then, I hate to be the one to break it to you, but Chief Deputy Lund says he found a bottle of booze in your glove box."

She laughed. "Sure, he did. What was I drinking?"

"Mr. Boston butterscotch schnapps."

"Ah. Of course."

"They took some of your blood at the hospital for routine tests earlier, I guess. I'm supposed to pick some up and take it to a lab down in Prairie du Chien for a BAC test."

Olaf the Handsome blinked too quickly for a moment.

"Sheriff, I'm really sorry, but apparently Marge Joss has the power to suspend you . . . and she did. I'm not even supposed to let you back in my car."

She felt her breath burst. So first Ladonna. Now Boog Lund was messing with her, and it all seemed to start at the library last night, continue through the stag party, and involve the assault on Walt Beavers.

"Works for me."

"No. What I'm saying is you're suspended," Yttri repeated. "No badge, no gun. Off duty." His posture had stiffened, his expression clouded. But suddenly she felt the sunshine. She was free to turn a rock over now, stomp a zombie as he scuttled after darkness.

I will find you.

"Works just fine for me," she said.

31

To Pepper's question at sunrise about Tianna's money—*What I gotta do to make her hundred too?*—she has heard no answer. Reasking it, reasking it, she finally gets from the camera troll a sideways response.

He says, "OK. You dang-darn betcha. Real good."

"Does that mean I get it?"

She keeps asking because if she can get $250, then she can eat on the Amtrak *and* bring gifts. Or $300—what about $300?—then she can eat *and* bring gifts *and* take a taxi from Whitefish to Hungry Horse. She won't have to hitchhike. Or steal a horse. Ha!

Tianna is long gone and they are taking a break. Pepper sits cross-legged on the studio floor wrapped in a beach towel, a little chilly, shivery but still floaty high. He sits before a desktop computer working with photo files. Talking to him, she thinks, is like talking to a talking doll. You ask a question, pull the string in his back, and he says, *You betcha.* He says, *Real good.* He says, *No worries.*

"I mean, like Tianna said, I'm not eighteen. So maybe you ought to pay me extra."

"OK, you betcha, no worries, I will make your dreams come true, everything you ever hoped for, real good, then."

"Dude, shit. I'm not asking you to marry me. Just get me to Montana."

"The Big Sky. The mountains. Very nice."

"You mean I already earned $250?"

"Not a problem," he assures her.

"Do you think my acting's good? Because I'm sorry, that Tianna was kinda gross. But do you think I pulled it off?"

"Your acting? Not a problem. Not a problem at all."

Right this instant, below Pepper's belly button, a hard cramp rockets through her guts, totally pops her floaty bubble. What the hell? Her period? Has she not even crapped since she left home last week? She has lost track of her body. Suddenly she can't stand up straight.

"I think I have to use the bathroom."

He nods at a closed door. "And to the left. Put some clothes on? How about?"

"Oh," she gasps. She is naked. "Right."

The door leads into a reception area, furnished with a desk and a phone and a sofa and samples of his photography on the walls, brides and grooms, senior portraits, kiddie soccer teams, family holiday shots, prize-winning livestock. Pepper is surprised by full daylight at the window. The sky is bright blue and everything is under snow and ice, prettily trapped like bottle caps under the surface of a bar. She can see where Tianna went, out a long driveway to a highway where a milk tanker sends water splashing high into the sunshine. Next on the highway a black buggy appears pulled by a gleaming black horse. A second cramp buckles Pepper. She hurries into the bathroom.

She waits on the toilet. The photographer decorates. Seashells. Driftwood. Cork and nets. Her gut cramp does a peekaboo. It jabs like a hot knife against some cincture inside her, threatens to split her in half. Then it retreats, vanishes, no release, not even gas. She counts to ten and forgets why. She decides that she is fine. All she needs is $250.

She comes out of the bathroom to find that a handsome Amish boy, about her age, is standing in the reception area. He looks a little hungry. His hands are large and raw. He wears a sweat-stained straw hat, a navy-blue jacket with thready cuffs, pants with ass patches. He has holes in his boots. Pepper might see him from a distance and think *poor guy*, but up close he looks like young Brad Pitt playing an Amish dude. Hand-*some*. Written on his face is exactly the same fragile rapture that Pepper, with the cramps gone, seems to be feeling. She flirts.

"I thought you people didn't do photographs."

He smiles remotely. She wows her eyes at him. She winks.

"But I can take a mental picture, right?"

He's got blue eyes and pink cheeks, exquisitely scraggly facial hair on tender skin that makes her want to grab him down there. She comes closer like she needs to see through the front doorway, check on something outside behind him. He smells like soil, horses, leather.

"Will that horse and buggy make it all the way to Montana, you think? Can I hire you?"

Same smile, looking her in the eye, not rattled, cool.

"He's pretty, what's his name?"

He shrugs. She laughs. Right? She's not after the horse.

"Can I marry you?"

At last he speaks—a weird little accent.

"Could you move, missus, please?"

Pepper feels startled—*missus?*—but she gets out of his way. He takes another step in, half closes the door. Behind it is a clear plastic sack with crushed Diet Coke cans inside. He picks up the sack, like five hundred cans that the camera troll emptied, fits it through the doorway, drops it into a wooden bin at the back of his buggy. He climbs aboard, snaps the reins on his horse, and never looks back.

This is when she crashes. This when a tiny voice inside her, a useless voice that Pepper hates, cries out, *Help me . . .*

She stumbles toward his reception desk, his telephone. Clumsy, blind, trying to remember Marie's number, she drops the receiver on the floor, it clatters, she fumbles for it, kicks it.

"OK, you betcha, then how about no way?"

This is what the troll tells her as he rushes out of his studio. He comes at her with that roll of silver tape from Walmart and Pepper tries to run for the outside door but only sinks onto her knees because she is so stupid and weak that she can't even run properly and just like before with Felton Henry she is so bad at escaping.

"You can't hurt me!" she tries to scream through the tape across her face.

32

Sheriff Kick—interim, suspended, in jeans and a sweatshirt, with the .38 Cobra in the pocket of her barn coat—sped the family minivan over Cliff Swallow Branch. The tiny spring creek, normally as clear as gin, was muddily opaque and swollen nearly to the deck of its iron bridge, about to spill beyond its boundaries. That was exactly how she felt, and OK with it. The hospital had told her that Tianna Ek had taken Brock Pabst home. Zombieland, here I come.

The community of Blackhawk Locks, where Pabst shacked up with his lady friend, was truly *on* the Mississippi, a lifestyle choice literally drowning in bad ideas. When she found the residence, it was a small, flat box, about as well built as a birdhouse, balanced on rickety stilts twenty feet high. At flood stage, in other words, the fourth-largest river on the planet was supposed to flow harmlessly beneath. What could go wrong?

She eased the van as far as she dared upon the slushy-muddy yard. At the extension of deep ruts beneath the house was Tianna Ek's silver Subaru. The twenty or so steps leading to the front door were sway-backed and buckled. She wasn't going up there. Pabst was coming down. She blew her horn. Nothing happened. She left the Kickmobile—gold Dodge Caravan, smudgy windows, sour-milk smell—and approached the steps while gripping the Cobra, glad she had hung on to it.

She kicked a metal stair tread. The whole house vibrated. Tianna Ek appeared. Dressed in a blue bathrobe, her hair wet, that boy-child on her hip, she stood on the tiny tilted porch and glowered down for a good long time. "Of course," she said at last. "It's you without your costume. I'll send the loser out."

She went inside, closed the door. The walls were thin. "Guess who's here, dumbfuck!"

In about thirty seconds Brock Pabst limped onto the porch, shirtless and barefoot, in pajama bottoms, an unlit cigarette between his fingers. "I didn't do nothing." The whole house jiggled as his wide-spaced heels thumped down the steps. "Hey, a guy can party, right? No law against that. How are you doing? I guess this is all gonna melt now. Is the river coming up? Shit, forgot my lighter. You don't have a lighter, do you? Hey, I was here with Tianna all night."

Take your time, she advised herself. "No, Tianna was 'here and there,' she told me. It was her night out. You were home with the baby. Is that what you meant?"

He turned to look up at Tianna. She stared dirty knives at him. Their child was out cold, his big head lolling over her elbow.

"Uh. Shit. Yeah, I meant I was here with the baby all night."

"Except you went to a party at Emerald Faulkner's barn."

"You *what*?" Tianna jerked the kid around to get a better grip. "I knew it. You left Garthy here alone. Where's your stupid car at, Brock?"

"My car?"

"*C-A-R*. You can't hear me or something?" For such a young woman her voice had the scorch of old rage, of too many trips down this same stupid road. "What happened to your fucking car? And who'd you go to the party with?"

He found a lighter in the pocket of his pajama pants. He lit up. "What party?"

"The one she just said. How'd you get your nuts burned? What's her name?"

Pabst was looking ever more twitchy, agitated. "Her *name*?"

"Yeah. What people call other people. The chick you went with. Dumbfuck."

"You guys are not communicating." The sheriff touched the pistol in her pocket. "Let's try again. You went to a party last night at Faulkner's barn. Booze, strippers, high times. Good so far? Later somebody beat up Walt Beavers." She stopped herself there. "I think you might know who did that and why."

"Coach Beavers? Somebody beat up Coach Beavers?"

"We have your plate number from the party, Mr. Pabst. It was on a gray GTO. We have a photograph. You were there."

"Shit. OK, OK, you got me. Yeah. OK." He began to pace on his bare feet in the slush. "OK, yeah, me and a friend went out for a while. Hey, shit, Tianna, go inside."

"Oh, no. You don't talk to me like that. You were at the stag party? With a friend? What's her name? That little Beavers chick again? Somehow you got your nuts scorched?"

"Can you just go inside?"

"That bitch will do anything for you, huh, Brock? What happened, she was so high she helped you turkey baste with a cigarette in her mouth? You're never touching me again."

"Go inside."

She did. She slammed the door, barely missing the boy's head. The stilt house rocked. Brock Pabst pulled on his smoke, squinting at the massive slab of brown water slipping past, a pair of sandhill cranes bleating along, paddling the air with their necks out and legs trailing.

"Thanks," he muttered just audibly, watching the cranes. "Thanks a lot. The fuck you think you are, ruining my life when I didn't even do nothing?" He glanced up at the house. Tianna watched from a window, the kid crying and wrestling with her. She seemed to aim her phone.

"Come with me," the sheriff told Brock Pabst. "Let's get ourselves a little space, talk privately."

She herded him ahead of her toward the riverbank. She kept her hand in her barn coat, touching the Cobra, urging him across swampy melting snow and mud onto what looked like a muskrat or a beaver track that twisted through the brush and riprap lining the river. She stopped him on a flat spot where a deep eddy swirled below, a littered spot where fishermen drank beer and smoked cigarettes down to the filter and chucked stink bait for catfish.

"I'm going to give you a choice right now. You assaulted a law en-forcement officer when you hit me with that bat. That gets you five to ten. Later, when you knocked me into the river, you were attempting to kill a law enforcement officer. That guarantees you life. Your whole shitty life, such as it is."

He added his cigarette to the mess at his bare feet. "You got no proof," he ventured.

"It won't be hard. Coach Beavers is going to recover. You left the bat behind. My car has your car's lipstick on it. The thing is, I haven't told anyone what all happened yet. My reasons. And so here is your choice. You tell me who sent you to hurt Coach Beavers and why, and I'll have no idea which of our many local meth heads committed such horrible crimes last night. Are you with me so far?"

He nodded, shivering.

"If you choose not to tell me," she said, "or you lie to me, that gets you somewhere between five years and life, not counting time for what you did to Coach Beavers."

This whole time the two cranes had been bleating and circling—waiting for a third and a fourth crane to join them. Now they coasted down to settle onto a midriver island. They aimed their long black beaks and stalked through melting snow like dinosaurs.

"Yeah, OK. I went to the party. I picked up a friend. Later she drove and dropped me off to wait for Coach Beavers. I was just told to bust him up a little. You showed up—I just freaked. I didn't mean none of that."

"Uh-huh. Told by who to bust him up?"

"Aw, man . . ."

"Your choice, five to life."

"Told by Pinky Clausen."

"I see." She reminded herself: there had been that weird break-in later at Clausen Meats. "Why did Coach Clausen want you to hurt Coach Beavers?"

"Pinky said Coach needs a good thumping now and then, keep him in line."

"Why does Coach Beavers need to be kept in line?"

Pabst shrugged. His scrawny torso was goose-bumped, his pale skin turning dull purple.

"Because he's a drunk and a moron? I don't know."

He was inching back, getting behind her right shoulder a little. She opened her stance to keep her face to him. She kept her fist around the gun inside her coat pocket. "You said when you were offering to fuck me with your baseball bat that since you beat him up, Coach Beavers wouldn't tell me anything. What was he not supposed to tell me?"

"I don't know. I really don't."

"Were you paid?"

"Nah, shit no."

"Then why would you do it?"

"I kind of owe Pinky."

"For what?"

As he searched for an answer to this, a door opened at the stilt house. A tiny back porch was just visible over the riverbank brush. Tianna appeared with the toddler dangling under her arm in a new grip that gave her mobility. Miscellaneous possessions began raining over the porch rail: a toothbrush, a can coozy, a wad of dirty clothes, a fishing rod, a white foam cup that exploded in midair with sawdust and mealworms. She went back inside to reload.

"I guess you're moving out."

He shifted again. She shifted to stay square. He could push her into the current, she realized. She might not survive the great river twice.

"So why do you owe Coach Clausen?"

"It's this weird thing."

"I'm sure it is."

"When we won state in 2010, Pinky had kicked me off the team for coming stoned to a game. But then he, like, totally forgave me. I got to dress for the tournament. I got to stay in the hotel. I got the per diem and everything." His voice cracked. "I got to be in the picture with the trophy. Ever since then, I just feel . . ."

Now tears. He wanted sympathy from her, someone he had assaulted and threatened to rape with a bat. Abruptly her heart was beating too fast. He was too close to her. Fucking zombie.

"I think of Coach Clausen as . . . as kind of like . . . a father to me."

"I see. That's very touching. New topic. Did you have any contact at all with a girl with long black hair who was at the party last night?"

"No."

"Do you know the girl I mean?"

"Yes."

"Did Clausen have any contact with her?"

"Not that I know of."

"How about Walt Beavers?"

"He just gets drunk and tries to dance along with the dancers."

"Did you see who the black-haired girl left with?"

"No."

"When you beat up Walt Beavers, who drove the car for you?"

Pabst glanced back at the house. Tianna had come out once more. This time instead of the baby she carried a large yellow snake. She flung the snake off the porch into a tree. It dripped down a few branches and then hung, writhing slowly.

"Damn, Tianna . . ."

"Who drove the car?"

"Brandy Beavers."

"Who's that?"

"His niece."

"She helped you beat up her own uncle?"

Pabst shrugged to answer. "She didn't know."

"How old is Brandy Beavers?"

He shrugged again. "Eighteen, for sure." Meaning, for sure she wasn't.

"Where is your car now?" One more shrug. Her voice felt thick. Her fist felt hot and slick on the pistol. "You don't know where your car is? Why not?"

"I think it got stolen."

"You think you'd like to spend your life in prison?"

"OK, OK. I told her take it home and crush it. Because, you know, I crashed into you. Beavers's junkyard. They have a machine."

She looped back on him. Walt Beavers had tried to hide something in the library.

"Let me quote you. 'Stupid old stumble-fuck,' or maybe it was *coon-fucker*, 'won't tell you nothing now.' Let's try again. Tell me what?"

"I don't know."

"You're sure?"

"I told you."

"Last chance."

"I'm telling you I don't know!" he whined. "Shit!"

She stepped back until her jacket scraped the crowding buckthorn behind her. "Stand right there," she told Brock Pabst, indicating where she had just stepped from, closer to the edge above the eddy.

"Turn around so I don't have to look at you."

He shakily followed her orders and she made him stand there for about fifteen seconds while the river flowed mightily past. Then she removed the .38 from her pocket and touched it to his skull. The black-haired girl, she was understanding, had been swept up in a swirl of secret events through the Bad Axe, a mass of bad actions bigger and older than one party last night, flowing forward and back. Ladonna Weeks, Walt Beavers, and now, if Pabst wasn't lying, also Rattlers ex-coach Pinky Clausen had something to hide from her. Was it all the same thing? As for Chief Deputy Lund, was he messing with her just to make sure he was the next sheriff? Or was he helping Ladonna? Or Clausen? Or both?

"Four years ago, the Rattlers lost a playoff game, nineteen to three. Did something happen during that game? Before it? After it? Anything that Walt Beavers was nervous about and Coach Clausen didn't want coming back to the surface? Something that happened after that game?"

He felt the gun and trembled. She trembled too. It would feel so good.

"I don't know. I was off the Rattlers by then. I mighta been in jail."

"If anything you told me turns out to be a lie, stumble-fuck, I'm coming right back."

33

"Yes, my queen?" Denise answered.

"Coach Clausen was at the party last night. We have his plates."

"Correct."

"Send that jpeg to my cell, please."

"Heidi, you're suspended. You're supposed to be at home. I think I'm not even supposed to talk to you. And Pinky Clausen is, if I may speak in my native tongue, a real motherfucker."

They were both silent for a long stretch of road. The Kickmobile ascended and cleared the river bluffs. On the ridges, in every direction, unplowed spring fields pushed up dark earth through the sloughing snow and ice. Water flowed beneath the vast melting slabs, like streams from glaciers. The flood was beginning. And the sky was clouding up again.

"So are you sending it now?"

Denise sighed. "OK. I'm sending it. Anything else?"

"Can Walt Beavers talk to us yet?"

"I'll call and check."

"Have we heard from the Dells yet? On the blue van?"

"Negative so far. But I'll make sure Rhino lets you know. And by the way, Olaf the Handsome volunteered to take your place to hear the Strong and Pritzle audit."

She went blank for a moment. Ahead of her, Coach Pinky Clausen's sprawling estate had appeared on the south-facing slope. She was looking at a big new house with architectural design, a landscaped yard the size of several baseball fields, a two-story multicar garage, and at least a mile of white vinyl fencing to contain the Meat King's thoroughbred horses.

"Sheriff Gibbs's Public Outreach budget," Denise reminded her. "The audit. Today we find out what kinds of sleazy things he was doing with all that money. I'll make sure Yttri reports out."

"Thank you."

"One more thing."

"Yes?"

"That booze in your car?"

"Yes?"

"That half pint of Mr. Boston butterscotch schnapps?"

"If you say so."

"We're withholding that detail. No one outside the department knows it. That bottle has an Iowa liquor control sticker on it. Rhino's got a call in to every outlet in a fifty-mile radius of the Lansing Bridge. He's gonna find out who bought it."

———

A battered red pickup with a snowplow blade cut swaths of black across Clausen's snowed-in driveway. She pulled into a freshly plowed corner and put her window down. The snow removal guy watched her from the shadow of his cab. In ghosts of stripped-off letters, the door of the pickup still said *Rhinegold Dairy*, the place down in Crawford County, defunct now, where she had worked part time one winter during high school.

"Where's a good place for me to park this?"

Cigarette smoke drifted from his window. She couldn't see his face.

"Hey? I don't want to be in your way. Where do you want me to park?"

He wasn't going to tell her. She shut off the engine, collected her cell phone from the cup holder, and headed toward Clausen's front door.

"I'll move it if you need me to."

But did she know him from Rhinegold? Her path brought her close enough to see beneath the cab shadow, and a glimpse of something only vaguely human took her breath away. She flinched, stopped, didn't know what to do with herself, found herself looking at him directly. Severe burns had left him hairless and without ears—without a nose, two open pits in the center of his face. He stared out at her, his only movement a faint but steady spasm in his neck and chin.

She tried to hold eye contact, be polite. "I'll be talking to Coach Clausen. Let me know if you need me to move."

Now he stirred. He raised a cigarette pinched between the knuckles of a scar-webbed hand. He put the cigarette to a nose hole. As he inhaled through the fleshless nostril, she had the sickly sensation that, yes, she knew him.

"I'm Heidi Kick. I used to be Heidi White. I used to work at Rhinegold. Have we met? What's your name again?"

Smoke gushed out his opposite nose hole. He nodded minutely, as if his skin were too tight for more. His voice was a hoarse monotone.

"Three thousand psi sounds about right."

What? She saw a smirk flicker across his melted features. He clubbed his stick shift into REVERSE. He spun the truck backward, swung it around, dropped its blade. She hurried out of the way as he rammed another half ton of wet snow into Clausen's yard. So here was another guy who worked for Clausen, she noted. Brock Pabst, now him.

The Rattlers Hall of Famer was uncomfortably surprised to see her at his door. He knew Harley didn't like him, and he correctly projected the animus onto her. But he recovered and glad-handed her inside his country mansion.

"C'mere, young lady. C'mere, c'mere. I won't bite. You gotta see this."

"No, thank you. I just came to ask you some questions."

He gave her no choice. He galloped his beer-barrel body ahead on crutches, his pinned-up pant leg swinging over the diabetes-related vacancy that had finally forced Rattlers leadership into Harley's hands. She followed him through a living room where people didn't live, down a trophy-lined hallway, through a family room for a man who had no family except for his grown son, Scotty, and two or three ex-wives, and finally onto a rear patio that looked over an empty in-ground swimming pool and across a storm-sheeted expanse of pasture.

"Look at that. I know you're into horses."

What he wanted her to admire was his wife number three or four, who was a hundred yards out astride a chestnut mare that she led across the glinting terrain. The horse stepped out with a clear distaste for the sharp ice crust and the unsuitable footing. Lady Clausen was coercing it into an odd, formal rigor.

"The Charleston canter. Isn't that a pretty sight?"

"You're right. I am into horses. The horse doesn't like it."

"What do you mean?"

"She's forcing it, looks like she's abusing it. But I guess it gets to why I'm here. Does she know where you were last night?"

"Say what?"

"Ducks Unlimited? Was that what you told her?"

He looked away and made a soft rumble inside his wattle of a throat. He took a little hop and a deeper lean into his crutches, which creaked. "Zero to crazy in six seconds," he said as if commiserating with a third person among them. "Just like they say."

Now he looked at her and steered a thin chuckle through his teeth.

"I give up. What's this about?"

"You went to a party in Faulkner's barn last night," she told him. "While you were there, you talked to Brock Pabst. You sent him to beat up Walt Beavers."

"Who said that?"

"Pabst told me himself."

"Hell," Clausen said, "I haven't seen that punk in years."

"You saw him last night. He shit his pants pretty good. He told me everything except why, which is what I'm here to find out."

"Never happened."

She showed her phone: Clausen's black Hummer with a crust of sleet on the top, Faulkner's barn in the background.

"You were there. Brock Pabst was there. Walt Beavers is in intensive care. Those are all the pieces." She nodded at his wife, out there aggressively goading the horse. "Kiwanis Club? Knights of Columbus? What'd you tell her, Coach? It looks like she's kinda on the verge of something, if you know what I mean."

He leaned into his crutches, making a face that she had seen a hundred times at the rail of the Rattlers' dugout, a latent explosiveness that kept everyone on edge.

"Here's what I think," she told him. "Something happened after a Rattlers game four years ago, when you were running the team. Then something happened last night to make Walt Beavers worry that it was coming back up. He said something to somebody, maybe to Ladonna Weeks at the Ease Inn, maybe to you at the party, and then *you* got worried. You sent Pabst to make sure that was the end of it. How about if you tell me what it's about? Or I can make sure that your wife gets this picture."

He muttered, she thought, the word *cunt*.

She waited. The snow-removal guy appeared on the drive from the house to the horse barn, slush curling from his blade. Now, as his face was struck by the sun, it was a misshapen red-pink-yellow blur, drilled with black holes. What was that famous painting? *The Scream*?

"I hear you're a drunk," Clausen said finally. "Drinking on duty. Butterscotch schnapps. That's pathetic."

A streak of sweat ran from her pits to her hip bones. He had talked to Boog Lund. No other way to know that. One question answered.

"I know you're suspended," he continued. "So you're impersonating an officer. And you're also extorting me. I should probably call the sheriff."

"That's funny."

He snapped at her, "You think so?"

"Like you say, I'm a civilian. So I think at this point our situation is more like one person lying to another person about something ugly in the community, Coach. They have my blood. There won't be any alcohol. I won't be suspended for long. Meantime, I'll send your wife this picture, so she can leave that horse alone and focus on what's really bothering her."

His thrusting face quivered at the jowls, his lips moving silently. Here came the snow-removal guy on his return trip from the barn. She felt him staring. *Three thousand psi sounds about right*. Why say that to her?

Clausen's throat rumbled more deeply than before, drawing something up. "Be careful, Missus Kick. You're done in July. I promise. And nothing you do now is gonna stick."

"July should be enough."

He spat. "And being married to a lady killer like Harley Kick-Ass, you'd better keep this in mind: you're not the only one with pictures. You might want to quit while you're ahead."

She tucked her arm to stop another streak of sweat. Direct line to Ladonna Weeks too. She and Clausen both wanted her to worry about Harley.

"Thank you, Coach. I think I have the roster straight now. Now I just have figure out what the game is. This has all been very helpful."

———

Back on the ridgetop road, her phone chimed. She dropped it on the seat and played two messages over the speaker.

"No go, as for talking to Walt Beavers," Denise said first. "He just stabilized enough that they're transporting him up to the head trauma center in La Crosse. Meanwhile, Yttri delivered your blood sample to the lab, now he's meeting with the audit people. Rhino found the store that sold the schnapps bottle. He's talking to the right clerk now and he'll call you. Still no word from Dells PD. I'll touch base with them again before I go home. Finally, acting sheriff Lund is a total dick and we miss you already. Over and out."

In the next message, her little girl's voice drifted up. "Mommy, Granny Belle is smoking in the kitchen and dropping ashes down the sink."

She surrendered to blind exhaustion for a moment, unsure where she was. Then she turned toward home.

34

Angus had escaped Boog Lund at the river, at the traffic pinch where Gibbs's old Charger was recovered, but he knew it would not be long before the deputy came for him at the scrap yard.

Now here he came, the brown-on-tan Tahoe easing down Lost Hollow Road from the west, straddling a meltwater gully in the gravel.

Angus watched this in nervous silence from midway up the acres of scrap. He had come home to find his dad upright and outside, wearing just a T-shirt and a diaper, pitching garbage into his big pipe, his waterslide. He would not shut up in the house, Brandy said, and so she had pilled him double, and then off he went to throw back other people's garbage. In the meadow across the road, where Lund's Tahoe now leveled off, drifted bloated kitchen trash sacks, a shattered plastic lawn chair, a microwave oven gulping as it sank. Angus grabbed his dad by his bone-thin wrist. He pushed Brandy ahead.

"That there is why," he told both of them. He aimed his chin at Lund coming. "See that? That ain't a friendly visit. That's why you two are going someplace safe."

As for Brandy, Angus had come home to find his little sister trying to operate the forklift. She had been planning, she said, to put Brock Pabst's piece-of-shit car into the E-Z Crusher machine and smash it flat, like Brock told her to.

"So that means you and Brock did what last night?"

Brandy had refused to answer.

"Something stupid," he had told her.

He shoved her ahead, looking back. Boog Lund rolled up beside Pabst's GTO, giving it slow consideration. Next he got out of the Tahoe and took a long look at the big pipe coming out from under the road, spewing brown meltwater and old cornstalks into the garbage already floating in the meadow. Finally he strolled up alongside the Beavers Salvage truck.

"Get Dad into the Quonset," Angus told his sister, "and keep him in there."

———

He was as ready as he could be. Coming down through the scrap, he watched Lund zip open his Jumbo Shrimp gear bag. Inside now were his Florida clothes, his cleats and his bat, his glove, his pillow, his radio, and the white straw cowboy hat he had bought in Corpus Christi and thought he might as well bring home for Brandy.

"Like I said, my stuff."

"Where's your family at?"

"Out."

Lund looked up the scrap yard. Brandy had failed to drag their dad much farther than where Angus had left them. There was Lyman Beavers in his diaper, showing Gibbs's chief deputy his middle finger.

"Uh-huh. Get in the car."

"What for?"

"Don't you want to see inside the jail again, just for old times?"

"What'd I do?"

Lund shoved him. Angus didn't move much. Lund reared back and blasted him with both palms in the chest. Angus had his feet set this time and he didn't move a bit. On his own, he turned against the Tahoe and spread his legs. Lund slapped him down.

"Unregistered vehicle, no driver's license, fleeing an officer. Being the latest dumbfuck Beavers to cause trouble. Have a seat in the car."

———

As Lund drove up out of Lost Hollow, Angus felt an old fear hatch like a worm in his heart. He had been a third grader when Gibbs had put his mom in a cell. Angus, his dad, and baby Brandy had gone to see her one time. Since then jail meant this to Angus: his mom had never been the same. After jail, she wouldn't let anybody touch her. She had lived just one month more.

But Lund headed southeast, away from town and the jail, toward the bluffs along the river. The melt was on. The ditches were full. The sun was out but the roads were skimmed with water. Everything gurgled and dripped. Lund eased the Tahoe along just beneath the speed limit while he made mocking chitchat about last night's storm, the wet spring overall, the saturated ground, the rain in today's afternoon forecast, the flood that was slowly building around them. Angus stayed silent. Ten minutes, twenty minutes. Finally Lund stopped in Bishops Coulee at the Pronto station. He chuckled, looked at Angus in his mirror.

"If I recall, it was a six-pack of beer, a box of maxi pads, and three cans of cat food."

His mom had been arrested here, at this Pronto, for shoplifting. She had scratched the face of the officer who arrested her. That was why she went to jail.

"Look there, Hotshot."

He was pointing his chin at the window of the Pronto, the deals written on butcher paper in large red letters.

"We can't just have cheese anymore. We gotta have organic local hippie cheese with fungus in it. We gotta drink hippie beers named after somebody's goddamn acid trip."

Angus's mom had worn a ring in her nose and didn't shave her legs. She had tried to make wine. They sat there another minute, Lund texting someone on his phone.

"What am I forgetting?" he wondered at last. "Grain Belt, pussy pads, cat food . . . and what else?"

His text pinged as it left. He chuckled.

"Oh, yeah, *and* Lady Speed Stick."

———

He steered the Tahoe away from the river. Sandrock Road took them back up through the bluffs and east along the border of Bad Axe and

Crawford counties, where Battle Bluff towered, sunstruck in the wind-shield. But Lund went around the landmark, into the coulee to the south. There, Rademacher Hill Road was pitted with deep puddles and sawed through with blades of rushing meltwater. The undercarriage of the Tahoe hissed and rattled. Lund whistled the Clausen Meats jingle. At Red Mound, he turned into the cemetery.

Angus's mom was buried here. Lund drove right between graves and stopped where he couldn't help but see her stone.

CHEYENNE BEAVERS. FLEW TO JESUS. 1971–2004.

"Doggone it," he said after a minute. "See those?"

He was pointing into the sky, bumpy and gray to the northwest.

"Are those rain clouds already? I tell you, Hotshot, we oughta sue Minnesota."

Angus stared at the dates. She had gone into the jail at thirty-two years old, spent her birthday in there, come home quiet and jumpy, and died at thirty-three. He had been eight, Brandy four. No one ever told them how she died.

Lund said, "I'm just gonna assume, Hotshot, that you came back to take care of your family. Like you said, your dad being sick and all."

He snicked his teeth. Angus stared at the roll of fat on the back of his neck.

"And if we start with that, then anything else you might think you're doing is probably a mistake. Any other choices you've been making are probably the wrong ones, things that would probably hurt your family instead of help. Are you with me so far?"

Angus did not respond. Lund picked up a *Broadcaster* from the seat beside him. He shook the newspaper wide and laid it against his steering wheel and began to read last week's news. A minute passed. He turned a page. Another minute. He turned another page.

"Well, it says here that I'm the only candidate that's filed for the sheriff's job, the election in July, and there's only a couple days left to get in. So it looks like I'm the one. You follow me, Hotshot? You'll want to make good choices. You hear what I'm saying?"

He started the Tahoe. His eyes came into the mirror. "One more stop."

He drove off Red Mound, schmoozing about the weather again, about last spring's flood, about some farmer's drowned cattle found against a rolling dam three miles down the Mississippi. He drove Angus up the coulee parallel to Lost Hollow, to the gate of the Battle Bluff overlook. The gate was locked, not Memorial Day yet. Lund unlocked it and bumped the Tahoe up the narrow dirt road a quarter mile to the top. They arrived at a small open space of root-threaded limestone where a few red pines stood over a feeble shelter and a picnic table. Nearby were the remains of a campfire, a dozen or so beer cans and broken bottles, and the Blackhawk monument, the plaque that stood before the overlook. Lund drove up close.

"Why don't you get out and enjoy the view."

Angus opened his door and went to the rock retaining wall. Most of the Bad Axe spread out before him. To the west, to the left, he could see the Mississippi. In the other direction, he could see the ridges and the hollows extending east until Wisconsin leveled out. But straight ahead, north, he figured, was the view that Lund wanted him to have. You could see Beavers Salvage from up here. You had to look straight down, almost lean over the wall. That was Lost Hollow down there, that narrow coulee, that little creek, that meadow. That was his dad's property, directly under Battle Bluff.

It had been a long time since Angus had seen it from up here. They used to picnic on the bluff when he was little, when they still had a farm, not a scrap yard. Angus used to throw pinecones off the edge, right here, imagining he could splash one in the creek. He had learned that was an illusion. It was a long way down. Then, when his mom died, they had stopped coming up here. Seeing the land below, the farm that had turned into what clearly was a junkyard, his throat filled and his eyes blurred.

But then as Angus watched, something separated from the mass of junk. An old red pickup with a snowplow blade pulled away from the scrap yard. Where was his dad's Beavers Salvage truck? Who was that pulling away? Angus felt frantic suddenly. What had he missed?

Lund said, "If you can't make good choices for your family, Hotshot, if you're gonna pull dumbass stunts and get them hurt, you might as well 'fly to Jesus' right now."

He was smiling out the Tahoe's window.

"From right here, off that wall, like your hairy-assed mommy did."

Angus knew then what had just happened down at the scrap yard. He vaulted the wall, landed on the scree of broken limestone, skidded, fell, skidded, ran, crashed through a lap of brush at the bottom. He forded the flooded crick, up to his armpits already. He wallowed across the filling meadow. He climbed up beneath his dad's spewing pipe to the road.

The Beavers Salvage truck had been hammered by that snowplow blade into the greater mass of junk. He went into the house. His dad and Brandy hadn't stayed up in the scrap yard like he told them to. His dad was beneath the kitchen table, moaning and slowly wheeling his feet, gashed on the back of his head. Brandy's door was locked. Angus kicked it in. She was rolled up in her blankets, her eyes swollen, her neck abraded, her tattooed ankles sticking out as she kicked at him and sobbed. "Why are you here, Angus? What did you come back for? What did you do?"

He snatched an ankle.

"Who was that?"

"What the fuck did you do?"

One of her ankle tattoos was a snake, a rattler. He had seen it before.

"You're a Cave Girl now? OK, then that's what I came back for."

"Get out!"

"Who was it?"

"I don't know who it was! What the fuck did you do?"

He let her go. He climbed through the scrap yard, clawed through the shrinking snowdrift in the shadow of the Quonset shed. The girl was still where he had buried her.

Her neck had drooped, her chin had puddled between her collarbones. Her dead blond hair had thawed into grizzled rags that blocked her face. She had begun to smell, a gummy smell, faintly like oatmeal. The hair clip, the blue plastic butterfly, had slipped down to where it clung above a knob of ice in her hair, about to fall.

With a clumsy anxious hand Angus fixed it. He felt the crunch of brittle fibers inside the friction of the clip. Her gold necklace had come unstuck from the mealy flesh of her naked chest. For the first time Angus saw that its pendant was a word. He reached, stopped himself, reached, and plucked the pendant from between her breasts. As he raised it to read, the chain was still frozen to the back of her neck and it broke away in his grasp. Now he held it dangling in the sun. The pendant said *Sophie*.

He looked at her. Through the weeping melt of ice crystals, she gazed back at him with one fog-blue eye.

Sophie.

Brandy.

And any other girl who came too close to that shit.

A Cave Girl.

Then Angus had it, what to do with her now. Rattlesnake Cave.

35

Because that is what they tell you to do, right? Report to someone what happened? Don't be silent? Don't hide it? Say what happened? When someone does sex to you and you don't want it? Because sex done to you that you don't want is not your fault?

Pepper hates to remember, but now as she lies captured with troll-talk beyond the door, the memory is happening, she can't stop it.

Aren't you supposed to tell your mom when someone hurts you?

So she does. The very first time, just beyond her thirteenth birthday, she tells her mom what her stepdad, Felton Henry, has just done to her upon the sleeper bed inside his tractor-trailer. *And this is what Mom says* . . . It all leaps forward. She is in Montana, she imagines, telling Marie. *Mom tells me, "Don't make things up."*

Right here she always thinks that Marie was lucky to be older. Marie never needed Bennie for protection like she did. Right here she always tries to stop the memory. She snaps a band against her wrist, bites herself, steals liquor and drinks it. Or she can be a runner when she wants to. They won't let her on the team anymore but sometimes she puts her shoes on and runs a million miles. Or she sings, or she screams. But she can't now. Silver tape binds her wrists and ankles and straps her mouth from ear to ear. So it happens all over again.

Because when Pepper is about ten, Felton Henry appears, a long-haul trucker, a huge man with a loud jolly style who drinks hard with her mom. He is wary of Bennie and so mostly leaves her alone, but sometimes he makes Pepper clean his cab. But then a week after that big game up here, the one she remembered when she was with Dale, after Bennie's six home runs, the fight, the long party home, her big brother wraps his Mustang around a power pole and is gone. Felton Henry waits a few months until she turns thirteen and then he's coming at her.

Her mom says, *Well, don't let him.*

Her mom says, *Don't lie to get attention.*

So Pepper tells Felton Henry, *You can't hurt me.* Then, as best she can, she can't be hurt. This goes all the way until when she turns sixteen and she decides to kill him and escape. But she fucks it up, both the killing and the escaping. She almost does it right—but *almost* counts in horseshoes, not rape. She hates to remember . . . but she can't stop it.

Felton Henry parks his tractor-trailer in front of the house. They live on a hill. Down the hill, the road turns sharply and runs along a bluff above the Wisconsin River. A hundred feet below is a swirling deep spot behind the Kilbourn Dam. Pepper Googles a few things at the library, studies how his emergency brake works, the yellow knob beneath the dash. The next time she cleans Felton Henry's cab, while he's inside drinking with her mom, and just before he comes for her, when she hears the screen door bang against the house, she puts his gear box into neutral. After his cock comes out of her, after he rolls off and starts to snore, she punches in the yellow knob and skims bare-assed across his driver's seat. She launches herself out of the cab and slams the door as she flies away from it. She lands and goes for his wheel chocks, two ten-pound rubber wedges on a rope. Then she runs.

But she fucks it up and still wonders what she could have done differently. The truck rolls maybe ten feet before Felton Henry comes across his seat. He slaps the knob in and puts the truck back in gear. He is fast like a bear, and he catches her running with the chocks. He beats her with them, holding their connecting rope and stoning her over and over with the heavy wedges.

Your little bitch tried to kill me.

And her mom never asks, *Really? Pepper tried to kill you—with all of her clothes off?*

36

"Mommy, what's a lady killer?"

She had banished her mother-in-law for smoking in the house, repeat offender. After that, she had meant to lie down for a few minutes and review her assumptions—Ladonna Weeks, Boog Lund, and Pinky Clausen were all on the same team, playing the same game. At least the black-haired girl from the Dells was caught up in that game, but surely there were more like her—and then she had been dreaming.

Her mom's and dad's slain bodies were laid out on the floor of the milk room—but the floor was putty-colored carpet, squishy with blood puddles, smoke billowing through the scene from the Bishops Coulee murders—her beloved cows were standing around talking in human voices about what a pity something was—*but only a farmhand would know where he kept his gun*, she was telling the bell cow, Ophelia, who said back, *Don't worry I will find you*—then an electronic traffic billboard was scrolling her list of suspect farmhands: Greg Schatz, Carson Troutman, Darrold Dinkle, Robert Who Slept in the Woods, all the rest—and then dream-Heidi had shot this really nice old man who used to fix the hay elevator for her dad, and in her blood-spattered boots she was standing over Wayne Pitzer's blown-out brains when Ophelia's question awakened her.

"A lady killer?"

She took a moment. That yearbook photo of Harley had been sitting on the kitchen table all morning, the kids looking at it. *Harley Kick,*

Lady Killer. Some woman issuing a "bomb threat," Belle Kick had advised her.

Flat on her back, head throbbing, she felt dizzy and sick. *Be careful, Missus Kick. You're not the only one with pictures.* She had to rouse herself, get back to work. A different photograph had to be reconstructed of what had seemed like a second shrine in Walt Beavers's home, the one *not* dedicated to his drowned daughter. That photo was lost, that phone ruined by her plunge in the river, but she aligned the elements in her memory: the calendar date, the blue butterfly hair clip, the mustard crock full of ashes. That arrangement, she thought, was her hinge between the past and the present. The calendar page was the same as the date of the baseball game that Harley said he missed and the Rattlers lost badly, the game that the girl had looked up in the library to win a bet, panicking Walt Beavers. *Get up*, she told herself. *You mean Rattlers first-base coach Walt Beavers, who kept a girl's barrette and a crock of ashes on his shelf—and last night got himself beat up by Coach Clausen, via Brock Pabst.* All of that was the past, and the black-haired girl from the Dells was the present.

"*Lady killer* is just an expression, honey. It doesn't mean killing, really."

"Why? What's an expression?"

This was Dylan. She felt all three awake now, quietly beside her. Goddamn Ladonna, she thought, the bitch knew what she was doing. But the Kicks were stronger than that.

"Like when Daddy calls you guys cookie monsters. You're not really monsters, right?"

"I am." Taylor started roaring. The sheriff opened her eyes. Bright sunlight streamed into the bedroom. Ice dripped everywhere. She found her phone. Shit. It was after two o'clock. She had slept three hours. She had three messages.

"Your daddy means that you really love cookies, like Cookie Monster on Sesame Street."

"Can we have cookies?"

"We forgot to have lunch. Let's do that first."

She struggled onto the elbow of her injured arm. Ouch.

"How about macaroni and cheese?"

The boys celebrated, letting go of semantic concerns. Opie was not that easy. She sat against the headboard, reading her book about dragons. "So that means Daddy really loves ladies?"

"Yes. Women. That's all it means."

"How many women?"

"All women. He thinks women, and girls, especially smart ones, are really cool."

"But he loves you special."

"That's right, sweetheart. That's why we got married and made you. First comes love, then comes marriage, then comes Opie in a baby carriage. Did you ever hear that one?"

Very solemnly, Opie said, "Mary Beth Sime sings that about me and Danny Wertzelbakken because she's jealous that Danny's desk is next to mine. I ignore her."

The sheriff dumped Taylor off her legs. She sat on the edge of the bed, testing her stiff ankle where Pabst's initial bat blow had connected. She was not quite ready to stand.

"You mean you're not going to marry Danny Wertzelbakken and be booger farmers?"

"Mommy . . ." her daughter warned her sternly.

"Well, if you're going to scold me, I'm just going to go make lunch."

Groggily boiling wagon wheels and grating Colby cheese, she played her messages. Day-shift dispatcher Rinehart Rog informed her that Deputy Yttri was headed out to the farm—unofficially, Rhino was clear—with a report. Yttri had attended the county board's Finance Committee meeting, and he had news about the auditor's analysis of Gibbs's budget. Next message, Rhino told her that Wisconsin Dells Police Department had called back. They had received the photograph Denise sent of the blue panel van and its plates. They knew the vehicle. They were looking for the owner and would be back in touch. "Oh, uh, and, Heidi? A clerk at the IGA in Lansing told me that he sold someone a half pint of Mr. Boston butterscotch schnapps last night, right before he closed. Um. Yeah. So if you want to know who the clerk said the customer was, just call me back."

She did. She asked him, "Who, Rhino?"

"You."

"I see. Then I should show up on IGA's security recording."

"But you won't," Rhino said. "Because he said their system was down."

God, what a bush-league attempt to set her up. It went along with sticking shit in her mailbox, baiting her with lurid hints about her husband, and vaguely suggesting that she would regret doing her job. But why? With this on her mind, a minute later she had overboiled the pasta. The wagon wheels were one solid formation. She dumped in cheese anyway, added milk, and tried her best to stir. Back into her thoughts circulated Walt Beavers's shrine. Who was dead?

"I have a riddle, and if you get it right, it's lunchtime. Why is cheese orange?"

"Because God loves oranges!" Dylan shouted.

"Because God loves cheese!" Taylor piled on.

"You are both absolutely correct."

"They are not. Cheese is made from milk, and milk is white. They dye it."

"And a score for Opie too. It's lunchtime, everybody. Wash up."

She hardly looked at their wet little hands, held out for inspection. She cleared the *Lady Killer* photo of Harley off the kitchen table and folded it into the back pocket of her jeans.

She set out bowls of steaming orange muck. It got very quiet, just the sounds of gummy mastication. She drifted to the front window. Should she drive back to Coach Beavers's place and double-check her memory? No, no, she was sure. But what if the shrine disappeared, or was destroyed?

She had to let these thoughts go because Yttri's cruiser was bumping and splashing along the driveway. She rushed to the kitchen. "Another riddle," she said to the kids. "Who is a big gray baby who can fly with his ears?"

"Dumbo! Dumbo! Dumbo!"

She herded them into the family room, started the video, and closed the door. She checked her face in the bathroom, checked her sweatshirt and jeans for cheesy wagon wheels, then let in Olaf the

Handsome. He put a folder on the kitchen table that said Strong &
Pritzle, CPA.

"I'm on dedicated rounds," he said. "That's my story, and Rhino's got
my back. Lund is telling everybody not to talk to you. But here I am,
and you're not going to believe this."

He opened the folder and put his finger on a sum. "I didn't let on to
the Finance Committee. I wanted to show you first. Look. This number, right here, is the sheriff's department's contribution to that Second
Amendment bullshit at the Ease Inn."

She exhaled. Ladonna Weeks and her brother, Dermit, annually
put on what they called a Second Amendment Celebration, essentially
an unlicensed gun show—a munitions swap, fueled by bratwurst and
beer—apparently with the unpublicized sponsorship of the Bad Axe
County Sheriff's Department, via the taxpayers. Wow. The figure, what
Gibbs gave to Dermit and Ladonna Weeks to sell beer, brats, and weapons, was $2,682.97.

Yttri said, "Weirdly specific number, right?"

"Sure is."

"Unless you look up the property tax on Faulkner's farm, where the
party was last night."

He showed her a printout from the county clerk's online records. The
official owner of the property, Emerald Faulkner's daughter, Prayleen,
had last year been billed exactly $2,682.97 for the taxes on an eighty-
three-acre farm on Bottom Road. Yttri spread his big hands on her
kitchen table as if to brace himself and to suggest that she do the same.

"So I called Prayleen Faulkner," he began. "She told me that 'somebody up there' pays the tax in exchange for hunting rights on the land.
So who is 'somebody,' right? I called the clerk's office, and Beth Lovaas
says to me, 'Oh, yeah. Ladonna Weeks walks in with Faulkner's tax pay-
ment in cash every year. This year I had to give her three cents back. She
says her family hunts the property.' In other words," Yttri concluded,
lowering his voice for emphasis, "the taxpayers of Bad Axe County are
directly funding the venue for secret stripper parties."

He wore his look of cold amusement very well. What stood out was
the lack of any common-sense effort to conceal what essentially was theft

and money laundering. Gibbs hadn't even smeared the numbers around a little bit. "It's not very clever," she said.

"Gibbs didn't need to be clever. He'd have been sheriff another twenty years if he hadn't bought the farm."

"Ha. Right. But what did he get out of paying Faulkner's tax and protecting the stag parties? I doubt he attended."

"Good question." Yttri preened his perfect blond mustache with subtle tugs of his lower lip. "There's another angle, for sure. We don't know what it is yet, but I'll bet Lund is part of the equation. If you solve that equation—I mean, if you're going to run in the election—then you're going to beat him by a landslide." He glanced out the window. "With this melt on, by a mudslide."

She heard the kids laughing to *Dumbo*. She would love to beat Chief Deputy Lund by a mudslide. *If you're going to run in the election.* In the last two days that big decision had dropped off her radar. Meanwhile Bob Check was out collecting signatures. Hadn't she already given up on the job? Then why was she worried? Did she want it? The questions clenched her stomach.

"I know the Faulkner property a little bit," Yttri interrupted her thoughts to say. "There's the house and the barn. But there's also a whole lot of wild and remote land. Rush Creek flows into the Bad Axe River out there. It's great trout water. They fence and post the living shit out of it. Whoever does that seems really freaked about someone getting in there, but . . ."

He paused and looked at her sheepishly.

"But you know how to get in?"

He shrugged. "Like I said, it's good fishing."

"And you want to look around?"

"There are other buildings deep in there, not close to where they have the parties."

"Do we need a warrant?"

"Not if I'm off duty, use my own vehicle, and go fishing. Then I'm only trespassing."

He grinned at her, his question in the air.

"Don't look at me," she said. "Right now I'm a civilian. But while you're trespassing in the neighborhood, can you go into Walt Beavers's house, take pictures of everything on his trophy shelf, and, when you get reception, text them to me?"

"Done."

She stopped him at the door.

"Who can I talk to about Walt Beavers? Somebody who knows him well."

"Lyman Beavers?" Yttri said. "He's Walt's younger brother."

"I've never heard of Lyman Beavers."

"I don't think anybody's seen him in a while," Yttri said. "He used to get drunk and holler at the Rattlers games. He thought his kid should play, and from what I hear, he was right. Then the kid went away to a baseball academy and ended up in the minor leagues. Angus Beavers. There's a girl too. Brandy Beavers. She must be a teenager now. The family runs a junkyard."

The alternative was waiting all day, she decided.

"Kiddies," she announced over the *Dumbo* video after Yttri had left, "I'm so sorry to interrupt you, but we're going for a ride . . ."

37

The scene stunned and appalled her. On the approach, trash littered the shoulders of Lost Hollow Road. More trash floated in the flooding meadow beyond. Then the tight gravel curve resolved and the actual junkyard came into view. She slowed the Kickmobile to a crawl. On the uphill side, where the house and barns were, the accumulated wreckage was dense, incomprehensible. From there it flowed downhill, straddled the road in a rust stain at least a hundred yards wide, and then resumed in a random strew of vehicles and other junk that extended across the valley bottom all the way to the underside of Battle Bluff.

The sheriff turned her engine off and looked up. At the southern reach of the Bad Axe, Battle Bluff was close enough to Crawford County that she knew it as a party spot, a place to drink and throw beer bottles off the retaining wall of the Blackhawk monument and listen to them crash on the rocks below. She remembered looking down on this exact place. It was not a junkyard all those years ago. But life created junk, and here it was. She touched Ophelia's hand on her shoulder, followed her daughter's gaze, and tried to answer her question.

"I don't know what's wrong with these people, sweetie. This is just how they live."

"But why are we here?"

"Because I need to talk to them."

"Why?"

The boys chimed in. "Are they bad? Are you going to put handcuffs on them?"

"I just need to ask a few questions. And speaking of questions, does anybody know why the old man never flushes his toilet?"

"Why? Why? Why, Mommy?"

"He just scares the poop out of it."

A cushion of giddiness enveloped her children. She enhanced it with a box of Cheddar-flavored Goldfish, put Opie in charge of that, and stuck the *Dumbo* DVD in the overhead player. She cracked the front-seat windows and put the child locks down. They would be OK. She was only here to talk. She would retreat from the first sign of danger. She had promised herself, promised Harley in her heart. But she touched the .38 in her jacket pocket as she shut the door.

No one had appeared to greet her yet, not even a dog. She crossed the rust-stained mush of the road and began her wary approach toward the house. It had shed all of its paint and half of its shingles. Cardboard and blankets replaced broken window glass. The chimney had toppled. Heavy smoke spewed from a stovepipe punched through a sidewall. Cinder blocks served as steps to a porch that had buckled like a roller coaster. The sheriff glanced back—they were fine—before she climbed the cinder blocks and knocked.

No answer. The door was unlocked. She pushed it open, took a gust of foul hot air, and faced catastrophic clutter—hoarding, nest fouling, complete breakdown.

"Is anyone in here? Is everyone all right?"

She stepped back to the porch, wanting better air, looking for signs of life in the junkyard. She saw only junk and went back to the doorway.

"Is everybody OK in here?"

She was overheated suddenly. Her lungs felt clogged. She widened the door, drew the .38, and stepped in. The tide of squalor parted three ways, one for access from a recliner to a flat-screen TV, another from the recliner to an overloaded woodstove, a cast-iron monster that cranked out oppressive heat. Any day now, she thought, the closest VFD would be hosing down a pile of smoking rubble. A third path led to a narrow hallway.

"Does someone need help?"

In the hallway, she opened a door. Facedown on the bed sprawled a girl in twisted, too-tight pajamas. One leg hung off the bed. One arm was bent beneath her torso. She looked like a smaller girl had been hurled down from the sky and now she lay there in this heat, bloating inside the pajamas. But she was breathing. Her back just barely rose and fell. Brandy, Yttri had said. Brandy Beavers was asleep.

She retreated, opened the door to the next room. On the bed, curled, she saw hairless skin and bones in a diaper. This was Lyman Beavers—alive too, breath rasping—but he looked injured. Some kind of makeshift bandage for his head had been made from a stocking cap and napkins. She rolled him gently. His emaciated arm unfolded awkwardly and heavily from beneath him—she leaned to hear what he was muttering—and he lashed out, a dim wide flash as she jerked back from what looked like a machete. The heavy knife, jagged with corrosion, carried his arm back to the bed. He lay still, gasping. He had just missed her.

From a safe distance in a dim corner of the room, she said, "This is Sheriff Kick, Mr. Beavers. Push that knife onto the floor." Slowly, with great effort, he did. One eye was swollen shut, but the other regarded her acutely through a pinprick black pupil. His dry lips split: "Dairy Queen."

"That's me."

"I thought you were gonna be the booger."

"I see."

But she didn't. The booger? Booger farmer? Boog Lund?

"It turns out the daughter gave away all my guns."

"I see."

"To the same punk boyfriend that's been eating my pills. She does whatever this fella says, I guess. He sold my guns for more drugs. So the boy says, Angus."

"Mr. Beavers, what happened here?"

"Hell if I know. Ask the boy."

"Where is your boy?"

"Hell if I know."

After a struggle he managed to sit up on the side of the bed. The old mattress nearly poured him off, but he got his feet planted and grabbed the bedclothes and hung on. He processed the challenge of verticality for a long moment, working his whiskery gullet and blinking in her direction like a nestling ready to be fed. "The boy said no more today, but I do think I'll have me a couple more of just them half pills." He pointed to a dresser top like it was a mile away. There was a pill bottle on it. "You mind to make the reach?"

Her phone jumped in her pocket: Yttri.

She headed for the porch to take the call, and hit the open air with a gasp. "What's up?"

"The trout aren't biting."

"What?"

"I'm on Faulkner's farm. There are two secondary barns way back in here, at the end of a tractor road. I've never seen them from the river."

She closed the front door and came down the cinder-block steps. She could see the kids were still fine in the van. The voice of Olaf the Handsome felt good in her ear.

"Sure, they have illegal parties at the main barn on the property. The evidence from last night is all over the place. It looks like Peter's Potties out of Zion even catered a shitpot for the event and they haven't picked it up yet. But these barns back here are another reason that Gibbs and the Ease Inn crowd have been keeping Faulkner's taxes paid up."

She took a deep breath of faintly rusty air.

"Go ahead."

"One barn is full of heavy equipment, farm stuff and otherwise, all brand-new. The other barn is crammed with building materials. I'm looking in the window at spools of copper wire worth a bundle. It's gotta all be stolen. There are ruts back here made by big trucks. Somebody's been shipping this stuff in and out."

"OK."

From the scramble of her thoughts, she tried to assemble a sensible, sherifflike directive. Yttri beat her to it.

"How about I see if I can get into the barn with the equipment and get some serial numbers? Then we can find out if this stuff is really stolen. If it is, we'll get a warrant."

"OK. Yeah. Sure." She caught him before he hung up. "Hey, Olaf?" She had surprised herself, calling him Olaf. Him too, it seemed.

"Yes . . . Heidi?"

"Any chance that Angus Beavers isn't playing baseball anymore?"

"I don't know."

"What kind of kid was he?"

"I remember quiet," Yttri said. "Big kid, good player, really, really quiet. Um . . . so is everything OK with you? You're still at home, taking it easy?"

"Yeah. Sure."

"You get the Walt Beavers pictures?"

"Got 'em. Thanks."

She dropped the phone back into her pocket. She gazed over Beavers Salvage. The beast that ate a hundred family farms—that's what she was looking at. But the longer she looked, the less monolithic the view became. Individual bits of wreckage began to stand out. Amid it all, a hundred yards out, breaking visually from a stack of crushed cars behind it, there was Brock Pabst's GTO.

———

The girl was still facedown on the bed. She was hot to the touch. She stiffened.

"Brandy, this is Sheriff Heidi Kick. I need to talk to you."

"I didn't do nothing," she muttered into her arm. "What'd I do?"

"Brock Pabst told me you helped him beat up your uncle. Then he said someone stole his car. But I see it outside. You want to tell me what really happened?"

"I didn't do nothing."

"Your uncle Walt is badly hurt. He might die. That would be murder. After that, Brock crashed his car into a sheriff's car and knocked it into the river. That's attempted murder of an officer. This is serious, Brandy. I know you were involved, but I don't think any of it was your idea. You need to tell me what happened."

Her body stiffened even more. Then she burst. "Tianna. That bitch. She started it."

"Started what?"

"She's such a bitch to Brock. He just needs to have some fun now and then. She takes all his money too. For their kid supposedly. Then she parties. Like he's supposed to stay home."

"I see. So because of Tianna, you and Brock went to a party last night? Is that right? In Faulkner's barn?"

The sheriff took the girl's hot silence as a yes.

"Entry was a hundred bucks. That's a lot of money to party with a bunch of old men. Doesn't sound like fun to me. Or did Brock take you there to *make* money?"

Another silent yes. So they were another pair—Brock Pabst and Brandy Beavers—like the pair from the library.

"Do you remember, at the party, was there a girl about your age with long black hair, wearing boots and a skirt?"

Silent yes again.

"Do you know who she left the party with?"

"I saw her get into a van."

A van. Good. "A dark blue van?"

"A white one."

Here was news. The girl had left with someone else. It was time to go through all the pictures that Buddy Smithback took, looking for a white van. The sheriff looped back.

"Did you know that Brock went to your uncle's house to hurt him?" She waited. "When you don't answer me, Brandy, I'm thinking you mean yes."

"No!"

"That's good. I wouldn't think so. Brock said your uncle was not supposed to talk about something. Do you know what that was?"

"No!"

"Would you look at something for me?"

The girl withdrew the arm that blocked her face. She had cried beneath it. The sheriff scrolled and then extended her phone, showing the photograph of the blue butterfly barrette and the mustard crock on her uncle Walt's shelf. The girl sat up to see better.

"Is that your barrette? Or could it belong to someone you know?"

"I don't think so."

"Do you know what's in the mustard crock?"

"Mustard?"

"OK, do you see the calendar page? Do you recognize that date? I guess you would have been twelve. There was a Rattlers game. They lost badly."

The girl slumped. "No."

The sheriff scrolled back and zoomed in on the barrette. "Do you have any idea why your uncle Walt would have that on his shelf?"

She shook her head. All of this was beyond her.

"It looks like you and your dad both got hurt. Can you tell me who did that?"

Fear welled in her eyes. "No."

"You don't know? Or you can't tell me?"

"I don't know."

The sheriff gave Brandy Beavers some space and returned to her dad's room, wanting to ask the same questions of him. But the air felt different, fresher. The bed was empty. The room had a door to the outside. Beyond was a million tons of junk, and into it somewhere Lyman Beavers had disappeared.

As she emerged a second time from the house, her eyes went straight to the Kick family minivan: three little faces, watching with wide eyes as a man who was *not* Lyman Beavers, who was young and healthy, hurried away across the road. She cut him off heading for the junkyard.

"And you must be Angus."

The young man stared at her through deep fatigue. His forehead was white, as was the imprint of sunglasses on his sun-scorched face, the same look Harley rocked April through October. This was Angus Beavers.

"What were you doing at my car?" she asked.

"I said hello."

"What?"

She glanced back. The doors were locked. The kids gawked, ripped from *Dumbo*. But they were fine. She returned her attention to Angus Beavers. He was looking up. The sky had clouded. A new breeze squeaked the junk behind him. His hands drew into anxious fists.

"You're the new sheriff. Right?"

She glanced back at the van. How would he know that? Had he spoken to the kids? Had his dad found him and told him? She gave herself a moment to see him. Angus Beavers looked fidgety and exhausted. He looked haunted.

"When exactly did you come back to the Bad Axe?"

Before he could answer, she heard a smack and shriek. Again she turned to look at the Kickmobile. Dylan had broken the tension by smashing a Goldfish against the glass. Taylor found it hilarious. Another orange explosion. Opie scolded both of them. Dylan wiped his orange hand in her hair. His big sister lost it, began to slap.

"You stay here," she ordered Angus Beavers. "You stay right here."

But by the time she had restored order in the Kickmobile, Angus Beavers, like his dad, had vanished into the junkyard.

38

So that Harley wouldn't notice she had burned half a tank of gas, so that he wouldn't notice the mud from Lost Hollow Road, so that he wouldn't ask where she had gone with the kids and bring up her list of her dad's old farmhands again . . .

She decided to fill the tank and wash the van. This was small-town life in a nutshell, she noted in grim bemusement as she turned into the Ease Inn and coasted between the gas pumps. Your neighbor held illegal gun shows and took graft and peddled tits and ass and pulled bomb threats and fenced stolen property and implied bad shit about your husband—but unless you wanted to drive twenty miles out of your way, you still had to buy your gas and your car wash from Ladonna Weeks.

Actually it was Ladonna's brother, Dermit, flinging salt at the entry to the tavern, who watched her park the mud-spattered Kickmobile and pop her gas flap. This was motherhood in a small town too. Her kids had perked up—the truck stop, yay!—squawking from the backseat could they please-please-please go inside the mini-mart and get corn dogs and dip them in barbecue sauce and play the deer-hunting video game?

Her head throbbed as she ran gas. Why again did she think it so great to raise children here? She pushed YES for car wash.

"OK," she said into the van. "I'm giving Opie five dollars. I'm going to wash the van, and then I'm coming to get you."

She idled in line for the car wash, scrolling through the photos of heavy equipment that Olaf the Handsome had attached to a text. She zeroed in on the serial-number tag from a Caterpillar front-end loader. She had worked a stolen-tractor case last year, a new Kubota that had disappeared from John Franklin's farm in Buck Grove Township, and she still had hotline contacts at the National Insurance Crime Bureau and the National Equipment Register. A minute later, Dave from the NICB was telling her that the front-end loader had been reported stolen from a U.S. Silica equipment yard in Williston, North Dakota, only three days ago.

"Where are you calling from again, Sheriff?"

"Bad Axe County, Wisconsin."

"And you've recovered the property?"

"Not yet. We know where it is."

"I'm looking at a map," Dave said, tapping keys. "You're on U.S. Highway 14."

"It passes through us, yes."

"That's the route folks are taking from Chicago and beyond out to the fracking fields when they want to stay off the interstate. They take U.S. 14 all the way to Pierre and then sneak north through the Indian reservation, or vice versa. All kinds of contraband move along there. Kind of a Silk Road, you might say. You've got a truck stop?"

"I'm at it right now."

"Right. I'm seeing it. The Ease Inn. Proprietors Dermit and Ladonna Weeks. Rhubarb pie is on special in the restaurant today. Diesel is $2.45 a gallon. Happy hour is three to six, half-price rail drinks and domestic beers, free popcorn, and today's discounted appetizer is deep-fried cheese curds with a choice of horseradish, barbecue, or nacho cheese dipping sauce."

"You nailed it, Dave. You might as well be here."

"You guys dip cheese in cheese sauce?"

"Only deep-fried cheese."

"Sure. That makes sense."

She had been watching a tractor-trailer pull past the diesel pumps and into the rest area. The trailer was nondescript and sooty. The tractor was red, with lettering too small to read from afar. It had tricked-out exhaust stacks and a black silhouette naked lady decal on the sleeper cab. The driver hitched down and went inside the tavern.

"So, Dave?"

"Yes?"

"Highway 14. You said all types of contraband . . . including human?"

He paused. Then he was tapping again. "I only track equipment, Sheriff. But if you've got an issue with that kind of trafficking, let me give you a number."

––––––

When the Kickmobile was washed, she parked it in front of the mini-mart. Goddamn it, Ladonna was in there, talking to the cashier. As she left the van she caught herself thinking that the girl behind the mini-mart register, Holly Hefty, a recent high school graduate, pretty and smart, ought to be somewhere better than the Bad Axe, doing something better than working for Ladonna Weeks. Yet she wanted to raise her own daughter here?

Of course Ladonna saw her coming. Of course Harley's ex-skank pretended she didn't, pretended to be too busy bossing Holly Hefty, who expressed her chagrin with a tight little wave. As the sheriff headed for the video game machine in the back, she slipped into an old rant. Sure, Ladonna was long legged, heavy chested, and darkly pretty, but at the rate she drank and smoked, her window on good looks was closing fast. Ladonna knew it, and she compensated with raunchiness. Men loved the way she talked dirty, and they behaved as if each drink purchase added frequent-flier points and someday they would earn enough to take her beyond the mini-mart into one of the Ease Inn's dank motel rooms. Harley said he hadn't even talked to Ladonna in years. But given who the woman was, that was a tough one to believe.

"Hello, Ladonna."

"Oh. Didn't see you there. What's up, Dairy Queen? You keeping my Harley Kick-Ass happy? You taking care of his needs?"

The sheriff swallowed a snarl that returned as a bolt of acid up her throat.

"I hope you know," she said, "that a bomb threat can go federal in a heartbeat these days. A bomb threat makes you a terrorist."

She had meant to walk on by. *Keep moving*, she now ordered herself.

"I make one call," she said instead, "I can send Homeland Security crawling up your fancy ass."

Ladonna's wide, blue-gray eyes showed nothing. The white letters on her tight black T-shirt said *Alcohol, Tobacco, Firearms . . . Who's Bringing the Chips?*

"Oh, dear," she said. "You sound upset. Someone made a bomb threat? I'm sorry. Where? I'll bet that keeps you really busy."

Off she went, fancy-assing though the glass connecting door to the tavern. The sheriff watched long enough to see her head down the entry hallway that led to the tavern's front door.

"Jeepers," said Holly Hefty, pulling the sheriff's attention away. "She read me the riot act, and I just started my shift. I haven't even done anything yet, right or wrong. I mean, the kids dripped a little barbecue sauce on the floor, but I was going to wipe it up."

"It's nice to see you, Holly. Sorry about the sauce. I'll get it. Aside from you working here, what's new?"

"Oh, I am so glad you asked. I'm engaged!" She held up her left hand. The ring was a small blue stone. "Hunter popped the question! I said, Are you kidding? The wedding is gonna be on Labor Day at the Lions Club pavilion."

The sheriff's dark mood got darker. Hunter Vikemeyer was a short-horizon kid with a twelve-pack of beer attached to one hand. His strengths were that he was handsome, he once made second-team all-conference football, and now he was almost a tractor-pull champion. And she wanted Opie to grow up here?

"I'm going to be Holly Vikemeyer! Isn't that gonna be great? I should probably wear a helmet and carry a sword. We're gonna take over my dad's farm. We want to start a B and B."

"Hang on a sec, Holly. I'm getting a call."

She stepped outside as Rhino said, "Great news, Sheriff. Your BAC test came back zero."

"I see. So that last drink I had, which was 3,005 days ago today, is finally out of my system."

"Ha. You're funny."

"If you say so."

"Anyway, you can put your badge and gun back on. Bad news is you still can't drive a county vehicle until that accident assessment is completed. Marge Joss is all over that. The Police and Fire Commission has a meeting tonight. They need to hear your story, because there's still some questions about how you ended up in the river. And, like, why you don't remember anything. And how the bottle got in there."

"Sure."

He waited as if she might slip him the answers.

"So that's the news," he said, giving up. "You still can't drive a county car. That, and we're about to get rain."

She looked up. Heavy clouds had closed the western sky.

"Warm, slow rain," Rhino told her, "on top of all this melting ice and snow. Flash-flood warnings for us and the five counties around us."

"Ten four, Rhino. Thanks."

Back inside the mini-mart, Holly Soon-to-Be-Vikemeyer had been waiting to tell her, "Hunter's really matured. You'd be surprised. Last night he went to this meeting, you know, about conservation, about, like, volunteering and taking care of nature, making sure it's still around for our kids. You know, Ducks Unlimited?"

———

She was now thinking darkly about her marriage to Harley—all 2,263 days of it—as she herded her kids out of the mini-mart. He knew all these guys, these Hunter Vikemeyers, these Pinky Clausens and Walt Beavers and Brock Pabsts. He probably knew a hundred guys at last night's "Ducks Unlimited" meeting. He had to know there were stag parties. He had to know about this whole male underworld in the Bad Axe. Maybe he had even been part of it. The night before she accepted the interim position, she had begged him, "You have to tell me *everything*."

Shit. Here came Ladonna again, vamping out the tavern door. "Hon, don't go," she called. "I've got a present for you." Just like Coach Clausen had threatened, she waved an Instamatic photo, no doubt one she had just unpinned from the Wall of Shame that lined the hallway entry to the bar—*Be careful, Missus Kick, you're not the only one with pictures—*

one of the hundreds of snapshots that documented Bad Axers getting drunk and acting stupid at the Ease Inn.

"It's such a cute one of Harley Kick-Ass, I thought you'd like to have it."

The sheriff snatched the photo from Ladonna's hand. Just like Clausen's sleazy hint had predicted, it showed Harley with a female that wasn't her. She knew at a glance that it was taken the summer the twins were born. She had given him that haircut on the deck of their duplex in Middleton. What Ladonna wanted her to see was her husband sitting at a bar table, wearing the white shirt with the orange three-quarter sleeves that went beneath his black Rattlers jersey. At the table with him, with a burger and a soda in front of her, was a busty blond girl with a ponytail, not more than sixteen years old.

"Isn't that sweet?" Ladonna said. "Isn't she special?"

The girl's face was pretty except for her eyes, which looked haunted and scared, with dark circles under them. They were fixed on Harley's handsome face. A thin gold necklace dangled between her heavy breasts and disappeared beneath a white halter top that did not look clean. At the bottom of the picture, the girl's pale thighs ran under the table. Pressed against the outside of one her thighs was Harley's big brown hand.

The sheriff's face burned. She stared into her husband's eyes as he showed his surprise at the appearance of the camera. Then it seemed like Ladonna spoke from a distance. "Listen, hon. You married into the Bad Axe, OK? You're kinda-sorta new here, and you kinda-sorta don't get the culture."

I was born thirty miles away. She ground her teeth and glared at Harley. *You have to tell me everything.*

"And you're only temporary, remember?"

She looked up. Ladonna was waving at the kids in the van. Then she crossed her arms beneath her tits and smiled.

"And you already can't handle it, am I right? They had to suspend you?"

"I've been reinstated."

Ladonna shrugged. "You keep that picture for looking at," she said.

"Help you remember that until July your job is playing donkey basket-ball and doing karaoke fund-raisers. Take a good look, OK, hon? Either chill out, or what you see is what you get. Do you get it?"

———

Did she get what? That they'd drag Harley and her family through the mud in an effort to shut her down? She glanced once more before she jammed the picture into her shirt pocket. They were playing chicken with the Kick family, and she wasn't going to flinch. Still, it seemed pretty clear that nobody had dragged Harley into that photo with that girl. It seemed pretty clear that he had made his own mud. Ladonna, Clausen, maybe Lund—they knew that picture would slug her in the heart. So what did they fear she was so close to knowing? She sat behind the wheel for too long, unable to answer the summary question now coming from Ophelia. "Mommy, what's wrong?"

Goddamn it, Harley.

"Mommy, what's the matter?"

"I was just thinking about something. Shall we go visit Daddy?"

As she started the engine, a few fat raindrops smacked the wind-shield. She started her wipers—then stopped them immediately as their tips lifted something from the bay. In the center of the windshield, dragged up just onto the glass, was a thin gold necklace.

To reach that far across the hood of the van, she had to go up on her toes, then up on just one toe, before she could just barely pull the blades and free the tangled necklace. She unwound the chain. It was a cheap thing, from a drugstore or a kiosk at a mall. The pendant at the bottom was connected letters in thin script that spelled *Sophie.*

For a moment she considered Ladonna's whereabouts over the last ten minutes. No, the bitch had not been near the Kickmobile until she had come outside with the picture. The necklace came from somewhere else, and from someone with longer arms than hers. She considered where the van had been: their barn, Pabst's place in Blackhawk Locks, Clausen's driveway, Beavers Salvage.

Angus Beavers.

39

She stopped the van at a distance and gathered herself. Ahead of her was Harley's baseball practice on the high school parking lot, surrounded by a moat of ditched cropland, the approaching rainstorm now massing slowly overhead. Her husband was hitting fungoes at his outfielders, smacking rubberized baseballs that sailed over the faculty parking stalls and drove the players back to a chain-link fence at the edge of what would be corn in a month. Other players held pepper games on the handicap spaces, lobbing, bunting, fielding. And, speak of the devil, there was Pinky Clausen, forced on Harley as a volunteer hitting coach, leaning into his crutches and tossing beanbags to a tall, left-handed hitter, who drove them against the brick wall of the school building. Beyond the margins of the parking lot, Harley's freshmen slogged after balls that had escaped into the mud.

Sated on corn dogs and the slaying of digital deer, all three kids had passed out on the short drive from the Ease Inn. She cracked the sliding door for air. Harley's outfielders lobbed baseballs back toward a five-gallon bucket. Most went long and settled against a parking cleat. She gathered as many as she could and dropped them in the bucket.

"We need to talk."

He hammered a line drive right at the throng of outfielders, not waiting for the next player to step out. She had thrown off his rhythm.

"Sure. Why not?" He tried to grin at her. "I'm not doing anything."

"This is serious."

"What is?"

He swung and skipped a weak grounder across the asphalt. Voices rose on the breeze, his outfielders giving him shit.

"You knew there were these stripper parties going on out in the hollows."

He checked his swing and caught his toss. "I knew there used to be."

He retossed and hit a weak pop-up. The razzing grew stronger, but Harley wasn't liking it right now.

"We've been married six years, Heidi. I haven't gone. I haven't heard. I haven't even thought about it. I never liked those parties in the first place."

"So you did go."

"I went twice. The team went, after games. I went with." He lifted his next ball from the bucket at his heel. "Not my kind of thing."

"Really? Then why in the hell wouldn't you tell me that this went on? There was a party last night."

"I'm sorry. I didn't think of it."

"You didn't think that Ray Gibbs and Boog Lund must be letting this happen, so as the next sheriff I should know about it? You didn't think about laws broken and girls in danger?"

"Heidi, I'm sorry. It would take forever to tell you everything that anybody ever did wrong in the Bad Axe."

"What good does sorry do me?"

He muttered. Then he swung hard and hit one square. A player turned and tracked a towering fly ball into what would have been left center on a baseball field. He settled under the ball and caught it. She touched the picture in her pocket but didn't want to show it yet.

"Let's go back to this game in 2012 against the Dells . . ."

"Again? Why are you interrogating me? All I do is support you, watch the kids, sleep alone half the time while you're out working all night . . ."

"According to the box score, you gave up a whole season's worth of runs and cost your team the state tournament. But this morning you claimed you were never even there."

Again he checked his swing and caught his toss. "Goddamn it, Heidi. I wasn't."

"You're in the box score."

"Coach Clausen was pissed off that I didn't show up. The Dells hit the shit out of Aspinwall and whoever else pitched instead of me. For payback, Coach gave me all the stats that he sent in to the league. My ERA ballooned up, and it knocked me off the WBA All-State Team. I took the loss in the scorebook, but I wasn't at that game."

"Why not?"

"I promise you it wasn't important."

"That game keeps coming up for some reason. And you keep coming up. It's important."

Crack. He nailed this one. It sailed too far. A body rattled the chain-link fence. The ball dropped without a bounce into the mire beyond. A small muddy freshman trudged after it. In that slow moment Ladonna's intentions came alive. She had never had a reason not to trust Harley. Now, suddenly, she almost didn't want to know if she had been a fool.

"I'm trying to hold a practice here, Heidi."

"I'm trying to do my job too."

A wail came from the van. Taylor had awakened. Opie, quickly alert, could manage her own car seat, and she tried to unbuckle her little brother while he wheeled his feet, kicking her.

"What happened to Mom watching the kids?" Harley asked.

"I sent her home this morning."

Here came Taylor in a postnap wrath galloping toward them. Harley checked his swing as their little boy came close. Taylor hesitated between them, then plowed his forehead straight into his mommy's groin. Harley stepped to a distance and ripped a ball to imaginary right center. His face was red, his jaw set. With a shaky hand, the sheriff caressed Taylor's sweaty head, pulled him to her hip, and stopped his ears. "Was there a stripper party that night, after the game that you didn't play in?"

"I think there was. I'm pretty sure. I didn't go."

Now she showed him the picture: at a table in the Ease Inn, his hand on the outer thigh of a troubled-looking teenage girl.

"What's this?"

"Lunch."

"Who is she?"

"Some girl."

"Did you pay her, or did you get it for free?"

"You act like you don't know me."

"Imagine that."

She reached into her breast pocket again, showed him his yearbook shot, *Lady Killer*.

"Why would someone leave me this?"

"To jerk you around. Make you jealous. Get you out of your lane."

"Why? Why today?"

"Heidi, honestly, I have no goddamn idea. You're the one with the information here. You're not telling me what this is about."

"Who is Sophie?"

"No clue."

"You had that little girl by the thigh. Is she Sophie?"

"I don't remember what her name was. She was hanging around by the gas pumps and I bought her something to eat. She kept wrapping her leg around mine. She wanted to leave with me. Go wherever I was going. Anywhere. Look at the picture. Look at my hand. I was pushing her leg away. Jesus Christ, Heidi, she was about fifteen years old. I called the sheriff's department. But guess what. Gibbs was in charge, Lund was chief deputy, you didn't work here then, and nobody gave a shit."

Here came Opie. Bless her heart, she carried her other little brother, forty-pound Dylan, piggyback. With their sharp-eared daughter on the way, the conversation, the fight, whatever it was, was nearly over.

"She was trying to get away from her pimp," the sheriff guessed.

Harley looked surprised. Then he exhaled hard.

"Turns out you're right," he admitted. "Sweetheart, OK. Here it is. It was the day of that game. I was getting gas and she came up to me. I took her inside and tried to make her eat. She wouldn't tell me who she was or what was wrong, she just wanted to go wherever I was going. La-donna took that picture without asking. You know how she is. I called, but the Bad Axe County Sheriff's Department didn't have anyone they could send, they didn't give a shit, so I tried to drive her up to La Crosse and give her to somebody who did."

He paused, squeezing a rubber baseball in his fist. "Go ahead. Say it."

"You never told me."

"Right. And here's why. Because putting that girl in my truck and driving was a bad idea. There was an Amber Alert. She had to use the bathroom at the Pronto in Bishops Coulee, and somebody who saw us there called the cops on me. I got pulled over by the state patrol on Great River Road. I got hauled out and arrested in front of about a hundred vehicles going by. Pandering. Sexual assault of a minor. Cuffed and hauled away. Your husband."

His face had turned splotchy red-white. His outfielders stared from a distance.

"I missed that game you're asking about, and no, I didn't spend the night with friends, like you thought I did. I spent the night in jail. It took La Crosse County until the next morning to believe that girl and let me go. You were sad and angry when I got home, Heidi. You thought the world was a terrible, dangerous place. You handed me all three kids and went to bed."

He tried to shake the memory off. He tossed the ball in his fist and smacked it with the bat. His startled players just stood and watched it sail.

"I was fine," he said. "It was weird, I was embarrassed at being so stupid, but it was nothing, and I didn't want to upset you. I just dropped it. I should have told you then. I know you're angry at me now. I don't blame you, except you never told me what any of this was about. End of story."

Opie was joining them now. "End of what story?" she wanted to know.

"No, wait," Harley said. "That's not the end of the story. A couple weeks later her mother tracked me down and thanked me. She made the girl get on the phone. I just remembered her name. Her name was Karen."

"Who's Karen?" Opie asked. With her flawless instincts, she drifted to her father and hugged him.

The sheriff's brain had locked. She tucked both pictures back into her pocket. She felt like she had stabbed herself.

"Come on, kids. Let's go. Daddy's doing his job."

Back in the van, she buckled the kids in and sagged behind the wheel. Opie had to tell her that her phone was ringing.

"Hello? Sheriff? You there?"

"I'm here."

"Wisconsin Dells PD is on the line," said Rinehart Rog. "One of their officers just found the blue van with the stolen Illinois plates. They've got the driver in custody, and they want to know how soon we can get somebody there to question him. Either Deputy Bench or Deputy Yttri can drive you."

She jerked upright.

"Tell them two hours, Rhino. Tell Yttri to pick me up at the farm in thirty."

"They also have a minor in custody, some girl this guy was pandering. She's one of ours, a seventeen-year-old from Blackhawk Locks."

She unleashed the kids, spun them toward the wider parking lot. "You can pick up baseballs for Daddy. He'll take you home. Mommy loves you."

She slid the doors shut, jumped back behind the wheel, turned the key. Overhead the sky snapped bright, triggering a long, low boom of thunder. The first warm drops popped against the van's roof. Harley's players raced one another for the awning over the school's front door as she sped the Kickmobile away.

40

Angus hurried as light faded from the dumping sky. The red pickup with the snowplow blade had struck the Beavers Salvage truck broadside and tipped it over and shoved it fifty feet on its side and pancaked the cab against a reef of tangled trailer frames. Angus made his decision and walked away from it. He was going to have to drive Brock Pabst's shit-can GTO.

He reached in and turned the key. The engine shrieked and shuddered. Exhaust exploded out the back. He let it run a bit.

He fetched her body from the dregs of the snowdrift behind the Quonset shack. He worked her back into the bag and layered in the jerseys. She smelled bad now. Not rotten. She wasn't rotten. She smelled like thawing meat.

He carried her in the bag to the GTO and opened the trunk. Pabst had jammed it full of other people's stuff: car radios, Walmart shopping bags, hubcaps, GPS systems with plug-ins dangling, a backpack, a purse, a leaf blower, a game console. Angus shut the trunk and fit the bag onto the passenger seat and forced the door shut.

Before he left he went inside the house. Brandy was watching TV in her pajamas, smoking a cigarette. His dad in his cap-and-napkins bandage sat in a tilted slump on a chair in the kitchen, where he could see out the window. That pill bottle was in his fist. His one open eye hit Angus like a bead of lead. His chest rattled.

"The goddamn hell you think you're doing?"

Angus flinched and lowered his brow. His whole body stiffened. All his life those exact words had given him about three seconds to run before he took a boot up his ass. But instead, his dad dropped the pill bottle.

"I came back," Angus said quietly, "because I want to be here. I want to live here. Someday I want to play baseball here. That's all I wanted in the first place. I want Brandy to be safe. That's what the goddamn hell I think I'm doing."

His dad's big hands, all bone now, fumbled in space, looking for the dropped pill bottle like a raccoon feeling in the crick for crawdads.

"I'm going to try to make it like Beavers never touched her, which we never did, and all the ones involved will have to answer. I'm gonna put her in that cave back on Faulkner's where the players like to take girls."

Angus watched his dad recover the bottle and uncap it, peer into it, rattle the few half pills left in the bottom, then upend it into his mouth. He chewed, swallowed.

"I just came inside to tell you, if you'll listen," Angus said. "I'm undoing what they did to us. Then we're really gonna have to watch out. They'll come after us. Do you understand?"

His dad grinned then. There was foam from the pills in his saliva.

"Bring it on," he said.

———

Through this new warm downpour Angus steered Pabst's wobbly car up Lost Hollow Road to the ridge, onto Bluff Road and around Battle Bluff into Dog Hollow, along Dog Hollow Road past his uncle Walt's place—it was Walt who took him to Rattlesnake Cave once, when they were out poaching deer—up and over the next ridge, then on Bottom Road past Emerald Faulkner's property to the Upper Rush Creek bridge. In the GTO's crooked headlights the creek streamed beyond its banks, brown and foamy and full of stick litter from the forest floor, sweeping whole branches along. Just beyond the bridge, an old dirt road led upstream to the cave, a quarter mile, maybe.

He couldn't risk it with the GTO. He drove in just far enough to hide from traffic on Bottom Road. He squared the headlamp on his forehead.

He shouldered the bag. The smell of her thawing body gagged him. The weight of her buckled his legs. As he hauled her up the road, the rain made him blink, washed sweat into his eyes, fractured his headlamp beam. He stumbled into smears and starbursts of light, tripped upon closed-eye patches of black. But at last he found the place where the road shanked around a jut of sandstone and began to climb out of the canyon. From here, the cave was down a steep ravine across the creek.

———

Later, inside the cave, he could not remember exactly how he made it there. Shaking with cold, his back cramping, wet to his armpits, he was bleeding somewhere. On the wade across, the bag had taken on water, doubled its weight. Midstream, a heavy branch gliding at deceptive speed had spun at the last moment and mauled him, snagged the bag handle, swung him around, and nearly pulled her away.

But here he was. As he staggered into the cave mouth, his headlamp fell on beer cans and campfire remains. Bottle caps and flip-tops and cigarette butts lay everywhere under shoe prints on the grainy limestone floor. He saw old high-water marks on the layered walls. He hadn't thought of that. The creek had come inside the cave before. But not this time. Please not this time.

Angus raised his chin and panned the headlamp through his own steaming breath. The cave walls were knobby and pocked, laminated eons of sea bottom shot with fissures and defaced with human testimony. His beam lit a cock and balls etched by knifepoint into the soft stone. From there he panned it over names and initials, boasts, oaths, and threats, ugly words for girls, cartoon pictures of their body parts. Here was *C.P fucks*. Here was *Durrell Sherry blows donkies*. Here were tally marks. Here was *Hollow Billy Lives Here, Get Out*.

He sloughed the bag to the cave floor. Deeper in, here was one shoe, here was a deflated vinyl air mattress with spent condoms strewn around it, here was a decomposing blue sweatshirt. He tucked his chin to see beneath the lowering roof, saw a fissure too small to crawl through. He aimed his light. Upon the powdery floor of a low-ceilinged second room his beam lit older signs of human habitation. Animal bones. Broken clay pots. A ring of fire stones. He raised the beam. Here were drawings in charcoal on pale-orange walls. Stick figures. Snakes and birds. A hunter with a bow. A bear with a spear through it. Human handprints, etched in ash.

He returned to the bag. Gently he unpacked her and laid her on the deflated mattress. He arranged the jerseys over her: *Strunk, Ossie, Clausen, Gibbs*. He undid the blue clip from her hair and slipped it into his pocket. He kicked through garbage around the cave rim—rotted clothing, liquor bottles, skeins of tinted plastic that had been sacks—until he found what he was looking for. Crumbling coil in the dust, diamond pattern faded, fork broken off its white tab tongue, rattle eroded to a pale shapeless sponge, here was the toy rubber rattlesnake, the unofficial team mascot for the guys whose jerseys he had stolen. They called him "Buster H. Johnson." Younger girls who wanted it badly enough, who wanted to run with the Gibbs and Clausen crowd, had to find the cave and pose with Buster H. Johnson across their naked chests for "ID" photographs, proof they'd been here—that they were worthy and loyal and ready to be treated like sluts. The *H.* was for hymen. They were Cave Girls now.

Angus left the cave with the blue butterfly clip and the toy rubber snake. His next move had to involve Harley Kick, who would tell his wife where the snake came from.

The rain falling steadily through darkness feels good at first, warm but cooling, because Pepper's skin burns where the troll ripped the tape off her face and wrists and ankles. But now there comes a moment where suddenly she is cold and there is no way that she can stop herself from getting colder. Her skin tightens and shrinks. She shivers and her teeth chatter.

She always thinks Marie was the lucky one . . . because Marie was older, so she never needed Bennie . . . and then when Bennie . . .

Don't make things up to get attention . . .

It starts again and Pepper screams against it. Then ferociously she blasts the wet brush and trees around her with a chorus of "Row, Row, Row Your Boat." She sings Felton Henry off her naked body, and there goes his truck, just the way she planned it, down the hill, off the bluff, sinking into the river. Ha!

But the shivers have her now, they control her. First the rain felt good but now it feels cold and she can't stop it, can't escape it. The troll has driven her half an hour into rainy dusk. He has stopped finally, puttered beneath an umbrella along the roadside for what seems like a long time. He has tied a pink plastic ribbon to the low-hanging branch of a tree. He has removed her from the van and walked her on a chain into the forest. There he has left her.

The handcuffs go to a chain. The chain goes to a tree. The rain feels good at first then feels cold and now she tries as much as she knows how not to feel anything at all.

"We observed Mr. Hill dropping off the girl at the Indian Bay Resort," the Wisconsin Dells chief of police began by telling his visitors from the Bad Axe.

"One officer followed his van while another raided the room. The girl was already doing business, going down on some old man from Chicago who could have been her grandpa." He paused for a grimace. "Bad choice of words. Sorry. That's who's on his way to get her, her grandfather, from a place called Blackhawk Locks."

Chief Jordan Johannsen was a polished young guy like Olaf the Handsome, not quite as camera ready, but comparably muscle bound and mustachioed. He observed her sympathetically.

"I know the look, Sheriff. We've got coffee and some leftover pizza in the break room. You want some?"

"Only if you also serve shots of Pepto Bismol."

He opened a drawer and set a bottle of the pink stuff on his desk. While she dosed herself, then declined pizza and accepted a cup of coffee—Yttri did the opposite—Chief Johannsen told them that their suspect had already been Mirandized for pandering and sexual assault of a minor, both of which he had denied.

"The girl's name is Bailey Voss. His name is Dale Hill. Mr. Hill tells me Miss Voss approached him at a gas station here in town and asked him for a ride to the Indian Bay."

"Sure. And she swore she was eighteen too."

"Right. As for her story, Miss Voss says that Mr. Hill approached her at a party over in Bad Axe County. He said he'd take care of everything for her, and here she is."

The sheriff cuffed her sleeve across her lips, erasing any pink.

"Let's go talk to Mr. Hill."

Chief Johannsen motioned for her and then Yttri to precede him. The hallway of Dells PD was spotlessly quaint, like an old elementary school. In its narrowness she felt oversize, and with coffee and Pepto in her stomach the illusion made her dizzy. Yttri almost walked into her. His touch just grazed her shoulder.

"Take a right," Chief Johannsen said from behind, "through that door."

Dale Hill slumped in a chair behind two-way glass in an interrogation room. Her pulse flared at the sight. He mimicked a man: blazer with the sleeves shoved up, shaved head and earring, high-top baller shoes, big ring on his pinkie finger, eyes sunk so deep that he saw the world through tubes of sickly shadow.

"He doesn't think he needs an attorney. He's his own lawyer, he says."

"Of course he is."

"He doesn't know that Miss Voss also gave us a room number at a different Dells establishment, the Pine Cone Motel, where two other girls admitted to selling sex for him."

Johannsen handed the sheriff a burner phone sealed in a plastic bag.

"On top of that, the old gentleman she was servicing led us to an ad on Backpage.com, where somebody with this phone number is offering the sexual services of underage girls."

She stared at Hill feigning nonchalance in the chair beyond the glass. She stared and she burned and then she erupted. She unsnapped her service Ruger and kicked the door open and fired, fired, fired again, pounded his zombie brains against the back wall. The vision was so raw it left her disoriented, her right hand crushed in a fist.

"You OK, Sheriff?" said Olaf the Handsome.

"Fine."

Chief Johannsen sighed and ran a thick hand over his haircut.

"Sheriff, the truth is, we could go through this routine every day of the week, especially in tourist season. A girl from your area is rare—you know, people call Milwaukee the Harvard of sex trafficking—but young ladies like Bailey Voss, they just flow through here."

Her brain still fizzed with the image of Dale Hill's skull exploding. Yttri was watching her. She could barely hear Johannsen.

"The internet just makes it too easy for these guys."

Chief Johannsen had paused with his hand on the door latch to the interrogation room, about to lead her in. Detecting the forthcoming action, Hill had posed himself, chin up, arms across his chest.

"Actually," the Dells police chief continued, "the web makes it easier for the women too. They don't have to hang out on street corners. And they can freestyle it. They can go solo, skip the pimp, work right out of their homes or apartments, the public library, a coffee shop, wherever. They can do internet porn and never touch anybody. Pimps are losing control, but the ones remaining have gotten more extreme."

He looked at her, his hand still on the door latch. "That's what Miss Voss told us about the other girl. She was too hard to control, according to Hill, so he went online and sold her up the food chain."

That startled Sheriff Kick back to attention.

"The other girl didn't come back to the Dells with him?"

"Miss Voss says Hill left the other girl there. We found eight hundred bucks in his van, rolled up in a soda cup from a Pronto station. Probably what he sold her for, and probably the reason he was in your area in the first place, to meet his buyer. Like I said, if the pattern holds, if she was too much for him to handle, then he sold her up the food chain . . ."

Her stomach churned. " 'Sold her up the food chain'?"

Chief Johannsen nodded.

"The way Miss Voss describes it, you're dealing with a whole network over in the coulee counties of folks doing drugs, making drugs, selling sex, making porn, robbing cars and houses and farms, fencing stolen goods. Miss Voss seems to know all about it."

"Let's see what Mr. Hill has to say," she said.

———

She glared back into the sneer of this monster who had used a computer, operating from distance, at the speed of light, to feed a juvenile "up the food chain" to a bigger monster in her own backyard.

"The old gentleman you assaulted in my library might die, Mr. Hill. If I were you, I'd save myself now. Tell me where she is."

"Who is?"

"The girl you took to the party."

"Some chick asked me for a ride, that's all."

"Fine. You only gave her a ride. And she was eighteen, for sure." She felt Yttri and Johannsen exchange glances. "Where is she?"

He smirked and shook his pink shit-balloon of a head. She felt out of breath as she continued. "Mr. Hill, you don't understand. I've got you for aggravated assault. That becomes homicide if my librarian dies. Chief Johannsen has you for pandering minors. That's a felony sex crime. Take a minute. Ask your lawyer what he thinks. Should you tell us where the girl is?" She couldn't stop herself. "Ask Counselor Dumbfuck."

Again she felt Yttri and Johannsen exchange looks.

"You give us her name and you tell us who she went with"—she pointed across the room—"and that door opens. You're good to go."

Now she felt Johannsen leaning, peering at her, felt Yttri practically jumping out of his skin. She doubled down. "You talk, you walk, asshole. Give us the girl, you're out of here."

"Well, then—"

"Hold on, Sheriff—"

Chief Johannsen had opened the door, but not for Hill, for her. He scowled. Yttri had his hands up and open, as if trying to stop some large invisible object from bouncing around the interrogation room. Johannsen said, "Sheriff, shall we?"

In the corridor against the polished bricks her voice sounded clipped and hollow.

"Shall we what?"

He offered her a paper cup of water from a cooler. She pushed it away. Johannsen said, "It's not up to you to clear my charges . . . for one thing."

"'*Sold her up the food chain.*' Did you hear yourself? We need to find this girl, and we need to find her now. An hour from now, I plan to be back in the Bad Axe looking for her. Do you understand?"

Johannsen looked bewildered. "What I understand, and I'm sorry, is that you're new to this—" Here it came. "And I understand that this is emotional, but . . ."

She threw her sore arm toward the two-way glass, actually seeking the bolt of pain, the memory of Brock Pabst hitting her with a bat. "Do you see a lawyer in there?"

"Heidi—"

She wheeled on Yttri. "Don't fucking Heidi me."

"I don't see a lawyer, no," Chief Johannsen admitted. "There is no lawyer in there. Just the one in his imagination."

"Right. Then, are you recording us?"

"No. I mean, if you want me to do that, I can do that, but—"

"I'm lying!" she seethed. "Do you understand *that*? Do you understand that he's dumb enough to think that I'm dumb enough to mean what I'm saying? Do you understand that he despises women, can't imagine one who might be smarter than he is? Or are you with him?"

Johannsen winced. Yttri stammered, "Let's . . . let's calm down."

"Emotional?" She bore down Johannsen. "Is that what you call it when a woman busts balls? Is that what you call it when a woman steps in and moves the goddamn furniture?"

"I didn't mean—"

"What's 'up the food chain' from a pimp, you think? You think we have time to play by the rules here?"

She kept her arm up—*I will find you*—felt it shaking as she pointed at Dale Hill. "He knows her name. He knows who he sold her to." She kept pointing through the pain. "You want to worry about your charges? You think you can't pick him up tomorrow for the same shit? What's he going to do, Chief, outsmart you? We do this job to protect people, and there's a girl in danger *right now*."

Johannsen winced again. He glanced at Yttri and ran his hand across the top of his head. By the time his palm had cleared his haircut twice, he was faintly nodding.

"Pepper," Dale Hill told them a few minutes later. "All I know. Can I go now?"

"Nickname or real name?"

"Don't know, don't care."

He was acting jaunty now that he thought he was about to walk away. He was shoving up the sleeves of his blazer, crossing his arms to show his prison tats.

"Last name?"

"Don't know, don't care."

"What were you doing with her in my library? And remember, I have two witnesses. First lie you tell, the deal's off. You're coming with me for battery. Homicide if you get unlucky."

"Settling a bet."

"What bet?"

"Little bitch said her brother hit six home runs in a baseball game up there. I mean, I know baseball, I played. But it turns out that really happened. Her brother really hit six home runs. Too bad the librarian helped her, so she cheated."

The sheriff felt her hands jitter as she scrolled through the photo gallery on her phone, looking for the box score. No, it was on the phone that went into the river. But maybe she could recall it. *Come on, the guy who hit six home runs.* She had said his name to Harley.

"Greengrass," she blurted to Johannsen. "Her name is Pepper Green-grass."

Johannsen said, "That's a Ho-Chunk name. There's an extended Greengrass family around here. Some of them are tribal leaders, good folks. There are a few others that law enforcement knows pretty well. I'll get an officer on it right away."

The sheriff said to Dale Hill, "You sold her to someone. His name."

He recrossed his arms and stonewalled.

"Nah, man. Like I said, she just asked me for a ride. I was going to this party so she went along. I never held no gun to her head. She went home with some other dude."

She leaned in so close she could smell his body odor, his breath. *Fucking dead inside.*

"My mistake, Mr. Hill. You never sold her. She left with someone else. You see that?" Behind her, Johannsen had opened the door. "Describe the dude she went with."

———

Back at the Bad Axe County Public Safety Building, she used the toilet. She splashed her face with cold water. Yttri had taken an accident call. Denise was just arriving. She demanded the keys to Denise's old flatbed truck.

The man Dale Hill had described?

He was the same man who last week came to the grade school in a white van to shoot Ophelia's class picture.

Hans Kling.

In Denise's truck she sped through the dense warm rain out County Highway C to Kling Kountry Kamera. She smashed through the flooded ditch at Hans Kling's turnoff. She turned out the truck's lights and drove the long length of his driveway toward his dark studio. She exited Old Alimony with her fingers on the snap of her holster, her heart pumping.

But no one came to Kling's door. She looked in the garage. A sad-sack Chevy sedan, but not Kling's white business van, his mobile studio. The white van was gone. She put the butt of her flashlight through a glass pane in his back door, opened it, and went in. The converted farmhouse was so small, so achingly familiar, so easy for a coulee girl to search.

Pepper Greengrass wasn't there.

————

"Nightshift crew meeting in five, Heidi."

"I'm back," she told Denise. "I'm just turning off the highway."

"Police and Fire Commission just gaveled in for the hearing on your accident at the river. I said they'd have to wait for you to get your crew out."

"Actually, tell them to pull up a stool and wait for the cows to give chocolate milk. What's a Crawford County cruiser doing in our parking lot?"

"Sheriff Skog just showed up. He plans to ask Police and Fire what you think you're doing down on his turf. Last week, did you try to talk his county clerk into pulling some old files for you? And then threaten to sue?"

"I was out of uniform, driving a minivan, a member of the public, and I got a little upset. That's all."

"I think the DA down there is on your side. She came to see you yesterday, remember? But Skog wants to bust your lady balls. You probably need to show up and tell Police and Fire what you just told me."

"Tell Police and Fire to tell Skog that after the cows give chocolate milk, they can all settle back and wait for strawberry."

"Heidi."

"What."

"Sooner or later, you need a better story about why you left Walt Beavers last night and ended up in the river."

"I don't have time for this, Denise. We don't. Pepper Greengrass doesn't."

———

"This'll do it for the Dairy Queen," Deputy Eleffson was suggesting as the sheriff entered the squad room with her phone to her ear. The call rang on the other end, she was asked to choose a language, then it rang some more. "She can't file for election now, while she's under investigation. Anybody know if she filed yet?"

"She's filed her nails, that's it so far. I'm just kidding."

Yttri's voice broke in. "Shut the hell up, Schwem." He was back from his accident call, blood on his pants. "You're not kidding and you're not funny."

Sick with urgency, the sheriff cut right through their noise to the window, hoping to connect the call before her meeting started. Did she know the extension of the party she would like to reach? She heard Eleffson ask the question she was wondering about. "So where's our former acting interim sheriff?"

Denise hustled in. "Boog Lund just called in dick."

"What?" Eleffson's eyes widened. "Did you just say *dick*?"

"I said *dick*."

"Hey," Schwem protested, "isn't that sexual harassment?"

"You wish," Denise corrected him.

"I feel threatened."

"Shut the hell up, Schwem," Yttri growled again.

"Heidi," Denise said quietly into her ear, "Harley just called me. He said you're not answering his texts. He said someone called the house and threatened you."

A third prerecording booted the sheriff down another phone tree. Rain pounded the window. The field beyond the ambulance had filled with water that reflected the parking lot lights. Denise whispered, "Threatened you in nozzle pressure, Harley said, pounds per square inch. Really weird, he said."

Vaguely the sheriff nodded and waved her away.

"Called in dick is when you can't come to work because you're a dick," Denise explained on her way out.

"I don't feel safe in my workplace," Eleffson said.

"Shut the hell up."

"Wait," Schwem said. "Did I forget my thermos?"

They continued to bicker and banter around Sheriff Kick while she climbed her way down the phone tree at the National Human Trafficking Resource Center, the number that Dave from the National Insurance Crime Bureau had given her. The center was in Washington, DC. In the end, at the root of the tree, it was after hours, the center was closed, and she was asked to leave a message. She backed out and dialed the hotline number linked to something called the Polaris Project. It was for victims, survivors, families, service providers—not law enforcement. But she had touched all those bases already, triggered the Amber Alert. She was putting the name Pepper Greengrass out into the broader web of NGOs. At last a person answered and began to ask the sheriff questions.

"We don't know yet," she told the operator. "Pepper may or may not be her legal name. The local police are working that end for us, trying to locate her family. I'll update when I can."

"Age?"

"We don't know yet. Her pimp says eighteen."

"Of course he did." The woman had a strong Southern accent. "Whatever the man says, subtract two. Last seen, where, and with whom?"

"Last night, Bad Axe County, Wisconsin, with a local man named Hans Kling."

"Height, weight, distinguishing features?"

The sheriff shared what Gabby Grimes had observed about Pepper Greengrass in the library, before Dale Hill had punched Harold Snustead and put everything in motion. "About five six, a hundred pounds, long dark hair and brown skin. She's at least part Ho-Chunk."

"I'm sorry, What-Chunk?"

"It's a tribe. Ho-Chunk. Winnebago is another name. We believe her family resides in or near a place called Wisconsin Dells."

"Missing since?"

"Nobody's reported her missing."

The woman went silent, except for fingernails on a keyboard. The silence became so sustained that the sheriff worried she had just disqualified Pepper Greengrass from the database. It gutted her that nobody close to Pepper Greengrass had reported her missing.

Finally the woman from Polaris spoke again. "But you have this girl confirmed in the presence of an adult male not related? And evidence of sex trade?"

Relief. "Actually, two men. A pimp, Dale Hill, and I'm betting that our local guy, Hans Kling, is a pornographer. So, evidence of sex trade, yes."

"And anyone with information should contact?"

"Tips should come to us. The Bad Axe County Sheriff's Department."

She ended the call and looked at her deputies. All the chitchat had stopped when she had laid down her wager that Hans Kling was a pornographer. The idea hung out there in silence until Denise rushed back in.

"Mudslide. That bluff above the Turkey Hill Trailer Park collapsed on one of the mobile homes. Somebody might be in there, they can't tell."

Caught in the middle of a shift change, she considered her options.

"Deputy Schwem, that's you, please. Hopefully everybody is accounted for. On the way back, check all taverns on the route for Hans Kling. Detain if found."

He left right away.

"Now, you guys heard me. That's our ten fifty-seven, a girl named Pepper Greengrass, missing and endangered. Deputies heading off duty, I want at least five taverns each before you get home, work it out amongst yourselves. Talk to the barflies. Detain Kling if you find him."

"I'm staying on," Yttri clarified for her. "Interim chief deputy to the reinstated interim sheriff. I won't file overtime."

The sheriff kept moving. "Deputy Eleffson?"

"Yo."

"Kling's mobile studio van was gone. Maybe he's on location somewhere. Maybe there's an event tonight, a reception, a game, a rodeo, whatever. Get to his website if he has one and find out who his big clients are."

When the rest of the deputies had gone, Yttri trailed her into her office. She slumped into her desk chair, her mouth and eyes dry. Yttri studied her. "You heard me, right? I'm filling in for Lund tonight. I know there's no money. And if I get hurt I won't file a claim."

"You should go home, get some rest."

"Not until you do."

She sighed. A few long seconds slipped by. She tweaked her computer mouse. Brock Pabst's blow to her upper arm had evolved into a deep ache that pounded through the rest of her soreness. She minimized screens to see her desktop background: bright light, bright colors, big smiles, her photo of Harley and the kids canoeing on the Kickapoo River last summer, shot by her from the stern, the Kick family in love with one another, and in love with this place.

She glanced up. Yttri was knitting his big hands together as he leaned back in a chair, his chest stretching open and his eyelids fluttering as if he were viewing something inside his head. He winced. The sheriff looked away, refreshed her screen on the Polaris Project to see if Pepper Greengrass had registered on the missing/endangered clearinghouse website. Of course not, not yet. Urgency and inertia had crashed together—law enforcement work in a nutshell.

She tried to change her channel, fill some time. "You never played baseball?"

Yttri's eyes came open, a startled soft gray. "Me? Nah."

"Why not?"

He shrugged. "Not a jock."

She looked at him: that size, that grace. "You've gotta be kidding me."

"Nope."

"What makes you not a jock?"

"Loyalty to my mom. My Pee Wee League football coach called us girls all the time—ladies, ballerinas, Girl Scouts, beauty queens, princesses. Little League, the coach called us pussies and twats. I finally asked my mom why. She said, 'Because women are disgusting, aren't they? They're meat? Isn't that part of sports?' And she was right. Not to every guy. Maybe even most guys in sports are not actually like that. But it's kind of a groupthink thing, and on every team there were always just enough guys on that same page that I'd rather hunt and fish."

All of thirty seconds had passed. The sheriff refreshed the screen. Not yet. She began to scroll through the database, composed almost entirely of missing girls and women, a few boys.

"Where'd you grow up again?"

"North of Green Bay. Lived around there until I got this job eight years ago."

"So you never went wild with the boys at some secret strip party in a barn?"

"Worst thing I did was read a stolen *Playboy* up in my tree stand." His lean toward her pulled her eyes from the screen. "Heidi . . . are you OK?"

"Why?"

"It looks like this is getting to you, that's all. Back there in the Dells . . ."

She raised a hand to stop him. "Let's just do the job."

She was looking into the face of a missing girl from Idaho, realizing she could sort by region, where a girl was from and/or where she was last seen. She filtered for Wisconsin-Iowa-Illinois-Minnesota and scrolled through the postings, transfixed by the roster of tragedies.

Missing/Endangered . . .

Missing/Runaway . . .

Missing/Abducted . . .

Her eyes blurred with tears at the snapshots of missing girls, all of them between eleven and seventeen, and their age-progressed photos.

Age-progressed . . .

The computer projections broke her heart, how the technology gave these girls futures, tracked them into lives they had never lived. The software seemed so sensitive and accurate that even personality traits revealed in the original picture evolved with digital precision. A real girl looked at the camera with a cold hint of suspicion at age fourteen. Ten years later, the bloated rage beneath her defeat seemed stirringly real.

Age now: 35.

Age now: 41.

Age now: 25.

These girls were dead. That was the unspoken truth. Their lives were over. It was their bodies that were missing. Their families . . . the grief they must feel . . . the fear . . . the incapacitating anger . . . knowing a killer is out there.

She stopped suddenly. She bit her bottom lip and leaned in, squinting into the screen, feeling her breath catch. In this lost girl's shiny blond hair . . . was she looking at a pair of blue butterfly barrettes, just like the one she had seen on Walt Beavers's shelf? She brought up the photo Yttri had retaken. It was the same barrette, or one exactly like it.

"What's up?" He had noticed her heightened distress. "Is our girl on the board yet?"

"No. Open that."

She pointed to the red-bound volume of *Bad Axe Broadcaster*s at the edge of her desk. "Where I've got the marker."

Her screen said *Missing/Runaway.* This girl was plain and pale, with a shy smile and shiny blond hair that was swept back from her temples and pinned with a blue butterfly on each side. A thin gold necklace, worn on the outside of a white turtleneck, disappeared across her shallow bust at the bottom of the photograph. This was a high school portrait, for sure.

She glanced up. Yttri was flipping the large, brittle pages of old newspapers. She looked back to her screen. Age-progressed, the girl looked heavier, bustier, plainer, her paleness seeming light deprived, her eyes distant inside deep, bruiselike circles. She read down:

AGE NOW: 20
DOB: 8/15/1996
GENDER: Female
RACE: Unknown
HAIR COLOR: Blond
EYE COLOR: Blue
HEIGHT: 5'2"
WEIGHT: 110
MISSING FROM: Waukon, Iowa
MISSING SINCE: August 3, 2012
LAST SEEN: Farmstead, WI, August 12, 2012 (unconfirmed)
CONTACT: Allamakee County Sheriff's Department, (563) 468-4900

She scrolled up to see the name: *Sophie Ringensetter*. She reached into
her breast pocket, touched the photograph of Harley and the girl, felt
past it to find the necklace beneath. She laid the necklace on her desk.
Sophie. Her fingers clumsily nudged the broken chain, spreading it as if
to make room for the girl's neck. Sophie Ringensetter had been sixteen.

Her hand felt damp and clumsy as she reached back into her pocket
for the photograph of her husband with the girl at the Ease Inn. She
touched it, stalled. She pulled it up and glanced. Age, hair color, eye
color—and the date—all the same. *Oh, God.* Karen, Harley had told her,
was the name of the girl he claimed he tried to help. Should she check
with the La Crosse County Sheriff's Department, check their records, to
see if his story was true? Why did trust keep slipping away? Pages riffled.
Yttri said, "What am I looking for here?"

"Story about a missing girl. It won't be on the sports page, but that
same issue." Her own voice sounded alien. "I'm going to guess it wasn't
just the game that Walt Beavers closed the book on."

"Here it is." Yttri read, "'Authorities in Allamakee County, Iowa, seek
information about a missing minor, female, possibly seen outside the
Ease Inn truck stop in Farmstead on August twelfth. Area residents with
any information should contact . . .'"

He interrupted himself, noting her intense focus on the screen.
"What's up? Is our missing girl on the board yet?"

She couldn't find the words. She turned her screen so he could see it. Yttri leaned in. She pointed out the blue butterfly barrettes, the gold necklace that said *Sophie*. She showed him his own cell phone photo of the items from Walt Beavers's shelf. Then, her nerves about to shatter, she dropped the snapshot of Harley and the blond girl in front of him.

Yttri leaned over it. She stared with him, focusing on the girl's heavier chest, her ponytail, no barrettes.

"This picture was taken at the Ease Inn on August twelfth," she said. "But that's not her, right?" She felt her face flush and turned it quickly away, worried he could feel the heat. "Is there any way that's her?"

After a long silence, during which she knew her deputy was inspecting the two photographs minutely, looking from the computer screen to the snapshot, Yttri cleared his throat and said, "That's a different girl." She looked at him. "Heidi, no. Absolutely not. It takes more than one girl to have a party. Right now, we need to know who talked to Allamakee County about Sophie Ringensetter."

"Right." She exhaled. "Turn back to the sports page. She was last seen on the day of that Rattlers game against the Dells, the one Pepper Greengrass and Dale Hill were betting on when Harold Snustead got punched. Something else happened that night, at a stag party, and I have to guess it happened to this girl . . ."

Yttri scanned the article again and sat back, scowling deeply at his own fists.

"So there are two girls missing in the Bad Axe. One, if we can find her at all, we're going to find her dead . . ."

"Yes," she said. "And the other one, unless . . ."

She trailed off.

Pepper Greengrass. I will find you.

44

The handcuffs go to a chain. The chain wraps around her waist and meets itself at a padlock around the back side of a tree that stands amid other trees beyond the flooded ditch of the deserted gravel road. An hour, maybe two hours, she has waited in the rain. Three times so far she has lunged to the chain's length and shit hot liquid. Here it comes again.

When the cramp is gone and her vision clears, Pepper can see through the trees and underbrush to the edge of the ditch. She can see the ribbon fluttering on the overhanging branch, marking where she is.

Now she hears an engine, a diesel truck. The truck rumbles into low gear. As it strains uphill, its headlights illuminate rain falling through the treetops over Pepper's head. Then the truck's black shape appears at the ditch. It is a long-haul tractor, no trailer attached. It stops with the same hiss as Felton Henry's truck. But that can't be. Can it?

For a few long minutes nothing happens. Rain keeps falling through the treetops. Pepper's ass still burns while a new cramp spiders through her guts. Her teeth clack together. Stuffed between them, her tongue feels thick.

At last a door slams. Boots hit gravel. A branch snaps. A stranger's voice, not Felton Henry's, twangs out, "Darlin'? My precious little Pepper Pot?"

Strange relief. "You can't hurt me!" she announces through the distance.

"Say what?"

"I cannot be hurt!"

NIGHTFALL

Jerry Myad @thebestdefense
@BadAxeCountySheriff should not be allowed
to breed more little feminazis #dairyqueen
#huntingseason #doyouknowwhereyourchildrenare

45

The trucker who picked Pepper up, face like a hatchet with a bad beard, turns on his dome light and opens a dirty palm. He is showing her two small silver keys. One is for the handcuffs connecting her right wrist to the chicken handle above the passenger door. One is for the chain lock, which he left at the tree. His voice twangs. His sideburns are groomed to knifepoints. He is uniformed like Felton Henry—jeans, wallet chain, big belt buckle, pointed boots, mesh cap that says *Redneck Lives Matter*, plaid Western shirt that he rolls up to show tats like fungus on his hairy arms.

"Keys to my heart, darlin'."

A minute ago he smashed the semi cab through what looked like a pond, beyond a sign that said WATER OVER ROAD. It keeps raining. All that snow and ice keep melting. His windows are cracked open. Between the engine and the rain hitting the cab and the splashing and hissing outside, he has to yell.

"You wanna know what I paid to get these?"

"I wanna know what you're gonna pay me," Pepper responds.

"Say what?"

"Unless this road goes to Montana."

"Say what, Pepper Pot?"

He spills the handcuff key back into the shirt pocket that gapes over his hollow chest. He chucks the other key out the window. "Are you

sassing me?" His twang comes out shrill between those knifepoints sideburns. "Because I do like some sass. I do like it hot."

He leaves the dome light on. The road seems to disappear behind
reflections in the windshield. He is a busy driver. He tweaks his blower,
his wipers, and his window gaps, spits tobacco into a liter Mountain
Dew bottle, restashes the Dew bottle in his crotch, shifts gears, puts his
high beams on and off, tweaks and spits and stashes and keeps reaching
for her left knee, pulling it toward him, which spreads her legs because
her right wrist is hung by the chicken handle.

"I seen your pictures, fresh out there, and I jumped for five large,
girl. You're gonna fetch me back boocoo many times that. You got a big
old black bush. You got gumdrops, girl." He shows his small gray teeth.
He decelerates with a thunderous Jake brake. "We're gonna stop just a
minute."

They have emerged from total narrow darkness into lesser wider
darkness. This is a crossroads with a two-pump gas plaza and a small-
windowed store with bundles of firewood and bags of salt and bark
chips piled along the face of it. He waits as headlights on a larger road
approach both left and right—Pepper thinks to reach out, smack his
horn—then the headlights are gone. She watches how he shuts down
and leaves the truck, gear in first, emergency brake knob out, just like
Felton Henry. He bowlegs toward the store, passes under the pump
plaza, his head looking a size too small beneath the mesh cap.

Inside the store five minutes, then he comes out trailing the clerk,
who is a big man in a rain slicker pushing a pallet of bottled water on
a hand truck. He twangs small talk while the clerk loads the pallet into
the sleeper cab. Then he hops back into the driver's seat with a fifth of
brown booze and a small plastic sack that he slings up on the dash. Soon
they are rolling again along the larger road.

Pepper reminds him, "You can't hurt me."

"I like it." He cracks the seal on the bottle, a long-neck fifth, and
takes a swallow. "I like your spice."

"You're supposed to take me to Amtrak."

"I'll take you to the moon, girl, you'll see."

He fits the Dew bottle with his chew spit into a console cup holder.

She can smell the whiskey as he takes another swallow. She sees it's George Dickel sour mash No. 8. He jams the bottle between his legs. "You keep that up."

"I will."

"I like mine spicy, as do gentlemen in general."

"I've never met a gentleman."

"Oh, you're gonna meet boocoo plenty."

A few miles down the road, exactly at a sign that says NO JAKE BRAKES BY TOWN CODE, he Jake brakes again. Down the tunnel of his headlights Pepper sees three houses, two of which appear abandoned, and across the road some kind of store that is definitely abandoned, and a bit farther ahead a dump truck and a school bus parked in front of a structure that has burned down. At the far reach of the headlights is a gravel pit in a hillside.

This time with the Dickel in hand, he heads out into the rain and enters the house with lights on. Stretching to the end of the handcuffs, Pepper can reach the plastic sack on the dash. She awkwardly fishes inside for the stuff he got at the store, finding a plastic sleeve of three Bic pens, a Sharpie permanent marker, a packet of baby wipes, and a snap-blade box cutter. She thinks, *Whatever.* She thinks, *You can't hurt me.*

He is gone a long time. The rain slacks. Pepper nods and enters some kind of fatigue-charged daydream where she is stripping at the casino. Her brother Bennie is in the audience, cutting himself to bleed every time she takes another piece of clothing off. Then Dale Hill is there, soothing Bennie, wrapping him in mummy's gauze.

Then the dream is done, and out of the house the trucker drags a fat lady. She is circus-level fat, a human parade blimp yanked by the wrist and paddling after him in flesh-and-aqua-colored billows across oily puddles that stipple and glow in the red sidelights of the tractor. He opens the door and pushes Dickel breath inside.

"My handwriting might as well be Chink scratch for what it looks like, so, darlin', stand down here on the running board, there you go, now bend in over the seat, 'cuz I can follow-draw OK, but I can't hand-write for shit."

Her wrist feels about to pull apart up at the chicken handle. He twists her hips and pulls her skirt down. The fat lady touches her back above her tailbone with the Sharpie.

"Write it pretty for me, that's my girl, there you go."

This big woman is silent, smells like mildew, wheezes hard, does not return his salutation through the thickening rain.

"Real good friend of mine," he lets Pepper know, driving off. "No bullshit, no sass, just a real good friend."

46

She waited for the Head Trauma Unit nurse at Gundersen Medical Center in La Crosse to come on the line. Finally here she was. How could she help?

"This is Bad Axe County sheriff Heidi Kick. We need to talk to Walt Beavers at the absolute earliest moment possible. I can be there within an hour. Can we make that happen?"

"He has regained consciousness, Sheriff, but whether he can talk is Dr. Patel's call."

The sheriff glanced behind her. Her printer was working from a remote command, sent by Denise from the dispatch room.

"Is that the same Dr. Patel who works the ER at Vernon Memorial?"

"Dr. Alka Patel is the supervising physician in rotation tonight, yes."

"Could you give her my number, and have her call me right away?"

Olaf the Handsome was studying a printout of Sophie Ringensetter's *Missing/Runaway* bulletin. "This witness is 'unconfirmed,'" he said. "But the newspaper says someone from around here told Allamakee County that they saw her at the Ease Inn."

"You're on that. We need the name of that witness, and everything else that Allamakee has on this girl. Something they have might get us to Pepper Greengrass."

Denise appeared in the doorway, flushed and breathless.

"The bridge washed out on Sandhill Road over Clover Creek in the town of Blackhawk Locks. That's the shortcut people use to get from the river to Highway 14. It's dark as hell in there. We need a barricade and a detour. I tried State Patrol but they're too busy. Our friends in Vernon County, same. Schwem is still at Turkey Hill, so he's nearby."

The sheriff's blank mind must have showed on her face. Turkey Hill?

"The trailer that's under the mudslide," Denise reminded her. "We're still looking for the guy that lives in it."

The sheriff glanced at Yttri. They had forgotten all but dead and missing girls.

"Send Schwem right away to get flares up on both sides of the bridge. Send a Roads truck to put up barricades."

"I thought you'd say that. It's done already."

"Find out if La Crosse PD can assist Turkey Hill with a search-and-rescue dog."

"Also done. They have to find their dog handler. Waiting to hear."

But Denise still stood there.

"Something else?"

"Heidi, sorry, I know it's crazy right now, and I know you don't want to be bothered with the social media stuff, and honestly it's mostly just cranks and one girl who defends you, but since Harley called earlier, and since the board has a policy that if any of this stuff ever gets to the family level . . ."

"What?"

"On Twitter. I think you need to see it. Pull that off your printer."

The sheriff rolled her chair back and pulled two pages from the printer. Denise had collected tweets with the department's handle and circled one. Someone calling himself "Jerry Myad @thebestdefense" had tweeted:

@BadAxeCountySheriff should not be allowed to breed more little feminazis #dairyqueen #huntingseason #doyouknowwhereyourchildrenare

Instantly, her heartbeat pounded in her ears. Deputy Yttri leaned in to see. She felt his heat rise as he read aloud, " 'Do you know where your children are?' Is that a threat?" His face was close to hers, his eyebrows up, his hands in fists, his chest inflated. She shook herself free and looked at Denise.

"Can we find out who this is?"

"It's possible. Shit like that usually comes from a fake profile. But Twitter has an emergency request form for law enforcement. We can ask for IP logs."

"Hell yes, it's a threat." Yttri rose and paced the floor. " 'Hashtag hunting season'? 'Hashtag do you know where your children are'? That's a threat of violence against your kids."

She watched him a moment. His outrage helped her find just enough calm.

"So, Denise, let's . . ."

"I've already printed and filled out the form. You autograph, I fax to Twitter. We wait."

Denise pushed the second printed page toward the sheriff for her to sign.

"But meanwhile," she said. She glanced at her own cell phone. "Come on," she said. "Come on, come on," scrolling and tapping. "Ta-da! Meanwhile, speaking of Hans Kling, I just found him."

47

Olaf the Handsome drove again. Kling's van was in the barnyard of Albin Metzger's farm, twenty miles south at the Crawford County border. How different the logo on the van looked to her now.

KLING KOUNTRY KAMERA
Bridals, Engagements, Weddings, Events, Family,
Sports, Pets, Livestock, Rodeos

Kling was here for rodeo glam shots. Albin Metzger bred bucking bulls. In the sheriff's Dairy Queen days, he had sponsored rodeo teams around the region. She remembered shaking his huge hand and accepting a check for prize money after winning a barrel race. Hans Kling had taken the picture of her that appeared in the *Crawford County Independent*.

Tonight, Kling had the interior of one of Metzger's barns set up for bucking-bull porn. Hay bales were artfully stacked before a sky-blue shooting backdrop. A pitchfork leaned against a bale. In the foreground was a phony powder keg stenciled *TNT*. The keg sprouted a fuse that sizzled with tiny LED lights. Behind the hay bales was Kling himself, crouched, his face made up like a rodeo clown. He had not yet seen the sheriff and her deputy enter the barn.

One of Metzger's strapping adult daughters steadied a cream-colored bull by its nose ring. The beast was cut with heavy muscles, brushed to a gleam. Metzger's daughter whispered in its ear, then she let go of the nose ring and walked out of Kling's shot. He triggered the photograph. A flash popped. The bull never flinched. They all had done this before.

Then Kling saw her and Yttri. When he scrambled upright it turned out he was wearing his rodeo clown face over his usual dumpy-gentleman street clothes. It was hard to say what his real expression was. But he turned suddenly, like he was going to bolt.

"I need to talk to you, Mr. Kling."

In the meantime, Albin Metzger had seen the cruiser pull into his barnyard, and now he was coming into the barn through a side door, a burly Vietnam vet who walked with a slight hitch and favored fresh denim and white Stetsons. He put his hands on his hips and watched Kling scurry out from behind the hay. He made an innocent joke.

"I knew there was some reason you were late today, Hans. What were you doing, holding up a bank somewhere? Now the sheriff is coming to get you?" He winked at her and Yttri. "Bringing along this big fella to wrangle you in?"

Metzger had a lethal handshake. Yttri could handle it. The sheriff felt her bones fold.

"How you doing, Sheriff? What I hear is that you're doing pretty darn well. My girls are big fans of yours. How can we help you today?"

"I just need to talk to Hans about a young lady he met at a party last night."

"Me? A young lady?" Kling made his clown face incredulous. "A party?"

Metzger laughed. "You all talk away. Stacy, let's give the law some room. Bodacious is done, is that right, Hans? Hon, put him away, will you? And let's get Freckles next."

In a minute it was just her and Kling and Yttri.

"Mr. Kling, I'm too busy to let you lie to me. Don't even think about it. Get a lawyer. Somebody from the Bad Axe County Sheriff's Department will be around to pick you up, and you know why. Right now just tell me where she is and I'll leave you alone with Freckles."

"Where who is?"

"You bought a girl named Pepper Greengrass from a man named

Dale Hill at a party in Emerald Faulkner's barn. We caught Hill. He told us. Eight hundred bucks. Where is she?"

"I . . . I just gave her a ride. Bought a girl? No way, OK? She had no place to go, so you betcha she spent the night, and then she wanted to go see her sister in Montana, so a nice guy like me, you know, I . . ."

Yttri moved between Kling and the nearest doorway. He kept stammering. "She needed a ride so you betcha I got online and found her a ride. She's gone. Why? Did something happen to her?"

The sheriff kept her hands gripped together. "I know you took pictures of her. You didn't pay eight hundred for nothing. Look at me, Mr. Kling. She's underage, a runaway. This is bad for you already. You're out of business. But it's going to be so much worse for you unless I find this girl before she's hurt or dead."

He was shaking now. Tears of a clown. Stacy Metzger was backing through that side door with a black bull by the nose.

"You passed her off to another predator. You know what the police chief in the Dells said? You 'sold her up the food chain.' A child."

Hans Kling slumped. The camera remote dropped from his hand. Stacy Metzger stopped with the bull. She called back through the doorway, "Dad, get in here."

Kling said, "The guy . . . his handle . . . I didn't hurt her, OK? . . . He must have been close by, I put her up online and, boom, I got a response, and he wanted to pick her up right away . . ."

Kling kept shrugging and mewling and peddling his phony, dithering innocence until the sheriff lunged, shoved him by the throat against a hay bale—Stacy Metzger gasped—drove his greasepaint chin up into the barn's high fluorescent lights.

Kling choked, "OK, sure, you betcha. His Backpage name was 'King Cream.'"

48

The semi tractor rumbles down a long curve. Pepper hangs from her wrist by the chicken handle and stares at segments of the guardrail ticking past. She sees WATER OVER ROAD again. The guardrail is puny, a thin weft of wavy metal on rotting wooden posts, a gesture at safety and a lie about what will happen when things get out of control. He is belligerent with his Jake brake and uses it at the bottom of the long grade as if to shatter the bones of anyone sleeping in the few drab houses with vehicle-cluttered yards on the bottomland. But no one sleeps. Pepper sees dim shapes with flashlights, staggering shapes in pajamas and boots, carrying children and possessions, loading pickups. He hits the water and it explodes sideways into a man carrying a large girl-child and washes over the hood and windshield as his truck decelerates with a backward surge that throws Pepper against the dashboard, leaves her dangling with her knees just touching the floor.

He bulls the truck through the water that's flooded the valley bottom and gears down as the road starts to climb again. He's been talking on a cell phone, losing coverage, getting it back. She should listen. It could be useful. He wants his trailer loaded right now. It's on low ground, he says. On the other end someone tells him it's on high enough ground that it can get loaded in the morning. He turns to her and says, "OK, then I guess you and me will have our fun early. Boocoo good times, girl, coming up."

Her wrist hurts, her shoulder, she feels a searing pain between her hips, she *knows* she shouldn't say this but she does: "When you say boocoo you sound like some douche bag in a casino, OK? It's pronounced *bow*coo. Just so you know."

"Huh."

He says this thoughtfully, gripping the Dickel neck with a hand that holds a burning cigarette between two fingers. The truck is just now leveling onto a ridge, its headlights long across a rain-swept field.

"Another girl with your kind of spice, I'd have to name her. Yours comes with."

A little ways along the ridge he takes a short spur off the road and stops at a gate. He finds a tool behind his seat, carries it through rain and headlights. His elbows bend as the tool scissors and a chain drops off the gate. He drives through the gate onto an uphill dirt road hardly wider than the tractor. He leaves the truck in neutral with the yellow emergency brake knob pulled out while he swings back out to close the gate. When he returns, Pepper hears his exertion, little Jake-brake rumbles coming from his heaving chest.

He steers uphill, the road becoming more and more narrow. Wet branches rake the windows. He keeps up that rheumy purring like a sick cat. He wants to speak, she thinks, but his lungs are shredded—meth, she thinks—and he can't catch his breath. At last they reach some kind of peak. The forest thins. The road opens into a little park on a bluff, against a void of rainy sky.

He seems familiar with the place. He backs without hesitation toward the void, pulls forward, reverses again into the void, pulls forward once more across the pitched surface, until the truck is turned around and almost level. Pepper feels its nose tilting slightly back down the road. Now its headlights shine on a shingle-roofed shelter over a picnic table. He pulls his brake knob, jumps down to chock his wheels. The door on her side opens. He stands on the running board, unkeys the cuff from the chicken handle, and claps it on her free wrist behind her back.

"Party time."

He pushes her through fat vertical raindrops toward the shelter. With both hands cuffed behind her she feels off balance. She stumbles and his hand comes up beneath her skirt.

"I gotcha."

"You think so."

He keeps it up there, pinching her.

"I also like mine all denty."

"You want to say *alfresco*."

"Do I?"

"Nothing you can do will hurt me."

"Gonna be fun to hear that when I'm up in your tonsils."

"I will bite that limp shit off."

He whips her around, slaps her hard across the face.

"I will bone you stupid, child."

"You can't hurt me."

"Tell you what." They have reached the shelter. "I do like all the big talk," he says, wheezing, "all the spice and the pizzazz, as I said, I like it, but then I get tired of it."

He shoves her under the roof. She stands on dry dirt, on her own long shadow. He whips her around. He is a black shape in a halo made by headlights through the rain.

"So here is what you and me are gonna do."

He leaves her at the picnic table, returns down his high beams to his truck. It occurs to her to run. Which way? She darts inside the rain curtain coming down around the shelter. Five seconds. Ten. Then his shadow pierces the curtain and that hatchet face looms back in wet and wheezing with a ruined cigarette dangling. He spits it to the dirt.

"Since I'm already tired of your bullshit . . . and your sass . . . and since you and me need to be . . . friends . . . here's what we're gonna do."

He carries a five-gallon bucket, plastic, orange, empty. He sets it under the shelter. He returns to the truck and comes back wobbly-legged under that shrink-wrapped bale of bottled water. Panting raggedly, he positions the bale by the bucket. He tears the wrap, a few bottles topple out. He lights a new cigarette, calms his lungs. He sits on the picnic table bench, unscrews a bottle, and pours the water into the bucket. He does the same thing again. Again.

"Turn around. You're gonna help me with this."

He takes the cuffs off her wrists. She sits down. He hands her a bottle. She unscrews it, pours the water into the bucket.

"You see this?"

He lifts the tail of his shirt: a silver pistol holstered squarely in the caved-in center of his chest. He hands her another bottle. She unscrews the cap, upends it over the bucket. The bucket fills another quarter inch.

"You like a smoke?"

She accepts one. Marlboro Red. He scorches it with a Zippo. She unscrews, pours, unscrews, pours. The rain lets up. Coyotes howl nearby. When the bucket is full, water slopping over the rim, he grabs Pepper Greengrass by the hair and shoves her head down into it.

49

Angus had just mentioned Harley Kick to an old-timer on a stool at the VFW who was drunk enough that he might not remember who asked him.

"Do you know where he lives nowadays?"

"Him and the Sheriff Dairy Queen moved out to Hank Pederson's old place. Hell, you look familiar. Aren't you that Beavers kid playing pro ball?"

Angus was out the door. He would have to ask someone else where the Pederson place was. At Kwik Trip, the big red-haired lady said to him as he came through the door, "How'd them chicken nuggets suit you? Ain't those the best?"

"Chicken nuggets?"

"Cheesy taters is on special today. You ain't by taxi like last night."

She recognized him too. He was leaving a trail.

She answered his question. "Where is the Pederson place? On Pederson Road, son, where else? Off County J. But watch out. I heard on the scanner the J bridge is under water."

He took Highway 14 to Military Road along the Vernon County border and dropped down north of the County J bridge. On Pederson Road he found the mailbox, *H&H Kick*. He parked Brock Pabst's sputtering shit can in a dark spot off the road and came down the long and winding driveway, wading through puddles, listening for dogs, not hearing any. He figured that minivan might be in the barn, and he was right.

He looked on the windshield. The Sophie necklace he had left for her to find was gone. So maybe that had worked. She might have guessed it was him, but at least she knew something was up. So try it again.

He had just pinched Sophie's blue butterfly hair clip onto a coil of Buster H. Johnson and laid the crumbly rubber rattlesnake on the hood of the sheriff's van when a light came on in the yard. A half second later, a light switched on in the barn. A screen door banged. Harley Kick's voice called, "Is somebody out here?"

Angus darted deeper into the barn and lay down behind a feed trough. Harley Kick's feet in rubber barn boots appeared. Then a small pair of bare feet appeared beside them.

"I said stay inside. Go back in."

"I want to talk to you."

Angus guessed it was the little girl he had seen inside the sheriff's van at the scrap yard.

"We can talk inside," Harley Kick told his daughter. "Go on."

"We can't talk about grown-up things in front of the boys."

"We can't talk about grown-up things period. You're five."

"Daddy. Tell me. Why are you and Mommy fighting?"

"We don't fight. We discuss."

"*Daddy* . . . at your baseball practice."

"Please go back in the house, Ophelia."

"What is the story? Who's Karen?"

"Back in the house, please. Now."

Harley Kick's boots moved. Angus watched the butt of a shotgun touch the dry dirt floor. Was he seeing wet footprints that weren't his? "Who's in here?" The boots began to circle the back of the van. Angus held his breath. "The heck . . ." Angus heard him mutter.

Was he seeing the snake? No, he was at the rear of the van. But if he did see the snake, then what? Holding his breath, Angus hastily processed his mistake. Maybe, once upon a time, Harley Kick had been more like Scotty Clausen and Wade Gibbs. If he had been, he wouldn't want his wife to know. If he recognized Buster H. Johnson, instead of telling her the nasty thing it meant and where it came from, he might just get rid of it.

"What the heck," Harley Kick said again.

He was at the side of the van now. He called after his little girl.

"She washed the car? Opie, when did Mommy wash the car? She never washes the car. Did you guys go somewhere today? Where?"

"Daddy," she called back sternly, her voice trailing away toward the house, "you're not the boss of where Mommy goes."

Harley Kick was silent for a while. Then Angus heard him pump the shotgun. Next thing Angus heard him do, he picked up a bucket and threw it, made a racket, what you did to flush a possum or a coon. Nothing moved. A minute later, at the house, the screen door smacked its frame. The barn light and then the house light went out.

Angus grabbed the snake and the hair clip and he ran.

50

She had been Googling "King Cream." The futility so far encompassed restaurants, cream ales, ice cream parlors, and Twitter handles for these places. There was a vintage dairy sign, KING OF CREAM, on eBay. Nothing so far. She was spinning her wheels, grinding her teeth. Hans Kling had told her King Cream was local. He said the buyer had picked up Pepper Greengrass right away. She was about to wade once more into Backpage.com.

"Mighty Heidi, whirly girly, how ya doing?"

She looked up to see Perry Gardner, a brief old flame, a guy from up here in the Bad Axe. She had met him while temping at Rhinegold Dairy in the winter of her senior year.

"You left a message? You wanted to ask me something?"

Perry was still handsome, sharply dressed in a business suit, half drunk, grinning.

"You're the sheriff now, huh? What'd I do? Or you just missed me?"

For a maddening few seconds she couldn't think of when or why she called him. Then she remembered. *The Scream.* The guy at Pinky Clausen's, plowing snow with an old Rhinegold Dairy truck. She had called him after that.

"I thought maybe your memory was better than mine," she told him. "At Rhinegold, when we worked there, was there ever a guy there that ended up with his face and his fingers burned off?"

He laughed. "S'more?"

"I'm sorry?"

"Naw, he never worked there. He just bought a Rhinegold truck when they went out of business. But yeah, you mean Jerrold Mickelson. He got toasted."

Her breath caught. Somebody Mickelson, no first name, was on her list. A Mickelson had worked for her dad. But there were too many Mickelsons in the Bad Axe. Now she added a first name. *Jerrold* Mickelson.

"What do you mean, toasted?"

"You know, marshmallow on a campfire. He blew up a meth kitchen a few years ago. No idea if he ever worked for you guys."

She saw that face again, melted off center, holes in it, Jerrold Mickelson saying to her, *Three thousand psi sounds about right. . . .* Hadn't someone called and said something like that to Harley?

"I hear now he's a major troll on the internet," Perry said.

"Does he call himself King Cream?"

Her old friend shrugged. Her phone was blinking. Denise hollered from dispatch, "A Dr. Patel on line one! Coach Beavers is cleared to talk! O the H is still over in Iowa talking to Allamakee County!"

She hesitated.

Denise hollered, "If you're going, take my truck!"

After she had put on her jacket and hat, Perry Gardner was still leaning in her doorway. He said, "So anyway, other than sheriff, what's new with you these days? You ever want to get a drink and catch up?"

"Good to see you, Perry."

51

An hour later, Walt Beavers squinted through medication-blurred vision at the sheriff's cell phone picture of his shrine: the calendar page, the blue butterfly barrette, the mustard crock with ashes. Dr. Patel had cleared him to talk. But was he even hearing her?

"Her name is Sophie Ringensetter," she repeated. "She was sixteen. She's never been found. You need to tell me what happened, Coach."

He released his bandaged head into the pillow. Finally he answered, "I dunno . . ."

"You do know something. This looks to me like a shrine to her, like the shrine you made for your daughter who died." She showed him Sophie's picture from the Polaris Project website. He skimmed it with half-open eyes. "Do you know what happened to this girl?" she asked him.

"I just dunno. . . . Lyman . . ."

"Lyman what?"

"My brother. I dunno."

"Is she dead?"

He nodded faintly. Yes, Sophie Ringensetter was dead. His confirmation forced her to hold still for a moment.

"Did she die that day? August 12, 2012?"

He nodded yes, Sophie Ringensetter had died that day.

"Was she a stripper at the party in Emerald Faulkner's barn? After the Rattlers lost to the Dells? And the team was there?"

Yes, he nodded, to all of that.

"Is this her? Coach Beavers, look again. Are you sure? Is this the girl?"

She held the *Missing/Runaway* photo in front of him. He took a longer look. A tear trickled down his ruined face. He smeared it sideways with the back of his hand.

"What happened?"

"We didn't kill her."

"That's good to hear. Who did?"

"Dunno. They tried to make it look like me and Lyman did."

"They?"

"Dunno. She was at the party, you know, getting with the men. The team was real drunk that night 'cuz they lost a big one and there was a fight. Some of the guys took her outside. She, you know, she could hardly hold herself up to walk, but I guess she pulled a train . . ."

The sheriff flinched. "They gang-raped her?"

"Dunno what you call it. Yeah."

"You saw this?"

"Me and Lyman was pretty ripped. But we saw them take her off somewhere."

"Do you remember who 'some of the guys' were?"

"Wade Gibbs, Sherman Ossie, Scotty Clausen, Curtis Strunk. They took her away from the party into another one of Faulkner's buildings. They were big-talking after. Next thing I really remember, I was waking up at Lyman's place and there she was."

"There she was? What do you mean? Where?"

"Aw, God, I just hate to remember it." A new tear leaked down his face. "Me and Lyman was drunk as skunks after. I decided not to try for Dog Hollow. I slept over at the scrap yard . . ."

He paused. His nurse had come in. She exchanged his drip and went away.

"Angus came inside yelling in the morning. Turns out, see, I had driven home with a girl's dead body in the back of my truck. Somebody had throwed her in there. I had seen my own daughter dead because of my own damn fault . . . and I had seen this poor girl at the party, so drunk she could hardly stand . . . and I shoulda . . ."

"What *did* you do?"

"Well, Lyman, he called Sheriff Gibbs directly. And Coach Clausen. Said them two's families was in on this. Gibbs and Pinky came out with Boog Lund. Their idea was they could make us get rid of her body, or else they'd charge us with killing her. But, well, Lyman—see, my brother, he will just dicker you to death. He just will. And he got a deal out of them."

"Meaning what?"

"Well, Lyman had already called Clinton Knobloch."

"Who is Clinton Knobloch?"

"He's just another fella that seen Gibbs's nephew and Clausen's boy and them others taking that drunk girl out in the dark. Knobloch don't even lie about fishing. Gibbs and Clausen, Boog Lund, them guys knew Knobloch would say what he saw. Next thing you know Lyman had a deal. He was going to get rid of that girl's body, sure, but only if Angus got a hunk of Clausen's money to go to that same baseball academy that Scotty went to, and only if I got to be first-base coach on the Rattlers. Lyman didn't take nothing for himself, just the satisfaction. But I guess me and him really shoulda . . ."

He lifted a corner of his bedsheet and wiped his tears.

"Later I found one of that girl's blue hairpins still in the back of my truck. I kept it."

"So your brother burned her at the yard? Is that why you have ashes in a mustard crock?"

"He was supposed to burn her. That's what he agreed to. I just took them ashes from his burn pile."

"But he might not have?"

"Lyman's got a big mouth, but he don't mean hardly anything he says. So I don't know."

Dr. Patel stood in the doorway. Coach Beavers saw her and said, "I'm gonna die now," and closed his eyes.

"You are not going to die, Mr. Beavers," said Dr. Patel as she entered.

"Angus and Brandy, them poor kids can have my things . . ."

The sheriff bore in on him. "Coach Beavers, listen to me now. Your niece was at that party last night. She's alive. Sophie Ringensetter died at a party just like it. Do you understand what I'm saying?"

He closed his eyes and nodded.

"Now I'm going to ask you about another girl, and a man who calls himself King Cream. There was a girl with long black hair who danced at the party last night. Yes?"

He nodded.

"She's missing."

He nodded.

"You knew that?"

"No. But I ain't that surprised."

"Apparently you spend a lot of time online, on Backpage.com. Is that right?"

"Some."

"Have you ever seen King Cream on there?"

Walt Beavers nodded. He gathered a breath. "He's a fella," he said, "always trying to buy girls. The way he talks, he's some kind of trucker, takes the girls out west. I . . . I ain't with that, Sheriff. I just like it when the girls dance. I don't ever touch them."

"Someone said he might be from around here. Is he, Mr. Beavers?"

"He seems to be."

"How do you know?"

"He talks about you all the time."

"He talks about me? Like what?"

He lifted the sheet and wiped his eyes again. "Folks at the bar show around them cell phone tweet things. Last one I seen, he talked about your body. I don't want to say them words."

He hung his head.

"When you go to those parties, Coach Beavers, you're part of that. Even the words."

"I'm sorry, Sheriff."

She was out the door and into the hallway before she understood what still nagged her.

"One more thing, Coach. Then you can rest. You shut that book of newspapers and ran out of the library. You didn't even try to help Mr. Snustead. Why?"

"What that girl said," he answered weakly. He looked toward the window in his room even though a heavy curtain blocked it. "The last time there was any conversation about the night we've been talking about, I got myself busted up almost as good as this, never even saw who hit me, and they got Lyman pretty good too. Coach Clausen kinda sideways let me know my little niece was next, Brandy. Anytime any of them guys gets worried about what they did, it comes down on us Beaverses. When that girl at the library called emergency and then she said Deputy Lund was coming, I shut that book and I scooted."

"Did you talk to Ladonna Weeks after that?"

"I went to get my ticket for the party and she said, 'What's the matter, Coach? You look like Hollow Billy chased you in here.' But no. I didn't say nothing to her about it."

"Does she know there was a murder at the party?"

He still stared away at that thick curtain, thinking about it.

"I'll bet she did. Them are hers and Dermit's parties. She was at that one, serving the drinks that girl was having too many of. I'm gonna guess . . ." He finally looked at her. The fear was unmistakable in his pain-exhausted face. "I'm gonna guess that what happened at their party got known to her and Dermit. Aw, hell, I'm done now. You get on the wrong side of Lund and Clausen and then you add in them two . . ."

On the way out, she called her dispatcher.

"Denise, contact La Crosse PD. Request a guard outside Walt Beavers's room . . ."

———

Hard to say what she thought about on the drive back to Farmstead . . . a swirl of mudslides and floods, signatures on nomination papers, freight trains, bullets exploding from the barrel of her gun, dead girls, live girls, lost girls, the person she was before she was lost, the Dairy Queen, happy and complete, right up to the instant when Mrs. Wisnewski said . . .

As she pulled into her parking spot, where the yellow paint on the asphalt still said SHERIFF R. GIBBS, her headlights struck something sprawled over the cleat. It looked real, and she recoiled with a gasp.

"That's a rattlesnake."

Olaf the Handsome was back from Iowa with everything the Allama-kee County Sheriff's Department had on file and in memory about the disappearance four years ago. He looked somber.

"A rubber rattlesnake. Wearing Sophie Ringensetter's hair clip."

"Why?"

"Hell if I know. Except somebody's leading you."

The sheriff hollered out her office door, "Denise! We need you!"

Yttri dropped the barrette into an evidence bag and dangled the snake by its rattle. It bounced in its coils, dusty and damaged by age but still lifelike. "You're getting led. The necklace. Those photos you received. Now a rubber rattlesnake with a hair clip. The problem with getting led—"

"I know what the problem is."

A headache spiked between her eyes. She reached across the Sophie necklace to pick up her coffee. "If someone had a straight story that checked out, they'd just tell it." She pushed the necklace open with her finger, as if to make room for a head. "This is not that simple."

"Or maybe you're supposed to be intimidated, to back off. You, spe-cifically." Yttri tossed the snake onto her side table. "Which isn't gonna happen, I can see that. Are you ready for what I have?"

She studied him over her foam cup. Was she being led? Or was it simply that Ladonna Weeks and Pinky Clausen believed she could be made to mistrust Harley and give up? But if that were true, why the snake and the barrette, which seemed to lead her toward, not away from, a crime?

"Go ahead," she told Yttri. "Who's the witness?"

"Otto Koenig, of Red Mound. I've met him on dedicated rounds. Odd guy, bachelor, lives alone, about fifty years old, used to be a successful dairy farmer, not anymore, drinks a lot, and three different women in three different counties have filed restraining orders against him. One of them is an ex-wife here in the Bad Axe."

"*Koenig* means 'king' in German," the sheriff said, thinking King Cream.

"Right. So maybe he's our guy. Four years ago, August 12, according to Allamakee, Koenig claimed to have seen a girl who looked like Sophie Ringensetter on the grounds of the Ease Inn the afternoon before the stag party. The detectives I talked to said they weren't sure if they should believe Koenig or not. They suspected him for a while, thought he might be smoke-screening them. I called the number Allamakee gave me on the drive home. Disconnected. I called his ex-wife. She suggested he was dangerous. She also believes he goes to stag parties."

"We'd better pay a visit."

"Right."

As she eased her sore arm into her jacket, her printer started up. She heard, "Yes, my queen, you called?" and Denise entered, spitting Skoal juice into her soda can. It took the sheriff a split-second to recall what she had wanted from her dispatcher.

"Would you please research Angus Beavers for me, find out where he was playing baseball, what the team colors are, whether he might have a big blue bag, and when he left the team to come home?"

"Can do. And now for something digital, by way of inoculation. You ready? So the husband says to the wife, 'We know that Google is a female. And how do we know? Because she starts suggesting things before you can even finish your sentence.'"

Yttri looked quizzical. The sheriff braced herself.

"And the wife answers, 'That must mean Bing is a man, because he tries to convince you he's superior, then does a shit job of pleasing you.'"

Denise continued right through Yttri's chuckle. "News from the cyber world. Grab those printouts."

Sheriff Kick took the pages off the printer.

"Twitter took us seriously. The Jerry Myad profile was phony, like I thought. Get it? Jeremiad? A list of grievances against the world? The best defense is a good offense? Attacking you first? Because you threaten him? The IP log shows those tweets coming from the cell phone of a creep you crossed paths with pretty recently."

Denise's stubborn cheer had vanished. Here came the hard part, apparently. Based on 'pretty recently,' the sheriff was guessing the Rhinegold truck, the snowplow, *The Scream.* "S'more," her old flame Perry Gardner had called the man with the melted face.

"Jerrold Mickelson?"

Denise was surprised. Then she winced. "Oh. Him? He's another monster. But no, not him." She sighed like something was hurting her, something worse that she didn't want to say. "No, it's a guy named Baron Ripp."

"Who's that? I crossed paths with him recently? How do you know?"

"He took a picture of you. Look."

One of the printouts was another Twitter screen shot. To accompany a tweet that said *drag that queen, I got the chain*, the creep with the Twitter handle Jerry Myad had posted a photograph of the sheriff standing behind her kids at the video game along the back wall of the Ease Inn mini-mart while she had been talking to Ladonna Weeks.

Her face burned, but she felt a chill.

"Though funny you should mention Jerrold Mickelson," Denise was saying. Her face had gone blotchy. Her voice sounded out of rhythm. "Because I went vertical on this, down in the direction of hell. One of the websites linked on this Jerry Myad account is Mickelson's, sovereign citizen bullshit with a side of snuff porn. Ripp and Mickelson retweet each other. There's a network of these guys. Ripp took the name Jerry Myad from a character in some nasty internet cartoon they like. In one of those tweets, Ripp says to Mickelson . . ."

She stopped and shuddered.

"Never mind. But it involves a body part of yours . . . and a nozzle . . . and guess how many psi?" Denise had gone red in the face. "If it's a joke, I don't know it yet—but the tweet gets a couple dozen likes."

A weird numbness had swept through the sheriff. She looked up from the picture of herself and her kids. "Either of you know Baron Ripp? I mean personally?"

"Only heard of him," Yttri said. "Big-name family, decent people. Don't know how they made a loser like him. How about you, Denise?"

Denise said nothing. In fact, out of character, she stood frozen, only blinking. At last she forced a little smile. She tried to speak but couldn't. She widened her eyes and blinked fast, then forced a bigger smile, but tears came anyway, filling her lids as she tipped her head back to contain them.

Yttri was turned away, getting his coat on, ready to visit Otto Koenig. He said, "Are you sure you don't know the guy, Denise? Don't you know everybody?"

Denise's lips had curled, bitten from the inside. She still tried to smile, but her face wouldn't play along.

"I'm OK," she said. "I'm fine."

Then she began to tremble, shaking her head *no-no-no* and fighting the tears. Sheriff Kick rose and put her arms around her friend.

Yeah, Denise knew Baron Ripp.

Poor Denise, she *knew* him.

Yttri had frozen with his coat collar rucked up around his head. He let the jacket slide down over his shoulders. "Maybe I should step out . . ."

Denise scorched him. "You think? You think I'm not freaking naked here?"

53

Pepper Greengrass screams her silent oath under water.

You can't hurt me!

Her cheek hits the rim of the tall plastic bucket. Her ear rakes the bail attachment. He drives her down, always a triple dunk, like there is a school of thought that he follows, a training for this that he has attended.

This is the fourth overall time that he has drowned her within the slow, rain-drilling hours. In between he smokes and raises the bottle neck to sip Dickel while she lies gasping on her back beside the bucket and the dirt becomes mud. He has brought out the sack of items he bought at the store and arrayed them on the picnic table: Bic pens, baby wipes, a snap-blade box cutter. He rants. One time in the middle of the goddamn night a lady got into his wallet. One time this poor dumb cunt believed she could run. One time four of his ladies got in a catfight over who was his favorite and the beaner bitch lost an eye to the jig bitch who thought she could damage his property but she had another thing coming, yes, she did. And speaking of property, one time this sad cock-hat thought it was hers to give away, and so he corrected her and it wasn't his fault she couldn't take what she deserved.

Pepper hears all this looking up into two bright black eyes, a cliff swallow silent in its mud nest in the shelter roof. She stares into those alert black beads. Then he jerks from a Dickel daydream, the bird shoots from the nest, and Pepper can't hold back a sob.

"There we go, darlin'. That's what I'm waiting to hear. Now you're getting the idea."

He reaches with his boot, the point of it, and just nudges her nipple, cold and tented up beneath her wet top. He leaves his boot there.

"See? Practice makes perfect."

As if he's been teaching her to swim, like there is a life skill here, important for her to know. She will never sob again, ever. She seeks out her memory of the time when Bennie really was teaching her to swim.

It becomes the afternoon of that game up here, hot August . . . and they stop at a river along the way to cool off. The Kickapoo River. The Here-and-There River, in the language her ancestors spoke. She is laughing because Bennie himself swims terribly, tries to do it in blue jeans, like any Ho-Chunk ever, and he can't even put his head under water, skims his face across the slow brown Kickapoo current and comes up sputtering and slinging his hair. In an hour Pepper swims better than he ever will, like an otter, he says. She attacks his ankles with fingernail bites from under water, sends him screaming back to the shore. They sit there getting warm and dry, twelve years old and twenty, and Bennie says, *I love you, girl.* He says, *If the current ever gets you, don't fight it, just go with it, keep your head up, keep breathing, stay alive, everything washes up eventually. I love you.* They drive on, and then, like the total freak that Bennie was, he hits six home runs. *Six!*

"That's a good girl. Real nice and easy." He draws his boot back from her nipple. "Now get them clothes off and wash up. You got a whole bucket of washup right there. Go on."

He watches her strip nude. He staggers, half the Dickel bottle inside him. He picks up her muddy clothes, walks off into a lull in the rain, and hurls them off the black edge of something. She hears them slapping down through tree branches. He comes back out of the dark passing that snap-off blade through the flame of his Zippo. He tells her to lie facedown on the table. She feels his high beams shining up her ass, feels his shirttail dry the skin above her tailbone where the fat lady wrote with the Sharpie, feels him use a baby wipe, then spit Dickel on the spot and trace what the fat lady wrote with his finger. Then Pepper feels the blade.

"Just you relax, darlin'. This is gonna take awhile."

54

"Shit!"

Her face against the sheriff's shoulder, Denise snarled to stop herself from crying.

"Like you said, Heidi. We don't have time for this!"

The sheriff turned her head to keep her chin clear of the bitter-smelling frizz of her dispatcher's perm. Her view now was of the rubber rattlesnake on her side table. If she was supposed to understand what the snake represented, she did not. Denise pushed away.

"But seriously, what is wrong with me? Am I not the biggest ATV you ever heard of?"

"I don't know what that means, but—"

"All-terrain vagina! Come on, Heidi. Baron Ripp! You read what he wrote about you. I screwed that piece of shit! On a picnic table!"

She pulled away. Her mascara had smudged from the corners of her eyes.

"I'm fine. Never mind. A day in the life of Denise. We don't have time for this." She reached for the tissue box on the sheriff's desk. "But, Heidi . . . while we're here?"

"Yes?"

Beyond the wall came the sound of coins trickling, then a *thunk*. Olaf the Handsome was getting a soda. Denise gave Yttri time to move away. When he was gone, she said, "While we're alone for a minute, I have to ask you a favor."

"Sure. I owe you like crazy."

"Well . . . it's . . . OK, here's the favor. Please don't fuck up."

"What?"

Denise blew her nose. "I want you to be the sheriff, Heidi. I need you to be the sheriff. If you're not the sheriff, then either Boog Lund cans my ass, day one, or I rip his balls off, day two, and I cram them down his throat. The whole Bad Axe needs you to be sheriff just about that bad. You gotta be the sheriff, Heidi. Please do not fuck up."

"How am I . . . ?"

Denise just looked at her, eyebrows raised.

"OK, I know. I lied about last night."

Here came Yttri's change, rattling through the machine. Olaf the Handsome was still out there. Had he heard? Now he would go. The sheriff gave him time. Then more time.

"I lied. I do remember what happened. I got my wires crossed. I've been that way since Bishops Coulee. I can barely stay professional, and there's more than you know, even worse than pulling on Randy Brundgart. I'm a danger to myself and others."

Denise shook her head no, then yes. The sheriff let a long silence pass.

"You know the guy from the hospital this morning? Brock Pabst? He's the one who beat up Walt Beavers. I was going to kill him last night. I chased him and I ended up in the river. I wanted to kill him this morning. I've been out of control."

Denise nodded and reached out to touch her shoulder, nodding to keep her talking.

"These people seek nothing. The boy zombies steal shit that amounts to nothing and hurt people for no reason. The girl zombies take their clothes off for strangers and they feel nothing. What do they get? What do they want? It's all about nothing."

Denise waited, still nodding.

"Fuck all this nothing. I'm at war with it."

"Yes," Denise said finally. "Yes, you are. And I can't blame you. But the favor is, Heidi, before it's too late, please stop."

She thought a soda can cracked in the hallway. She thought she heard hissing, drips on the tile. Was Yttri still out there? She waited, heard nothing more.

Denise said, "Can you listen now?"

"I can try."

"You have to stop. People are talking. The Randy Brundgart thing. Your cruiser in the river. Then Skog comes up here from Crawford County, and supposedly you're suing them. The board is taking notice. You can't go around in a cloud of secret vengeance investigating a closed case from another county, not on Bad Axe time, and not on your own time either. It doesn't matter about Bishops Coulee, it doesn't matter if you might be right and there's a killer still out there, it doesn't matter if you're wearing blue jeans and driving a minivan with your kids and pretending not to be the Bad Axe County sheriff. You *are* the Bad Axe County sheriff, and you need to stay that way."

Denise stopped for breath. She took the sheriff by the shoulders.

"Heidi, nobody is cutting you slack for your pain from the past. You're in charge here. You're the boss. It's not OK to be trigger happy. It's not OK to drive into the river and not remember why. You can either do this job or you can't. We need you to do it, we need you to file for the election, but if you can't separate the past from the present, even the people who support you are going to freak the fuck out. I wouldn't vote for you either. And Lund will flush your entire career down the toilet. He would love nothing more."

Denise had moved to the window. She used her reflection against the rainstorm to dab up her smudged mascara. "OK? So here's the plan," she said. "So that you don't fuck this up, here is what I'm asking you to do."

The sheriff waited uneasily. Was that the squeak of Yttri's shoes? She took a step closer to the door, cocked her ear.

"Give me the list."

"What?"

"I know you have a list."

"List?"

"Harley called. He told me. You have a list of names and you're going through it. He gave me the idea. Your suspects. Your zombies. Your war plan. Guys who could have killed your mom and dad. Give it to me."

"But . . ."

Denise scowled as she loaded in a dip of Skoal. Her bottom lip swelled. "Give me the goddamn list. I mean it."

"But what would you do?"

"Are you kidding me?"

Denise found her can and spit with force.

"Are you fucking kidding me, Heidi? You think I don't have a talent for sniffing out the very worst men in a tricounty area. I got this. And nobody will know a thing. Do your job."

In relief, the sheriff's shoulders fell, her eyes filled, and she closed them.

"I'll give you a thumb drive tomorrow."

"Good girl. Now let's get back to work."

The sheriff stopped at the door. She lifted the rubber rattlesnake from her side table and dangled it. "By the way, any idea what this means?"

Denise was surprised. Then she made a face and she nodded. Yes, of course she knew.

The sheriff was still trying to wrap her head around such a sad and degrading idea. A visit to a cave, a rattlesnake named Buster Hymen Johnson, bare breasts, a photograph, and then you were a Cave Girl, which apparently earned you the right to be exclusively molested.

"The point, Denise thinks, is that the snake is kept in a cave on Rush Creek."

"OK," Yttri said. "I think I know where that is."

"As a reformed Cave Girl herself, she's almost positive that it's the same snake. At least it's one just like it. Either way, she thinks the intention is to tell me I should go to the cave. She said it's on Faulkner's land upstream from the bridge over Bottom Road. Is that the one you're thinking of?"

"I fish through there a couple times a year," he said. "I know it well."

She and Olaf the Handsome both fell quiet for a while. They were getting close to Otto Koenig's place.

"I know you know this," Yttri said at last, "but you've had people throwing curves at you since this whole thing started. I'm not sure you want to get led. You want to stay under control."

She glanced at him. Stay under control? Had he heard from the hallway?

There was no vehicle on the premises of Koenig's small ridgetop farm. No one answered the door when they knocked.

"Let's check the barn," the sheriff said.

They stepped back into the rain. It rattled off their yellow slickers as they passed through the barnyard. It smelled like fresh manure, so Koenig still had an animal or two. Sure enough, they heard hoof-sucking noises in the dark. Then they could see spots of white through the rainy gloom. Then some plane in the darkness was broken by three massive black-and-white creatures with steaming nostrils and rolling eight-ball eyes, hungry for attention, bowing the barbed-wire fence for a scratch on the nose.

Yttri paused to satisfy one. He said, "It's almost like someone has figured out how to get under your skin, how to make you dangerous to yourself."

Yes, she was thinking, and it's almost like someone lingered in the hallway.

55

She updated Olaf the Handsome on Walt Beavers's story as they drove toward Otto Koenig's place in Red Mound. The warm rain was surging and ebbing. Every low spot on the road sent up a huge splash. Here and there Yttri had to steer around a minor mudslide or a tree limb in the road.

"Rattlers players?" he repeated. "They gang-raped her, then killed her?" He couldn't quite believe it yet. "And they tried to pin it on Walt and Lyman Beavers? What was the deal again?"

"Walt Beavers got to be a Rattlers coach. The kid, Angus, went away to an expensive baseball academy. And for that, Lyman Beavers would take care of the body. His brother is not sure what he did with it."

Yttri processed this through a long curve where the road was half under water. "And now jumping to the present," he said, "Walt Beavers confirmed that Pepper Greengrass was at the party. And he's seen King Cream doing business on Backpage.com."

"He thinks the guy is from around here, like Kling thought."

Her deputy slowed, looking through his wipers for a turn. "Dark out here. I'm sorry if I made Denise upset, pushing her about Ripp. But she'd seen that rubber rattlesnake before?"

"Right. Personal experience. It's a team thing. Some kind of initiation for girls who want to show their loyalty to the Rattlers. It goes back a ways, Denise thought maybe thirty or more years, back to the eighties sometime. She knows it from the late nineties."

"You're the one in charge," he went on. "We're all in trouble if you get your wires crossed. Lund will ruin you."

That made her eye him sideways, frowning beneath the cowl of her slicker. He scratched the cow's nose. "This job can really trigger your emotions."

She couldn't contain it anymore. "You know, it's nice that you left me and Denise alone. Thanks for that. Emotion makes us stronger. It's something men don't get."

"OK. You're welcome."

She shined her flashlight at the side of her deputy's face, bisected by his dripping hood. The cow began to lick the sleeve of his rain slicker.

"You had no business listening."

"Listening? I got a soda. Then I took a call in the dispatch room. Some guy jackknifed a horse trailer over a gully in Dutch Hollow. A flash flood hit him broadside, flipped the trailer, which torqued the truck onto its side . . ."

He finally put a hand up to block the beam. "I'm not sure what I'm doing wrong here."

She kept the beam on him. The cow's twelve-inch tongue got too close to Yttri's face. He backed away. She sighed and released him. "Never mind."

She moved her beam across the door of Koenig's small, tilted barn. Its emptiness chilled her, and it looked about to collapse. She shined her light up the road. She listened to her deputy exhale, like he was waiting to see if he was safe to continue. He finally did.

"Koenig isn't here. If he was, his cows wouldn't act like this. His vehicle's gone. We'd be better off canvassing the bars."

"No," she said. "Take me there."

"Where?"

"To that cave."

She sensed his hesitation. "What?"

"There are a lot of rubber snakes, Sheriff. There are a lot of psychos and haters out there too. And you know somebody's been messing with you."

She put her flashlight back in his face. He said, "I'm just saying maybe we should stick with basic police work and find Koenig first. And with flash floods, I don't think we should try to get to that cave tonight. It's dangerous even at low water in the daylight."

"Let's go."

Yttri looked at her too long.

"Lead me, Deputy."

He winced as he shrugged. "Somebody sure is."

56

She rode with Yttri across the Red Mound ridge and down into Snake Hollow, her second visit in two nights. The storm clouds bellied low, dropped sheets of rain, and it was all dark along the sluicing gravel roads, the headlights of Yttri's Tahoe boring like drill bits through the drop-speckled black. He stopped at a bridge where the swollen Bad Axe River boiled through the upstream guardrail and skimmed at uncertain depth over the road. They got out and looked.

"If we cross this," Yttri judged, "we may not get back."

She splashed out to the center, surprised at the push of the water as it flooded into her boots. "It's only hubcap-deep. Let's go."

"Sheriff, I don't know."

He shined his flashlight upstream. Normally a dainty spring-fed river, the Bad Axe looked ominously wide and flat and brown. The lower boughs of stream-bank trees swept and bounced on the current. Heavy flotsam spun through Yttri's beam.

"I think we should turn around and see if we can get in from the other direction. Maybe that South Fork bridge isn't breached."

Her boots squished as she passed him. "Let's go."

Yttri's gaze lingered on the swollen Bad Axe as he folded back into his cruiser. His Tahoe forded the floodwater. In the next hollow, he slowed at another inundated bridge, this one overcome by Rush Creek, a few miles upstream from where it fed the Bad Axe. Taillights receded ahead of them, disappeared in the rain.

"This is it?"

"This is the other end of Faulkner's land right here. That's Rush Creek. That cave is on the creek, up that canyon. No way we should go up there."

"Lead on."

"Sheriff, this could cut loose any minute. That canyon could fill up in seconds. That cave will be under water."

"With a girl in it, if I'm guessing right, maybe Pepper Greengrass. Let's go."

"We can't leave the cruiser this close—"

"You wanna wait here and watch it? Catch me when I come floating down? Or just park it uphill a little?"

She hiked behind him up the ill-used road, so narrow that branches raked their shoulders. The road penetrated dense woods for several hundred yards, staying just above the creek's flooded margins. Then the canyon tightened and the road elevated to rocky ground, continuing on crumbling road cuts that must have been traveled by horse-drawn milk trollies and logging sleds. The roar of the creek below was deafening. At last Yttri stopped. His tone was neutral.

"The trail goes down here."

He shined his flashlight down the ravine side of the road.

"The cave is on the other side of the creek."

She followed his beam down a steep tumble of brush and rocks. A hundred feet below, mud-brown water coursed from right to left, its pace measured by a length of shattered tree that spun through the beam.

"A flash flood will fill this ravine. All these side gullies are draining the ridgetops, all the farmland up there. It's a timing thing. It all hits at once. This will fill up in seconds."

He held his light on the spot where the trail met the water and disappeared beneath foam.

She thrust her phone toward him. "Hold my beer."

"Ha. Sure." She saw his perfect teeth, bared in an anxious smile. "Sheriff, seriously—"

"Oh, I'm totally serious. When you fish, how do you get down there?"

"On my ass. I use a stick. Look, there's just way too much water. And it's only getting started. This is not worth the risk, Sheriff."

"A stick like this?" she asked him, grabbing a broken branch and heading down.

57

She unsnapped her own flashlight at the bottom and shined it on Rush Creek at close range. She was a coulee girl. She had seen high water. She had once forded Cress Creek on her family's farm after ten inches of rain had flashed the creek out of its banks and separated a week-old calf from its mother. Nothing about that rescue had been pretty. Maybe in some ways it was stupid. She had cut herself on something under water, and she had badly dislocated her thumb. But she had brought the calf back.

At close range the creek was opaque with mud, fast and inscrutable. It could be two feet deep or ten. But either way it was no more than twenty feet across, and her beam reached the cave, about four feet above a foam-swirled eddy. There, an overhanging lip of limestone looked eroded by the oily touch of human handprints. A shoe, half charred by fire, bobbed in the eddy, nearly caught by the pell-mell current before it spun back upstream past the gulping throat of the cave. She put her stick in the water ahead of her and stepped in.

She was drowning instantly. The current flipped her so fast that she was midinhale when her face hit the water, quicker than her brain could stop her diaphragm. Water rushed into her lungs, and as she was tossed downstream she had no chance to open her mouth and expel it. This was drowning, so sudden, this was what drowning felt like—this stifled coughing, this retching stuck inside her, her own air exploding in her neck and face and blowing up inside a brain that launched signals that her helpless body could not answer. She was drowning.

She spun and her legs struck a rock. The current stood her up—for a split-second she inhaled more water—and then the water's power tossed her headfirst. Now she was somersaulting, her hands raking up the stream bottom, the current a thousand times stronger than gravity or her own failing grasp.

Next, a lightning bolt inside her heart muscle, a dull chill after it. She spun, losing awareness, the water feeling strangely hot as she drifted feetfirst with her arms and legs loose, her eyes open on nothing . . . then jarred back to consciousness by a sticky, bristly sensation, the pressure of the current folding her against the fulcrum of her waist, bending her up into sharp objects.

Then her blind head emerged. She twisted with all her strength and grabbed anything while the water levered her until she thought her spine would snap. At last she was pushed as far as she could be pushed. Her eyes came open. The current had jammed her into the madly jittering top of a downed tree, beside another body.

She heard Yttri hollering. She coughed water, vomited so hard it burst into her ear canals. She fought her head around to see. The current pinned her to another body. Side to side. A small body, cold and bent. A girl's gray eyes gazing into hers.

She ripped the dead girl through branches, dragged her halfway ashore by her thick and mealy ankles. Was this Pepper Greengrass? Yttri's light flashed. He was working downstream, hanging on to limbs and brush.

It seemed like forever that she hung on to the body rather than protect herself as she was shoved and bumped along by the rising creek. She hit a tree, sieved through a submerged thicket of buckthorn or wild rose, took a cruising deadfall branch to the back of the head. Then Yttri got there. He pulled her ashore by her uniform belt. He put his beam on the body as it hung facedown across her lap.

"Look," he panted. "Look at that."

Etched crudely with a knife into the small of the girl's back, written in wormy old welts: *KING CREAM*.

She was a short-legged blonde. She was half frozen. This was Sophie Ringensetter. And King Cream, whoever he was, wherever he was now, had Pepper Greengrass.

58

He spits, cuts, wipes. He smears ink, wipes, hisses Dickel through his teeth. He cuts, smears ink, wipes, spits Dickel. He tells her one time this silly little cuntling forgot who she belonged to and thought these young pricks were hot shit and thought it was hers to give away and how did Pepper think that idea worked out for little miss cuntling? That's right, not at all.

"You're mine now."

"I know."

"You're lucky."

"I know that."

———

Later, inside his sleeper cab, she can't lie on her back, on the fresh tattoo. She has to take him on her hands and knees. He keeps the light on. Whatever he does back there is brief and drunkenly performed and leaves him sucking air through his ruined lungs. When she turns around his shirt is hanging open on that silver pistol holstered in the pit of his chest.

"You ain't never been loved like that before."

"I know," she says. "I know that."

"You had more than you could handle."

"Way more. I know."

He buttons his shirt. He smacks the light off and collapses beside her.

Several dark and heavy minutes later he is confessing in gasps that he is bad sometimes, but not as bad as he seems, because he just needs to be respected. People need respect. Why can't people just respect each other the way they're supposed to? He's bad sometimes, but that's only what he does, not what he is. Respect him, everything is fine. Why won't she say anything?

"I know," she whispers.

"I understand," she purrs.

"Shhh," she soothes him as her fingers travel in a searching caress. She finds the box cutter retracted in his back pocket, slips it out and palms it, easy.

———

Later again, all is black inside the sleeper. The rain stops tapping. Coyotes begin to howl. Then from somewhere below she hears a *whip-poor-will, whip-poor-will, whip-poor-will,* relentless in the greater darkness.

I have the blade. Pepper sings along toward dawn. *I have the blade, I have the blade, I have the blade.*

59

The rain stopped. Barn owls hooted. Coyotes hollered behind the scrap yard. Angus heard the whip-poor-will up on Battle Bluff. He said, "Dad, come on. I left her over in the cave on Faulkner's and tried to help the new sheriff find her. Now come on."

"Next snufbitch tries Lyman Beavers is gonna take a waterslide."

"OK. Sure. But let's get somewhere safe."

"Down this pipe, whoosh, all the way from here to Norlins."

His dad was reeling on his pills. He was feeling no pain. "I'm going to get Brandy," Angus told him. "We got her friend's car still. We'll go over to the Pronto station in Bishops Coulee. They're open all night. Let's get some of those mini egg rolls and a soda. We'll just stay in there for now and be safe."

"You know who. Flush that fat snufbitch like a turd."

"Let's go."

Angus stood exhausted in the waning dark and listened to the bird calling from the bluff beyond the meadow. *Whip-poor-will, whip-poor-will, whip-poor will, whip-poor-will*. He remembered being up at the outlook with Boog Lund just hours ago, looking down here. So close but so far.

"Come on, Dad. Before you fall in and go to New Orleans yourself. Leave that. That ain't gonna work. Come on."

When he came home from the cave, Angus had found his dad slinging more of other people's garbage down his waterslide, or so he thought at first. By now a torrent of meltwater crashed through the pipe. It roared two hundred yards beneath the scrap and under the road. It was too dark to see yet, but Angus could hear it disgorging from the pipe mouth, a retching spew of sound, gushing and splattering into the meadow. But instead of sending garbage down to Bishops Coulee, his dad had claimed to be making a trap.

"Lookit this," he said again proudly.

"That ain't really gonna work," Angus said. "Let's go."

"Hell it ain't. Your granddaddy Beavers used to pit trap black bear back when there was black bear in here. He caught one too. Me and Walter killed it throwing rocks."

He had stretched a tattered sheet of canvas across the hole above the opening in the pipe. He had weighted the corners with tires. When Angus had first found him up here, he was feebly kicking clots of mud and gravel onto the canvas, trying to make it look like the scrap yard ground around it, the way you disguised a pit trap. Now he twisted out of Angus's grip and kicked more. The canvas slipped its corner weights, crumpled down, and with a whoosh it was sucked away down the pipe, gone. His dad had more old canvas. Feebly he began to shake it out.

"Dad, they're going to find her body now. I waited in that quarry off Bottom Road. I saw a sheriff's car, and two of them went up there."

"Your granddad got a lot of deer too, ain't wasn't any season. That way the government never heard any gunshots."

"Word is going to get out fast. We can't stay here."

"Sawdust," said his dad. "Fetch me a barrow of that goddamn sawdust in the Quonset."

Now down the west end of Lost Hollow came headlights.

"Dad—"

As the vehicle pulled under the pink spray of the yard light, Angus could see it was the same faded-red pickup with the snowplow blade that he had seen from up on Battle Bluff, when Boog Lund had kept him away from home while his dad and Brandy got hurt. And he hadn't got Brandy out of the house yet.

He ran. In his headlamp-jarred field of vision, a figure in a hooded sweatshirt nearly fell from the pickup. He got his balance. Angus kept running. The figure reached back into the pickup and took out a gas can. He had trouble holding on to the can. Angus kept coming. Now one arm was looped through the gas can handle. It hung from his elbow like a purse while his two hands weirdly gripped a pistol and he tottered toward the house. He hadn't shut his truck off. Angus hollered at him. "Hey!" He turned and fired and Angus twisted to avoid it, a batter's box pirouette, a bullet at a thousand feet per second. He was hit before he moved.

He was down, dazed, hearing that gun banging off inside the house. He forced himself up. Two more shots. He was on his feet. No pain yet. As he hunched toward the porch he heard a fourth shot. He lifted one of the cinder-block steps—now he felt a scorch of pain—but he hung on and took the block with him, a heavy, sharp-cornered weapon wielded in his big fist, that pain exploding into rage. A fifth shot from the gun.

Inside, that gas can spun on its side on the kitchen floor, draining out amid the hoarded trash. Angus heard a scuffle in the hallway to the bedrooms, Brandy still alive because now she was screaming. He found her riding the attacker's back while he staggered. His hood was off. He had no hair, no ears, no nose. He had holes. Brandy's fingers plugged those holes like the holes in a bowling ball and she rode him as he lurched backward and slammed her into the wall.

Brandy lost her grip. He flung her off. As he turned to finish her with the gun—clumsily, his fingers short and webbed with bright pink flesh—Angus gathered off his back foot and swung the cinder block against the side of his head. The blow dropped him on the spot, a sack of flesh inside his clothes.

"Come on, Brandy. Come on, let's go."

"That's S'more. That's mine and Brock's friend."

He lay there twitching, muttering filth, his face like melted wax around those holes. Gasoline trickled under him. Angus saw movement at his side, those half fingers snapping at a lighter. He stomped the hand, crushed the bones, splintered the lighter.

"Come on."

He pushed Brandy outside.

"Where's Dad?"

"Up the yard. Messing around. I'll go get him." Angus bent where the bullet had struck him. "Get into his truck. He left it running."

"That was S'more. Yesterday he said don't tell no one he was here or he'd kill me."

"Today he came to do it."

"But he was mine and Brock's friend."

"Get in that truck. I'm fetching Dad. That won't be the last of it."

He shoved her at the truck. He pulled his shirt up, saw a crease of open flesh above his hip. It hurt but not enough to stop him. At the top of the scrap yard, his dad had covered the hole over the pipe again, anchored more canvas with more tires. He had wheelbarrowed moldy sawdust from the heap in the Quonset shed. He had scattered the sawdust over the canvas. As Angus saw it in the dim predawn, as a pit trap it did not look half bad.

"Let's go."

"Get some chairs."

"Dad—"

"This is gonna be a good show."

"We gotta go somewhere."

"Hell no. Get some chairs. We know who's coming next. We're gonna watch that snufbitch take a ride."

He strutted the uphill side of his trap, cocking his unswollen eye at the road. Angus touched his wound and winced. His hand came back bloody. "He ain't gonna step on your damn trap, Dad. He's just going to shoot you."

"Naw, he ain't gonna shoot me. That ain't his style." His dad wheezed a laugh. "Snufbitch is gonna come up here making threats and trying to cut another deal with me. He don't think enough of me to shoot me. But this time he's gonna take a ride all the way to Norlins, dead as a crawdad in a coon turd. Go and call him up."

———

That melted face gasped in the hallway. His twitching body had sponged up spilled gas. Angus pickup up his pistol and opened the cylinder. There was one round left. He pushed the cylinder back in place. He rolled the wax man over, slapped his pockets, found his phone. His last received text said *Go finish it*. Angus touched the number.

"We're still here," he said. "We want to talk."

"Who does? Who is this?"

Angus held the phone away and shot the man with the wax face through his forehead. His brains blew back across the floor, greasy and pink, spreading in the puddle of gas. Angus brought the phone back in.

"Beavers," he told Boog Lund.

Sophie Ringensetter thawed in lurid brightness on the logging road.

The Bishops Coulee Volunteer Fire Department, deploying ATVs that towed utility trailers, had brought in a generator and floodlights. Deputy Eleffson circled the body with an evidence camera, while Schwem led VFD searchers along the near side of the raging creek. She had taken Yttri's Tahoe keys and sent him on foot upstream to find a crossing point over smaller water. If he could get down the other side and into the cave, the sheriff would send more people to search it. Vernon County was sending mutual aid deputies. She had alerted Groetzner's Funeral Home, the de facto county morgue. The county coroner, Herb Elder, was on his way to Groetzner's to wait for a body that he would not know what to do with. Time of death: four years ago.

The sheriff was on hold for Rick Rogers, the sheriff in Allamakee County, Iowa. Sheriff Rogers came on. Their connection wasn't good.

"I need you to notify family," she told him, "and send someone to the morgue over here."

"Aww, God . . . those poor people . . ."

She felt it too, swallowed a surge of sadness. "We need a positive ID. It seems like she was frozen and just moved to where we found her. She still has all her basic features. There may still be physical evidence preserved."

"Aww . . . hell. . . . God help us . . ."

Deputies Bench and Dowel had been called on duty early, overtime issues be damned. Crawford County had agreed to help with flood-related calls and traffic as much as they could. All this time, the sheriff's mind had been on Pepper Greengrass—and on Angus Beavers, who was coming into focus as part of this. That was him at Clausen Meats, she felt sure now, trying to put Sophie Ringensetter into the freezer. She gave Deputy Dowel control of the crime scene and hiked back out to Bottom Road. There she had a shock. Rush Creek had swallowed the bridge. It flowed a hundred feet wide, only the bridge's reflector posts sticking up. She took Yttri's Tahoe.

On the ridgetop, as she detoured south to pick up U.S. 14, the long way around to Lost Hollow Road, her phone stirred against her skittering heart. A message had drifted in from sometime earlier in the night. "Heidi," Harley began through static, "I'm sorry if I haven't told you everything you need to know. I guess there's a lot of bad stuff that I just want to deny is out there, because I can't stand thinking that you might have to deal with it. But I'm going to try. I'm sorry. I love you." He paused and there was background noise. "OK, kiddies, hit it."

They sang her "Llama Llama Red Pajama" until the connection was lost. She covered the wet highway sniffling and gripping the wheel so tightly that her elbows went numb.

Then Denise was calling.

"OK, Heidi. Here's what I have. Angus Beavers played for the Jacksonville Jumbo Shrimp. They say he just disappeared two days ago. They say he had a big blue gear bag."

"OK. That was him. I was just now heading to the junkyard. "

"But also, Heidi?"

"Go ahead."

"We found Otto Koenig."

———

The most recent wave of rain had just stopped as she finished the circuitous drive and pulled into the Kwik Trip in Zion. A disheveled man slumped at one of the two small café tables inside, scratching his way through an impressive stack of lottery tickets.

"Been here all night," the clerk said.

He looked harmless, depressed, and exhausted. It was hard to imagine he had the willpower to commit any crime, let alone two acts of sexual violence. Still, she approached warily.

"These are the fresh ones," he informed her as she arrived at his table. "I been waiting on the fresh ones."

"I need to see some ID, please."

He had his driver's license out already. That was interesting, as if he knew she was coming. Yes, this was Otto Koenig.

"Today is when the fresh ones come in. The fresh ones are the best."

"The scratch-off tickets get stale, do they?"

"They get the stink on them."

"The stink."

"Yes, ma'am, the stink."

"Mr. Koenig, Allamakee County has a report from four years ago saying you saw a girl at the Ease Inn, a runaway, somebody they were looking for."

"I used to get my fresh tickets at the Ease Inn. Now the delivery stops here first."

"Mr. Koenig, listen," she said sharply. She waited for his attention. "You're a witness in an Allamakee County sheriff's report about a missing girl a few years ago. Yes?"

He slumped more deeply over his tickets, looking down at them. "Yes."

"Can you tell me what you saw?"

"A little blond girl with blue hairpins."

"How did you know they were looking for her?"

"I saw her picture at the Pronto station over in Lansing," he said and sighed deeply, "where I get my fresh Iowa tickets. I saw her face on a poster and recognized her from seeing her at the Ease Inn. I called it in to Allamakee." He began to grip his oily hair. "They sent a deputy to Red Mound to talk to me."

Was he nervous? Lying? She couldn't tell. She took a half step back and put her hands to her belt. For now, keep him talking.

"When you saw her at the Ease Inn, she was doing what?"

"Oh, yeah, well, she was hanging around, chatting with a fella next to his pickup. It looked like he was mad at her. He kept pulling her by the neck and kinda hissing at her." He looked up with sad eyes. Did he want her to pity him? Or chase someone else?

"What else did you see?"

"I came back out with my tickets, he had got her inside his truck."

"Did you know who he was?"

"I didn't."

"But you told Allamakee what he was doing with the girl?"

"Yes, I did."

"You described the man?"

"Yes, I did. Kinda long hair in the back, I guess. Mustache that went down around his mouth. Jeans, boots."

The sheriff looked away. Otto Koenig had just described half the young men in Bad Axe County, including just about any player on the Rattlers, including her own husband. It was an easy lie, if he was telling one.

"Can you describe his truck?"

"I didn't pay attention to it."

"You talked to the deputy from Allamakee County on August 13. Did Allamakee ever come back and talk to you again?"

"No," he said. "But later that day Sheriff Gibbs did."

That startled her. Gibbs did?

"And you told Sheriff Gibbs?"

"No, Sheriff Gibbs told *me*. He came out to my place to tell me that they found the girl and not to worry about it. Later the same day Deputy Lund stopped by and said the same thing. They were both in street clothes, just dropping by neighborly. She was found, they both told me, don't worry."

"So you didn't worry about it."

"Until now."

Otto Koenig looked up at her with surprising clear intensity. No, he wasn't lying. No, he was not King Cream.

"Ma'am, I know you're talking to me about that little girl for some reason. And I'm guessing it's because those two sonsofbitches took off their badges, Gibbs and Lund, and lied to me."

"Yes. They did. We found that girl's body a few hours ago. She was murdered."

"Then . . ." He fiddled with his tickets, stacking and restacking. "Then it's a good deal that I can tell you who he was, this fella who acted like he owned her."

"You just said you didn't know who he was."

"I'm not a liar, ma'am. I'm a lotta things. You probably looked me up and you know that. But I didn't know who he was at the time when Allamakee asked me. Then I did, the next day, after Sheriff Gibbs and Boog Lund talked to me. But by then it didn't matter who he was, if the girl was found OK, which is what they told me and what I believed. It wasn't no longer any of my business."

His eyes had clouded. He was tearing up, stung by the girl's death and by the lie that Gibbs and Lund had told him.

"I need the name. And how you know it."

"I won a hundred bucks on a Powerball ticket. I went back to the Ease Inn the next day to cash it. I saw that same fella gassing up his truck. Black truck, now that I paid attention. He was going somewhere. It looked like everything he owned was in the back of that truck. Just to be friendly I said, 'Off to seek your fortune, I guess.'"

Suddenly her face burned and she could hardly hear his voice. Harley had been driving from Middleton to the Bad Axe for Rattlers games. They had two new babies, were outfitting a double nursery. He had been hauling back furniture from the estate of an uncle who had passed away, using an old black Ford F-250.

Koenig continued, "Well, that fella just about shaved my ass with the look he gave me. I got inside the store, I was just curious, so I asked the clerk who the gentleman was. She said, 'Him?'"

The sheriff's breath stuck.

"She said, 'Him? That's no gentleman, that's Baron Ripp.'"

She blinked at Otto Koenig, her mind already racing away.

"The Ripps of Dutch Hollow," he went on, "the youngest son of Roger Ripp. I heard his dad ran him out for using drugs and stealing. He used to truck cattle. You know who I mean?"

She was all the way out of the Kwik Trip and into Yttri's Tahoe, already with an idea of how to find Baron Ripp, when she said to no one, "Yeah . . . yeah . . . I know who you mean."

A bad old idea had just become her best new one. She turned her cruiser toward the Rolling Ground Shooting Range and smashed the gas.

DAYBREAK

Cindy Lemke @groundbeef
@BadAxeCountySheriff don't listen to the haters,
you are a real bad axe #dairyqueen #yougogirl

61

He snores sprawled across her legs, across the sleeper doorway, his arms crossed over the pistol at his chest.

Pepper Greengrass waits for daylight.

Waits. Waits.

Listens to the *whip-poor-will, whip-poor-will, whip-poor-will.*

Breathes in his Dickel sweat, his fungal feet, his tavern-Dumpster exhalations. Her brother Bennie told her if the current takes you, go with it. Don't fight it if it's too strong, just go with it. *Keep your head up, keep breathing, everything washes up eventually.*

———

At last the new day breaks for Pepper, first as a linty gray that fills the half-moon window of his sleeper, then as a column of lighter darkness breaking over the lump of him where the sleeper opens into the tractor cab. Within minutes the whip-poor-will shuts down and in the plain new light she can see his face better than she wants to, a fortysomething hag of a man with bad teeth, big ears, lips flapping as he snores.

Pepper has the box cutter. She catches the tab with her thumb and snicks the point out. The blade is made to break off in brittle half inches. But she could cut an artery. She pictures the slash, his oily blood, the fight for the gun. But go with the flow, Bennie said.

She sits up, crosses her legs, watches him, snicking the blade point in and out. She has no clothes on. The carving on her back is hot and sticky. It stings. But what is the flow? This is what she waits to know.

Now she has it. So many times she has reviewed how it all blew back on her with her stepdad, Felton Henry. Now she sees the flow is trust. The flow is *he* gets out first. Everything changes then. If he gets out first, because he trusts her, his choice becomes chase her or chase his truck. And men, as Pepper knows them . . .

She nudges him awake.

"I found this."

"Huh?"

Into the shaft of gray light she extends the palm of her hand with the box cutter on it, its blade drawn into the yellow plastic sheath still crusted with blood and ink from her back.

"I found this. I guess it fell out of your pocket. Don't you want it?"

He pries up on an elbow. He pats his chest to feel the gun. God, what a rat-faced little shit he is, squinting at the knife, finally taking it. He returns it to his back pocket and falls back asleep. Afloat in the flow, Pepper waits.

62

She felt less sure as she sped toward Crawford County. A horrific old idea had become the best new one she could think of.

She was Heidi White then, fallen Dairy Queen. Twelve years ago, lost in grief and rage, high on booze and weed, and desperate to find a bad guy, she had presented the wrong gun, the .38 Cobra that Crawford County gave back to her, to Cecil Mertz at his Rolling Ground Shooting Range. Did he know the gun? Mertz had said yes. Did he recall who he sold it to? Mertz had said he recalled, and his answer, a lie, had sent her off with the intent to kill Dalton Rockwell, an innocent man.

But that old story had a new point. The point was no longer the evil of Cecil Mertz's lie. The new point was this: Mertz had known exactly where she could find Rockwell. Every zombie lowlife in a tricounty area, Mertz knew where to find them. That was her gamble.

Sheriff Kick tore south on U.S. 14, detouring around the flooded Kickapoo River through a string of high-ground villages, using her siren twice to move milk trucks. She crossed into Crawford County, plunged back down alongside the Kickapoo, sped past what used to be Cress Springs Farm, her family's place, crossed the swollen river on the new bridge at Gays Mills, then climbed again, at last careering along the hogback ridge toward the phantom town of Rolling Ground and Cecil Mertz's shooting range. With five miles to go, Denise called and read over speakerphone everything law enforcement had on Baron

Ripp. After a string of offenses in the Bad Axe and neighboring counties, Ripp's rap sheet had moved west in 2012. In Williston, North Dakota, epicenter of the fracking boom, he had been busted for methamphetamine possession, pandering, battery, and check fraud.

"Denise, I have to ask."

"Please don't."

"I need anything germane to finding him."

"I got nothing."

"You're sure?"

"Exclusively drunken sex on his favorite dirty picnic table, the same place every time. He was needy and possessive, and he blamed me for making him feel that way. He broke my arm."

The sheriff exhaled, let the cruiser coast into Rolling Ground. Ahead was Mertz's range.

"He broke your arm? I didn't hear that on his rap sheet."

"I never told anybody. I said I fell off my horse."

They shared a silence.

"We need to contact people in North Dakota, let them know we want him if he shows up there. We need an APB between here and there and we need to extend the Amber Alert."

"I'm on it."

"And, Denise?"

"Yes, my queen?"

"You don't deserve anything he did to you."

"I know. I know, I know, I know . . ."

She wrenched the cruiser to a stop on potholed gravel outside the range. She burped her siren to call out Mertz. Waiting, she gazed at the fog-shrouded shabbiness of the range, where nothing had changed: Mertz's perimeter of cinder blocks, sandbags, and snow fence, his graveyard of bleached and busted deer torsos, the abandoned apple orchards that flanked the sick old man like the black-limbed invaders he needed to keep his paranoid fantasies alive.

Here he came, shuffling out of his collapsing house in a bathrobe and slippers, mouthing curses in her direction. One thing had changed: he was much frailer, looked pathetic and defenseless at a distance. When he reached the shooting range he hooked a claw through his sagging fence and glared fearfully at the Tahoe. She could read his mind. All these years, the Crawford County sheriff had left him alone. But now here *she* was, that damaged girl he'd done his best to ruin, coming at him as the sheriff from the Bad Axe.

She was out of the Tahoe. He scuffed away into his shooting shack. She followed into a grim cold space that still smelled of rat poison, bullet brass, and cigars. A poster lit by dirty window light pictured Ronald Reagan bottle-feeding a monkey. Mertz had gone behind his counter.

"I'm here about Baron Ripp."

"Who's that?"

"I'm sure you know. He killed a girl."

Mertz retrieved a pack of Phillies from a pocket of his bathrobe. As he shucked one cigar from its plastic he eyed her up and down, his nude head spotted with necrotic brown.

"Killed one, huh? Was she cute?"

She had no time to feel that. "He has another girl right now."

Mertz snapped a Zippo. He twisted the cigar between his lips and the flame, squinting at her through the eruption of smoke.

"I see. Another girl. Well, same question. Is *she* cute?"

"I'll ruin you, Mr. Mertz. It's way overdue."

"Ha." He spewed smoke and coughed—and spat—and tried again to laugh and coughed more. She had to look away. The caption on the poster showing a president bottle-feeding a monkey said *I'll be damned . . . Reagan used to babysit Obama.*

When Mertz recovered he parked his cigar in an ashtray.

"*You'll* ruin *me*? How so?"

As he was asking, both hands drifted beneath the counter. She had no time to gamble on his intentions. She shot her left hand across and caught the throat of his robe. Sure enough, as she hauled him across the counter he was spraying mace toward the ceiling with one hand and with the other hand wildly firing a pistol as if shooting at his slippers flying off across the room. She slammed him to the concrete, heard his skull hit. His grip opened. She batted his weapons away and jammed her Ruger behind his ear.

"You tell me how to find Baron Ripp, Mr. Mertz, or I'll leave your brains on this floor right here. *That's* how so."

A mace cloud descended over them. Her eyes were tearing. She was starting to gag.

"Tell me where to look for Ripp. Why is he in town? Where would he be?" She worried she had knocked him out. She dug in with the barrel. She slapped him. He wheezed and his rheumy eyes came flinching open. "Tell me *now*."

——

Five minutes later she was reporting to Denise.

"Ripp traffics stolen construction equipment from out west. He works with Dermit and Ladonna Weeks. They broker the stuff out of Faulkner's barns. He drives a red tractor cab. He takes girls back the other way, apparently. I'm on my way to Faulkner's now."

The farm gate was chained. She plowed her cruiser through and heard the gate strike a tree. The Bad Axe River had risen nearly into the driveway. She spun through fresh tire ruts in the mud. At least one heavy vehicle had entered since the party two nights ago.

She cornered the main barn and found the swampy tractor road that Yttri mentioned, which led deeper into the property. A quarter mile in, she saw the gray roofs of the two hidden barns. She stopped and approached behind the tree line, on foot.

But there was no red tractor cab—just a sooty trailer like she had seen in the lot of the Ease Inn yesterday. Down a ramp out of the trailer backed a forklift. On its tines hung a huge spool of copper wire. At the forklift controls was the blimp shape of Dermit Weeks. She crept closer, made sure. No, Ripp was not around.

Then she was running, reaching the cruiser, jerking it through a Y-turn and heading out. She tossed her phone on the passenger seat and hollered toward its speaker as she snaked out the muddy farm road.

"He's still in the Bad Axe!"

She hit the end of Faulkner's driveway, Bottom Road ahead.

"Denise, I'm sorry . . . but you had drunken sex on which picnic table . . . his favorite dirty picnic table . . . where?"

"I beg your pardon?"

"Where did Ripp take you?"

"Really, Heidi? How much do I need to relive that trip to hell?"

"He's waiting for his trailer to get unloaded. He's hiding somewhere with Pepper Greengrass, taking her west when he's done. Come on, Denise. Where is his favorite spot?"

"Oh, God . . ."

"Yell at me, Denise!" The Tahoe's engine roared as she waited for direction. "Tell me where to go!"

63

She should have made Felton Henry chase his truck. This is the flow she went against the first time. A man and his truck. Truck versus woman. This is the flow she rides now.

Pepper Greengrass has light enough inside the sleeper cab to see some other girl's skirt and top and panties wadded on a shelf below his tiny TV. This is good, because she won't get very far nude. She stretches to reach. Her back stings but she ignores it. She snags a corner of the clothing wad. Tugging gently, she makes it fall down into her lap. This doesn't stir him, still sprawled across her legs. Taking her time, she aligns a hole in each garment, shoves the clothing up her arm, storing it for later. She puts that arm behind her back. She bends at the waist and blows into his hairy jug-handle ear.

Now he stirs.

Another puff. She whispers, "Pee-pee."

"Huh?"

"Sorry, hon, I gotta tinkle."

He jerks up to sitting, touching the gun beneath his shirt. Breathing hard, he glares at her with lethal rage, his bloodshot eyes showing no recognition, no idea who she is.

"You lost this again."

For the second time she hands him the box-cutter knife.

"You keep losing it. I keep giving it back to you."

"Unh."

He slumps against the sleeper wall with his chest caved around the holstered gun, eyeing her naked body like something he might need to kill to protect himself. She keeps the elbow-threaded wad of another girl's clothes behind her back. He doesn't notice because he follows her other hand down between her legs. She pinches herself and squirms.

"I really gotta go pee-pee. Don't you?"

With both hands he rubs his hatchet face. "Shit." One more time he has lost track of the box cutter. One more time she gives it back.

"Jeez. Put that thing away somewhere. You keep losing it."

He yawns rot. He rubs his face again but can't erase the deep exhaustion. He pulls his phone from his pocket and looks at it.

"Huh."

He scowls at her. Confusion. He does this to a lot of girls. Which one is she again? The stupid one, who keeps giving him back the knife.

"Don't you gotta pee-pee too?"

"Like a goddamn racehorse. Then we're moving."

Easy as that, he heads out first. He jams his feet into his boots. He wobbles into his cab, slides across his seat, and slings down with an angry squeal of a fart.

Behind him Pepper, scooting fast, slings out the arm with the other girl's clothes accordioned at her elbow, shakes the wad down around her hand to muffle the sound, and punches in his yellow brake knob. She steps on his clutch and works his gear shift into neutral. She keeps her foot on the brake pedal. He stumbles off toward the shelter and the picnic table, fighting with his zipper. She waits until he has it out. When he starts spurting, she lets the brake pedal go, jumps down, snatches out wheel chocks—she hesitates one second, two seconds, watching, making sure—yes, the truck begins to roll—and she runs.

She hears the truck snapping branches. At the rock wall above the bluff she glances back. See? He chases it, not her, his promises to kill her fading as he disappears down the swath of forest cut by his plummeting truck.

She surveys beyond the stone wall. Loose rock tumbles down the sunlit flank of a treacherous, brush-clogged descent. Way down at the bottom, a brown-water flood spreads across a foggy bottomland strewn with rusty farm machines.

Beyond that, a junkyard, a house. *Go.*

64

Sheriff Kick had one fraction of a second to see that she and Denise had guessed right—Ripp had taken Pepper Greengrass to Battle Bluff—and the remainder of that second to understand that his truck was going to crush her.

The tractor cab sheared a small tree as it shortcut a narrow corner of the overlook road. Then it hit Yttri's Tahoe head on.

As her spine snapped forward and the airbag inflated into her face she could feel the car driven backward down the narrow access road. Then the Tahoe's tail end struck something that made it pivot. Ripp's truck pushed through and past and then the weight of it was gone. A collision below shook the earth. Then everything was quiet.

Her airbag deflated. The Tahoe's engine died. Slowly her senses reconnected. Her door worked. She staggered out, saw that Ripp's truck had kept descending, mauling its way through another hundred yards of forest and underbrush until a huge red oak had stopped it cold.

She drew her weapon and approached. The engine was off. The driver's door was open, no one inside. A howl of wrath came from uphill, at the overlook.

On her way up, based on the drinking she did here in high school, the layout came back to her. The dirt road she now ascended at a tortured sprint left the county gate at the bottom, zigzagged up the forested south flank of the bluff, and ended where there was a picnic area at the top. The overlook faced north, a panoramic view of the Bad Axe from a deep bluff that overhung a creek, a meadow, Lost Hollow Road, and the eyesore of Lyman Beavers's junkyard beyond.

The little park at the top was strewn with cigarette butts, empty plastic water bottles, a pair of tall black boots. The girl's soggy clothing hung randomly from trees down the slope. The sheriff headed for the stone wall behind the Blackhawk memorial plaque. She looked over. Ripp skidded down the rock face below. The risen sun glinted off a large silver handgun as he disappeared into a tangle of buckthorn and sumac where rockfall had collected.

Where this scrub forest opened at the bottom, the entire hollow was flooded. A black-haired girl in a pink top and white skirt waded into the wide sheet of brown water.

She holstered her pistol and vaulted the stone wall.

65

Pepper looks up at the steep descent she came down, boulders and brush, the top out of view. She can hear him screaming. She can't see him. She looks ahead at a creek flooded way beyond its banks, a wide meadow full of water flowing from her right to her left, the road and the junkyard on the other side. Now she sees there is an old red pickup with a snowplow blade parked there. As she wonders if this means there are people there who will help her, another red vehicle appears on the road, an SUV. It stops near the house. A heavy old man gets out, looks around but doesn't see her waving, looks the other way when she whistles through her fingers. He lumbers up into the junk. OK, so now she needs to go.

As she steps in, she remembers water like this, thick brown, in the Kickapoo where Bennie taught her to swim. She has no idea where the bottom is. She waits for each step to come down on nothing. At hip-deep, the water hardly pushes. But at roughly the center of the expanse she needs to cross is a seam of chop and curl and froth. She keeps an eye on this as she feels along the bottom. Out there a full-size log bobs and twists, then strikes the rusty bin on some kind of farm wagon that is moored in fast water. One of the log's shattered branch stumps punches through the bin wall, turns the wagon over and drags it along. The wagon's flat tires spin out mud in the sunshine. Then the log and bin separate and the log plunders on.

As she wades in, her plane of vision changes and she can no longer

see the house, the vehicles, just the mass of junk that climbs the opposite side of the valley. But out there. Across that. She needs to aim at
something. Beneath the road, amid a beard of last year's dead weeds,
a corroded pipe spews a jet of orange-brown water. That. She needs to
aim there, where that jet of water arcs in the sunshine before it crashes
onto the flood. *Go*.

Now filthy names for her come screeching off the bluff. She looks
back but the angle is too steep. Then she remembers Bennie. *Flow*, he
said. *Don't fight it*.

She retreats to swampy ground and moves upstream. Through suck-
mud, over wobbly tussocks of dead marsh grass, she less walks than
wallows, can't ever get her balance. But the current will take her, and the
farther up she goes, the more room she has to flow with it and end up
where she needs to be.

She hears him screaming again as she reenters the flood two hundred yards above. She pushes through a thicket of underwater briars.
Thorns tear her legs, sharp streaks of pain that the current whisks away.
When she looks back she can see him now, stumbling out the bottom
of the bluff. She penetrates deeper. Just as the flow takes her, she flexes
her knees, squeezes her eyes shut, claps her palms above her head, and
pushes off the bottom. She kicks and wheels her arms until the fast water
flips her over. She tumbles once. Then she gets her head up. Her eyes
open. Her legs drop. She spreads her arms and tries to steer against the
spinning.

She spins anyway. On one circuit she glimpses him. He has waded
in up to his chest, holding his pistol high and dry. On the next spin she
can't find him. Next time around she fixes on the spewing pipe, and
she sees that she is moving too fast, she is too far on the wrong side of
the current. On the next spin, the blunt black lunge of an old sawed
log aims to crack her in the face but she ducks it. She feels it glide
along her back like the heavy tongue of some great beast. She feels the
slap of catching it. She throws a leg, grips. Up she bobs, riding it. He
is taking aim at her with his pistol clapped in two hands.

But he can't hurt her. Not from there. She slides behind the far side
of the log, raises her middle finger for a target as he fires. No way.

But she will flow too far. She twists to find the pipe again. Nearly past it, she is stunned by what she sees. That same heavy old man comes slinging out the pipe mouth. His body tumbles sideways as the jet of water spreads and flattens. One boot flings off. As he rotates, flailing his arms, she sees flashes in the sun—keys on his belt, holster in his armpit—then he belly flops. She can't tell if he's still moving. His soggy mass decelerates and eddies back toward the pipe, sinking. Pepper lets go and swims.

66

In the end, his dad never got to see how perfectly his pit trap had worked.

Angus had whistled to direct Boog Lund. Sure enough, Gibbs's old chief deputy had come wearing street clothes and driving his own red Silverado, like when he had come with Clausen and Gibbs to make the first deal. Angus had whistled and Lund had hauled his old bulk up the scrap yard running his mouth instead of drawing his weapon.

"Well, if it ain't Hotshot and Potshot—"

His dad had set up a chair exactly uphill of where he wanted Lund to walk. He had jabbered excitedly for a good long time while he waited. An hour had passed. The next hour had begun. Brandy had gone inside the Quonset shed to sprawl sullenly on an old truck seat, and then she had fallen asleep. Angus had gone back down to the house and looked at the wax man Brandy had called "me and Brock's friend." He had never seen a man shot. He had shot animals, but never with a pistol in the head. Blood and brain had leaked from the wound into the gasoline spilled around his body. The woodstove still cranked out too much heat. Angus had wondered if the house would blow up, burn down. He had wondered if that might be a good thing. If he had come back to start things over, maybe that should happen.

He had gone back up to his dad, who had become exhausted and fallen silent. Then finally Lund had arrived. Angus had whistled to direct him. Lund had walked right up the line of the pipe, all that floodwater coursing six feet below his boots.

"Well, well, well," he had continued, every step bringing him closer, "if it ain't the happy Beavers family, just sitting up here in the junk where they belong. Lyman, you ain't got any pants on. Hell, is that a diaper?"

Angus had tried not to look at the trap because Lund was heading right for it. Once it was under the full light of day it hadn't look very good. Under the weight of the sawdust spread over it, the canvas had sagged slightly into the hole beneath. Earlier, waiting, Angus had revised his dad's original approach, replacing the four tires that anchored the corners with four random pieces of heavy junk, each one different. But a bear, a deer, any animal you were trying to pit trap, would have sensed it by now and changed paths. But his dad had been right about Boog Lund, a man so full of himself, so eager to intimidate Beavers, that he had never even noticed.

"You folks are gonna want to reconsider all this trouble you've been causing." He had looked at Angus. "Hotshot, you didn't listen to me, did you?"

His next step had been the one. The sawdust puffed. The canvas buckled. The anchors at the corners slid. Lund's arms had wheeled desperately as he tilted in. Then the high current in the pipe caught his leading foot and flipped him headfirst. He was gone in an instant. There was no sound then except the water in the pipe, washing him down beneath the scrap yard, a hundred yards, two hundred yards. Ten seconds later, there he went, spinning out the pipe into the meadow. But Angus, hearing no celebration, had looked over and seen his dad had missed it. He had touched the leathery side of his dad's neck. He had lifted the stranded bones of his dad's wrist. He was gone.

Now Angus stood stunned as the wet black head of a girl popped from the flood. Who was that? Where had she come from? He watched her swim into the eddy under the pipe. Then she was snatching out Boog Lund's huge wilted mass, beaching him on a spit of high ground below the road. She rolled him over on his back. No doubt what Angus saw next: she robbed him. She took his keys. She took his wallet. She took his gun.

Then more. Far across the flooded meadow a man fired a pistol at the girl, then stumbled into the flood and began swimming like a house cat. The girl ignored him. She climbed to the road. She had Lund's pistol and his wallet on its chain. She aimed her hand. Lund's Silverado flashed and chirped. She was going to steal it. Then she saw something upstream and she began to run toward the car. An officer in a brown Bad Axe uniform sloshed through slow water at the upstream end of the meadow. The wet uniform clung to a woman's shape following the fence line toward the road.

Brandy had appeared beside Angus. She was looking at their dad. No strength left, Angus put his arm across his sister's quaking shoulders.

67

The sheriff had crossed the flooded meadow to the junkyard side. But still there was nothing she could do about what was happening too far in front of her. She could be glad that the girl was alive. She could pray that Pepper Greengrass would be safe and not get far before someone found her and helped her. That was it.

The girl had Boog Lund's keys, for sure. His Silverado flashed and beeped as she loped toward it. The gun in her hand had to be Lund's too. That was his wallet hanging from the chain looped around her elbow. With the sheriff running but still too far away, the girl hopped in. The engine roared. She plowed Lund's truck through the stream coming down the west end of Lost Hollow Road and was gone.

Now she assessed as she limped along. Lund was somewhere. And that was the old Rhinegold Dairy truck that plowed snow at Pinky Clausen's yesterday, so Jerrold Mickelson was here somewhere too.

So was Angus Beavers. She still wasn't sure if he was with or against her.

And she could see Baron Ripp. He was thrashing in the flood, trying to get across.

She drew her weapon. She did not expect Mickelson to be in his truck. He was not. The door of Beavers's house was open. She headed that way behind the Ruger.

Inside, the house smelled of spilled gas. That woodstove glowed and snapped. With her boot, she shut its iron mouth. This place was going to go up. Now here was Mickelson in the hallway, an additional hole through his forehead. She left him there, checked the bedrooms, no one else.

She returned to Mickelson. She stared . . . and blinked . . . and stared. It looked like her zombie fantasies, blowing brains out in her imagination, but no, this was real. His brains were blown backward, a mass of gray-pink gelatin dissolving in a puddle of gas. She stared for a moment into his weirdly pale eyes, like old ice.

She backed out. She came off the porch scanning the scrap yard above and saw Lyman Beavers still sitting mostly naked in a lawn chair and his two kids, Angus and Brandy, sitting in the mud beside him, Angus with his arm around the girl. Ahead of them was a gaping hole in the ground. She was heading toward them when she heard Ripp scream for help.

She saw him downstream of a disgorging culvert, about a hundred feet out, clinging to the tire of an upside-down hay wagon that bobbed ponderously downstream. He had an armpit hooked over the tire. The tire kept spinning out beneath him. He screamed and waved with a big silver handgun.

She made hand signs: throw the gun in the water.

He didn't.

She yelled, "Throw it! If you want help, throw it away!"

That wagon tire kept rotating beneath his armpit. It kept dunking him. He held on to the gun. Then the tire peeled off the wheel. Ripp gargled a shriek of panic. He went under.

Shit. She stripped her duty belt as she skidded down off the road. She shucked her boots and socks on a lump of high ground beneath the spewing culvert. She tore out of her heavy sopping shirt. Like the old Mighty Heidi White at a bonfire on the Kickapoo, she sprinted at a downstream angle until the water cut her stride. Then she dived.

She had no idea where Ripp was until she was swept over the blur of him on the bottom. Through the churning murk she saw his white skin and the filigree on his cartwheeling boots. She caught one boot. It came off in her grip. But the tug bobbed him up. She caught him around the neck, let the flow lift them, and began to scissor-kick out of the current.

As they caught the eddy, things slowed down, and she wasn't surprised when he tried to thrash a shooting angle on her head. She got one foot on the bottom. She grabbed an ear and shoved his head under. She held it under. She felt him go boneless. She lifted her foot and collected him by the neck again and stroked through a deep slow eddy back toward the patch of high ground under where the culvert spilled out. Again one foot touched bottom. Then the other. She wrenched the big silver automatic from his hand. She threw it up where her belt and boots were. She dragged Baron Ripp ashore. She sank to her knees, shaking and breathless.

"What a hero you are," said Boog Lund behind her.

68

He loomed unsteadily, straddling her discarded gear. He looked soggy and feeble and out of his mind, huffing and spitting, snot trailing from his nose. He staggered two steps back and tipped forward over his huge gut. He snagged her duty belt, unsnapped her Ruger. He leveled it at her. Then he staggered three steps to his right and picked up Ripp's gun. He popped the magazine and looked at it. He replaced it and fired once into the air. The explosion echoed through the hollow.

"So, here's what happened," he slurred.

He looked at the two weapons as if to keep them straight.

"You shot Rippy."

He tilted his big raw head, confirmed it was the sheriff's service pistol in his right hand. He was going to shoot Ripp with that one. Ripp lay gasping, barely conscious.

"The problem being, of course, that Rippy shot you too."

He squinted down his shaking left arm at Ripp's showboat silver gun. She would get her bullet from that. He aimed it at her. But he was unsteady on the saturated ground where he stood. His bootless heel sunk beneath his weight. Feebly, very carefully, he began to change his footing. While he tried to get satisfied, the sheriff searched for the energy to charge him. Five or six steps across the mud seemed like so far away. She had to look down to see if she was standing up or not. She was not.

She had just gotten off both knees onto one knee, had one bare foot planted, was understanding she wouldn't make it but was forcing herself to try, when behind Lund out of that vomiting pipe shot a tangle of black sticks and then Angus Beavers on his back. He flew smoothly for one second. Then he corkscrewed with the shattering water. His hands pinned something narrow and rust red against his chest.

The splash distracted Lund. He turned. But Angus Beavers was well beneath the surface. Black sticks floated where he had gone under. There was nothing for Lund to see, so he went back to work on his footing. He didn't quite have his balance yet. Now hearing distant sirens, he took his time to gloat a little.

"I could have stopped the whole thing, if only I had gotten here earlier. It's a shame. Hell, look at me. I had to fish you out half dead but anyway you shot him while he lay there helpless on his ugly face. Like folks are starting to say, you seem to have your issues. But anyway, I did my best."

"You covered up a murder."

"Says who? If it's a Beavers telling the story, that worm won't fish."

He raised Ripp's gun to shoot her first.

"I just wish to hell I could have saved such a fine young officer as yourself—"

A new splash turned him. Angus Beavers brandished an iron fence post as he exploded from the water. His speed was almost invisible, three hard strides, his big hands loading a swing as he covered the twenty feet to Lund. A firearm in each hand, Lund tried to respond, but he could do nothing before the uppercutting fence post caught him in the ribs with a crackling thump. It was a sound of ruination, final. The guns fell to the mud. Lund collapsed. Angus Beavers flung the post toward the flood and it splashed into the shallows. He sank to his knees. He dropped his head between his heaving shoulders.

Fighting for balance, the sheriff came to her feet. She collected the weapons. She stood over Lund, wondering what she needed to do. His face was in a soupy swirl of dead meadow grass, his lips releasing pink bubbles. She listened to the sirens getting closer. She turned to evaluate Baron Ripp and got one more shock.

Ripp was on his feet. He held the fence post that Angus Beavers had flung in his direction. The seconds slowed into a gluey, dreamlike progression. The man who had cut his name into Sophie Ringensetter's flesh and bought Pepper Greengrass like an animal was twenty feet away, armed with a fence post, stalking toward her. This made no sense, because when she looked down to check—yes, she had not one but two firearms trained on him. Baron Ripp was bringing a fence post to a gunfight. Between his chinstrap sideburns, his small gray teeth fit together in a lurid grin.

"Go on, Dairy Queen. Kill me if you think you can."

She found herself flushed with eerie calm. For how long had she ached to shoot a bad man through his filthy brain? Time slowed even more. Baron Ripp was grinning, like he thought he would be the one to close the deal.

"Even though I could tell you some shit," he offered.

He kept coming. A fence post against two firearms. "Some shit about your past, Dairy Queen, that if you killed me you might never know." He thought he could get close enough. She leveled both weapons at his center mass. Ripp kept talking.

"But go ahead and kill me if you can. I ain't worth the pants I'm wearing. I know it. But be it known that I sure did get some fine young ass before I went."

He thought he could con her into distraction. He took another step. She took one step back. "Like you could tell me what?"

"Whiz-Bangs."

That startled her. The rounds that went with her dad's Colt revolver, Whiz-Bang brand .22 shells, had disappeared when the gun did. But Ripp knew Mertz and Mertz knew these details.

"What about Whiz-Bangs?"

"I know who stole your dad's old Colt and tried to sell it, Whiz-Bangs and all."

"Who?"

He laughed. "Slips my mind at the moment." He took another step toward her. She stepped back. "Now, I *could* remember some shit, though. Oh, Miss Dairy Queen, yes, I could."

"Like what—that you didn't just hear from Mertz?"

"Like every cow you folks had was named from that English faggot. Shakespeare."

This startled her again. It was true. "You never worked for us."

"I drove your cattle to Sunnyfield for rendering. Same fella who had that gun, working there at the time, he named every one of them bossies getting off the truck. He thought it was funny as hell."

"Who?"

"The name just keeps slipping my mind." He took another step, grinning. "But I can tell you another thing this fella had for sale that I'm gonna bet he had ripped off of your dad. Prove I know what I'm saying."

She wasn't backing up anymore. Nothing had been stolen, nothing had been missing aside from the gun. She lowered Ripp's weapon and steadied the Ruger. He was eight feet away, nearly close enough to reach her with the post.

"You're a liar. You don't know anything."

"Then I guess you won't know nothing neither."

He lunged and swung. As she ducked the lashing post, she guided her aim down his chest through his groin to his leading knee—pulled and grazed him—pulled again—and blew his leg apart.

———

Ripp screamed. Sirens wailed in close. She stepped away. She put her shirt back on, her radio and badge, she strapped her duty belt back on, holstered her gun. She knocked out Ripp's clip and stuck that gun in the baggy side pocket of her wet pants. She unclipped her handcuffs. She circled behind Angus Beavers. He sat with his head hanging and shoulders heaving. She cuffed him.

"You don't know what they did."

"I will when you tell me."

"Good."

After she handed Angus Beavers off to Deputy Eleffson, she realized by the sharpness of gravel that she was still barefoot. That same moment, Deputy Schwem appeared with her socks and boots.

She sat down to put them on. She forgot why she sat down. She lay back on gravel in a puddle grown warm under the sun. The spring sky was scrubbed cloudless, sapphire blue. Next moment of awareness, Yttri's breath was in her ear.

"Sheriff, you're going to be all right. Bishops Coulee EMS is a minute out, I can hear them coming. Just stay down."

Then she was in a bed. The bed was moving toward flashing blue-and-red lights. Shiny white doors swung open to a place where she could rest.

FIVE DAYS AFTER

Robert V. Check @bobcheck
Tweet tweet a little bird is asking you to sign for
nomination of Interim Sheriff Kick she's a keeper
VFW 4-9 Mon #dairyqueen #yougogirl #kickherin

69

"You sit right here, young lady," Bob Check told her, pulling out the chair next to his. "Next to a friend."

She did so. She squared her uniformed shoulders, drawing the sore shoulder up to level, and sent a tight smile around the conference table. Bad Axe County board chairperson Marge Joss made an announcement to the audience beyond.

"Now that the sheriff is here, the Bad Axe County board of supervisors, as required by state law, will proceed to closed session in order to consider a personnel matter."

Chairperson Joss looked over her reading glasses at the modest crowd of Bad Axers who sat in the gallery on folding chairs. One of them was Deputy Yttri, looking exactly Olaf the Handsome in slacks, a blazer, and a tie, his hair stuck straight up and shining like gold. The interim sheriff had put him up for special commendation by the board. When she walked in he was just tucking his certificate into a folder he had brought with him. The district attorney, wheezy old Baird Sipple, remained seated beside Yttri, the two of them talking with their heads together, not paying attention until Marge Joss rumbled her throat.

"State law, gentlemen. It doesn't matter who you are. If you're not a member of this board, out you go."

When Yttri and Sipple had followed the other spectators out of the room, Chairperson Joss passed out copies of a document to the board.

"Every one of these copies comes right back to me at the end of this discussion."

Supervisors were present from seventeen of the county's twenty-one townships. As the copies made their way around, the sheriff silently read over her statement one more time.

The recent formation of a special county commission to review my conduct in office brings to light the need of any community to have confidence in its leaders, especially those whose job it is to protect that community and enforce its laws. Routine inquiries are required anytime there is significant loss of county property, and also, more important, anytime an officer injures or kills someone.

She had worked hard on the wording, Harley and Denise as her reluctant editors.

It is because these routine inquiries have raised legitimate doubts about my conduct that the commission was formed. However, before the commission begins to put precious resources toward this work, I wish to respect the efforts by some members of this board to move past a history of mistrust and problematic behavior within the Bad Axe County Sheriff's Department.

Did she really mean it? It was twenty-four days after she had accepted what should have been the job of her dreams. It was five days after she had shot Baron Ripp. And, yes, she really meant it.

For this reason, I ask that you accept my resignation as interim sheriff of Bad Axe County, effective immediately.

She heard the murmurings of surprise as board members skimmed and got the gist. Chairperson Joss said, "Sheriff, resignation may seem appropriate to some on this board, but it's still unexpected. Will you explain?"

The idea had come to her in stages over the last few days, beginning a few hours after she shot Baron Ripp in violation of department protocol, of protocol anywhere, clearly to maim him. Sophie Ringensetter's body was still at the morgue, her family on the way. Pepper Greengrass was still on the run, her family also notified. The sheriff had walked out of the hospital a second time and gone home to see her own family.

Harley had met her in the yard. He had hugged her long and hard. She had swallowed what she had to say, not sure how to say it. When secretly and helplessly you mistrust someone you love, and you are wrong, and you are ashamed, do you try to put into words the weakness of your soul? Or do you just hang on for dear life?

She had held on, and held on, until his neck was wet with her tears. She had whispered into it, "I'm always so afraid to lose you."

———

She had hugged the kids, taken a shower, hugged them again, and gone back to work. That afternoon in a meeting with District Attorney Sipple, she had admitted what had really happened with Brock Pabst— thereby opening herself to multiple questions of misconduct—and then she had arrested Pabst on a long list of charges. That evening she had difficult meetings with the mother of Pepper Greengrass, negligent and sullen, and the family of Sophie Ringensetter, devasted as their daughter was confirmed dead, her body under medical examination. The next day she had talked with the FBI about Dermit and Ladonna Weeks, their interstate transport of stolen goods, their potential human trafficking. The FBI advised her they would open a case. That same day, she had remembered to give Denise the thumb drive with her list of could-haves.

"I'm on it," Denise had told her, "like a duck on a june bug."

"I should just let it go," she offered. "I know I should. I let it go once before."

"No, you didn't. You can't let it go."

The thesis of her offer to resign as sheriff had occurred to her right then.

"Then I should probably leave. We should probably leave the coulees."

Denise had looked back at her with the gritty refusal of a coulee girl to back down.

"The hell you'll leave the coulees. Heidi, we want you here. We need you here. You need to be here."

Denise had gone to the door of the dispatch room, looked up and down the hall to make sure they were alone.

"I know this one guy," she began. "Well, I know a lot of guys—but I know this one guy down in Crawford County. He's tight with that new preppy chick district attorney who came to see you last week. He talked to her, and she's on your side. You don't need to fight the open-records exemption. Here's a copy of the case file on your parents. It's open now to you privately, if you know what I mean. What you'll see is pretty basic. Sheriff Skog considered hardly any suspects, dicked around and dragged his feet, and when the trail led past Cecil Mertz, he just shut the whole investigation down and settled for murder-suicide, rather than expose the fact that he knew for decades that Mertz was selling illegal firearms and that he took bribes to look the other way. Here you go."

Her hands had trembled as she accepted the file.

"Her name is Cindy Puma, the DA, I mean, and she's awesome. She plans to push Skog out of office by the end of the month."

———

One day later, after Lyman Beavers was laid to rest beside his wife in the Red Mound Cemetery, she had questioned Angus in more detail. His version of Sophie Ringensetter's murder agreed with his uncle Walt's, and she had worked with Sipple to make sure Angus was released on his signature. She had driven him home, and she had tried not to feel appalled by the mess of Beavers Salvage. Maybe Angus would work on it. At least the house hadn't burned down yet. Angus said he was thinking about building something new.

"Take care of your sister," she told him.

"I will."

"My husband heard you're back in the Bad Axe. He's player-manager of the Rattlers now. Depending on how things work out, I'm sure he'd love to have you in the lineup."

Angus had blushed. "We'll see."

"OK. Good."

"Depends on what I need to do to get things right for me and Brandy. And how much trouble I'm in with the law."

"We'll work on that," she had promised.

———

The next day was when the misconduct questions began to catch up with her. For one thing, she had given DA Sipple multiple complex legal problems with her retraction of her "don't remember" story and her admittedly extralegal handling of the whole Pinky Clausen / Brock Pabst / Walt Beavers crime wave. For another, she had totaled two sheriff's cruisers in a twenty-four-hour period, one while under strict prohibition not to drive a county vehicle. She saw no point in denying her disregard for rules or her recklessness. Could there be something wrong with her judgment—so went the argument—if it came with a two-cruiser price tag? And so the special commission had been formed to investigate what she had already asked herself: did she have *any* business being the Bad Axe County sheriff? She had decided to spare the resources they would spend in saying no.

———

She had been driving back from Beavers Salvage that afternoon, wondering if Denise could really do anything with her list of men who might have murdered her parents, thinking she would just ask for the thumb drive back and start talking to Harley about their next move in life, when her cell phone buzzed in her shirt pocket.

"Go ahead, Rhino."

"It's good news, bad news, I guess. We just got a call from Sergeant Louden of the Minnesota State Patrol. They found Lund's truck at a travel plaza in Albert Lea. It had been sitting there at least two days. A witness saw a girl with long black hair catching a ride with a trucker heading west. A *female* trucker. Sergeant Louden extended the Amber Alert out through Montana, but I'm thinking maybe she's OK."

"Let's pray. Keep me posted."

"Then Marge Joss called. She wants to know what our internal investigation protocol is—you know, for officers shooting people."

"I'll bet she does."

"She wonders if you were trained by Hollywood."

"Of course I was."

"Me, I don't wonder, Sheriff. I would have shot him in the nuts. Then the face. And *then* the chest, like I'm supposed to. I'm just telling you."

"I know, Rhino. Thanks."

70

Later on the fourth day she had ridden with Olaf the Handsome to interview Ripp at the ICU in La Crosse, where they were prepping him to have his shattered leg amputated.

Ripp had completely startled them with his story. He was conscious, but drugged up to the point of feeling delusionally expansive, as if they had come to listen to a great man share the noteworthy events of his life. He seemed unconcerned that his leg was about to be gone, more concerned to set the record straight, make sure that credit was given where credit was due.

Yes, he understood that he had been arrested, charged with kidnapping and rape. Yes, he understood that they could use anything he said against him. But how stupid were they? Then he laughed at them.

"Them players never killed her. Hell, you got it all wrong."

"Could you say that again? They *didn't* kill Sophie Ringensetter?"

"Oh, hell no," he said proudly. "I did that."

Yttri, taking notes and operating a recorder, had to look at her, both of them struck speechless. Finally she said, "You killed her, because . . ."

"Because what's mine is mine. Dumb girl just didn't get that."

The sheriff felt sick and had to look away, seeing in her mind Harley with that different girl at the Ease Inn, begging him to take her anywhere else—anywhere away from Baron Ripp, she guessed now.

"So you killed her because she was unfaithful? By getting raped? Do I understand you correctly?"

"You do understand that correctly, Dairy Queen, yes, you do."

"You strangled her."

"With my goddamn belt, yes, I did."

"And then you threw her in Walt Beavers's truck? Why?"

"I figured the way those two fellas was standing out there talking like they knew every damn thing about baseball, who shoulda played and who shouldn't, that they had to be with the team. It didn't matter to me. Hell, stupid little bitch woulda cowgirled every one of them. But when you're mine, see, you don't play like that. I believe I made that understood."

The sheriff had to look away from him. "Then you left town," Yttri managed to say after a long and brutal stretch of note taking. "Otto Koenig saw you. You worked in the fracking fields in North Dakota."

"I did."

"You were gone until sometime this winter."

"I was."

"What made you come back?"

A weird shift had occurred. Ripp had changed his angle in the bed. He had sort of backed up and relaxed as if to get cozy, focused his druggy eyes on her, like this was a seduction and he was making good progress. She had shivered as she glanced at Yttri. Olaf the Handsome had turned ugly with rage and disgust.

"Hell, I was rich out there until I was laid off. Then I got into the shard and the shaboo and all that. I started stealing copper wire, equipment, shit all over the place out there, and I got wind that Dermit and Gibbs and Lund and them had a thing going back here and they could fence it. One time Ladonna sent me back west with a girl, and I thought, shit, I can do that myself, boys out there'll pay big money for fresh meat if it comes in tenderized."

Yttri had nearly choked. "Tenderized . . . ?" His big hands gripped the corners of his legal pad like he was hanging on to keep himself from lunging in. Ripp gave him a clueless little nod, man to man. "You know, all the gristle pounded out of their stupid little minds."

———

"Wait out here," she had told Yttri after they had left the room.

She had gone back in and closed the door. This time, without Yttri around, Ripp had looked afraid of her. She set her phone down, touched RECORD.

"You are just barely alive," she reminded him.

"I know."

"You're alive because you claimed to have information I want."

"I do."

"Every single syllable you say to me had better ring exactly true. If not, I'll come back. What'll happen then is you'll attack me, and this time I'll blow your infected brains out all over that bed. Now, speak."

71

But she still hadn't believed him.

Jerrold Mickelson, Ripp had told her. S'more. Mickelson had killed her parents.

But that was too easy.

He knew Mickelson was a terrifying freak who was dead and could never be questioned. Ripp was still saving himself with bullshit, in the same way he had first gotten his hooks into her by mentioning the Colt and Whiz-Bang bullets, which he could have learned about from Cecil Mertz.

A stolen pressure washer, Ripp had told her. A barn burglary gone wrong, a faked murder-suicide by Mickelson to cover his tracks, dumb-shit Sheriff Skog lapping it up. Mickelson had tried to sell Ripp her dad's stolen pressure washer. This was Ripp's claim. But it was bullshit. Her dad had never owned a pressure washer.

She knew that. After the wrong gun was returned, trying to prove that *something* else was stolen, *anything* else, she had gone through her dad's machinery maintenance checklist. Everything had been accounted for. Nothing was missing but the Colt and the bullets. She had searched the barn, the house, her mom's jewelry boxes, *nothing*. Nothing was gone except for the Colt, the bullets—and life as she had known it.

———

She had left Ripp in the hospital and gone after the players that after-noon, hoping for rape charges now instead of murder. The medical examiner had found the semen of four different men preserved inside the girl's frozen body. On a first-degree rape charge, the sheriff knew, it was going to be *he said, she said*, and Sophie Ringensetter was dead. But there wasn't going to be any way around the fact that the girl had been a minor, and therefore could not consent. Statutory rape and sex-offender status for life, at the very least.

She had picked up third-basemen Curtis Strunk in Vernon County coming out of the Viroqua Walmart with his wife and baby daughter and a cartload of soda pop and packaged food. He had stood there in his wife's gaze of disbelief and then disgust, and then he had popped wide open on the spot, telling her what happened, calling their gang rape a "train," the girl so drunk she couldn't walk on her own. His wife pushed the grocery cart away to their truck across the parking lot and left him standing there.

Sherman Ossie, located at The Pickle Jar, a pub in the town of Hefty, had said the same, in tears. He had heard rumors she was dead, Ossie said. He had always figured one of the other guys had done it, to keep her quiet. He had always known he should say something, but . . .

Next she had gone after Wade Gibbs, right fielder and nephew of deceased sheriff Ray Gibbs, at the public boat landing in Blackhawk Locks. Word had traveled fast. Gibbs knew why she was there, and he had tried to run—squealing out of the parking lot with a half-trailered boat shedding fishing poles and minnow buckets into traffic on the Great River Road. She had let him go. Two hours later he had turned up at the Public Safety Building and confessed to the same thing that Strunk and Ossie had told her. Yes, they all had sex with her. No, they didn't kill her. No, he had no idea where Sophie Ringensetter had disap-peared to later, Wade Gibbs said. He had always figured Scotty Clausen had done something with her.

That was her next arrest, at the Clausen Meats central office in La Crosse. The son of Pinky Clausen, free of consequences like the rest of them for 1,337 days, had already lawyered up. He and his dad.

72

"I call the vote," interjected Bob Check. "Gosh darn it, you folks are gonna jaw about this all day while the sheriff's got work to do. I can't believe you'd even think about accepting her resignation. It never bothered most of you when Gibbs made mistakes, wrecked cars, blew county money, hurt people that didn't need to be hurt, made his own rules. Listen to yourselves. I call the gosh darn vote."

By voice, yays and nays, the verdict wasn't clear, so Marge Joss polled the supervisors. The sheriff watched carefully. She had five clear supporters. Another five rejected her resignation because they wanted the inquiry to proceed and perhaps to skewer her officially. That left only seven who purely wanted her gone, against ten who at least for the moment did not. She was on thin ice. But it was a technical win.

Olaf the Handsome was pacing the hallway when she stepped out.

"Back in open session," she informed him. "The personnel discussion is over."

He studied her face. She must have looked as drained as she felt.

"So you're finished?"

She could read what he thought. She guessed he and District Attorney Sipple had done different math.

"No. I'm still your boss. Ten to seven."

Yttri looked away and began to scratch at his mustache. One of his thumbs nervously tapped the folder in his other hand.

"Wow . . . I didn't . . ."

Sipple came out of the restroom, the kind of old gentleman who still dried his hands on his personal handkerchief. He never even looked at her. He took Yttri at the elbow and turned him toward the boardroom door.

She was several steps down the hall toward to her office when Yttri called after her.

"Hey, uh, Heidi?" Then, "I'm sorry, but . . ."

She turned and saw him raise his folder. He was submitting his nomination papers, she realized. He followed Sipple back into the boardroom.

———

Olaf the Usurper. This was what Denise began calling him when she heard. They met in the sheriff's office. Given her exhaustive knowledge of the coulee region and the men in it, Denise had winnowed her list of suspects down to seven names. The guy Denise knew in Crawford County, an ex-deputy, had confirmed that Sheriff Skog had looked into two of her winnowed seven and found alibis that held up. That left five.

"So, my criteria," Denise said. "One, he had to have worked for your dad at any time, or done significant business with the farm, such as an equipment service contract or veterinary work or milk pickup. Two, he was in the region at the time. Three, he had to have, as you say, zombie potential, a drug background, a criminal record, mental instability, violent behavior, all of the above. Four, either he gave Skog an unchecked alibi at the time, or Skog never asked. Criteria number five: the asshole couldn't give *me* an alibi that checked out."

Denise had paused and scratched her frizzy head.

"I know you think there needs to be some element of resentment toward your family, Heidi. But I'm not sure. Think of Bishops Coulee. Isn't that part of what set you off? Horst Zimmer used to live across the highway from the couple that he killed. No history of conflict. He went to their wedding. He was just high as fuck and needed money to stay that way. Your guy was just smarter, or maybe not quite so high, and he gave himself a better chance to get away with what he did. So here are your five: Vernon Eckert, Wesley Thibodaux, Jerrold Mickelson—"

"Denise, stop. I know I can't believe Ripp, but . . ."

Her phone was slippery as she fumbled it from behind her badge. The display seemed fickle beneath her fingers. At last she got the recording to play. *Prove it*, her voice was demanding of Baron Ripp. *Prove what you're telling me.* She remembered Ripp sprawled on his hospital bed like Hugh Hefner, or so he seemed to think, as his voice rasped from the phone's speaker.

Hell, you know how it is, Dairy Queen, hauling stock, petrified cow shit stuck on everything. My trailer always got to be a goddamn mess. So me and this fella that was laughing at your Shakespeare cattle later, we was sitting there at Mudcat's about five or six cocktails in—this is the same day your folks was shot—and I already said no I won't buy your little toy pistol for a hundred bucks, go to Mertz, you'll see, Mertz won't give you more than fifty. But I tell you what, I said, I will take a look at that pressure washer. See, darlin', according to him he had also just acquired himself a brand-new Briggs and Stratton, three thousand psi, gas engine, four hundred bucks new, and he wanted a hundred for that too . . .

She paused the recording.

"Oh, Jesus," Denise said. "'Three thousand psi.' Where have we heard that before? Violates my parts just hearing it, like it's supposed to."

"But he's full of shit, see? Because my dad never owned a pressure washer. If the farm was bankrupt and he was freaking out about money, I don't know why he would buy one either. Or why anybody would bother to steal one, if one existed."

"But it makes a weird lie for that same reason, doesn't it? And remember the big haul at Bishops Coulee: two lives, for an Xbox, a toaster, and a chainsaw? Isn't that the other thing that set you off? Actually, a nice new pressure washer is exactly the kind of thing a meth head would grab and try to turn into quick money. And sure enough, Ripp was interested in buying one on the cheap."

"But we didn't have one. He's a good liar, more likely. But listen."

I said I'd come by his place the next day, take a look, see if we could make a deal. I get there, his place down over the Crawford border, thinking I'm about to get me a bargain on a pressure washer, hose all that cow pucky off my truck. But guess what. The sonofabitch says too late, he already sold it to his Amish neighbor down the road . . .

The sheriff heard her voice say, *Give me his name.*

Amos Zook.

Not the buyer. The seller. His name.

Hah. Jerrold the marshmallow. But this was before he blew himself up.
Jerrold Mickelson.

"See? So easy to say," she told Denise, "because it just so happens that he's dead and can't deny it. So is Amos Zook, probably dead. He was ancient, if I remember. Not to mention: would the Amish even use a pressure washer?"

Still, against her own logic, she was suddenly overcome by a surge of hope that it was Mickelson. She had seen him, shot by Angus Beavers, his brains curdling in a pool of gas. If it *was* him, he was dead—and it was over. Suddenly she felt like she would weep. Denise was reaching out, gathering in her shaking body.

"Ripp is lying, Denise. I know it. He's playing with me."

"Hon, I know what you mean. I do. But I'm going to check it out."

———

At the end of the long fourth day, she took her time driving home, twelve miles out to their rented farmhouse, through a beautiful April evening. This had been the sunshiny warm day when spring had popped in the hollows. White and purple phlox had opened their first buds on the flanks of sunward ditches. Warblers flitted in the green-tipped brush, chasing insects. Last week's flood was down, the streams scoured and rearranged but running clear. She saw trout fishermen gearing up at the bridges.

When Denise called, she said, "Call you right back," and pulled over at the bridge where Spring Hollow Branch went under Pederson Road. She needed a few deep breaths. A guy in half-mast waders waddled toward her with his gear-laden vest creaking and chiming. She vaguely knew him as a former classmate of Harley's, now a fishing guide. People called him Chub. "I wasn't urinating off the bridge, Sheriff, I swear. I was just—"

She put a hand up to stop him. "Good luck out there."

When she called back, Denise asked, "Are you sitting down, Heidi?"

She put her butt against the cool iron bridge rail. She gazed into a ripening sunset over a ridge of leafing hardwoods. The stream scrolled out, a thread of reflected gold within green pasture grass. "More or less. Hit me."

"Number one, your dad *did* own a pressure washer. He bought one from True Value in Gays Mills on credit, July 8, 2004, the day before he and your mom died. Dick Krueger, manager there, remembers him being pretty ticked off because he had to wash down his milk room, based on a new FDA rule made for big producers."

Nervously gnawing at her lip, she admitted that she did remember this general complaint by her dad: money he had to spend based on things the bigger guys did wrong.

Denise said, "I don't think he ever even took the tags off or cracked the owner's manual. His receipt must have been with it. Then later everything got auctioned off. Am I right?"

"Except the older cows that went to Sunnyfield."

Ripp had claimed he trucked them there, Mickelson on the receiving end reciting their *faggot Shakespeare names* as they came down the ramp, according to Ripp. Now her pulse raced. An awful memory cycled back. The farmhand herding in a snowstorm who had hit her dad's old bull Samson in the face with a shovel and got his ass fired—was that Mickelson? She recalled the guy's pale cold eyes and his smirking, tobacco-crusted mouth. Mickelson had lost his face. But those eyes . . .

"Right," she told Denise. "Everything else got auctioned."

"OK. Everything except cows. That's important, because, number two, I checked with Dairyland Auction Service. They went back in their records and there was *no pressure washer on the auction manifest*. So it disappeared before the estate was settled. Most likely it disappeared about five minutes after your parents died. As in, it was stolen. Now, number three, I had to connect the washer to who stole it. We got lucky, Heidi. Amos Zook is alive."

She felt tears rush to the brims of her eyes.

"Sweet old man, ninety-some years old," Denise said. "I asked and he gladly showed it to me. It's gas powered, like all their sawmill stuff, so it's OK by Amish rules. His family still uses a Briggs and Stratton three-thousand-psi pressure washer that he bought in the summer of 2004 for a hundred bucks. Heidi, guess who from?"

"Oh, my God . . ."

"Ripp wasn't lying to you. Zook bought your dad's pressure washer from Jerrold Mickelson. And that zombie is dead, Heidi."

As she put the phone away, her eyes finally spilled. In colors made even more vivid by tears, she watched a hawk circle in blue sky over emerald pasture. She followed the progress of fishermen up the glittering stream. By old habit, sometimes a day counter but always a head counter, she tallied, one by one as they appeared, a herd of barn-bound black-and-white Holsteins, twenty-three strong as they crested a green rise in the distance.

Bob Check was waiting at the Pederson place, visiting with Belle Kick on the porch while the kids played with a litter of new kittens.

"I've got all the signatures," he said, raising a folder to wave good-bye to Harley's mom, who had wasted no time getting in her car, heading off for happy hour somewhere. "See you later, Belle."

As the dust of the sheriff's mother-in-law settled on the driveway, Supervisor Check said, "It's now or never, Sheriff." He extracted the nomination paper and a pen, laid them on the rickety homemade table between porch chairs. "The deadline to file is noon tomorrow."

"You want a beer, Bob?"

"Does a one-legged duck swim in circles? Heck."

She handed him one of Harley's Leinenkugel's. She sat down where Harley's mom had sat, surprised to feel that Belle Kick had left behind some warmth in the chair.

"I'm sorry, Bob. I'm almost there. But I don't know yet."

"Olaf Yttri filed at the board meeting today."

"That I do know."

"We certified him as a candidate. You'd be the challenger now. I guess I don't understand why he did that, when you tried to resign and we wouldn't let you."

They sat quietly.

"Well, yeah, so anyhow," she said eventually, "Harley's still at baseball practice. The diamond's finally dry. I guess we should wait until he's here."

Bob Check held his beer in the hand that missed two fingers. He raised it and took an old-man sip, one teaspoon, and set the bottle back on the porch floor. She wasn't sure what she was really waiting for. Not for Harley's permission or support, which she had.

"Is it OK if we hold off just a few more minutes, Bob?"

"He goes late, huh?"

"He loves what he does."

"I can sit here until the cows come home."

The expression sent her back. The poor doomed cows that Mickelson had once named as they staggered off his truck, the killer laughing at her family's ways: *Cordelia, Cleopatra, Desdemona, Queen Mab, Rosalind, Juliet, Mistress Quickly* . . .

The kids romped with the kittens. Four kittens, three kids, no fighting. The mother cat sprawled proudly in the explosive spring grass, bowled over by her own full teats. The sheriff and Supervisor Check watched without comment. The sun slipped over the wooded ridge at the west end of the old Pederson farm. Slowly, the sky blushed deep red. Interim Sheriff Heidi Kick watched as, with inexorable grace, everything close by slipped into warm and easy evening shadows. This moment was it, what she waited for, the soft ending of a long, hard recollection.

She reached for Bob Check's paper and his pen.

EPILOGUE

Crawford County, Wisconsin

Night, July 9, 2004

After the horrifying, unbelievable news, while her Dairy Queen chaperone, Mrs. Wisnewski, drives her home, Heidi White's entire world is no. And never.

A thousand kinds of no and never, across two hundred miles of landscape, and it might be an insane time to think about geography, but what she notices, what she feels for the first time, is that the coulee region where she comes from is in all ways below the rest of the state. She sees that she is from wilder, from poorer, from lower elevation. What looks like uphill from inside the coulees is downhill from out. What she knows as hillsides and bluffs, as sky-closing towers of densely forested land, these are eroded slopes cut from the prairie, and trips down the coulees are trips down toward the raw core of the earth. No wonder this is where the caves are, where the snakes are, where the wild trout live, where the Indians ran to hide and die. She returns shattered to a home place that is so much deeper than she thought.

As if she feels this too, Mrs. Wisnewski rides the brake. On the straightaway into Boaz a milk truck blasts around, its horn blaring over the elderly chaperone's tremulous words.

"Stay with me and Mr. Wisnewski. You can't go home now."

"No."

"Sweetheart—"

"No."

"I just can't take you home. We'll go to our place, we're just outside Soldiers Grove, we've got all kinds of room, and we'll talk to Mr. Wisnewski, and then maybe later he will—"

"I said no. Never."

"I know how hard this is."

"You don't know. And you don't know what happened either. You're just repeating whatever bullshit lies you heard."

"It was Sheriff Skog himself who informed me, Miss White."

"No. Take me home."

She closes her ears and her mind. Being from lower, poorer, wilder, from deeper, she finally understands all the hoopla about her being the statewide Dairy Queen. People are surprised. But to her it means that her mom and dad were even stronger than she ever thought, were even more worthy of her love and admiration, must have worked even harder and more bravely and more stubbornly than she ever imagined in order to raise her on a farm because they believed that was the best they had to give. Her dad would never do what they are saying. No, they are wrong. Mrs. Wisnewski is lying. Sheriff Skog is lying. It didn't happen. No.

An hour later, installed in a sterile bedroom with a bathroom attached at the rear of the Wisnewskis' house, with no clothes on her back but the yellow gown she traveled to the reception in, she turns on the shower and goes out the window.

———

Later she will clock the journey with a trip odometer, drunk-driving her dad's Ford pickup that she inherited. So established, that terrible night, first of many, she walks 13.92 miles home. She understands the Wisnewskis would have called the Crawford County sheriff's office, and maybe the old couple is out looking too, so she travels some in roadside ditches but mostly cross-country, just how Blackhawk fled two hundred years before, except in a shredding yellow gown and spikes with the heels snapped off, over fences and through cornfields, across private property and empty roads. This is not, will never be, a story she will ever tell any-

one, not even the man she will come to love, because this is the secret core
of herself that she carries forward from that day on: shattered, enraged,
denying, bleeding, crying, screaming, plunging through hostile darkness
toward a vision of what used to be, a journey that will never end.

The farm is still a crime scene when she gets there. From the crest of
the south pasture, through fireflies from sixty acres away, she sees lights
that don't belong. Red and blue, strobing, scorching the side of their
white barn. She has shed, miles ago, the gown and the slip and the panty
hose and the shoes. She crosses Cress Creek in bare feet, bra, and panties.
She is bruised and bleeding in a hundred different places. On the near
side of the creek she finds the cattle, unmilked, bunched in a corner of
the fence. Every cow points its nose toward the barn except Ophelia,
the bell cow. Ophelia stands watch at the back of the herd, facing the
darkness that now produces not a coyote or a wolf or some other cattle
demon but a shattered version of her bovine heart's beloved, Heidi the
Milkmaid, Heidi the Dairy Queen, and the cow trots toward her, snuf-
fling and moaning and butting, then licking her chest and her arm.

"I know. I know," Heidi tells her, trying not to sob for the cow's sake.
"But they're all lying. He never did that. Go on, get the girls. I'll take
care of you."

––––––

Sheriff Ken Skog doesn't seem all that surprised when Ron and Darlene
White's headstrong daughter, supposedly missing, exits the house fully
dressed in barn clothes. Or when she effs him off on her way to open
the pasture gate. Skog has yellow crime-scene tape across the wide barn
door, but Ophelia leads her ladies right through it and into the milking
parlor—twenty stanchions, twenty-one cows, the slow one, Duchess,
standing in the doorway splat-shitting as if to keep official Crawford
County from following into the barn. Skog backs off.

Heidi White walks under the beam where her dad keeps his old Colt
revolver and his box of Whiz-Bangs. She doesn't think about these items
then. What Sheriff Skog says happened did not happen and she doesn't
even think about proving otherwise, seeing if the gun and bullets are
still on the beam. Of course they are. She can see deputies beyond the

strangely lit doorway to the milk house. She does not believe her mom and dad are in there. Or ever were. Not together anyway. It is a small tight room that her dad deals with alone. All of this is bullshit.

At Cress Springs Farms they milk the old-fashioned way. She shoves her head into Mistress Quickly's warm flank and paints her teats with Purell and squeezes the far pair and gets started. Her dad always plays the radio, the public station from Prairie du Chien, but the radio is off. It's a long time before she realizes that what she is absorbing instead—the same way she has always soaked up stories about elections, about Iraq, about arts and interesting people—is the sloppy casual chatter of the officers working in and around the barn. They gossip and joke, yawn and complain. They evaluate yesterday and forecast tomorrow. In a while, after she has milked a half dozen cows, one deputy takes a smoke break, checks in with his wife on the phone. "Yeah, I don't know, I guess it'll go up for sale. The land is worth a bundle. Except if you farm it, I guess. You watch, some lawyer from the Twin Cities is gonna buy it so he can shoot his Bambi once a year."

She finishes Cordelia. She effs off Skog again and goes past the milk house into the back barn. Knowing that all of this is a bullshit lie, that her dad never owned more than one firearm that wasn't a hunting rifle, she stops beneath the beam and puts a hand up. The Colt, the Whiz-Bangs, gone.

It chills her, the vacant dusty spot atop the beam. Her dad's gun is gone. It confuses her. Did he use it? But the whole box of Whiz-Bangs is gone.

She has cows left to milk and she does it, weeping silently into their flanks. Later she stands in fireflies on the black expanse of the south pasture. She is sorting out what will never be true, and what will be true forever. She understands the farm is lost. She believes that she is lost. All of her relationships, to every place, to every thing, to every person and creature, including to herself, she believes that these are lost forever. She can't imagine how or why to live.

She gets a warm, wet nuzzle. The bell cow, old Ophelia, has found her. She doesn't know it yet. She wouldn't believe it. But the old cow has found her, keeps finding her, and the nuzzle tells her something she will finally come to remember: beloved girl, someday you'll be OK.

ACKNOWLEDGMENTS

To those bravely there from the very beginning: Ben Leroy, Blake Stewart, and Alison Dasho; to all the friends and colleagues who generously gave time and attention to some phase of this book along the way: Bob, Mike, Craig, Osman, Kristy, Michelle, Keir, Linda, Natasha, and Larry; to the best editorial team I could have asked for: Sean Delone and Peter Borland; to my outstanding agent, Joanna MacKenzie, whose faith, patience, and vision made it all come together; and, for their loving forbearance against the mostly invisible work of the writer, to Joe, Sam, and Ya-Ling, . . . thank you.